W9-CUT-700

THE SPANISH SEASON

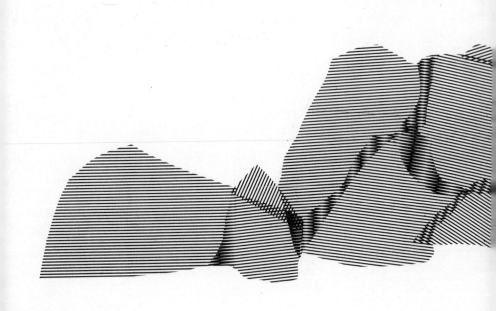

BERNARD OLDSEY

THE SPANISH SEASON

HARCOURT, BRACE & WORLD, INC.

NEW YORK

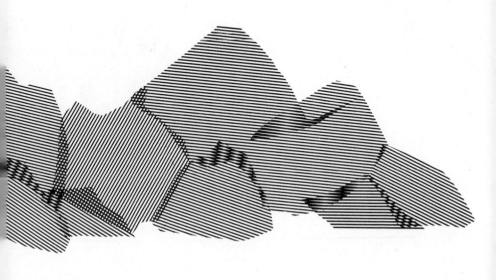

The places in this book are real, as places are real in remembrance; the personages in the book are not, except in a fictional sense. There is, to the author's knowledge, no such modern and *sub rosa* organization as the Legión Azul.

TO MY WIFE, ANN;

MY SON, BILL;

AND MY DAUGHTER, JAN

PART ONE

1

The Brothers Swiatski

His eyes shifted involuntarily from the examination booklet he was grading. The June afternoon had turned muggy, as though it might rain, and he felt bored to the edge of restiveness. His line of vision shifted across the desk and up the wall to a reproduction of Breughel's "Carnival." Of late, he realized, the painting had become not so much a refuge as a sufficient comment on life. As usual, he glanced past scores of figures, all of them hell-bent on carnal pleasure, and fixed his gaze on the fat man in the lower left quadrant of the picture. It was inevitably Fatso that got him—that sack of flesh astraddle a hogshead on skids, meat speared out in front of him on an iron spit, a pot dangling from his right ankle, and a bird pie balanced on his flat head. Old Breughel had depicted him as the father of us all. Fatso rode, his codpiece bulging. But where had he come from, on his pork barrel of despair? And where was he going?

Curt swiveled slowly around in his chair so that he could see the gross bulk of D. Elmo Whitaker, situated at his desk in the front left corner of the office. Whitaker was dressed in a summer suit of light gray cotton, and as he sat hunched, whacking away at some unfortunate's booklet, he resembled a butcher chopping meat for the next day's sausage.

D. E. W., or Dew Drop as some of the students called him, was certainly not one of Curt's favorite people. He could be pompous and stiffly officious and often was, like some colonial

3

plantation owner who wanted eventually to govern a province of indentured servants. And yet, since Curt's divorce, Elmo had been as understanding as possible. He didn't pretend nothing had happened, which would have been the worst reaction, but he didn't act funereal about it, either; and now when he brewed tea on his hot plate he offered it with a bit more enthusiasm than before, and when Curt propped a tennis racket against a corner bookcase, Elmo no longer winced at the thought of creeping athleticism.

At this point, Whitaker gave a snort of derision, a grim smile on his face as his red pencil cut into someone's hurried prose. A bead of perspiration broke across his forehead and he brushed it away nervously with his left hand. One of the plantation workers was about to receive twenty lashes and be sent to bed without supper.

Curt shut his eyes. He felt tired, stale. He became aware of the knocking at the door at the same time he heard Elmo's imperious "Come in!"

The man who appeared in the doorway did not look professorial. For one thing, he wore a dark blue suit in the afternoon. He might have been one of the older graduate students, one of those small-town teachers who worked toward master's degrees in the summer sessions—or, as the strong face suggested, perhaps one of the federal investigators who came around occasionally to check on former students. But his tentativeness made Curt decide he wasn't that either.

"Is there a Dr. Fielding here?" He looked toward Curt, then Elmo, then back again.

"I'm Fielding. Come on in."

"I am Stanley Swiatski," the man in the navy blue suit announced, making it sound as though his name should have a definite effect, and if it didn't he wasn't coming any farther into the office.

He stood loose-hipped, with his weight to one side, his right hand still on the doorknob. In his left hand he held a gray hat.

His shoes were black and highly shined. Suddenly Curt remembered the uniform dress of young Slavs back home in Hazleton —on their way to mass on Sunday morning, and then an hour or two later, continuing their bending-kneeling-standing exercises, playing dice on the back porch of a neighborhood store, ties loosened, jackets folded over the left arm, trousers hitched up carefully to preserve the crease.

"How are you, Mr. Swiatski?" Curt stood up and offered his hand to the visitor, who came forward and gripped it with the firmness of a worker. Swiatski had gone all out sartorially for this visit to the university: his tie was a cosmic whorl of purples and greens, anchored to reality by a clasp shaped like a baseball bat. Curt made a silent bet that the white shirt collar was held by a wire M that pronged the tips out into rigid perfection. Swiatski was definitely Anthracite Bowl, as identifiable a member of his clan as any Ivy Leaguer in the regalia of rep tie, button-down oxford, and J. Press jacket with real bone buttons. He had probably saved his two or three thousand dollars and now, though he might be in his early thirties, wanted to make the big leap into academe.

"Have a seat." Curt offered a chair by the bookcase next to his desk. Swiatski sat down. His bullet-shaped head, framed by Hemingway, Faulkner, and Fitzgerald titles, looked out of place. What it needed, Curt thought, was Tolstoy or Conrad or Dostoevsky.

"I'm sorry to have to bother you this way, Doctor." He nodded at the heaps of examination booklets on Curt's desk.

"That's all right."

"There's somethin' personal an' important that I gotta talk to you about. Anyways, it's important to me and my family."

Out of the corner of his eye Curt could see that Elmo had stopped grading. Now, with an exaggerated yawn, the fat man rose and said, "I'm going down to Petry's office for a bit, Curtis. If there are any calls, direct them down there, will you?"

"I'd be glad to, Elmo," Curt said. Which really meant:

"Thanks for allowing me the privacy they don't provide, but which we make possible when we have enough decency to make the effort—a decency you're showing more and more of these days."

When the door closed Curt said, "Now, Mr. Swiatski, what's on your mind?" He hitched a cigarette up out of the pack, offering it to the stiff-sitting applicant.

"No, thanks," Swiatski smiled. "I give it up a couple a months ago."

Curt lit the cigarette for himself and settled back in his swivel chair.

"Well, first of all," Swiatski began, "I don't mind telling you the only reason I come here was because my brother said you'd remember him and maybe do us a favor."

It was a preamble and the rest would come of its own accord; but it couldn't be to apply for college. The more Curt listened to Swiatski the surer he became that that wasn't it at all.

"Joe—my brother living in Cleveland—says you'll remember him."

Curt's face was blank.

"He played for Hazle Township when you were at Central. You played each other. Then you both played together in the Anthracite Bowl. Joe said you'd remember. . . ."

"Joe Swiatski, Joe Swiatski. . . ." Curt ducked his head down to one side and blinked his eyes, waiting for memory cells to produce some kind of picture. Nothing resulted except some fuzzy and overlapping images. "Joe Swiatski," he said once more, and then got a mental shot that looked right: a tall, rangy end. He saw himself and this tall boy double-teaming a big tackle. Red, Red, Red—Vukash. Vukash, from Kingston. The tobacco-spitting expert, who also specialized in twisting face masks. Curt, from his wing-back spot and Swiatski—it definitely *was* Swiatski—from his end position had worked Vukash over two or three times with elbows and knees.

Christ, how you remember some things! He could still smell the tobacco juice. . . .

"I remember Joe," he said. "How's he doing?"

"He's doin' good. He graduated Georgia Tech and now's a engineer out in Cleveland. He's married and got three kids and a nice home there in Shaker Heights and all."

Well, Curt thought, one of the Swiatskis had made it. He was glad for Joe. He could remember now that they had talked at someone's graduation party about plans for college, and he had gotten an impression Joe was bright, or bright enough.

"I'm glad he's doing well," Curt said. "Now tell me what I can do for you."

"First off, I got this here letter from Joe that I'd like for you to see." Swiatski put his hat carefully on the floor beside the chair and reached inside his jacket. Curt was about to draw his attention to the hat-and-coat rack in the corner, but he was already busy pulling a small leather notebook from his coat. A number of items had been packed in the notebook. Swiatski removed a rubber band from the packet, fingered out a gray envelope, and took from it a single sheet of stationery, which he handed over with a serious look on his face.

Curt noted that the letter was dated a week and a half back, May 22, 1964. He began to read the firm but rather boyishly large script:

Dear Stan,

I am glad you sent me the clipping about Curtis Fielding. You are right about him being the one I knew in high school. I remember that he went to Nittany and played a year of ball there before the war. It was the same year I went down to Tech. I'm pretty sure he will remember me, and if he doesn't, just remind him of the big s.o.b. we played against in the Anthracite Bowl, the tobacco chewer. He will remember then.

Tell him hello for me, and then if everything is all right show him the stuff about Teddy. Explain the whole thing to him. Tell him everything we know, even about Brutkevich and the girl. If there are any questions maybe Professor Fielding will call me collect at the office or at home.

Marie is taking things all right but little Nancy is not any better. We do not know what we are going to do. But I guess it is not up to us now. We are not giving up though.

Give our love to Bronny and the kids. Tell Stella if she can take her vacation and would like to come out here any time this summer we would like to see her and I think it would do a lot for Marie. But she knows the situation she would be coming into.

Your brother,
Joe

Curt placed the letter on the corner of the desk near his visitor. He hadn't meant to read the part where he sensed a switch to personal matters, but the impetus of curiosity had carried him on to the end and now he was even more curious. "What's it all about?"

"It's kind of a long story, Professor. It's about our kid brother, Theodore, that is—that *was* in the Air Force. Maybe the easiest thing is for you to take a look at these here." He handed Curt a batch of folded material with two news clippings on top and some envelopes beneath.

The top clipping proved familiar. It was the release put out by the university press service about Curt's having got a Fulbright to Zaragoza in October. It stated what his degrees and publications were, how old the University of Zaragoza was, what he would be lecturing on, and so forth. But the handout had been transformed into a hometown-boy-makes-good story by the Hazleton *Record*. Some staff writer had pulled out morgue material, added "the son of Mr. and Mrs. Alfred C. Fielding of this city," and topped it all with a photograph taken ten years ago, which made Curt look like his kid brother—if he'd had a kid brother.

He pushed it aside to see the other clipping, which was a two-column story with an 18-point head:

LOCAL AIRMAN KILLED
IN NORTHERN SPAIN

The accompanying photo showed a young, square-faced version of Airman First Class Theodore Swiatski. The nose looked broken and tough and the smile youthfully cocky. Otherwise, the face peering out of the clipping was much like that of the man staring at him from beside the desk.

"Teddy?" It was a useless question, but Curt asked it.

Swiatski nodded.

Curt's eyes took in the dateline of the *Chronicle* story: *Saragossa, Spain, April 15.* As he read the account, he began to get a glimmer of why Swiatski had come to visit him:

A1C Theodore J. Swiatski, 22, late of this city, was the victim of a fatal highway accident fifteen miles east of Saragossa, Spain, on Wednesday of last week. Swiatski's body was discovered in the wrecked shell of his 1959 Chevrolet on Spain's National Highway 2, leading from Saragossa to Barcelona. He was reportedly on a three-day pass, returning from Barcelona on the morning of the tragic mishap.

Spanish and American military police stated Swiatski failed to negotiate a turn on the highway and plummeted to his death a hundred feet below. They said the body of the young airman might have been thrown free except for the seat belt he was wearing.

Spanish authorities stated that this section of the road between Saragossa and Lérida is especially treacherous. Only two hundred yards from where Swiatski was killed there is an accident marker showing where a Spanish couple were killed less than a year ago.

Theodore J. Swiatski was the son of the late Mr. and Mrs. Joseph P. Swiatski, 23 Ashland Avenue, Hazle Twp. He attended St. Mary's on the Mount Grade School and Hazle Twp. High School, where he will be remembered by many as a star halfback on an undefeated team. After training at Lackland AFB in Texas, Swiatski was assigned overseas duty with the 3972 SAC Squadron of the 16th Air Force, stationed just outside Saragossa.

Swiatski is survived by the following members of his family: Joseph, Shaker Heights, Ohio; Stanley, 23 Ashland Ave., Hazle Twp.; Mrs. Rita Grasso, South Brunswick, N. J.; and Sister Stella Maria, OSV, Smithfield, Va. His brother Sgt. Casimir Swiatski was killed in Korea in August, 1952.

Curt handed the clippings back to Swiatski. The two envelopes remained on his desk and he wondered what might be in them, but he thought he should say something consoling in the face of death. "It's really tough about your brother," he said. "I'm sorry. But I don't understand what you want me to do. Is it something about the body? I mean, burial or anything of the sort?"

Stan Swiatski's face was squared and tough, and you didn't expect anything crybaby from him, but his voice was husky with emotion now. "Yeah, it's sorta about the burial, Professor. You see we got this here friend, Brutkevich, who's always done the family burying business—my father, my mother, aunts and uncles and the rest. Well, he called me soon's the Air Force turned the body over to him, and he told me come right down to his parlor 'cause he's got something important for me to know. So I get down there in a hell of a hurry, you know, and this is what he tells me. He says, 'You could look at that body with me in the embalming room, and maybe it's a good idea you do.' 'Why?' I says. 'Is there anything wrong?' 'Tell you the troot, I don't know,' he says like that. 'Maybe yes and maybe no.'

"So I says O.K. and in we go." Curt could see the lines of the face grow tighter, as though the bones had become suddenly larger under the skin. Swiatski shoved against the back of the chair and took a deep breath like someone about to dive below the surface of filthy water.

After a moment he continued. "I don't know if you ever

seen a burnt-up body, Professor, but I'll tell you one thing it's a goddamn lousy sight. I'm sorry to say it like that, but it's the troot and I hope you never have to. Anyways, I take one look at *it* and almost heave my cookies right then and there. Finally I says to Brutkevich, 'Holy Jesus, Bronc, don't tell me that's our Teddy.' Then he shows me this here rubber cover and the tag on it which the Air Force sent—ah—everything in. And 'course it had on there Teddy's name and rank and all.

" 'But I don't have no idea whether this is Teddy or not,' Bronc says. 'And I don't know how the hell them guys in the Air Force can tell either. So all's I brought you down here for is to ast whether they have told you how they made the positive idenification.'

"I moved into the other room there, the parlor, trying to think, and Bronc follows me. And then I tell him, come to think of it—no, there's nothing like that with the papers they sent. Just how it happened and all and here are his things, which they sent in a cardboard box. So Bronc tells me no use'n getting too excited about it. All's he's saying is that he can't tell one way or the other, and couldn't I maybe write the commandin' officer and get the information."

Curt took a last drag on his cigarette, stubbed it out, and then asked, "*Did* you write?"

"Well, as things come out, no. 'Course when Joe got home from Cleveland, which was next day, I tell him about this and we talk to Bronc again, who says, 'Don't get too excited or nothing, but just a formal request for information from the Air Force,' like that. And Joe says he understands and sure we'll do it."

"But you didn't? Why not?" Curt was getting caught up in all this despite himself. Roads, he thought, roads. *Who makes them? Who takes them?*

"You got the answer there by your elbow," Swiatski said, jerking his chin as a facial pointer.

Curt looked down at the two envelopes. Both were loaded with foreign-looking stamps. One was purplish gray; the other plain white with the red, white, and blue slash edgings of an airmail envelope.

"Maybe you'd get more outta the purple one first."

Curt examined the graceful, girlish script on the envelope, the letters tilting—as he could tell from numerous student papers—in the manner of left-handed script. The stamps turned out to be portraits of Franco. And there was a *Por Avión* scrawled diagonally across the upper left-hand section. He extracted the folded sheet from within and read:

Dear Family of Teddi:

I spek the Inglish but no write bery well. For to write I mus use diccionario. Please to excuse for bad writing. But I love Teddi and he say he love me to. For this reazon you now I write. What Air Force of Unite States tell you over Teddi and me is no the truth. Teddi is no bad. I no bad. We love and are good peoples togeder. We no look for troubles. They make troubles. Policía Espanish no good y policía Americans no good. What it is that makes bad is, I belief, somaons kill Teddi. No a accident. I no ask you money. I ask you somaons come to España. I no care now Teddi dead. I care for his family. Is no right that they kill him.

Con mucho respecto,
María Maite Xavier-Peralta

Curt let the words sink in, reread a few phrases. He turned the envelope around and saw there was a return address. Then he looked at Stanley Swiatski and said, "It's for real? Not a joke?"

"We don't think so."

"Had Teddy written you about her?"

"No. Ted was always with the chicks and he didn't write much anyway, 'cept now and then he'd send a present to the kids, and cards around the holidays."

"And what about the Air Force, did they write you about

her—this, ah"—he looked at the signature again—"María Maite?"

"Not a damned thing."

"Well, you certainly can't go off half-cocked because of a single letter from a girl you don't know anything about. It could be a racket. There are a lot of these rackets."

"That's what Joe and me thought and 'course we're not sure of nothing. But then we got that other letter there and we begun to wonder."

"May I?"

"Sure, that's why I give it to you."

The other letter was typed, all in capitals, and contained neither signature nor return address. It was accompanied by a clipping from a Spanish newspaper. Curt read the letter first.

DEAR MR. SWIATSKI,

YOUR BROTHER, TEDDY, AND ME WERE GOOD BUDDIES AND I THINK MAYBE HE WAS GIVEN A BUM DEAL. THERE IS SOMETHING VERY FISHY ABOUT THE WHOLE THING AND I THINK YOU OGHT TO WRITE TO YOUR CONGRESSMAN OR SOMEBODY. BECAUSE THE WAY THINGS ARE RIGHT NOW NOBODY KNOWS THE REAL SCORE ABOUT TEDDY AND WHAT HAPPENED. I COULD GET MYSELF IN A SLING FOR WRITING TO YOU THIS WAY. BUT I THINK TED WOULD HAVE DONE IT FOR ME IF THE SITUATION WAS REVERSE.

A FRIEND OF TEDDY

P.S. I AM SENDING A SPANISH NEWSPAPER CLIPPING THAT WILL MAKE YOU SEE WHAT I AM TALING ABOUT. I AM SURE YOU CAN GET SOME- ONE TO READ IT TO YOU. THEN YOU WILL SEE THAT SOMETHING STINKS IN DENMARK.

Curt looked up from the letter. Swiatski said, "If you don't read Spanish, I can tell you what's in the clipping, 'cause we asked this Mexican that works on my shift to translate it."

"I read it a little. Let me go through it and then you can fill me in if I get stuck."

The clipping had been cut large enough to show that the story came from a newspaper called *La Verdad*, and it bore a Barcelona dateline of April 9.

"What was the date of the *Chronicle* story on your brother?"

Stanley checked it. "April fifteenth."

"And when did the body, the remains, come?"

"Two, no, three days later."

"You had a letter from the Air Force before that?"

"Yeah. Like a telegram, a couple days before the story come out in the *Chronicle*."

With the exception of two or three phrases, Curt was able to pick out the meaning of the Spanish story. According to it, someone named Cipriano Farlo Trigo, thirty-two years old, of Zaragoza, had been killed in an automobile crash on National Highway II between Lérida and Zaragoza. The body had been burnt and was difficult to identify. But the coroner had finally identified the body as that of Farlo. It *was* Farlo, Curt remembered, because the family name came in the middle. Trigo would be the mother's name.

"I wrote down what Lopez, the Mex, told me."

"Go ahead."

Swiatski read in effect what Curt had deciphered, with some details clarified. Farlo had owned a paper shop, or probably a stationery store, as Curt translated matters. And he had handled small printing jobs. He had left behind a train of aunts and uncles, nephews and nieces, but his parents had been killed in the Civil War and there were no other children. Only one uncle lived in Zaragoza.

"That's about what I was able to make out, too," Curt said, when Swiatski stopped. "Now the question is, what do we make of the whole business? The letters could have been fakes and part of some racket, but this clipping looks authentic, although it should be checked, too."

Curt realized that by using the word *we* he had in his own mind accepted a mission of trust without stopping to consider it. But in the back of his mind was Joe Swiatski, and in front of him was a man who bluntly asked for help. It was a request from the homeland, from a landsman, made in naïve honesty and with a force of implied friendship not to be denied. Besides, Curt thought, I'd like to know what the hell this is all about.

"Will you do it for us, then?"

"Stanley, I'll do what I can. But you can't expect too much. Your brother is probably dead and the body you received is his." Curt remembered reading about people who still expected loved ones to reappear, out of the "missing," from World War I. Distance simply added doubt in these cases, and *missing* was always more bearable than *dead*.

"If that is Teddy, we already give him a proper burial. He's in St. Mary's graveyard, where all our family gets buried. But we will all sleep better at night if you can make sure for us. I'd go myself, but I got the wife and kids and the job to take care of. Tell you the troot, I *would* go if it was absolutely necessary. Joe said he'd chip in with the cash. But he says seeing as you're going there in October and know the language probably . . ."

"Sure. I understand, and I'll do what I can. Everything I can."

"Wonderful. You'll never know how much we appreciate it. And speakin' of cash—"

Curt waved a hand in refusal. "Don't worry, my trip is fully financed by your tax money and mine."

"Well, for telegraphs and like that."

"Really not necessary, but thanks."

"I guess you already know that Joe's got enough trouble of his own. Otherwise you'd a asked why he ain't going himself."

Curt realized quickly that he had, indeed, dimly figured some of it out. The conclusion of Joe Swiatski's letter had been enough to keep him from asking anything more.

"I thought maybe there must be something wrong or he'd certainly go."

"Well, the family's got another rotten deal there," Stanley said, and more than ever his square face looked strained. "Joe's got a little daughter, Nancy, and the kid's got leukemia, and they don't expect her to last long." He said it as though the world and its ways might not exactly satisfy his sense of justice.

"I see. I'm sorry. That's terrible."

"That's why this other stuff about Teddy comes at a bad time. Not that—" He stopped himself and changed to another tack, deciding to keep his woes to himself. "So we'd be mighty thankful for whatever you can do, Professor. Joe says to tell you we don't expect no miracles and we don't want you should get in trouble. But he thinks you could do the right thing and —ah—since I met you now, I think so, too."

At this Curt could see the mask of toughness crumble into a smile, showing the boyish face of someone who must have hopped freights, slid down culm banks, and played follow-the-leader around mine caves in a regional variation of Huck Finn.

They shook hands. Stanley collected his hat. At Curt's suggestion he left the material with him, since he and Joe had had all the stuff photostated. Then Swiatski took his leave.

Curt watched the blue suit move down the foreign halls of academe, saw the blocky shoulders move away, and only then realized he hadn't offered to take Stanley down to the Cornerstone for a meal or at least a coffee. He really knew very little about the man—what his job was, how many children he had, whether his wife was pretty or ragged with housework. And yet in one hour he had been brought deeply into someone's life, like a priest behind the sliding door of a confessional box, who hears a murderer's story without ever knowing the surrounding elements of his life.

Well, he thought, watching the man disappear out the end doors, I'll do my best in other respects and, closing the door to his office, sat back down at his desk.

The sultry warmth of the afternoon was unalleviated by the open windows, which brought in nothing but the same hotness.

The file cases, the books, the telephone on the small typing table, the pencil sharpener on the wall, the number 318 printed on the frosted safety glass of the door—all gave a heavy sheen of reality to the place: cubes, lines, and surfaces reflecting hot light only partly blocked out by the heavy dun-colored shade at the windows. But the corporeal absence of Stanley Swiatski left behind a trail of unreality in the clippings and letters which now lay on the desk, claiming far more attention than the all but forgotten examination booklets.

The office door opened and Elmo Whitaker entered, saying, "I believe your interviewee has departed."

"Yeah. He's gone."

"If he's to be a new graduate student we must change that tie." Elmo was smiling social conspiracy against the unwashed.

"*And* his accent."

"Of course," Whitaker said grumpily, something in Curt's tone making him feel he was not being agreed with, as on those occasions when he read howlers from freshman themes, or others when he betrayed an attitude roughly equivalent to that of a physician who wants to treat only those patients with refined diseases.

As Whitaker waddled toward his desk, Curt realized more than ever that it was he and several of his friends—the inevitable other faction in any English faculty the size of Pennwood's—who had helped make him decide to apply for a Fulbright. Divorcing Helen had been bad enough, but he couldn't go through yet another year of committee haggling over rank, tenure, policy, curriculum, and the rest. Last September he had asked to be relieved of all committee assignments and at the same time applied for a Hays-Fulbright grant. He had had to get away. During the divorce everything within the university had shrunk. He had gone back to the big outside world of jet planes, lawyers, courts, and massed humanity, and found that Pennwood was not simply Happy Valley. It was also what Eddy Stone called it—Dead Center, Pa. That's what it had been for

Curt from September to June. The football games had come and gone, the students had filed through his mind, the cocktail parties had given him hangovers, and the early tennis had made him feel old and arthritic at forty. Only Mary Masters had rocked and soothed the pain into tumbling quiescence, and even there the arching joy was shot.

He and Marta Torres at the Fulbright offices in Madrid had been exchanging letters for months and all the arrangements had been made. It was time for a change, time for another fork in the road. And, he thought, looking once more at the items left on his desk, what about Teddy Swiatski's road? Was he still on it, or under it? Had that burnt meat in St. Mary's graveyard once traveled under the designation of Airman First Class Theodore Swiatski? Or was it the residue of some other flesh?

2
Departure and Arrival

He pushed the buzzer a second time and leaned against the doorjamb. The September heat in the hallway folded around him like warm dough. He felt dizzy as well as tired. The events of the night flickered through his mind in an alcoholic haze. Strongest of all were the impressions of J. Palmer Bruton and his traveling companion, Christine Bergman. Forget about her. Concentrate on Bruton. Tell Mary all about Bruton. . . .

He heard the squeegeelike sounds of bare feet on hardwood floor. The knob turned and the door opened to the limits of its safety chain. A sleep-puffed wedge of Mary's face appeared. Then the chain rattled free and he walked into her outstretched arms and felt the slump of her body as she clung to him.

"You're late," she said, disengaging herself from his arms and knuckling sleep out of her eyes. "What time is it?" She tried to keep from sounding reproachful.

"I don't know. My watch stopped."

She turned away and headed across the room toward the divan. For the first time he noticed the new outfit she had put on for their private farewell. It consisted of sheer, clinging, orange-tinted pants and a flowing, lemon-colored blouse that had sleeves of the kind Russian peasants wore. The pants fit too close to the flesh to have wrinkles, but the blouse had been crumpled into random lines and hatchmarks.

As he followed her across the white tasseled rug, which resembled llama fur, his eyes took in the familiar objects of

19

the room—the leather-topped coffee table, the imitation Giacometti on top of the white-painted bookshelves, the five-foot high canvas of a medieval monk done in the stained-glass-window style of an obscure Austrian painter named Hautfelt. But it was the unlooked-for objects, suddenly standing out from the others he knew so well, that tapped his reservoir of guilt.

Mary, who had decided not to go to the Beaverses' for his farewell party, had obviously planned Our Own Little Party. Atop the coffee table stood an ice bucket containing a bottle of champagne in a high tide of water. Next to it was a silver dish with four compartments, in which had been heaped black caviar, chopped chives, slices of lemon, and mashed egg yolk. These were nearly inundated by a shallow pond of water inside a china dish, where the silver plate had rested on a bed of cracked ice.

Mary had already thrown herself on the divan, as though to resume her sleep. The back of her head and her orange rump were accusing signs of neglect. Curt flipped his jacket over the canvas sling chair and sat on the divan beside her, stroking her hair gently, tentatively, not sure how she would react. She seemed the girl child who'd been denied a new doll or bicycle. As his hand moved down the line of her neck, he felt almost incestuous, and said, "I'm sorry, baby," in sudden awareness of the ambiguity.

"Wah it a goo parry?" The sounds came up muffled from the pillow.

"Not good, not bad. But I wish now that you'd come with me."

"To hell with them—all your academic friends who won't grant me rank or tenure."

"There was someone else there I think you'd like to have met. Eddy Stone brought him to meet me, *and* I'm now two thousand bucks richer."

She turned over on her back, fully awake now. "What do you mean?" she said, puzzled.

Carefully omitting the blond Christine Bergman, Curt told her that Eddy Stone had brought J. Palmer Bruton, president of Horizon House, to the party. Eddy had shown Bruton some of Curt's essays and his book on American literary naturalism. He had told him Curt had agreed to hunt up information for the book Eddy was doing on the Spanish Civil War, information about Roy Campbell and other writers who had treated Franco favorably in their English-language accounts of the war.

"Bruton said he was grateful, and he wondered if I would be interested in doing a piece for one of their affiliates, *Phaeton* magazine."

"Oh, Curt!"

Curt reported their talk, which had taken place in the privacy of the Beaverses' kitchen, almost verbatim. What Bruton wanted was an analysis of the American image in Spain as it existed at present. Once it had been better in Spain than perhaps anywhere else in the world, but now that the military had been there awhile, and the number of American tourists and businessmen had increased, that image had begun to alter. Bruton wanted the change analyzed: how it started, what started it, where we stood now, and where we might stand in the next five or ten years. Bruton made it seem that there was more at stake than our altered position in Spain. If Curt could trace it and document it in Spain, he could tell something about the way we stood elsewhere—in West Germany, South America, Vietnam—the whole works.

Bruton, Curt said, was almost too much. He described him in his Italian-cut suit, with his brown wavy hair turning gray, quite like Leonard Bernstein. But, as usual in the glossy, surfaces were deceptive. The man knew his stuff. When Curt had mentioned that *The Ugly American* had perhaps covered the same ground as the proposed article, Bruton replied: "Burdick and Lederer did a good job for their purposes. It's a stinging book, a good book, but fictional caricature done out of polemic rage. Graham Greene's *Quiet American* is more of the same. I want a straighter piece, an objective job of coming up with answers—for the tourist, and the businessman interested in Spanish investment, but for the military and political observer as well. Naturally it must be fresh. Otherwise we could ask some *Time* stringer to run through his files. . . ."

When Curt finished his account of Bruton, Mary said, "He sounds quite something."

"He was. And he had quite a something with him."

"Oh!"

He described the Swedish-looking Christine, Bruton's "companion," as a hundred-dollar-an-hour model type who sounded as though she had also been educated.

Mary didn't like her too well. Curt could tell that she wished now she had accompanied him to the party.

"I guess you wouldn't want anything to eat," she said, somewhat illogically, looking with resentment at the stuff on the coffee table.

"Yes, I would."

She swiveled up to a sitting position. "You're just saying it."

"No, I really would."

She made him a canapé with one of the tiny crackers, and he popped the warm bottle of domestic champagne.

"To some kind of remembrance," she said as they clinked glasses.

Her voice was still surly. He felt wary but very tired. "What does *that* mean?" he said.

"Oh, just that I know you'll have a good time in Spain, and I don't expect I'll be on your mind every hour of the day."

"No one's ever going to forget you."

She looked at him askance. "Ever?"

"Ever."

She put her glass on the table and threw her arms around him. He felt a tear warm his neck. He moved her against the back of the divan and kissed her, his hand moving down from her shoulder.

Her lips buzzed against his face. "I think it's time we said our own farewell."

Some twenty minutes later Curt fell asleep with a *déjà vu* dream about a *déjà vu* dream, in which elements of Christine Bergman and Mary were strangely intermingled, and his own effort at connubial farewell came off like an undercharged bottle of champagne.

After getting his flight confirmed and bag checked in, Curt moved over to the currency exchange window and bought two hundred dollars' worth of pesetas. The wallpaper-sized bills that the clerk handed him made it seem as though he were entering an international Monopoly game. The Spanish money was hard to treat seriously and, after making a pretense at counting it, he folded it into his passport carrier, promising himself to check the pesetas later against the exchange booklet that the clerk had given him.

Back out in the main lobby of the TWA terminal, he located a spirally, free-suspension stairway. A pedestal sign advertised a cocktail lounge on the mezzanine floor. He climbed the stairs, and as he neared the top he could hear a hum of voices, like tiny motors idling in anticipation.

Inside the lounge everything was softly lit and cushioned—plush red carpeting, leather-topped tables, well-padded bar. A long tier of picture windows admitted angles of outside reality through partially opened drapes, but almost everything in the room was oriented toward the bar, a high altar raised two steps up from the bottom row of tables. Modern man knew how to propitiate the gods of flight, Curt thought and, spying an open stool near the corner of the bar, moved toward it as an additional supplicant.

Ordering a double Scotch and soda, he swiveled around on the cushioned stool and surveyed his fellow pilgrims. For the most part they seemed to be businessmen in conservative gray suits, but he caught sight of two Stetsons and a clutch of mink, and a man and a woman, near the piano, who easily ran off with the fancy-dress prize. The man wore a yellow linen suit and his companion had on the damnedest outfit he'd ever seen: a steeple-crowned hat, like a witch's, with a pink veil that fell, hiding face and neck, to a long duster made of the same candy-striped material as the hat.

Consigning them to Miami or Bermuda or wherever birds of that color flew, Curt searched around until he found the Table Most Worthwhile Sitting At, and found it, near the potted palms. It featured a top-notch brunette, starlet or model class, attended by three indistinguishably good-looking young men who might have been left over from an old Judy Garland routine.

The girl reminded him of Mary and his promise. So when the barman arrived with his drink, he paid with a five and asked for the change in silver. With medical judiciousness he drank off half his Scotch in easy stages. When the barman returned, he followed his directions, stepping around a decorative screen to the phone booths, which were as plush and subtly lit as the lounge.

He decided on a duty call first and got his father's number in Hazleton. His father wasn't in. It was Mildred who answered; she was sorry Alfred was out, but she would be glad to relay the message. Curt made it short and formal. Mildred was the third Mrs. Alfred C. Fielding and he'd never had much to say to her, especially since she was only a year or two his senior, and he had known her when she was sleeping with the old man, even while the second Mrs. Fielding was still on the premises. He was tempted to say "Good-bye, Mother" but settled for "Mildred."

Sins of the father, he thought, as he waited for the operator to get him Helen's number in Harrisburg. Should he leave some hint of reconciliation hanging in the air? He started to formulate a little departure and good-will speech. If the conversation went right he could still place his bet at the insurance counter before take-off. Helen's phone was ringing, a hollow, echoing ring, one that convinced him the apartment was empty. The ex-Mrs. Curtis T. Fielding was out. Out where, and with whom? When Helen was out, someone was probably in, like Flynn. You bet. The hell with it.

When Mary answered her phone after the second ring he felt both relieved and grateful. She seemed to have been waiting for his call, and the thought calmed him. He found himself saying all the things you're supposed to say in taking continental leave of someone you're supposed to be in love with.

The operator cut in to say the three minutes were up, and Mary began speaking hurriedly.

"Don't forget, Curt, you're going to cable the minute you get to Madrid."

"I will."

"I don't mean to be fussy. I'd just like to know you're safe."

There was a tenderness and a concern in her voice that he associated with funerals and surgery. "I won't forget," he said, his own voice not quite making the grade.

"All right," she said.

"All right."

"Take care of yourself."

"You too."

"I *love* you."

"I love *you.*"

"Good-bye, Curt—or should I say *hasta la vista?*"

He thought he heard a sob and almost managed one himself. "Good-bye, Mary," he said, and broke the connection gently with his index finger.

The electric fan whirred softly at the top of the booth like a captured moth. He could hear the sound of his own breathing. It was like being in some modern kind of confessional, he thought: the additional charges would be a penance due; and he would have to say, "Bless me, Operator, for I confess to the Eternal Electron and to you, Operator. I confess that I can't manage it with Mary, Operator. She has plenty of what it takes—body, mind, soul—to make a total human being. And she's probably in love, but I'm not, Operator, not with her or anyone, not even myself. . . ."

The operator rang back and announced in her musical-chimes voice that there would be "an additional eighty-five cents on that last call, sir."

He paid the three quarters and the dime into the slots slowly, deliberately. Each bullfrog plunk pulled him back to reality. Time, patience, cash! Old Melville had had the right formula for sanity.

When he returned to the bar he found his stool unoccupied and his cigarette burnt out at the filter. He drank the rest of the Scotch and signaled the bartender for another.

He made up his mind to take out a policy in Mary's name before departure. Even by phone, she had managed to depress him and buoy him up at the same time, an effect which he now realized had become constant in their relationship.

In getting his passport folder out, before paying the bill, he decided this was a good time to check the pesetas. He counted the notes and then checked against the exchange list. The sum came to just under twelve thousand pesetas. With the exchange fee deducted, that should be about right.

"You must be headed for Spain."

Curt thought it was the bartender, until he looked up and saw a tall man about his own age sitting one stool away. The man had a wide, grinny mouth and dark brows that jutted out over wide-open eyes. The eyes reminded Curt of a Boy Scout offering a magazine subscription, and the voice certainly sounded American, with a touch of Midwestern flatness and friendliness. But the man appeared somehow foreign.

"Yes, I am," Curt answered, trying to sound equally friendly, not suspicious. "As you see, I'm trying to get my pesetas straight."

"No trouble these days," the stranger said. "Sixty's the magic number, as you probably know. Sixty to the dollar."

It wasn't the face that was foreign, Curt thought, though it had its own peculiar quality, pleasant looking, large boned, looming. It was the suit, made of a heavy dark cloth, very different from the synthetic sleekness of American warm-weather clothing. And also the hat—maybe that was what made him think Boy Scout. It was brown instead of the gray expected with a suit that color, and it had a broader brim than anything fashionable in the United States, except in Texas.

"I take it you've spent some time in Spain," Curt said.

"The last five years, apart from flying trips home like this. As a matter of fact, I'm headed back tonight."

"Well," Curt said, "we may be on the same flight if you're flying TWA."

"Flight 902?"

"That's it," Curt said, and decided to reciprocate the stranger's friendliness by moving over to the vacant seat between them.

Introductions revealed that the man's name was John Bowers: he was assistant bureau chief for UPI in Madrid and had been in Spain since 1959, "the year Ike visited Franco."

Curt told him it was a real pleasure to meet such an experienced hand. He filled him in on his own background, and somewhat sheepishly offered him one of the cards he'd had printed up on the advice of a faculty friend who had made several research trips to Europe. The card was replete with his Pennwood title and a list of his degrees. "Strictly for export," he said in handing it to Bowers.

Bowers looked it over, a smile spreading across his face. Then he reached into his breast pocket and withdrew a card of his own. "Here," he said, "you haven't seen anything yet."

It was a fine linen-based card with cursive letters raised as high as braille. Curt was somewhat puzzled as he read it:

> *John Bowers Furbisher*
> *Jefe Auxiliar de UPI, Madrid*
> *Asociado de EFE*
> *B. A. Universidad de Missouri*
> *M. A. Universidad de Northwestern*

"According to this," he said, "your name is really Furbisher."

Bowers laughed pleasantly. "Not really. The Spanish custom is to give your father's name—your family name, that is—right after your first name. Then comes your mother's maiden name. It's lucky for you that your card has only your middle initial or you'd have everyone calling you by your middle name."

Curt was nodding his head. "I understand," he said. "How about this EFE?"

"That usually gets Americans. It's simply a Spanish news agency. *Efe* is the letter *F* spelled out."

"What's it stand for?"

"Some people say it's an abbreviation for the Falange party, others say Franco. All I know is it's the only Spanish news service that's worth anything, and they use me for certain American material. That little designation has gotten me into and out of places where my regular *carnet* was useless."

While Bowers was talking, it occurred to Curt that he might have covered the Swiatski accident, but on second thought that seemed improbable. Zaragoza was two hundred miles away from Madrid. What was probable was that Bowers knew the story and had perhaps even relayed it to the States. Curt thought of bringing up the matter in some way, but then decided against it for the time being. Instead, he began to talk about the piece he had contracted to do for *Phaeton*.

"So you can see," he later concluded, "I'm really glad I ran into you this way. You can probably fill me in on a lot of things, if you don't mind having your brains picked."

"Heck, no," Bowers said, confirming Curt's opinion of Boy Scout. "I do the same thing all the time."

They ordered another drink. A half-hour later the subdued but insistent public address system announced that passengers for TWA flight 902, bound for Madrid, should report to loading ramp seven. They left the lounge, agreeing that they would try to arrange seats together on the plane.

Bowers' press card did the trick, and an hour later they were air-borne, with New York's brilliant circus of lights diminishing tailward.

3
To POL and SAC

According to the captain's report, they were cruising at seven hundred miles an hour, some forty thousand feet above the Atlantic. Curt and John Bowers sat on the two-seat side of the economy-class compartment. They had already ordered a Scotch and a cognac from their stewardess, a Miss Jameson.

"This is much better than the last trip I made to Europe," Curt said. His head rested comfortably against the cushioned seat; his eyes squinted, almost closed, as though peering into the smoke screen of the past. "A couple thousand of us footsloggers boarded a converted coastal liner in Hampton Roads, Virginia, back in forty-three."

"Well, you can relax," Bowers said. "You're in TWA's hands now."

"And very capable hands at that." Curt looked up into the professionally smiling face of Miss Jameson, who had arrived with their drinks. She placed them on the fold-down trays with the precision of an automaton.

When she had gone, Curt sighed. "What wonders our American assembly line produces," he said. "That smile never wavered a micrometric bit."

Bowers grinned and raised his brandy. *"Salud, dinero, y amor."*

"The health I've got, the money I could use, and the *amor*— well, the *amor* is tough all over." It had been with Helen and Mary, at any rate, Curt thought.

For a while the men drank in satisfied silence. Then Curt

opened up the subject of the American position in Spain. He said that he had done some reading and understood that the Madrid Pact, begun under Truman and completed by Eisenhower in 1953, provided for defense and economic aid.

"What I don't know are the specifics," he said, "about the bases, number of men, and that sort of thing. Either it's classified information or I've been looking in the wrong places."

Bowers seemed to gather his thoughts for a moment, then reached forward and took out a dinner menu from a slot in the seat in front of him. "I might as well do this right," he said, and taking out a pen began to sketch something on the back of the menu.

Curt watched it take shape as a map of the Iberian Peninsula. The Pyrenees and the Cantabrian shore formed the flat head, and Portugal the Vandyked profile of a rugged grandee, with Cádiz an Adam's apple extension to the southeast. The drawing was completed by a line representing the Costas Blanca, Brava, and del Sol, which eventually swept up around Barcelona to Port Bou at the French border.

"You sure you're not a cartoonist instead of a reporter?"

Bowers smiled. "This," he said, making a heavy dot just west of Cádiz, "is Rota. Our Gibraltar, so to speak. And it's here that the POL begins—oil pipe line, to civilians. Rota is the key to our Sixth Fleet in the Mediterranean. What most people don't know is that naval interest began all of our negotiations with Spain."

"And not the Air Force?"

"No, that came later. Now, of course, we have only about six hundred naval people in the country and over six thousand Air Force. And there were more than eight thousand Air Force before our shift in strategy."

"What kind of shift?"

"We changed our minds about the effectiveness of SAC bases overseas. The ones we built here"—Bowers drew three small circles at locations he labeled Seville, Madrid, and Zaragoza.

Then he connected them with a line of dashes and marked it POL.

Roads, Curt thought, who makes them and who takes them?

"These were built to handle complete wings of B-47's, as well as fighter planes and support craft. They were to be full partners in the Strategic Air Command's ring of defense around the world. But at the time these bases were completed, the manned aircraft part of our defense was minimized by the appearance of ICBM's. SAC's 'Reflex Operation' shrank. As a result we've never had more than about fifteen B-47's based at Torrejón, which is this one near Madrid, and one of the largest airfields in Europe. You'll see it when we land at Barajas. Torrejón was built to take care of hundreds of planes on a rotation system of ninety days—crews, back-up people, the whole shooting match. But all we ever had there were small reflex crews on three-week rotation. And these bases near Seville and Zaragoza, which have nearly the same capability as Torrejón, are just on stand-by orders now."

"When were the bases completed?" Curt asked.

"Late in fifty-eight."

"And when did the phase down begin?"

"Well, the shift in strategy began the same year, and since sixty-three we've been phased down real low."

"Then what you're saying is these bases were obsolete by the time they were completed."

"Not quite. We got three or four years' use out of them."

"It's not much."

"No, but military strategies are like weapons. When something more efficient comes along, they're obsolete."

"How much did these bases cost us?"

"Well, if we leave out Rota—which has become increasingly important—about $300 million."

"That doesn't sound too bad."

"Low cost of construction in Spain. We've paid triple that in other countries."

"The question is how long can we go on paying out that kind of money all over the world?"

"That's our diplomacy. It's based on the idea that we can afford these things better than Russia or China or anybody else. Look at the thousands of dollars we pay to kill a single Viet Cong. Besides, you're forgetting that we've helped Spain as a country. The Madrid Pact has had some of the effect of the Marshall Plan. Spain is moving into the twentieth century, as our ally."

Curt decided to wait and see for himself how much of a Marshall Plan effect there had been in Spain. It was something to be weighed against the fact that we had assisted a fascist regime that was supposedly weakening at the time.

"Let's go back to something you said before," he said. "If we de-emphasized the use of manned bombers, do we now have offensive missile sites in Spain?"

"That's the jack-pot question, isn't it? We're not supposed to have any sites here, but you'll hear it said we do. The Radio España Independiente blasts away from across the French border, and they say we have the sites through a secret agreement with Franco. But it's hard to keep anything like that secret for long. I don't mean just espionage, aerial photography, embassy leaks, congressional investigations, but by now some shepherd would have stumbled across something and spread the word."

"You sure one hasn't?"

Bowers' face became serious. "Look," he said, "I've done some checking on my own. I felt it was my job to follow up certain leads. Once I was told we were stockpiling missiles at Torrejón, only to find out that what my informant really saw was gas tanks. So, I'd say the odds are that if your shepherd stumbles across anything it'll be one of our radar sites. And I've visited all of those. There are a good batch of them: one up here by Irún, one near Huesca, and another over here by Gerona." He dotted the menu map three times across the northern tier of the country, along the Pyrenees. "The last one is out here"—he freehanded an island off the eastern coast—"here on Puig Mayor, the highest mountain on Mallorca."

"Looks as though we're well set up in Spain."

"Yes, and our military like it there. For one thing, Franco is geared to military operations. He can do things the way no democratic leader can. This pipe line, for instance. It runs through some prime real estate. He got the land for it in less than three months—five hundred miles of clearance."

Curt resisted the temptation to ask Bowers if he approved of such efficiency. He couldn't help wondering what sort of American correspondent the Franco regime could tolerate for five years.

"Over-all, then, you think our alliance with Spain has been successful?"

"I think so. We had four or five objectives and we've pretty much achieved them."

"Namely?"

Bowers began counting on his fingers as he spoke. "One, develop military bases that would help in common defense of the West. Two, keep Spain non-Communist and in close relations with us. Three, improve the country's defense of the Iberian Peninsula in case of limited land warfare. Four, move Spain closer to joining NATO. And five, assure internal stability in the country, at least to the extent necessary to achieve the other objectives. This is the way it's been spelled out for me, and I'd have to say we've done all right, from this point of view."

"You sound as though you might have some reservations."

"Well, you always do. You can't come into a country with a military force and escape some bad results. Servicemen aren't the best good-will ambassadors. We've got them in Germany, France, England, Italy, Turkey, Taiwan, Korea, Japan, and in all those places we're disliked. The military can't help it—it's in the nature of things. The Russians are hated in the satellite countries, too. In Spain we've become known as the *Peligro Yanqui*, the Yankee Peril. The Catholic authorities won't allow

Spaniards to attend any church services on our bases. The old Cardinal of Seville—Segura—has openly opposed the Madrid Pact, accusing Franco of bartering Catholic conscience for 'heretical dollars.' The Spanish army is jealous of the highly paid Americans. Some high-ranking officers resent the presence of foreign troops and want to return to traditional neutrality. And the university people, the intellectuals, see the United States as the main prop of a corrupt regime. All of this adds grist to the Communist propaganda mill, and—" Bowers stopped abruptly, as though catching sight of himself in a mirror. "I'm not boring you, am I?"

"You sound like an escapee from Carlisle and Georgetown, but go ahead. I want to know how Europe's becoming Americanized, and this seems to be a big part of it."

"Well," Bowers said, shifting his legs, "you might even find out how some Americans are becoming Europeanized in the process."

Once again Curt became aware of Bowers' clothing, seeing it this time as a Hispanophilic sign. "I suppose a man who's lived five years in Spain must have found something worthwhile," he said. "How about your family? Are you married?"

"Yes." Bowers grinned. "But I'll skip the photos. We have two daughters, ages twelve and eighteen. And the whole family likes Spain, although Milly's beginning to get anxious about the girls. She wants them to have an American education and date American boys. I think she'd croak if one of the kids got involved with a Spaniard."

Curt was about to ask what might be wrong with Spaniards as husbands, but Miss Jameson, who had for some time been working her way down the aisle, arrived just then with their dinners.

As she reached a tray in to Bowers by the window, she leaned over Curt and he was engulfed by her scent. His nostrils flared and caught the combined essences of *filet-mignon*, asparagus, baked potato, and Miss Jameson.

Bowers pointed to the red wine listed on the menu, saying he'd have a glass of that. Curt asked for the same thing, and Miss Jameson crinkled her nose and said, "Miss Williams will bring that round in the cart right soon."

The men ate the compartmentalized meal and chatted about food aboard planes being almost always better than expected. Bowers gave Curt some tips about restaurants in Madrid. The wine was served by Miss Williams; tiny bottles of an excellent Bordeaux.

After they had finished their éclairs and sat back, relaxed, with their coffee, Curt said, "There's something I'd like to ask you, but I'm afraid you might resent it."

"After a meal like that it would be hard to feel resentful."

"Well, it's about your work. And what I'm wondering is how you can stand being a correspondent in a country so dominated by censorship."

"It's not as bad as you'd think," Bowers said, and took a slow sip of his coffee. "After I got my master's degree I stayed on in public relations at Northwestern. After that I did a four-year stint with AP in Washington. And I don't see much difference between what I did then and what I'm doing now. Don't get me wrong. As a member of the fourth estate, I'm as determined as the next man to preserve freedom of the press. I'd fight for the right, and all that, but—have you ever done public relations work?"

Curt shook his head.

"Public relations is censorship, pure and simple. You put in what's good and keep out what's bad. And it's all a matter of timing. If you let something appear too soon or too late you ruin the effect. Doesn't matter what. It can be the hiring of a new football coach or a scientific breakthrough of Nobel Prize proportions. I lived through both at Northwestern and the amount of finagling each time was unimaginable."

Bowers took a packet of cigarillos from his coat pocket and offered one to Curt, who refused it. When he'd lit up, Bowers went on. "Washington is even worse. There you have news conferences and interviews where everything is off the record and others where only part of what's said is off the record. There are deliberate leaks and semideliberate leaks. There are trial balloons and old sausage stories that are limp from being in the files so long. Now, as a reporter, you have to know what you can write and what you can't. I spent my first year getting my ears unfurled after the bureau chief pinned them back. The point is, any newsman in Washington could have a scoop any day of the week—except for collusion between the press and government. I personally must have had twenty stories from office malcontents that would have made entertaining and even important reading, but I didn't get permission to write more than three or four of them, and not until the office involved had been informed."

Curt burst the bubble of resentment and impatience growing within him. In a level voice he said, "But what you're talking about is voluntary censorship. There is the right to inquire. Someone *could* have ripped the lid off those stories, if necessary. It seems to me there's a big difference."

"Maybe so," Bowers said, "but that difference in Spain is felt mainly by their national press. They don't bother us much. I can write anything I want and have it printed in the States. Just cable it right out."

"You've never had any trouble?"

"Well, once, a couple years ago, and the whole affair was silly."

"I'd like to hear about it."

"It was nothing, really. I covered a San Fermín parade and wrote a paragraph about a flare-up between the crowd and the Gray Police—you'll see them, they wear long gray military coats. They got busy with their clubs when the crowd turned surly, and I gave it a one-paragraph treatment about eight paragraphs down in the story. A rewrite man in the States moved it up as a lead, with a headline to match. Salgado was then what we called the Minister of Misinformation. He called me into his office and told me the story was intolerable, a stab in the back, and typical of the way foreign journalists misrepresented Spain to the world. This time it was really serious, he said. Some officers in Los Grises maintained that I had insulted the honor of the corps and should be gotten rid of, 'one way or the other.' Salgado said he thought it best to have me declared *persona non grata* and have me shipped home. I said, sure, have me expelled. I said it would take me twenty years to write anything that could harm his country more than he could by having me deported over such a triviality. I told him it would be worth $25,000 in publicity for me, and I'd pay him an agent's commission. I was a little scared as well as sore, but I was on the right track. Since then, I've written a number of stories much more damaging to the regime than that, and I've never been bothered."

"But newsmen do get bounced out of Spain," Curt said. "Seems to me there was a Frenchman last year, had something to do with student demonstrations."

"That was Menon of *France-Soir.* Salgado insists he was an *agent provocateur.* He also did an anti-Opus Dei piece for the *Economist* that brought the roof down on Salgado."

Curt had read about the Opus Dei and knew it was a Catholic lay organization that had become very powerful behind the scenes. The Menon article would be something he'd definitely want to check.

"What about Spanish newsmen?" he said. "You must see a great enough difference of degree in their censorship to make it a difference of kind."

"I'm just not sure," Bowers said. "It's all relative. Censorship stems from the idea of how much is good for the people to know. It goes back at least as far as Plato's *Republic.*"

"Hell," Curt said, "if you want to view it that way, it goes all the way back to the Garden of Eden. God was the first censor and Eve the first girl reporter."

Miss Jameson appeared with more coffee. When she went on to serve the people in front Curt watched the strain of her militarily severe skirt.

"Our Miss Jameson," he said in a low voice, "inspires me to believe God was also the creator of the first planned news leak."

Bowers laughed good-naturedly. "Sort of a trial balloon to see how the constituents would take it."

"And how do the Spaniards take *it?*"

"Well, as you may have heard, they're rather prudish. When you land in Spain you'll be in a country unlike any other on the Continent. It's like going through a time machine. Some places you're back in the fourteenth century, others eighteenth or nineteenth. And women come in for special consideration. In ͺone class you have mothers and wives and young ladies of good family. Under the cult of the Virgin they're idolized. In the other class there are maids and prostitutes and all foreign women, who are looked upon as fair game. Don Quixote still lives on, and so does Don Juan."

"You often hear that every Spaniard has his mistress."

"Maybe so," Bowers said, "but you need money and time for a mistress. It seems to me that for every ten Americans who have a secretary girl friend there may be one Spaniard with a mistress."

"How about prostitution?"

"Brothels were outlawed in fifty-four and there are very few streetwalkers. Barcelona's a slightly different matter and so's Madrid. Occasionally there are call-girl types around the hotels. But most of the activity takes place in the night clubs, *salas de fiesta*. I have a friend who's collecting material for a book on the subject."

"Interesting research."

"That's what I tell him. All he says is, 'Hope I live to write it.'"

They both laughed and then dropped into relaxed silence. The hidden tension of the flight and the solid dinner were taking effect. Curt dropped the back of his seat down several notches and shucked off his loafers. As he loosened his tie, he thought of Bowers' comment about a time machine and felt that he was going through it under drowsy pressure.

The next morning Miss Jameson served their breakfast of coffee and croissants. She said they had just crossed the Portuguese border and were only about a half-hour out of Madrid, well ahead of schedule.

John Bowers suggested changing seats so that Curt could look out the porthole of a window. At first all he could see was a thin, wispy layer of clouds about a thousand feet below, but then by cupping his hands and pressing against the glass he was able to make out the surface of the earth, mottled brown and green, like the irregular bottom of a deep lake.

"It could be Idaho or Montana," he said.

"Sure," Bowers replied. "And when we land you'll see why Spain is great for low-budget westerns."

Continuing to peer out the window, Curt found it hard to imagine this as the land of Don Quixote, where the gentle knight had once traversed the plain of La Mancha. For one thing—no plain. And for another, you just couldn't leave Long Island late one night and the next morning accept the news that below you was a section of Cervantes', and Franco's, Spain.

He turned back to his breakfast, vaguely excited. Bowers had finished his croissant and was now smoking a cigarillo with his coffee.

Several times the night before Curt had considered introducing the matter of Teddy Swiatski to Bowers, but had rejected the idea. Now in the light of day his traveling companion's face was so boyishly open and reassuring that he had a strong urge to confide in him. He had known Bowers for only eight or nine hours, but he liked him, thought of him as one of those big, capable Americans who might have all the earmarks of overgrown boys but were by no means naïve. As far as he could tell, Bowers was probably good, honest, loyal, clean, and trustworthy.

Nevertheless, he decided to keep the Swiatski matter under wraps. To use Bowers' phrase, it was all a matter of timing and how much good it did to let people know. For the present, indirect questions might be best.

As he began buttering his croissant, he said, "By the way, John, there are a couple of things I'd like to ask you about before we get separated."

Bowers put down his cup of coffee.

"For one thing, I'd like to know how reliable a paper *La Verdad* is. Do you know anything about it?"

"It's probably the best in the country, most liberal, most enterprising, best edited. They handle stories that *ABC* and *YA* and others never touch and they're always in hot water with the Office of Information. It's typical Catalan."

While Bowers was speaking Curt thought of his portfolio in the rack above, containing the news clippings and letters Stanley Swiatski had given him. It seemed that *La Verdad's* account of Farlo's death was worth checking.

Bowers puffed at his cigarillo, and then, suddenly blowing out smoke, looked at Curt with unexpected sharpness. "Why do you want to know about *La Verdad?*" he said. "You have some special interest?"

Anyone sensing that much must have a nose for news, Curt thought, and took another bite of his croissant before answering. "No," he said, "no special interest. It was just a paper that George Orwell praised in *Homage to Catalonia.*"

Bowers' face hardened momentarily, and Curt knew he'd hit a clinker.

"The other thing I wanted to ask you about," he said quickly, "is your own handling of American stories in Spain."

"What kind of stories?" Bowers' good will seemed to have fled.

"About military personnel, for example."

"You mean R-R-R and M."

"What's that?"

"Rape, robbery, rackets, and murder."

"All right, I'll take some of that."

"We cover them freely. Sometimes it takes a while to get the story straight from our own military and embassy people. But we get it eventually and cable it home if it's important enough."

"What about the other way around—when it's our people who are raped, robbed, racketed, or murdered?"

Bowers grinned in spite of himself. "We've never had one of the first and not many of the others, but we've cabled those also when they've been newsworthy."

"If some of our people are killed in a highway accident, is that newsworthy?"

"Not a routine accident. We leave that to the sixteenth Air Force notices. But if an airman runs his car into a village square, knocks over a statue, and kills three pedestrians before wiping himself out, then we do something with the story."

Bowers paused, butted his cigarillo in the seat-handle ashtray, and then began to speak again in a voice that was rather high-pitched: "Now," he said, "I want you to know I've enjoyed making this trip with you. In fact, I'd like you to meet Milly and spend some time with us in Madrid. But I'm not sure that you're just an English professor on a Fulbright to Zaragoza. You seem to have some kind of angle. If I'm wrong, let me know. But I'd really appreciate it if you didn't just try to use me."

Bowers' face was set and his eyes wide open, not belligerent so much as alert. Eagle scout, Curt found himself thinking, certainly not tenderfoot.

"All right, I won't lie to you," he said, and saw Bowers' jaw line loosen somewhat. "There is something I mean to investigate in Spain, but this isn't the right time to talk about it. When and if I need help, you'll be the first to hear from me. But first I want to feel my way into the situation and see what happens."

Bowers regarded him steadily for some time, then finally said, "All right, but I hope you're not doing a stint for the CIA or anything like that. If you are, I don't want anything to do with it. I don't want my credentials jeopardized."

"You have my word that it's nothing like that. When I tell you about it someday you may find the whole matter silly. But right now it's important to me and a few other people."

When Bowers spoke again he had recovered his boyish grin. "One thing," he said. "Don't tell anyone else you're interested in *La Verdad* because of Orwell. *La Verdad* wasn't established until after the Civil War and Orwell probably never even heard of it."

"I knew it was something stupid," Curt said. "And now may I give you a tip?"

"What's that?"

"You'd better work on your poker face. I knew immediately by your expression that I'd said something wrong."

They both laughed, and Curt realized that he probably wasn't telling Bowers anything he didn't know.

PART
TWO

4
At Oskar's

Oskar's was not hard to find. The bartender at the Fénix corroborated the directions Marta Torres had given on the telephone. From the hotel you walked three blocks east on the Castellana, just past the Biblioteca Nacional. Then you turned left at the corner, and across the street you saw Oskar's— or "Oskar" as the vertical neon sign had it.

Curt went across the street and into the restaurant, down three or four steps to a wide vestibule. This was separated from the main dining room by a buffet that gleamed with heaps of shrimp, lobster, ham, cheese, and pastries. To one side stood an illuminated glass tank, alive with the steel-dark bodies of trout.

A waiter in a tuxedo approached. *"El señor está solo?"*

"Ahora, sí, pero en un momento encuentro a dos señoritas," Curt said, wondering whether "to encounter" was the right verb.

"Perfecto," the waiter said, his smile implying that a man should always be fortunate enough to be meeting two *señoritas*. He started leading the way toward the center of the interior room. When Curt asked if he knew Señorita Marta Torres, the waiter turned quickly on his heel, and said that if the *señor* was "encountering" the Señorita Torres, he should come this way. He led him to one side of the room, where wide leather booths provided some privacy and additional comfort. From the table he whisked away a tented card marked *Reservado*.

47

The Señorita Torres should be here in a few minutes, he said, as he seated Curt. Would the *señor* meanwhile care for an *aperitivo? "Whisky-sifón, ginebra y tónica?"*

Curt ordered a Scotch and soda, *"escocés y sifón."* The waiter pivoted smartly on his heel and set off toward the bar like a soldier under orders. Curt sat back in the booth, keeping his eyes on the entryway. His inner ear carried tracings of Marta Torres' voice as it had sounded on the phone the night before, sharp in its British English, officially bright, and personally welcoming. He remembered especially how she had said, "I do hope you won't mind my bringing along a young countrywoman of mine. I assure you she's a person worth meeting."

Almost as though evoked by his thoughts, two women came down the stairs just then and entered the vestibule. One, in her fifties, seemed a combination great-aunt and superannuated schoolgirl. Gold-rimmed glasses contrasted with the olive darkness of her face. She was dressed in black, except for a wrap of orange net material draped over her shoulders. Her companion was a copper-skinned girl, perhaps in her late twenties, who wore a blue knit suit that clung to her slender frame. She was a beautiful girl without being pretty. Her breasts were elegantly small. Her legs just escaped thinness. Her dark hair was accented across the front with a silver streak, and her narrow nose was thinly arched. Her eyes were large, wide-set, and the brows curved inordinately high, like those of a modern Nefertiti.

As the women stood poised in the entryway, Curt felt sure they were the people he was supposed to meet, and by the way they glanced in his direction it seemed obvious that they had picked him out also. The waiter, returning with his drink, ended the suspense by pointing toward his booth and indicating that they were to follow.

Curt watched the girl as she followed the older woman.

She walked with her head and breasts high, like those native women who carry water jugs balanced on their heads.

"You are Dr. Fielding." The older woman approached with her right hand extended.

"I am, and, after all our correspondence, it is so nice to see you, Miss Torres."

They shook hands, and Marta Torres said in Spanish that she had the pleasure of presenting Señorita María Victoria Mandar y Saenz.

"*Encantado, señorita.*"

"It is my pleasure, Dr. Fielding. I hope that I do not intrude on you and Miss Torres. She has been too kind to invite me here, and I have been too forward." She offered her hand to Curt.

"Nonsense," Miss Torres said. "Dr. Fielding has no way of knowing how daring an adventure this is for a Spanish girl. He's probably used to France and England as well as his own country."

Curt couldn't tell whether she was warning him to behave, or satirizing the customs of her own country.

"I know only that you both do me a great honor and that I am delighted to be here in Madrid with such lovely and intelligent companions."

He helped them get seated.

Miss Torres took a corner seat between him and María Victoria. The waiter pulled the table out and then eased it back.

When they were settled, Miss Torres said, "I believe, María Victoria, that we have on our hands a *norteamericano* who is definitely *un caballero.*"

"Definitely," the girl answered, smiling pleasantly.

The waiter asked whether the ladies would require an *aperitivo.*

"Please do," Curt said. "I've anticipated you." He lifted his Scotch and soda.

"Well, I think we shall, then. María Victoria?"

"*Sí. Quiero un Tío Pepe,*" she said to the waiter.

"*Y para mí, un whisky-soda, Luis.*"

The waiter bowed slightly and departed.

"I'm curious to know," Curt said, "what kind of whisky that'll be?"

"Oh, it's always the same, Dr. Fielding. Here in Spain it always means Scotch. You'll have difficulty trying to find bourbon or rye."

There was a pause after the explanation. They had gotten by the opening introductions, and now it was as though they were all catching their social breath before plunging on.

"I'm glad you chose this place for us to meet," Curt began. "It's very pleasant."

"And the Hotel Fénix, do you like it also?" Miss Torres asked.

"Very much. Fine bar, the garden restaurant is lovely. And the clientele seems tweedy-proper, with consulate overtones. Also, there are very few Americans."

"Then," the girl said, "you are one of those who do not like to be with your own countrymen in a foreign country?"

Curt sensed that she asked things less precisely in English than she might in her own language, and he could see that she did not mean to be critical.

"Yes, you might say so. It's not that I'm anti-American, or even antitourist. But I've an idea that I will get to know more about Spain by staying away from my own countrymen. Do you think that strange?"

"Oh, no. I think it wise."

"You will find many Americans in Zaragoza, too, as you know," Miss Torres injected.

"You mean at the base."

"Yes."

"And how do the people in Zaragoza get along with them?" he asked.

"I believe rather well," Miss Torres said. "But perhaps

María Victoria can be more explicit. As I told you on the phone, she is from Zaragoza and is simply visiting in Madrid at the moment."

Curt turned toward the girl expectantly.

"At first when the base came, there were some difficulties, but now, as Miss Torres says, things go well."

"Do you know many of the Americans?"

"That is part of my purpose in having you two meet," Miss Torres put in. "You see, María Victoria is a five-year graduate from the University of Madrid and—"

The waiter returned with their drinks. They decided to order their lunch somewhat later and he left.

Miss Torres picked up the thread of what she'd been saying: "María Victoria has been teaching Spanish at the base to your servicemen and their children. Now she wants to prepare for her *oposiciones,* that is, competitive examinations, in order to teach English in a Spanish college or institute."

"What do these *oposiciones* involve?"

"In this instance, they are an examination on all English and American literary periods, as well as English philology," the girl said.

"And you must take these to get a job teaching in any college or university in Spain?"

Miss Torres said, "You will find, Dr. Fielding, as you get to know our country, that *oposiciones* are necessary for all professions."

"Yes," the girl added, "when my father wanted to become a lawyer, he took the *oposiciones,* and when a *juez,* a judge, for that, too."

"Your father is a judge in Zaragoza?"

"*Sí.*"

Something buzzed in his mind like an alarm. All Marta Torres had said on the phone was that she was bringing someone from Zaragoza to meet him, a lovely young person she was sure he'd be glad to know. *That* much was certainly true; but now the girl represented a danger, or at least a question, as well as a lovely opportunity. If her father was a judge, he probably knew something about the Swiatski case, and maybe the girl did, too. How *much?* You're being hypersensitive, he told himself; you've seen too many movies.

"How long will it take to prepare for your examinations?" he asked.

"I am to have them in August of next year."

"And," Miss Torres said, "since I have known Victoria's family for years, and knew also from your letters that you were anxious to perfect your Spanish, I thought I might bring you two together for an academic *quid pro quo.*"

Curt looked at the girl, catching the eagle proudness of the nose, the aristocratically arched brows.

"*Estupendo,*" he said, "it would be perfectly to my liking." His voice kept to a flat ambiguity.

Victoria said, "I am so glad. I hope that I can be as much help to you as I am sure you will be to me."

"Good," Miss Torres said, "then that's settled. Why don't we have our lunch now?"

Curt let her order the lunch, which included two specialties of the house, *caldo gallego,* a thick meat-and-vegetable soup, and broiled lamb chops marinated in wine.

During the meal, Marta Torres did most of the talking, describing the situation at the University of Zaragoza, vouching for Vice-rector Durán as a highly capable scholar and administrator, a Basque with a fine mind who was responsible for the American studies program. Later María Victoria described the amusements in Zaragoza—the museums, theaters, night clubs. She said he might find it all tempestuous at first, because he would be arriving at the time of the Fiesta de la Raza, a two-week festival celebrating the most important religious figure in Spain, Nuestra Señora del Pilar. There would be bullfights and processions and *fútbol* matches and competitions in *jota* dancing—the *jota* being Aragon's special dance form.

As they were having dessert, a flan flaming with brandy, Curt maneuvered the conversation around to Victoria's job at the air base, asking her how she had liked working there. She said she enjoyed it quite well; she had made some friends, especially among the teachers and with Lois Harte, who was an education officer at the base. The teachers lived in the city, and she had been to some of their parties. Many of them spoke Spanish fairly well and had become acclimated to life in Zaragoza.

"What about the military themselves?"

She had known few of them socially. She had been to the homes of two or three officers, and knew the wife of a first sergeant. But she had not gone to any of the base parties or to the officers' club.

Curt sensed hesitancy and pushed. "Was there any stigma attached to your working at the base?"

"Not as an instructor of the language. At first my mother objected but my father said that it would be all right, if things were done properly."

Which meant not fraternizing too much, Curt assumed. "And what of others who work at the base, the Spaniards?"

"It is not thought to be degrading, if that is what you mean."

Miss Torres had been toying with her glass, and now added her explanation. "I imagine it is somewhat different in Zaragoza than in Madrid, since Zaragoza is a bit more provincial. But honest labor is respected throughout Spain, and if someone works for the American military that fact does not make him an outcast. I think you'll find our real concern is how long you will be able to provide fruitful employment for our workers. Do you, by the way, have some special reason for asking?"

"As a matter of fact, yes," Curt said, and began to explain

about the article he had been commissioned to do for *Phaeton*.

"So you see," he concluded, "I can't simply have polite answers about Spanish-American relations or I'll end up with a useless article."

"Are you accusing us of being overly polite, Dr. Fielding? If so, you're reversing the criticism most often leveled at your countrymen." Marta Torres smiled in such a way as to indicate she was not offended, nor was he to be.

"Touché," he said. "Perhaps I myself am being somewhat impolite."

"Not at all," Miss Torres said. "And the article sounds like a wonderful idea. I will help you arrange any interviews you may want in Madrid. But I do hope you will be fair and honest in your writing. So many journalists give erroneous pictures of Spain."

"I think I know one who doesn't."

"And who is that?"

"John Bowers of UPI."

"Oh, I know Mr. Bowers. A wonderful fellow."

"I met him coming over."

Victoria joined the conversation. "Did you have a good trip?"

"Very pleasant," he said, "and uneventful."

Miss Torres asked for his first impressions of Madrid.

"I like it very much—its spaciousness, wide *paseos*. It reminds me of Washington, D.C., in some ways. You can see more here than you can in New York or Chicago. You're not always looking up to the sky."

Later the conversation swung around to personal plans. Curt acknowledged he would be staying in Madrid for the rest of the week, and then would leave on Monday for Zaragoza.

Marta Torres said she hoped that he would stay for the party at the embassy on Saturday night for all the Fulbrighters, and that he would listen to some of the orientation lecturers, although she was sure some of them would be too basic for him.

While she was talking, Curt searched for some way that he might properly ask María Victoria if she would attend the party with him, or perhaps act as girl guide around Madrid, but he found no appropriate way of doing so, especially in the *dueña* presence of Miss Torres. He wished she would hurry off to the powder room.

He did manage to ask when the *señorita* was going back to Zaragoza, and she confessed that she, too, was leaving early next week. He took this as a legitimate opening.

"Well," he said, "I'll be picking up the Volkswagen I ordered in a day or two, and perhaps I could drive you back to Zaragoza."

María Victoria looked from him to the older woman and back again, obviously confused as to how she should answer. He wished now that he had waited.

"I am so sorry, but my ticket is arranged for the Talgo. I go by train. My parents expect it."

"When did you order your car, Dr. Fielding?"

He decided to go along with the abrupt switch. "Two months ago," he said, "and I was told it would be here for me on the fifth of this month."

"That's wonderful," Miss Torres said. "You'll see so much more of the country than you would by train or bus. Don't you think that's nice, María Victoria?"

"Yes, it will be wonderful—for Dr. Fielding."

Marta Torres began listing a number of places in the Pyrenees and on the Costa Brava he might like to visit. Then María Victoria excused herself, saying that she had to return to her aunt's house for a fitting: she was having some dresses made in Madrid.

Marta Torres told her to run along; the doorman would get her a cab. She wanted to speak to Dr. Fielding about some Fulbright matters.

The girl's eyes were full on Curt. "It has been a pleasure to meet you, Dr. Fielding."

He stood up, wondering whether he should accompany her to the door, but decided against it. As they shook hands, he realized that she was tall, perhaps five eight. It *was* nice, just to look at her.

"*Adiós, señorita.* You have given me much to look forward to in Zaragoza. Your help will be appreciated greatly."

María Victoria addressed herself to Miss Torres, speaking very swiftly in Spanish, thanking her for her kindness, mentioning that her father would certainly wish to thank her when she next visited Zaragoza.

Then she left. It was like watching a cool flame vanish.

"She's a lovely girl," he said, as he sat down again.

"Yes, and her family is one of the best in Zaragoza. They can do much to help you there—open doors otherwise unopened to *extranjeros.* If—"

"If what?"

"*If* you play by the rules."

The headwaiter appeared and asked whether everything was satisfactory. Would there be anything else?

Curt said he would have another Courvoisier if Miss Torres would join him. She said she would have a Marie Brizard.

"Maybe," he said, "you'd be willing to coach me in the rules."

She accepted a cigarette from him and put it into a short amber holder.

"First of all," she said, blowing out a funnel of smoke with direct force, "you must realize that I have lived in your country several times, and I have known many Americans here in Spain, from the embassy, the military, and of course in my job. So I am not unaware of the difficulties involved in going from one culture to another."

She took another drag on her cigarette. "Secondly, I must assure you that I have never acted in the capacity of marriage broker or *anything of the sort*—"

"Of course, I—"

"Please let me finish," she said quietly. "You will find in María Victoria most of what is fine in Spanish womanhood. A generation ago, you would not have met anyone like her under such circumstances as these. But a slow change is in process. A girl in her social position may now enter the professions. It has become, if not fashionable, eminently acceptable. And it is on a professional level that you have met her. You must be very careful to keep it that way. Any untoward act— excuse me for my frankness—will simply embarrass her and her family, and you."

Curt was getting sore. Torres was not his goddamned aunt, or the girl's guardian.

"I see that I am annoying you."

"No, not really. But I'm not sure I understand you."

"If I can explain myself now, you will know that I intend being a friend. If not, we will simply not understand each other—and there has been plenty of that between our two nations."

"All right, I'm listening."

"You saw that María Victoria was confused when you asked her to accompany you to Zaragoza."

"Yes, but for God's sake—"

"Please, Dr. Fielding. I know that yours was a fair and open suggestion. It would be perfectly correct in the United States. But for a girl like María Victoria to accept your offer would have been like accepting concubinage. If a girl gets into a man's car in Spain, without someone else in attendance, it is admitting that she has *slept with him.*"

It sounded as though Marta Torres had plucked the last phrase from a nineteenth-century novel and had used it daringly.

"You're kidding."

"No, I am not 'kidding.' If you two were to arrive in Zaragoza together that way, her chances of marriage would be practically nil afterward. It would be true if she were to have traveled with a Spaniard, and with an American—" She let the words dangle, indicating how much worse that would be.

"Well, I'll be damned," he said.

The waiter had returned and placed their drinks before them.

Curt sipped some of his, then said, "I thought the days of the *dueña* were over in Spain."

"*Dueña* as *dueña,* yes. But in a place like Zaragoza, you will not find a single *good* girl going to a movie alone. She will move about in company with a girl her own age. We have what I believe your soldiers call the 'buddy system.' And you will not see such girls on the streets after ten o'clock at night. Not that there is a legal curfew, but an unwritten rule rigorously adhered to."

The brandy had mellowed him; he could see that Marta Torres was not simply speaking about his own forwardness.

"I shall go slowly and properly," he said.

"Shall I speak even more frankly, Dr. Fielding?"

"I wish you would, Miss Torres."

"I say this to you as one with whom friendship is possible."

"All right."

"I noticed that you were taken with María Victoria—as which man would not be? She's beautiful. I know also, from your application form, that you are divorced. So I wish you to know that even were you to go 'slowly and properly,' nothing ever could exist between you and her. Neither she nor her family would countenance it."

Curt looked at her straight and hard. "Miss Torres," he said, "when I spoke of Spanish-American relations before, you and Miss Mandar were careful to remain polite. In fact, I found you both a bit evasive. But you aren't pulling any punches now. Why?"

"Because I have a responsibility to that girl and her family. I introduced you. Besides—I have taken a definite liking to you. It is one of my weaknesses. I meet many Americans during the course of any given year, and always I have one or two pets—like a teacher. Also I have lived in your country and have learned a kind of Yankee forthrightness which I use from time to time. You will perhaps find yourself acquiring Spanish mannerisms and methods in turn."

He said nothing for a moment; then he raised his glass to her, smiling. "I see I have much to learn."

She raised her drink in return, and he realized he was sitting with a woman whose company he enjoyed as much as that of any man's. Marta Torres was complete within herself, as sexless as a mother superior, but she was someone worth being with.

"May I ask one question?" he said.

"Of course."

"I mean it to be as direct as your statements. No punches pulled."

"Shoot," she said, deliberately using an Americanism.

"Did María Victoria ask to meet me, or did you just happen to see how we could be of service to each other and suggest your good offices?"

Her face went serious. She took a deep breath: "I have promised to play the game of truth with you, so I must keep my end of the bargain. All I ask is that you do the same thing with me, should I ask as direct a question of you someday."

"It's a promise."

"María Victoria came to my office four days ago. We had a lovely chat, and toward the end of it, she happened to mention an article that had appeared in the *Heraldo de Aragón* about your appointment to the *universidad*. Since she was coming into Madrid on a visit, she and her family discussed the possibility of your taking her on a tutorial basis. It was I who mentioned the exchange."

"And may I ask another question? It's really part of the first."

She nodded.

"Would you say that Señorita Mandar and her family were acting in a typical—I mean, proper—manner for such a family?"

"There are two things you must know, Dr. Fielding. One is that most matters are managed in Spain through *enchufe.* I'm sure you'll hear that word used often. It means connection—literally an electrical plug or connection." She smiled broadly. "In this case, I am the plug, the *enchufe.*"

"And the second thing?"

"Something I said before. Much is changing in Spain. María Victoria is headed toward a professional career. She intends to be useful as well as decorative."

He broke the ensuing silence they allowed each other. "This has been an interesting luncheon," he said. "I like Oskar's very much." He waved his hand in the direction of the main eating area, which had filled to near capacity since their meeting. Most of the clientele, he noticed, were men, sitting in groups of threes and fours. One or two groups had rolled some little dice out of cups as though deciding who should pay for the meal.

"It's very convenient for me, being this close to my office. I come often for lunch, and I'm glad you like it."

"Is it a man's place mainly?"

"At lunchtime, yes. Actually, as you may have seen on the sign, it's Oskar rather than Oskar's; and until three years ago it was called Recoletos. From where we're sitting you'd never realize that behind the rear wall there"—she pointed—"is another section where you can eat and watch *jai alai,* or *frontón,* as we call it."

"There's no sound."

"They don't play until evening, but even then you could sit here and know nothing about the *frontón.*"

"Miss Torres," he said, smiling, "I'm beginning to think there is more to Spain than meets the eye."

"I am glad that you are beginning to get the idea. But, if I may be permitted an observation, you mustn't feel that everything in my country takes place behind walls, in the shadows. We also have sunlight—direct, warm, and clear. So be ready for the truth when it is made visible."

"*Muchas gracias, señorita maestra.*"

"It is nothing, *señor.*"

They chatted for ten minutes more about business matters. He was to come into the Intercambio the next day and meet the director; at that time there were some forms for him to sign, and he could pick up his initial allowance. Once again she reminded him of the embassy party and offered her aid in getting any interviews he might want for his article. If he had any difficulty with papers on his car, he was to let her know. And as for the apartment in Zaragoza, everything there had been taken care of: Dr. Durán was handling matters, and he should be back from Santander shortly.

Curt insisted on paying the bill. They left together. He walked Marta Torres to the Biblioteca, where they parted in the courtyard. Instead of going back to the hotel, he took a short stroll, and eventually found a sidewalk café shaded by plane trees.

Settling into a wicker chair, he ordered a gin and orange, and sat there contentedly watching people go by. The girls were not always beautiful or even pretty, but they were invariably well dressed. He had expected the Spaniards, both male and female, to look like Mexicans, but found instead that they resembled Italians more than anyone else. Many were slender and fairly tall. Their faces lacked the bulldog roundness of Mexicans'.

One girl who went by reminded him of María Victoria, and he recalled how she had looked, standing there in the vestibule of Oskar's with Marta Torres—so tight and beautifully self-contained. And suddenly he felt that if he could only unlock María Victoria, the secrets of Spain would lie open before him. As for Miss Torres' advice to proceed slowly and properly, he would take at least that much of it. But beyond the social shadow why couldn't there be personal sunshine?

5
Nacional II

Not until Tuesday did the Agencia de Motores deliver his car. An agent drove it to the Fénix about ten o'clock that morning. With the unsolicited help of the hotel doorman Curt checked over the shiny red Volkswagen. After test-driving it around the block, he and the agent went into the hotel dining room to take care of the papers. The agent was fat, well dressed, and very serious. Over a cup of coffee he lectured for more than a half-hour about insurance, international documents of ownership, and the regular mechanical inspections necessary for the proper maintenance of this superb little automobile. In taking his leave he was very formal. He bowed. They shook hands. He turned over the keys and documents with all the seriousness of an ambassador providing a *laisser passer*.

When he had gone Curt ordered another coffee and asked the waiter if he would have a sandwich made up for a road trip. Then from his portfolio he took out a *mapa general de carreteras de España*. He lit a cigarette and began studying the map with the joy of mathematical certainty that maps gave him. Everything looked sane and logical when you worked with a map. Distances were exact. Routes were inevitable. You saw a section of the globe as through the wrong end of a telescope, reducing thousands of square miles to inches. You understood the power of a staff general who removes a tiny flag from his vectored chart and says, "That's the end of the Fourteenth Battalion."

What interested him mainly on this map was a red line that

63

ran some seven inches on a right diagonal from Madrid to Zaragoza. It was designated N. II. All the national highways radiating from Madrid were designated in this fashion. N. I ran north to Burgos, N. II northeast to Barcelona, N. III southeast to Valencia, and so forth, boxing the compass all the way around to northwest and La Coruña with N. VI.

Punctuating N. II almost exactly halfway between Madrid and Barcelona was a red dot placed inside a black circle. This was Zaragoza, with a population of some 350,000 (including one María Victoria Mandar), squeezed into a symbol that was no bigger than a sturgeon's egg. All very manageable, he thought, from a distance. . . . He turned the map over so that he could see a flap which gave large-scale treatment to Madrid and its environs. Once more he traced the route the desk clerk had recommended for leaving town and tried to set it in his mind so that once he was out in traffic he wouldn't have to check. Alcalá de Henares was his prime target, about twenty-five kilometers out of the city. From there on it should be clear sailing, just following N. II.

A half-hour later he was strapping himself into the VW and rolling down the window on his side of the car. His suitcase and typewriter were neatly wedged together in the trunk, up front. He had the driver's seat pushed all the way back for plenty of leg room. On the seat beside him was the road map, tucked under his portfolio, which contained car papers, note pad, Fodor's guide to Spain, and an advanced Spanish grammar with a glossary of difficult idioms. In front of the passenger seat, on the floor, was a net bag bulging with two bottles of wine, a corkscrew, and a seven-day sandwich of cheese and hunter's ham, which the cook had wrapped in oily brown paper.

He turned the key and started the motor. The gasoline gauge showed full. Ahead of him lay the northern half of the Iberian Peninsula—and beyond that all of Europe. All he had to do was keep his hands on the wheel, his right foot on the accelerator. On a day like this, with the Spanish sun shining in a cloudless sky, anyone could believe he was the captain of his soul, especially with a passport folder that contained five hundred dollars in travelers' checks, as well as forty thousand pesetas, and an international license certifying him as a competent driver. To the road once again, Rosinante.

From the Fénix he drove onto Calle de Serrano, past the American Embassy, to the Calle de María de Molina, which soon ran diagonally into the Avenida América. It was now close to noon and the avenue was packed with SEATs and Renaults, some Mercedes, Citroëns, and Peugeots, and a few Fords and Chevrolets, which looked whale-big among the smaller fry.

Traffic remained constant for some distance. Then it thinned out and quickened as vehicles turned off into the outskirting apartment areas, and others at the circle leading to Barajas Airport. About five miles out of town all the Fords and Chevrolets turned left onto a special road that led to the SAC base at Torrejón. What John Bowers had designated with a dot on his makeshift map was here a huge complex of hangars, towers, and brick buildings. The entrance area at Torrejón itself was an American transplant of service stations, used-car lots, diners, and jerry-built apartments. Kilroy was here, Curt thought, making his mark on Spanish history. It was a history running from the Roman arch to a B-54 hangar.

He touched down on the accelerator, passed several trucks, and a few minutes later entered Alcalá de Henares, which lay almost adjacent to Torrejón. Alcalá was the earliest center of learning in Spain and the birthplace of Cervantes. But now it was a disappointing huddle of gray and dun-colored buildings, which gave no sign of whatever greatness it might once have possessed. He decided against stopping. Maybe on a return trip to Madrid. . . .

Four hours later he arrived in Calatayud. Behind him lay Guadalajara, Medinaceli, and miles and miles of rough mountainous road. He stopped for gas and then headed for the even higher mountains ahead. The landscape now became lunar. He was in the province of Zaragoza. The city itself lay some forty miles beyond the high bald mountains that humped up like white elephants.

The VW whined along in third gear. N. II climbed to five thousand feet. Each truck passed was an adventure. The road was narrow; there were no guard rails in many places, and the drops were seven or eight hundred feet straight down. Finally, he reached a pass at the top. He pulled the VW over to a clearing and got out, taking in the panorama to the north.

There were isolated houses and huts on the dun-colored plain, with the road running like a black string across it. Green vegetation followed small streams in strips. Off to the west two towering castles, or forts, formed a compound hub to which dusty roads ran. Cars and trucks spaced themselves on the highway like shiny bugs. A miniature railway line came out of a tunnel, heading in the same direction as the highway but on a straighter path.

After a twisting descent he drove through sparse wheat farms. At the pueblo of La Muela he saw a sign saying that Zaragoza was only twenty-five kilometers away.

Some ten kilometers farther on he slowed down when N. II abruptly widened to four lanes. To his right was a motel of sorts, called El Cigne. To the left was a large billboard devoid of writing—just the picture of a large jet plane. On an impulse he turned off to the left, reasoning that this smooth branch road had to be the way into the SAC base. The psychology of the billboard was simple: to announce the presence of something, but not too flagrantly for Spanish eyes.

Kilroy's touch was subtler in the provinces, Curt thought. The road was dreamy smooth. He was back in the States. The VW hummed along. Two or three American cars went by in the opposite direction, held to fifty miles an hour by imperious signs, the more noticeable here because there were no speed limits on Spanish roads.

A couple of miles off he could see low white buildings, and

some high red-brick ones. Soon he could make out hangars and some humped shelters that looked like Quonset huts buried in the ground.

The road broadened to four lanes at the entrance to the base. There was a guardhouse out in front of the wire fence. Signs demanded in two languages that all vehicles halt at this point.

As Curt drove slowly to the barrier, an American sergeant stepped out of the guardhouse. He was dressed in light sun-tans. A Spanish soldier in heavy olive uniform followed at his heels.

The American spoke: "Can I help you, sir?"

"I'm not sure, Sergeant. I'd like to go on base."

"Are you seeing someone, sir?"

"I'm afraid not."

"You're not on official business?"

"No."

"Then I'm sorry, sir. To get a visitor's pass you have to be on official business or seeing someone specifically. And then they'd have to come out to the gate and escort you in."

"O.K., Sergeant. I understand."

The sergeant indicated how he could turn around the guard-house to the exit lanes.

As Curt swung the VW around he caught sight of rows of pleasant houses surrounded by green grass. He made a token salute to the two soldiers and started out toward the highway again. Within those gates was not only an American oasis but possibly someone who could tell him about Teddy Swiatski. Through his mind flitted the faulty all-capital typing of the friend who thought "SOMETHING STINKS IN DENMARK."

He would have to find some excuse for getting onto the base, and soon.

6
Villalta

"Hello, Dr. Fielding?"

The voice on the other end of the line was definitely Spanish in intonation.

"Yes, this is Dr. Fielding." Curt's first thought was that he was being welcomed by the hotel manager.

"It is good to speak with you, Doctor." The accent sounded more American than British in training. "I believe we have a mutual friend."

"Oh?"

"Señorita María Victoria Mandar y Saenz."

Curt squelched an exclamation of surprise. "Yes," he said, "Señorita Mandar."

"I am Francisco Villalta. I am calling from downstairs at the desk and I wonder if you would wish to have a drink before dinner."

Curt glanced at his watch. Almost six o'clock. He hadn't been in Zaragoza more than a half-hour and already he had social ties.

"That sounds fine, Mr. Villalta. But I have just finished unpacking and will need twenty minutes to get cleaned up."

"Perfect, Dr. Fielding. I will wait in the bar."

Curt hung up. The first thought that crossed his mind was that Villalta was either a member of María Victoria's family or her fiancé. He had come to check out the American professor and decide whether he was fit to associate with. Of course, he

68

might just be someone from the university that María Victoria had mentioned him to. In any case, he certainly hadn't wasted any time.

As Curt showered and dressed he kept thinking about how casual and friendly Villalta had sounded on the phone, and wondered what the hell he wanted.

Fifteen minutes later he was down in the lobby. The elevator man pointed the way to the bar—through a huge glass-domed lounge, past the dining room, and then along a narrow passageway.

There were perhaps ten people in the bar. As he entered, Curt realized he had no way of recognizing the person he was to meet, no gardenia in the lapel or anything of the sort. But a man sitting at the near end of the bar raised his glass in acknowledgment. He wore the national uniform of early evening informality. Navy blazer, white shirt, dark tie, gray slacks, and the inevitable white handkerchief fluffed up in the breast pocket. His smile was wide, white teeth showing.

Curt got the impression of a hunting hawk. The eyes were brilliant and small, the brows angled back sharply from a point above the nose, where they joined and formed a continuous line like a set of black wings.

"Dr. Fielding." The Spaniard was on his feet, offering his hand. He was about five ten, a welterweight, light through the body and heavy in the shoulders. "I am Francisco Villalta."

Curt caught himself thinking this one could be either a real friend or a real bastard. *"Mucho gusto,"* he said.

Villalta signaled the bartender. "What will you have? Are you a Scotch or bourbon man?"

"Una ginebra con naranja," Curt said to the barman.

Villalta pointed to his glass. *"Otro borbón-sifón."*

"Sounds as though you're the bourbon man," Curt said. "Have you spent some time in the States?"

"Yes, seven years. New York, Florida, Louisiana, Texas. I studied for four years in Texas."

"And what is it that you do now?"

"Of course!" Villalta flashed a smile. "I call you on the phone, right out of the blue!"

"Well, you do know Señorita Mandar."

"Oh, yes, I am an old friend of her family. In fact, I was at dinner with them yesterday. María Victoria had just returned from Madrid and spoke of you in a very favorable manner. When she told me that you would be staying for a while at the Gran, I said that I would welcome you to our country. Always the Americans who come to our country say that we are a cold people, distant and formal. But since you are to help María Victoria in her chosen profession, and since I kiss the ground on which some Americans walk, I tell myself I must return the hospitality of those who were so kind and helpful to me in the States. Anything you need, I want you to call on me."

"That's awfully nice of you," Curt said. The Spaniard's friendly charm impressed him, but one small doubt nagged at him. He couldn't remember whether he had mentioned in María Victoria's presence that he would be staying at the Gran. Perhaps he had. Or perhaps Villalta had checked at various hotels and was too embarrassed to say so.

The bartender returned with their drinks. Curt started to pay, but Villalta cut him off, telling the bartender to put it on his bill.

"Thanks," Curt said, and raised his gin and orange.

"Welcome to Spain."

"Glad to be here." Curt took a long pull at his drink and then set it down. "You were going to tell me what you do for a living."

"Ah, yes." Villalta took out a card and handed it to Curt.

According to the card, Villalta was a lawyer, a graduate of the University of Zaragoza and of Texas.

"Does this mean you can practice in both countries?"

"Fortunately, yes. Much of my practice is with American companies that come to Spain."

"Sounds good. Are there many of them?"

"Oh, yes. Everything from Chrysler Corporation and Monsanto chemicals to Schlitz beer. At present I am working with the Boise Paper Company. They are trying to arrange a deal with a local manufacturer of paper."

Thinking of his *Phaeton* article, Curt said he was interested in Spanish-American business arrangements. Villalta was not at all reluctant to talk. He explained that no foreign firm could own more than forty-nine per cent of any business in Spain, but that the law was often circumvented through dummy stockholders. He also spoke wryly of the way in which Spanish industrialists, who bragged about the number of American consultants they were connected with, often dumped the experts and returned to their own inefficient ways.

"But what can you do?" he concluded, shrugging. "Men must have pride as much as larger profits, no?"

After they had ordered another drink, Curt asked Villalta about how he had gone to America. Villalta said it was a long story.

His father, it seemed, had owned orange groves near Sitges in the province of Catalonia. As a large landowner, strict Catholic, and anti-Communist, he had been non-Catalan in his politics. Francisco had been sent to a Jesuit school in Zaragoza, where Franco elements were in control. After the war he had stayed on, entering the university and eventually graduating in law. The trouble was that almost everyone graduated in law— that being the equivalent of liberal arts as a gentleman's degree.

Spain, he said, had thousands of these *abogados menores*, lawyers without license to practice. So he had worked for a while at the American air base, learned to speak English better, and through the patronage of a captain who took an interest in him, obtained a student visa to the United States. There he entered

Louisiana State University and, the family fortunes being at low ebb, maintained himself with various jobs, eventually rising from shrimp peeler to lighting-effects man in a New Orleans night club. He was doing just enough academically to retain his visa, when a friend helped him obtain a position teaching Spanish part time at Austin College. This made it possible for him to get a degree at the University of Texas and to take his bar examinations. He joined a local law firm as a very junior member, dealing mainly with Mexican matters. Then his father died and he returned home to help get the estate in order. Three years ago he had come back to Zaragoza, taken his oppositional exams, and had been living there ever since.

When the narrative ended, Curt asked how Villalta had liked it in the United States. What were some of his impressions?

"Well, *hombre,* the first thing I must admit—and I hope you take no offense—is that there is nothing like American girls. You cannot imagine how interesting it is to be a foreigner in the States if you like girls! They are fascinated by Europeans. . . ." He shrugged, as if there had been nothing else to do but satisfy their fascination.

"I hope I can repay the favor," Curt said. "But I'm sure there must have been something else that interested you."

"Of course. I was impressed with New York. When I landed there, I can remember thinking how could a country do so much in so few centuries? And to tell the truth, I thought everything in America would be like New York. When I left in a train and was traveling through New Jersey and I saw that there was open space and no more tall buildings, I could not understand. And in Texas, more open. Now I know that no European can understand what is America unless they have made a visit. Even then they will not understand because it is too big, too many kinds of Americans."

"We had a writer who said that only the dead know Brooklyn. Even that one part of New York is too big for anyone to know."

"He was right. But I try to get to know all I can. That is why I did not want to live any more in New Orleans. Too European, not enough Anglo-Saxon. And when I was in Texas I try not to associate with Mexicans. I wanted to speak English only. Also I know what the Texans are feeling about Mexicans."

"Did you run into much of that stuff?"

"Yankee-ismo?"

"Yes."

"Sometimes, mostly from the poor people, the uneducated. But there are some Americans that I kiss the ground they walk on, like Captain Wilson and Mr. Klenninger."

"*And* all those American *señoritas*," Curt added.

"*Ay, hombre,* and some of the *señoras,* too. Many fine wives want to be like mothers, to help poor me. I hope you don't mind I'm saying this. But every Spaniard is a little bit *pícaro,* you know."

"Don't mind at all. But you must tell me how Spanish women feel about foreigners, too."

"I am going to do better than that. Do you have something planned for tonight?"

"No. I just got here and don't know a damned soul, except for María Victoria."

Villalta looked at him sharply. "We are talking about other kinds of girls, no?"

"Naturally."

"*Bueno.* This is Tuesday night. The *salas de fiesta* are sometimes closed Tuesdays to give the girls a rest. But this is the start of the Fiesta de la Raza and so everything will be open. And I am going to be your cicerone. We are going to go on the town, O.K.?"

"*Y por qué no?*"

"*Bueno.* I make up for all those Yankee cocktail parties."

7
La Cancela

The next day, Wednesday, Curt woke refreshed, glad he had postponed night-clubbing with Villalta until tonight. There was a lot to do and he wanted to get an early start. He had breakfast sent up to his room, and over coffee and croissants planned his campaign for the day, checking addresses in his notebook against certain items in the blue portfolio. The desk clerk had given him a map of Zaragoza and he studied it, getting it set in his mind: the Río Ebro running like a blue lizard as a slightly diagonal northern boundary, the inner city clustering underneath like a yellow sac, and the gray outer city falling away into sections of oblong eggs, the modern spawn of a muddy ancestor.

He drove to the Paseo de la Independencia, turned left, and headed toward the Paseo de Calvo Sotelo. According to the map, the *universidad* lay in the southwestern outskirts of town, near the Primo de Rivera Park. To get there he had to drive out Calvo Sotelo—the *paseo* that still had its grass and trees, as well as patient governesses sitting on benches, watching their little charges, who scampered among the shrubbery like well-dressed squirrels.

As he cut past a swaying *tranvía* Curt realized one of the buildings to his right, *número* 28, was the one he'd be living in. What he managed to see of it he liked. It was a seven- or eight-story building that seemed no more than five or six years old,

with a brilliant blue-tile façade, and a fancy bonbon shop downstairs beside the glassed entrance. If he could find Vice-rector
Durán, he might be able to move right in.

Several blocks later Calvo Sotelo changed to Fernando el
Católico, which became Isabella la Católica, in typical Spanish
fashion. Past the Plaza San Francisco he turned off to the right
and in a few moments passed through an arched gateway. Inside he could see that the university consisted of four struc-
tures arranged around a parched mall thaŧ contained in its
center a shallow pool of lackluster water. There were no signs
of life until a man emerged from some nearby shrubs, raking
pebbles and debris. He came to the curb when Curt called, and
identified the buildings at his request: there across the way was
the Faculty of Sciences; here on this side the Faculty of Philosophy and Letters; between them the Faculty of Law.

"Is this all of the university," Curt asked, "totally?"

"Minus the Faculty of Medicine," the man responded, "which,
as one knows, is located at the Plaza del Paraíso."

"Clearly," Curt said, and looked once again at the fourth ele-
ment in the quadrangle: it was a huge wall, a monolith of concrete, fronted by high-relief soldiers involved in a death struggle.
Impressed in the concrete, letters beneath the soldiers recommended dying for one's country as part of one's duty.

At the Faculty of Philosophy and Letters a gray-uniformed
portero met him at the door. Stiffly officious, he became ob-
sequious when Curt introduced himself as the new *catedrático
de literatura norteamericana*. The *portero* was then pleased to
welcome Professor Fieldee. Of letters, there were none as yet.
As for Vice-rector Durán, he could be found, if at all, in the
Faculty of law, which housed the administration.

Durán was not in the law building, either. An ancient
major-domo there, looking like a tipstaff out of Charles Dickens,
said the vice-rector was presently at Santander and was not
expected back until after the fiestas.

Marta Torres had said this might happen. The apartment

had been arranged through Durán, and Curt might have to stay at a hotel until his return.

On an off-chance, he drove back to 28 Calvo Sotelo—only to discover from the *portero* there that Durán had left neither orders nor keys for anyone to enter the apartment. This *portero* was a cheery brown ball of a man, his face looking like a balloon on which some child had painted a thin mustache, and he agreed sympathetically with the tenant-to-be that all of this was frustrating, but one would simply have to wait until after the fiestas.

"Clearly," Curt said, wondering whether everything wouldn't have to wait until after the fiestas. But, pulling out his notebook, he checked the address of María Maite Xavier-Peralta, and asked the *portero* what was the best way to reach the Calle Obispo Mardín.

Something in the balloon face changed, a pucker in the direction of wariness, or sly amusement.

"Qué número?"

Curt told him the number and the *portero* gave him directions. There was something knowing in the man's attitude. As Curt drove away he tried to figure out what it could be.

After several wrong turns he had to be redirected. A young boy about fifteen said he would be glad to show him how to get there. Curt opened the door and the boy got in, appraising the interior of the VW, asking questions about maximum speed and gas utilization, giving directions where to turn. They traveled no more than four blocks. Then the boy pointed to a sign on a corner building identifying Calle Obispo Mardín.

"Aquí," the boy said, and got out at the corner.

"Gracias," Curt said, and tried to give him a tip. But the ride in the *coche* was plenty, the boy said. He wished the *señor* a very pleasant afternoon, and the way he said it reminded Curt of the roly-poly *portero*.

Number 235 Obispo Mardín turned out to be the next-to-last building on the street. Just beyond it was some kind of barrel-

or cask-making shop, with two trucks backed up against its corrugated steel doors. Some workmen paused and watched Curt curiously as he got out of the car. One of them shrugged, another smiled. Then they went back to their task of rolling a huge steel hoop out to a muddy lot which brought Obispo Mardín to a dead end.

Curt thought to hell with them, and took a good look at 235. The yellowish glazed-block exterior was stained, and even though the building was newer than the others in the neighborhood it somehow looked shoddier. He walked into the entry. There was no *portero*. He found Maite's name over one of the mail slits: number 5, level 3.

There was no elevator either. As he climbed the stairs he noticed dirt impacted into corners. In places the rough plastered walls had been scribbled on. Readers were encouraged to follow certain international directions in sexual release.

He found the apartment and rang the bell, hearing it echo inside. A moment later feet shuffled within and then the grating slid open warily.

"*Quién es?*" There was a small round grating and a peephole in the door.

"*Un amigo de la Señorita Maite.*"

The grating rasped closed. The feet shuffled away and Curt was left wondering whose aged voice it was that had asked just one question. "*Quién es?*" he thought: who is it who asks who is it? Oh, do not ask to know, let us go and make our visit. . . .

Again the feet shuffled close and the grating opened. Through it he caught sight of the wizened face of an old woman.

"*La señorita no está aquí,*" the face said, and the grating started to close.

"*Por favor,*" Curt said quickly. "Please, even if the *señorita* is not at home, will you give her this card? It is very important."

There was some hesitation, then the grating opened fully. "Yes," the face said, "if it is important."

Curt fished a card out of his passport carrier and quickly scribbled a line above his name: *I am a good friend of Teddy's.*

The door opened to the extent of its chain catch. Curt pushed the card into the opening and a blue-veined hand took it.

"*Un momento,*" the voice said. "You may wait a moment if you wish." All pretense of María Maite's not being in was dropped.

"*Bueno,*" Curt said, and the door closed.

As he waited, he thought of the letter Stanley Swiatski had given him. He had read it at least ten times since then and had each time tried to imagine what kind of girl María Maite might be. Someone who had been in love, certainly; someone who had the courage to fly in the face of what looked like official barriers; and someone who wrote: "Dear Family of Teddi . . . We love and are good peoples togeder. . . ."

This time when the door opened the hand offered a folded sheet of violet stationery and the old voice croaked, "The *señorita* is not feeling well. This note will explain."

"*Gracias,*" Curt replied, and as the door closed—just as the grating slid shut—he thought he heard something inside that sounded like the cheep-cheep of a canary.

He opened the note and read, recognizing the handwriting as that of the letter: "*Señor,*" it ran, "*Venga a la Cancela esta noche a eso de las once. Me conocerá allí.*"

He puzzled over the words again. What was the Cancela? And how would he "know her there"? He could find out about the place from the hotel or Villalta. And he would find out about María Maite at about eleven o'clock that night. At least this didn't have to wait until after the fiestas. You're making some progress, he told himself, as he went down the gloomy stairs.

But that was all the progress he made that day. About an hour after leaving Obispo Mardín he finally located the tiny shop of Cipriano Farlo. It was on Calle de Prudencia in the inner city, about two blocks away from the river and the Catedral del Pilar. The search proved fruitless. Behind the sign *Imprenta* painted on the window there was nothing but cobwebs, dust, and drawn curtains. The shade had been drawn down on the door and dirt caked around the handle indicated that no one had used it in weeks. Curt tried it without success. If Farlo was in Zaragoza he'd have to be found somewhere else, and the chilling question was whether he was even alive. One of the items Curt had reviewed in his room that morning was the story from *La Verdad* reporting Farlo's death. His parents were dead, according to the story, but there were some relatives left, including an uncle in the city. Curt decided to try him tomorrow.

From the print shop he walked to the Plaza del Pilar and took a table at one of the outdoor cafés facing the gigantic mud-colored cathedral, the most famous religious shrine in Spain. He ordered a gin and orange and sat watching the plaza. At this hour it was alive with people—most of them older-looking, wearing dark clothes, the women with veils and shawls, some carrying rosaries. Here and there walked small squadrons of priests in long black outfits, shaded by the wide brims of their flat-domed hats. An occasional soldier or two—burdened with uniforms that looked as though they would render a man helpless in the brilliant Spanish sun—joined the throng of pilgrims that entered various doors of the giant cathedral like ants in search of sustenance. The baroque pile loomed, thrusting domes and spires toward the perfect sky. It dwarfed everything else in sight—trees, cars, people. Curt's eyes worked like a camera, trying to photograph the Catedral del Pilar in sections, hoping to get the whole thing to fuse, but finding it impossible. Either he was too close, or the structure had its own built-in separations. Like much of Spain, it was best viewed from a distance.

After another drink he checked his watch, then went into

the café and phoned María Victoria. She sounded genuinely glad to hear from him but said she could not possibly accept his invitation.

"Always," she said, "we have lunch with my father. It is a regulation."

"Well, how about a drink somewhere later this afternoon? Say the Vegas at three-thirty."

"I am truly sorry, Dr. Fielding, but all afternoon I will be here with my sisters and our dressmaker. I hope you understand. It is the time of the fiestas and we are always so terribly busy during this time. There are all these friends of the family and my father's official social engagements that we must attend to."

"I understand," he said, inwardly cursing her constant dressmakers and her father.

"Please do not feel offended. I know this is not like your American hospitality, but there is nothing I can do."

"I understand."

"I shall see you at the university on Monday morning next, no?"

"Yes."

"Please do not be angry with me. After the fiestas we will have more time and everything will be more pleasant."

"*De acuerdo.*"

"Good. Then we are in accord."

"We are in accord."

"By the way, I am wondering if Señor Villalta has been—"

"Yes, he's been very kind. We had dinner last night."

"*Bueno.* He is a friend of the family. Mainly of my father. But I think you will find him very interesting."

"I do find him very interesting. In fact, we are going out to some night clubs tonight."

"That is good."

"Yes, that is good."

"Until Monday, then."

"Monday."

"Good-bye."

"*Adiós, señorita.*"

The phone made a small ringing sound as he hung up and he had a feeling that he had lost every round. Within the shade of the café he felt momentarily dizzy. Later, two more gin and oranges, along with a potato-and-peppers omelet, assured him that the world was not all defeat. About eleven o'clock he'd be seeing María Maite, and if the *portero's* knowing smile meant anything at all, maybe she wouldn't be as goddamned virginal as María Victoria. María, María! What the hell could you do in a country where half the female population was named after the Holy Mother, and the other half after the Virgen del Pilar, and some of them even doubled up with María-Pilar!

"*Vamos a ver,*" he mumbled to himself, glaring at the mammoth cathedral across the way: "We are going to see."

Villalta showed up at the hotel bar at about ten-thirty. Over a cognac, Curt told him about going out to the *universidad* and trying to get in touch with Durán and looking into the apartment situation, but he omitted everything about going to María Maite's and the print shop.

"I called María Victoria this afternoon," he confessed, "but even she is tied up by the fiestas. So I had a look at the Ebro and the Catedral del Pilar and took a long rest this evening."

"Well, tonight and tomorrow you will see that the fiestas are a good thing. I have two *billetes* for the *corrida* tomorrow. And we will see one of the best matadors in all of Spain, Paco Camino."

"That's damned nice of you," Curt said, meaning it, "but you have to let me pay for the tickets."

"No, sir. For the good things that have happened to me in the States, this treat is on me. Don't say any more about it."

"O.K." Curt smiled.

"O.K. And now we have to decide where to begin the evening. The Capri is good, and the Pigalle, and also the Cancela. What is your choice?"

"It doesn't matter," Curt said calmly, "but the desk clerk told me the Cancela is *muy divertido.*"

"*Bueno.* It is a good place to start. They have some beautiful tomatoes there." The smile was that of a young hawk, a boyish hawk, if there was such a thing.

The cab took them to a side street not far from the Plaza del Paraíso. A quiet, subdued neighborhood. Only two places showed signs of activity, a café across the street, and a brightly lit place about as wide as a small house, featuring a large iron grill, or *cancela,* like a gate to a church, at which stood a doorman in a gray-and-red uniform that marked him as at least a field marshal among his kind.

Curt paid the cabby, overtipping him by a half-day's pay, and they went into the club, past the field marshal, who put two fingers to his cap and said, "*Buenas noches, Señor Villalta.*" His bulk was great enough to assure Curt that he probably doubled as bouncer.

"You're a well-known customer," Curt said, as they went into the rather small entryway, whose walls were loaded with glossy prints of females.

"*Sí,*" Villalta answered. "This place is run by a friend of mine, but I must warn you he is a *maricón;* so you must be careful, no?"

"Thanks for the warning, but I think I can resist his charms."

"And how about these?" Villalta's right hand swiveled in a gesture that included the photos on the walls.

"That, as they say, is more my meat."

"*Claro que ese es un hombrón.*"

Curt followed Villalta down the carpeted steps, which turned and turned again and ended at a subterranean foyer. He was amazed at how large and cavernous, like the second or third deck of a ship, the night-club area was. A doorway led into a

83   LA CANCELA

passage to the left, another into a bar straight ahead, and a
third down some more stairs to a sunken dance floor and
scores of small round tables all dimly lit, some of them
shadowy deep under a gallery.

"Very intricate," Curt said.

"Yes, and there is more to it. Later we can go back this
way"—he pointed to the doorway on the left—"to the back
room for the flamenco. It is like two clubs in one, and with
double entertainment. Two shows going on at the same time.
You will see."

"There doesn't seem to be much going on now, though."
Curt looked down at the main floor, where two couples swayed
to the strains of a Latin-American number played by a three-
piece ensemble. Twin spotlights from the gallery cut through
a pale blue haze, outlining the taut curves of the girls, pulled
into crotch-straining attitudes by the men who seemed more
intent on closeness than fancy footwork.

"We are very early," Villalta said. "Things do not get
started until about twelve, and the entertainment not until one.
Not even all the girls are here yet."

There were six or seven in the bar, two of them sitting on
a bench near the back, the others standing at the bar with
male customers. Curt followed Villalta. They took places near
the entryway. In a moment one of the three men working
behind the bar looked toward them, gave a flutter of a hand
in recognition, and, after putting some change in a cash register,
started in their direction.

"*Mi mariconcito*," Villalta whispered.

"*Salud, Francisco*," the man said as he approached, holding
out a prettily shaped hand.

"*Qué tal, guapo*," said Villalta, taking the hand almost as
though he were about to kiss it, shaking it horizontally rather
than vertically. "It gives me pleasure to introduce a friend of
mine, Señor Fielding."

Curt took the proffered hand, saying "*Encantado*," and at

the same time getting a mental picture of himself shaking a fairy hand and uttering the word "enchanted" in English.

"This is Pepe," Villalta was saying, "the *patrón* of this considerable establishment."

Pepe's eyes were large, brown, and sad-looking. He had the sullen guardedness and the hopeful seductiveness of the predatory homosexual. "You are always welcome in the house of Pepe," he said.

Curt recognized the ambiguity of the words and the tone of voice.

"I think Pepe is going to make a treat of the first round. Not true, Pepe?"

"*Qué quieren ustedes, Francisco?*"

"You see what a welcome we are getting, Curtis? *Whatever* you want."

"*Quiero un whisky-soda,*" Curt said.

"Honny Walkair?"

"*Estupendo.*"

"*El rojo o el negro?*"

"Yes, Curtis, do you want it red or black?"

"*El rojo está bien.*"

"*Lo mismo,*" Villalta said.

"Weren't you being a little rough on him?" Curt asked, as Pepe moved away.

"On Pepito? You are such a puritan, *hombre*. He loves it when you talk that way. It warms his little drawers. Tonight when he goes to bed he will dream of the big Yanqui who will maybe make love to him and he will be in heaven."

"You are a son of a bitch, aren't you?" Curt smiled when he said it.

"The trouble with you Yanquis is that you have not yet lived long enough with life. You make hard and fast rules about life and you do not bend—or you pretend not to bend—and then you break when you realize the largeness of life and the *hipocresía* that it can make. On the other side, we

Spaniards allow for everything because we have seen the hard necessities. We do not have allowance in politics and religion, that is true, but in other ways, yes, maybe even more so because we do not have it in politics and religion. The bullfights tomorrow will show you something of this. And you know what will happen if Pepe goes to the *corrida*—how he gets his kicks? He will be thinking how *macho* the matador is and how *macho* the bull is and how he would like to have both of them. And when the matador puts the *espada* into the bull, he is going mad. *Olé!* We know this and it is all right. That is why Pepe can run an establishment like the Cancela and be successful. Besides, he takes care of the girls like *una madre superiora.*"

"You're taking an old anti-Anglo-Saxon line," Curt said. "We have as many homosexuals per capita as you do, though it's a hell of a thing to brag about."

"Yes, you do. Plenty. I *know*. But you do not accept them as part of life. You push them together the way we used to push the Jews and the Moors. Now we have a society that can accept all kinds of *morenos,* mixed bloods and mixed sexes."

"But no Jews."

"And no Communists."

"You mean they're one and the same?"

"No, it is what I have already said of politics and religion."

"Then we all have our shame."

At this point Pepe returned. He placed a Scotch and soda in front of each of the men and, from the small silver tray which he carried, took a tiny glass of liqueur for himself. With a smile of seraphic servitude, he said, "For your pleasure, *caballeros,*" and quaffed the purple liquid.

"And for *your* pleasure, Pepito."

"*Salud,*" Curt said, "*y gracias.*"

Pepe invited them to enjoy the diversions of his establishment; he himself had now to attend to matters monetary, in preparation for the night gala.

When he had gone Villalta said, "You are making a hit with all the *patrones* in Zaragoza."

"Because of *mi maestro*," Curt said with a mock bow.

"No, no. You are too modest. You are a North American *muy simpático*, and they feel it. I am not kidding you."

"Yes," Curt said. "I'm our secret cultural weapon, loaded with *simpatía*. Spain's just a trial run for me, you know. They want to see if I can overcome the damage done by our military presence. Then they're sending me on to Hiroshima."

Curt supposed that he did have a somewhat sympathetic nature. It had brought him and Stanley Swiatski into accord, for instance. But it was the kind of sympathy that ran close to the surface of life. It came from the realization that we're all in the same goddamned boat together, with the only enemy death. He never got very far under the surface of things; he was in great need of pricking his own surface to get under the skin of things. Androgynous that, he thought. The equivalent of screwing yourself. Yes, or loving yourself. Go love yourself. Love yourself as you would your neighbor. And a little bit more if you can manage. . . .

Villalta was observing him over his glass. "Also," he said, slowly, "I think you are like the Spanish because you are driven by the *gusano*."

"The *gusano*, eh?"

"*Sí*."

"And just what is that—*your* secret weapon?"

"In a way, perhaps. It is a worm which eats into the intestines. It is what we say some matadors have that drives them on and on to what kind of perfection they can achieve. And you have it. The *gusano*."

"*Leche*," Curt said, "*de una gran puta*."

"That's what you need—something to drink and a *gran puta*."

"In that department, we're being ignored."

The bar had begun to fill. Several customers had come in

and also more girls, singly and in pairs, trailing clouds of per-
fume. Some had joined men at the bar. They twitched their
flanks against the men, running an occasional hand over a
shoulder, cajoling for a drink. The rest of the girls stood
together round the bench at the rear. They were bank clerks
before the vaults opened, surgeons during the wash-up.

"We are not being ignored," Villalta said. "They are showing
us respect."

"That's about all."

"We will get a better view if you wish." Villalta flicked an
index finger.

A buxom brunette caught the signal, looked startled, indicated "Me?," and then looked half-relieved when Villalta made
another sideward motion. She tapped the bare back of a tall
girl with titian hair. The girl turned and looked at them. She
hesitated for a moment and then obeyed Villalta's fillip. As
she walked toward them in her white sheath dress, she was as
taut and musical as a tuning fork, vibrating with titillating
tremors.

Watching her, Curt suddenly remembered a time when, as
a child, he had stood with his father at an amusement park
where some ponies were available for a trot around an enclosed
ring. He had finally chosen one—a brown one with an almost
platinum mane—and his father had indicated his choice to a
gnomelike wrangler, who grabbed the pony's halter and led
it to them. Curt had mounted, feeling the living flesh quiver
under his own, as the pony's tail flicked away a fly, and the
dwarf of a man, his whisky face sullen in the sun, led them
off at a slow canter. . . .

"Good evening, María."

Curt snapped back to the present, thinking—another María.

"Good evening, Señor Villalta."

"This is a friend of mine. Señor Fielding."

"*Mucho gusto,*" the girl said, her voice soft, her eyes hard
and opaque. She was staring at Curt in a strange way.

"*Encantado,*" Curt said. "May I buy you a drink?"

The girl smiled ironically and nodded.

In English Villalta said, "It is she who expects to ask you to buy the drink."

"So I figured," Curt said. He felt there was something awkward in the relationship between the girl and Villalta. There was none of the gay playfulness expected of the man about town.

Villalta patted him on the shoulder and said, "You two have a drink. It is necessary that I see someone in the *sala.*"

"O.K.," Curt said.

Villalta moved to the entry, turned, smiled, and then dropped down the steps to the main room.

When Curt turned toward the girl again, she was standing with one elbow on the bar, her wide-set eyes trained piercingly on him. They studied each other for a moment. There was a Sophia Loren bigness about her. She was taller than most Spanish women, lithe and tawny-skinned, with eyes, made up in the latest emphatic fashion, tilted in an almost oriental slant.

"Would you like *it?*" she asked in nearly perfect English.

"What?" he said, startled.

"The drink."

"Oh," he said, "sure."

She beckoned to one of the bartenders and they ordered two whisky and sodas. Then she turned to him once more and said, "What do you do in Spain, Señor Fielding?"

He explained about the Fulbright and the University. He also said that he was a writer of sorts and intended to do an article on Spain.

"And how about you, *señorita?* How do you come to speak English so well?"

"From school I learn some of it." Her eyelids fluttered coquettishly. "And from Americans I learn more."

"Have you known many Americans?"

"Enough," she said.

"And Señor Villalta, do you know him well?"

Their drinks came. Curt paid for them. Then they both made little salutes with their glasses.

The girl's smile was tight-lipped as she put her glass on the bar. "I was going to ask you the same question about Señor Villalta. Is he a good friend of yours?"

"To tell you the truth I don't know."

"You don't *know?*"

"That's right." He offered her a cigarette, which she accepted with long-nailed fingers of reptilian grace.

"*Gracias,*" she said as he lit it for her, and then blew a thin stream of smoke toward him.

"I have known him only since yesterday, through a mutual acquaintance. Since then he has been guiding me around Zaragoza, and I've enjoyed his company . . . but I don't know much about him."

"I see." She seemed to be making inner calculations.

"And you. Are you a friend of his?"

"Not exactly."

"Good."

"Why do you say that?"

"I guess I'd like to know you better and I wouldn't want you to be anything to him."

Her smile encouraged him.

"In fact," he said, "I would very much like to see you later tonight."

Her eyes seemed brighter now, as though some film had been dissolved. "Maybe it is possible. At the end of the show you come here to the bar by yourself. You can make an excuse."

"Wonderful," he said, feeling himself warm at the thought of how easily her breasts could be freed, how quickly he could . . .

"He is coming."

Villalta appeared at the entry.

"One thing," Curt said quickly. "Do you know a girl named María Maite Xavier-Peralta, who comes to this club?"

"Yes, she works here. I will introduce you later if you wish it."

"Well, don't mention it to him, please."

She gave him a swift glance. "I won't."

Villalta joined them. The girl excused herself, saying she had to make a change of clothing.

"*Es una puta?*" Curt asked in a low voice.

"*Una artista,*" Villalta said. "She sings and dances."

"And how should one treat *una artista* at the Cancela?"

"With money, *hombre!*"

"I know but—"

"It is like with your high-class call girls. Sometimes, yes. Sometimes, no. *Claro?*"

Curt smiled and said, "Clear."

"And now," Villalta said, "if you can wipe that dirty smile off your face, we are going to meet some of your countrymen and watch the show."

8
María Maite

They went down the steps into the main room and walked across a corner of the dance floor to one of the tables just under the lip of the balcony, where a couple were sitting. The man stood up and they shook hands all the way round.

"Lois, Major, this is Dr. Curtis Fielding. Dr. Fielding, Lois Harte and Major Thomas Pardee."

"How do you do."

"Glad to meet you."

"Francisco has been telling us all about you, Dr. Fielding."

"He's a nice man."

"A very nice man, even for a European."

You'd probably know, Curt thought. Miss Harte was almost a caricature of tiny sexuality, like one of those little dolls that tumblers and trapeze artists throw around.

"Sit down and join us." The major's hair was crew-cut, his neck thickly jutting out of a tight collar, his face tautly red even in this light.

"Francisco tells us you'll be joining the *universidad* after the fiestas."

"That's right."

"What'll you teach?" the major asked.

"American literature."

"They need economics and agriculture."

"Man doesn't live by dough alone."

"It helps."

91

"Curtis is returning Europe's gift of culture."

"And I approve." The girl's round eyes and pouty little mouth were definite. "If we listened to Tom it would be all tractors and bombs."

"Books are nice for relaxation—after a man's work is done."

"I'll bet you like Mickey Spillane," Curt said.

"Sure, and James Bond."

"Were they required reading at the Point?"

"Citadel, Professor, where I spent my time on Von Clausewitz."

"Try 'The Battle of Maldon' sometime, Major. That's tougher than Mike Hammer, Von Clausewitz, and you."

"What the hell—"

"Would you like to dance, Dr. Fielding?"

"Delighted."

The men stood up. Lois Harte came around the table and took Curt's arm. They moved out onto the floor and began dancing among the five or six couples who were leaning into a slow rhythmic piece.

"Are you nervous because of the nearness of me?"

"*And* the major."

"Yes, I thought you two were going to dance in a minute." She came only to his chest and as she leaned her blond head against him, she let her small muscular legs scissor in close. As they swayed together it was he who gave ground.

"If you're his girl I may still have to 'dance' with the major."

"Was." She smiled, pulling back and sucking in her cheeks in a comic version of a model being photographed.

"And Villalta's?"

"Was." She moved in close again and they danced, and Curt thought, Christ!

"And now Miss Harte is at liberty?"

"Mrs."

"Married?"

"Was."

"Me too."

When the music stopped, they walked slowly back toward the table; she continued holding his hand and said, "Later I have an interesting proposition to make you."

"You're stealing my lines."

"Not *that* kind. Just take it easy with the major. We'll need his help."

"You're kidding."

"Shush."

The two men rose at their approach. Curt looked the major over carefully. He'd be tough—about two hundred pounds of red meat on a five-ten frame, running-guard type.

Villalta must have quieted him down. The edge had gone out of the major's voice. The conversation moved along easily about the Fiesta and what one ought to see, like the parade of the "big heads" and the procession of the penitents. Curt relaxed under the little paw of Lois Harte, who patted his thigh beneath the table to emphasize some of her statements. He listened politely as Pardee recommended his taking a trip to the Monasterio de la Piedra and its waters.

"It sounds like a place I knew in Italy," he responded. "Near Rapallo."

"Have you spent much time in Italy?" Lois patted him.

"Two years."

"During the war?" Villalta asked.

"Yes."

"What were you in?" Pardee said.

"Infantry. Thirty-eighth Division." Curt sensed his own juvenile satisfaction. "And you, Major?"

"I made the Korean affair. Those were my flying days."

"Now Tom's a swivel-chair pilot."

"What kind?"

"He's our sheriff."

Jesus, Curt thought, how these things do run to type. "Provost marshal?"

"Right." Pardee's face squared. "That's how Sisco here and I became acquainted. Ain't that—"

"They are about to begin," Villalta said.

The lights cut to a single spot as three other members of the band now joined the pianist, bass, and guitar man. A slender MC, wearing a white suit and black turtle-neck shirt, emerged from the curtains and, adjusting the microphone, began to address the room.

"*Señoras y Señores,*" he began, "I want you to think of me on this festive occasion as your town crier, one who brings you all the notices of good news." The word he used was *pregonero.* "And do we not know what a *pregonero* is? There is a story of the way most *pregoneros* are born. You remember? Just one phrase." He cupped his hands to his mouth: his voice rose and quavered in town-crier style: "Mo-o-ther, can you—tell me WHY—my father—SHOT—the town crier?"

The crowd was silent for a moment; then the laughter burst forth.

"I don't get it," Lois said to Villalta.

White suit was going on with his introductory prattle and Villalta began to explain the joke. "It is very Spanish. The little boy is what you call a bastard, no? He asks why his father has killed the town crier, and he asks it in a way that suggests who is his real father."

"Oh!"

"Very funny."

"Listen. This may amuse you more—"

". . . and the North American wife says to her husband: '*Your* children and *my* children get along well, but they are beating up *our* children. . . .'"

As Villalta began explaining again, two Americans came in with girls from the bar and took a table just behind theirs. Pardee had his eyes on one of the men, who grunted something as he went past. He was a tall youth, who couldn't have been more than twenty—lanky, with blond hair. He seemed to have been drinking heavily, and moved with the loose-limbed lurch of someone who didn't care what he bumped into.

"Bastard" and "crud" were two of the words Curt picked out of what the tall boy was saying to his shorter companion, and the other voice saying, "Easy . . . careful."

"Careful, shit," the tall boy said.

Pardee turned his chair in that direction and stared hard. Villalta patted him on the shoulder and said, "Look, Tom, you are missing the show." And Pardee turned grudgingly back in the direction of the space set off as stage area.

White suit was introducing a troupe that had come all the way from Mexico to be back here in the motherland. It gave him great pleasure to present them in all their native finery, with their vigor of song and dance—"Los Gritadores!"

Out came Los Gritadores with a whoop and a holler, bright orange-and-yellow skirts flaring, gigantic spurs and twenty-gallon hats spinning and revolving—"Yee-ee-ha-ho." When the commotion settled, the two men in the troupe chorded their guitars and four voices rose in falsetto tremolos that gave way to sharp cachinnations—"Ya, ha, ha," and then into plaintive melody. The Mexicans' pug faces and tanned-leather coloration under the spotlight made it easy to see how they differed from most Spaniards.

Curt drank the rest of his Scotch, relaxing with his hand on Lois Harte's under the table on his thigh. Once or twice he heard Villalta mutter something to Pardee, and although he couldn't quite make out what it was, dimly fathomed that it had to do with the kid who had made all the racket. It was strange how Villalta seemed to take charge of Pardee, the way he had cut him short when the major was going to say something about their connection. Well, he'd find out what the score was soon enough, he concluded, and gave Lois' hand a little squeeze, and she smiled that sucked-in cheek pout of the photographer's model again.

The Gritadores were having a hell of a success. They ran

through an initial repertoire that moved from *ranchos* and *ríos* to Granada and Guadalajara. Tying their program together was a string of songs featuring *corazón, mi cora-zón,* and Curt whispered to Lois that almost every Spanish tune ever written was a tribute to her.

"What do you mean?" She leaned close.

"Harte—heart," Curt said. "*Heart* is to Spanish song writers what moon-June-spoon was to tin-pan alley. I think I'll call you Lois Corazón. Do you mind if I call you Lois Corazón?"

"Clever," she whispered. "You are *very* clever." Her left breast cushioned against his right arm.

The Gritadores did another encore and then left the stage in a series of diminishing skirt and hat whirlings, agitating the smoky air in breezy patterns; and when the curtains closed behind them it was as though a small cyclone had been damped out.

Into the calm circle of light stepped white suit, who announced that Los Gritadores would be back later, but meanwhile he was anxious to present one of Aragón's most lovely, most melodious, most rhythmic, most enormously talented performers. He paused at the lip of discovery. "Our very own," he said, "María MA-I-TE!"

Curt sat straight up. At almost that same instant he realized that he had dislodged Lois from her intimate position, that she was regarding him quizzically, and that Villalta, who had been engaged in conversation with Pardee, was now regarding him closely.

Curt reached for his cigarettes in the middle of the table, as though they had been the reason for his sitting upright. Then, as he offered one to Lois, he almost dropped the pack, because the girl who glided into the spotlight was the titian-haired beauty he had talked to at the bar. Villalta smiled at him broadly.

"Would you like one?" Curt asked him, trying to keep his voice even.

"*Gracias.*" Villalta reached across the table. "You seem disturbed," he said. "You are not feeling well?"

"Feeling swell."

"I'd sure like to know this Maeetay a whole lot better." Pardee was sitting slant-backed in his chair, feet straight out in front of him, appraising flesh like a slaver at market. "Can you arrange that for me Sisco?"

"Curtis will introduce you. He already knows María Maite, don't you Curtis?"

"How *well?*" Lois said.

"Well, how about it, Professor?"

Curt let the questions hang in the air. Maite had begun to sing in low plaintive tones: the song had something to do with a *muchacho a la medida,* a boy just made for her. It had a samba beat, with a slight roll of traps in the background at the end of each phrasing, a sax staying on melody with her, and a muted cornet playing high over it and around it. She wasn't bad, he thought, not bad at all. Teddy Swiatski had had himself quite a woman, and he must have been quite a boy himself. *Is?* Anyway, she *is* something, even more lovely set apart from the crowd in the spotlight, her face alive to its own beauty in isolation, her skintight gown scintillating like the spangled scales of a mermaid, her mounded breasts almost spilling out of the gashed décolletage which ended just short of her navel.

She handled the detached mike like an instrument of pleasure and swept softly from one table to another, whispering the line about a "*muchacho* just made to measure," twirling the long cord with her left hand as though it were a lasso of entwining love. When she reached their table she eyed Curt almost defiantly for a full five-count, then glared at Villalta and Pardee and ended the song on a high wailing note. Under the wave of applause, she moved back to her position in front of the band, her head hung low, as though presenting herself for the axman's pleasure.

What happened next was something Curt had to piece together the way you straighten out the pieces of a spilled jigsaw puzzle.

Everybody had been clapping and the major had tilted himself back in his chair and was saying something like, "Boy, I tell you, that is one—" and never got to finish it, because the chair was out from under him and clattering out on the floor of the dance area, and there was an enormous guffaw from somewhere behind him, and then a room full of laughter. He was up in an instant, his face beef-red in the gleam of the spot, and Villalta made a quick grab for him under the pretense of helping to brush him off, but the major dived past him and was on top of the tall young airman, who never stopped laughing, even when the major and Villalta pulled him through an aisle of tables and up the steps, where they were met by the uniformed doorman. Then there was a wrestling event starring the tall airman and his friend against several of the club personnel and the major, swinging a clubbed fist, and then they were gone up the stairs.

Curt became aware of Lois Harte's clutching weight on his right arm. She hadn't let go once during the scuffle. Now, as they listened to the cries filling the *sala*—certain phrases of which sank in with a peculiarly chastening effect, like *"todos los norteamericanos"* and *"borrachos"* and *"locos"* and *"animales"*—she was asking him to please sit down.

"Come on, dear," she said. "Let's sit it out. You don't have to get mixed up in it. Let's show these people. Sit down, Curt. Please."

They did sit down and she handed him her drink and he drank some and offered her another cigarette. People resettled themselves and the cries sank to a hum of conversation. The band started playing and the house lights, which had been turned on, were doused. María Maite hadn't moved from her spot. She began to sing another piece, this one beginning with the line *"Me siento tímida. . . ."* It was either an extraordinary coincidence or she had cued the band purposely; but she was singing "I feel so timid, so awkward."

The waiter came to the table of the gallant Americans who had stayed in the face of national shame—or so his manner seemed to indicate—and asked if they would like another round. They ordered, and then Curt turned to look at Lois.

"What the hell's going on?" he said sharply. "Do you know?"

"No, I don't. But keep your voice down, and smile. You're on Candid Camera, darling. Look as though you're having fun. Mustn't lose face before the natives."

He laughed at her good-naturedly. She had good sense and much better quality than he had expected from a teasing piece of fluff. "O.K.," he said, "I'm having fun. See?"

She began laughing. "God," she said, almost choking, "didn't Tom look funny getting up off his butt!"

"Who was the kid he swung on? Did *he* kick the chair?"

"I don't know. He's from the base. I've seen him around, and I think he's had it in for Tom. Something about a girl, I think. Tom was fuzzy about it. He said something to Francisco once before, but I didn't pay much attention."

Curt had a feeling there was more to it than just a girl. Vallalta was too concerned. He hadn't acted the way he had simply to keep an American officer from making an ass of himself. Maybe the girl out there singing could answer some of the questions that the girl at the table could not. He had to see her as soon as possible.

Villalta came back as the waiter was bringing their drinks and he ordered another for himself.

"Well," Curt said when he was seated, "what happened?"

"Everything is all right. The Air Police have been summoned and they are taking the man back to the base."

"Tom's going too?" Lois asked.

"Yes."

"To press charges?"

"I suppose so."

"Who is the airman?"

"A troublemaker. He behaved like a fool."

"So did the major."

Vallalta smiled briefly. *"Verdad."*

"Is there trouble between those two?"

"I think once Thomas had to chastise him."

"About a girl?"

"I really do not know." Villalta's smile ended matters. "I am glad you two behaved properly."

María Maite finished singing and, after throwing a kiss to the applauding audience, disappeared behind the curtains.

When white suit came out to make his next announcement, Curt excused himself by saying he had to find the *servicio* and, after a short stop at one of the W.C.'s, made his way into the upstairs bar, which was packed.

He ordered a Veterano and waited at the bar. About five minutes later María Maite entered from the other end of the room. She had changed from her silver gown into a simple black dress. Several men tried to detain her but she smiled, made excuses, and came to him.

"You're very good, you know."

"Thank you."

"But why didn't you tell me who you were earlier?"

"Because I wanted to know you before you knew me."

"And now you know me?"

"No."

"But you do know I'm a friend of Teddy's family."

"Is this true?" Her eyes were fixed on his.

"I have a copy of your letter."

"We cannot talk here. Come with me."

She put an arm through his and led him out to the passageway going back toward the flamenco room. It was dank and dark there, like a hall in a prison, and you could smell the urinal effects of poor, untrapped plumbing from the nearby *servicio*.

Curt felt her thigh brush against his as they walked, and thought once more how lucky Teddy Swiatski had been. She was a head taller than Lois Harte, and hers was the fullness of ripe womanhood rather than that of muscular girlishness. It was hard to think about business in her presence. He wished they were in bed, exhausted, talking matters over in the calmness of mutual relief.

She stopped in the middle of the hall and turned to face him. "Tell me something that was in my letter," she said, obviously intending to surprise him.

"Well," he said. "Let me see . . . you speak English but don't write it very well without a dictionary . . . you believe Teddy's death was not an accident . . . you don't like the military police. . . ."

"*Bastante.*" She put a hand to his lips. "We cannot stay here to talk. I do not want to see Villalta or the *mayor*. You must come to my apartment tomorrow. At two hours, no . . . at three."

"O.K. But tell me just one thing, will you? Is Villalta mixed up in this somehow? Why does he bother you—"

"Kiss me!" She pulled his right arm toward her.

He kissed her, soft, then harder. Lucky Teddy, he thought, lucky me. Luck, luck, Christ, he *had* been drinking. . . .

"It was him," she said, disengaging herself.

"Who?"

"Villalta. Take me back to the bar, as though we have made a rendezvous, and then leave me."

He left her in the crowded bar and then made his way back to the table in the *sala*. Lois was sitting alone. He took her arm and led her onto the dance floor.

She kept a distance between them. "Where were *you?*" she demanded.

"Powder room."

"We thought you fell in."

"Almost," he said. "Where's Francisco?"

"Said he was going after you. Thought something might have happened."

"Nothing happened."

"Then why don't you wipe that stuff off your lips? Some *pow*der room."

"Oh!" He rubbed with the back of his hand.

"You're just smearing it." She took his pocket handkerchief out in a proprietary way and wiped his lips hard.

"Thanks," he said pulling her close. "One of the *putas* made a pass at me."

"I'll bet."

"I thought you and I had a deal."

"Strictly academic, Professor."

"I hope not," he said, pulling her in closer and feeling her respond. She must be a little drunk, too, he thought, listening to her sibilant breath just under his chin, smelling the alcohol fumes puffing up from her pouty little mouth. It was always somehow odd to smell alcohol on a woman's breath. He never thought about them that way. He never thought of them dying, either.

Villalta met them at the edge of the dance floor as the music stopped.

"Can you take Lois back to the base, Curtis?"

"Of course."

"Something has come up. You must forgive me, Lois."

"Certainly, Francisco."

"Business," he said to Curt. "I will see you at the hotel to-morrow for the *corrida*."

"O.K."

When he left, they sat down to finish their drinks. Her left hand rested in his lap. "Would you like to go now?" Curt said.

"Definitely," she said.

He waved to their waiter and tried to pay the check, but Villalta had already taken care of it.

At the door the field marshal put them in a cab, saluting as they pulled away. In the short drive to Curt's car, which was parked near the hotel, he knew he could do anything he wanted. He couldn't remember much about the ride out to the base, except that Lois curled up with her head resting in his lap, caressing him occasionally, making it hard for him to drive. She sat up when they approached the gate and managed matters with the sentry, and they drove down several rows of standardized houses to her place.

Inside, they moved through a dreamy sequence that went in and out of focus. He had no exact remembrance of getting into bed—just the easy reception, and the sleeping and waking and resumption, and then at about four-thirty her sobering tones, telling him he should really leave. And so he got dressed and got into the VW and went past the sentry with a salute, and drove through another dream to the hotel.

9

The *Barrera*

His head ached. A slant of sun cut across his face. He shifted onto the other pillow and his eyes fluttered shut and he hovered in the middle distance between sleep and waking and his body tensed and relaxed as the figure of Lois Harte ghosted in and out of his skull.

When the sun caught up with him again, his eyes opened wide and his tongue flicked bitterly against his teeth. He reached for his Vulcain "cricket" on the side table. It showed after one and he said "Jesus" aloud, surprised at the croaking sound of his own voice.

He shaved, showered quickly, and dressed in the light cord suit, which had been laundered and pressed and left hanging on the closet door. From his locked two-suiter he took the blue portfolio, and from that extracted María Maite's letter, putting it carefully into his inside breast pocket along with the passport folder. Then he put the portfolio back in the suitcase and locked that once more and slid it into the closet.

Downstairs at the desk was a note from Villalta. *Amigo,* he read, *you must have had a good time! I will come back at four.*

"At what hour does the *corrida* commence?" he asked the desk clerk.

"*En Zaragoza todas las corridas empiezan a las cuatro y media en punto.*"

Four-thirty on the dot. "*Gracias,*" he said, and headed toward the side dining room. There would be plenty of time if he went

104

to Maite's a bit early. He ordered a flan, hoping that the custard would help settle his stomach, and when the bottled water came he slipped out the two aspirins he had put into his pocket and swallowed them. By the time he got to his tea and the first cigarette of the day he was feeling pretty good, with a plan for questioning Maite all worked out in his head. *How long had she known Teddy Swiatski? Why had the Spanish and American police made trouble? Why did she think his death was no accident? Was she convinced he was dead? What about Farlo, did she know him? Where was he now? Who might have written from the base as Teddy's unidentified friend? Was there anyone there who might help?*

If she had the answers, his troubles might be over and he could knock off a quick letter to the Swiatskis giving them the straight stuff. *If.* Of course, she might not have the answers, but one thing he felt pretty sure about was that she was not involved in a racket. . . . Or was she? he asked himself.

As he drove to Obispo Mardín the question that bothered him most was how Villalta figured in all of this, if he did. . . . And why had he gone to the trouble of befriending him? The story about wanting to repay a debt of gratitude for favors received in the States seemed phony. And if there had been any kind of nascent friendship, it had absorbed a couple of dull blows last night. . . . In any human relationship both parties want something in return: from Villalta he wanted the kind of companionship that could open up a place like Zaragoza in ways otherwise impossible. But what did Villalta want in return? The pleasure of his English-speaking company? The pleasure of showing off his country to a foreigner who might be capable of appreciating it? Maybe María Victoria had instructed him to be nice. Maybe.

He parked across the street from 235 Obispo Mardín, and as he disentangled himself from the slope-roofed VW felt relieved to find no one working at the barrel factory. Its corrugated steel doors were shut tight. The men had probably gone home

to the long midday break that Spaniards take as combined lunch
and siesta from about twelve to three. A very inefficient system,
he thought, crossing the street. Like the British with their tea.
All right for colonization but not industrialization.

As he climbed the stairs to the third level of the building his
heart thumped heavily with effort and the excitement of seeing
María Maite. He could still feel the press of her body against his
in the dank hallway of the Cancela. Christ, can't you ever keep
your mind on business? He knocked on the door of number
five. In much flesh there is much weariness, he told himself.
Yes, that self replied, and a hell of a lot of pleasure. . . .

He knocked again, expecting soon to hear the shuffling of the
old woman's slippered feet. There was nothing. He checked his
watch: he was early by about twenty minutes. He pounded
harder this time. In a moment the door across the hall opened
part way and the boiled, brown face of a middle-aged woman
appeared.

"Do you wish to wake the dead?" she demanded, whining.

"No, *señora,* only those who live within."

"That is impossible, thank God!"

"And why?"

"Because they have gone away."

"Gone away?" he echoed. "Where?"

"What is that to me? What does it matter to anyone of a
decency where *that* takes itself? She and others like that—"

"*Perdóneme,*" he interrupted, "but is there not someone in
this building that knows her?"

"Knows her!" The woman mumbled something swiftly.
"Who in this considerable *lechería* does not know that one and
the others of her kind!"

The door slammed home like a musket blast. Curt decided not
to knock on Maite's door again. From what the good Christian
woman had said, there might be someone else in the building
who knew her, and besides, maybe the old bag was just crotchety

enough to get rid of him under false pretenses. He decided to retreat one floor and inquire there.

On the second level he knocked at number three. A bald-headed man wearing glasses answered. From inside someone's voice demanded, "Who is it, Manolo?" And the man, seeming frightened, told him quickly to try number two: there was someone there who would know about Maite. The door closed and Curt could hear the man starting to make an explanation inside.

The girl who answered at number two made him realize fully what had been behind the *portero's* smile the day before. This was obviously a building in which a number of girls had set themselves up among families, and it had acquired some no-toriety. She was the answer, in the flesh, as to why the woman upstairs was angry, and why the man across the hall was timorous. She was wearing a loose-fitting house coat that did not quite make it around the enormous breasts which sloped down without any visible means of support.

"*Ah,*" she said, "*el señor!*"

"You know me?"

"Clearly that yes. At the Cancela, with Señor Villalta."

He couldn't remember her, but it wasn't important. "Is it possible to enter?"

"I am sorry, but no." Her violet-shaded lips curled into a fat smile. "I have a good friend here now."

"*Comprendo.*"

"*Otra vez,*" she whispered, the lips curling again. "Another time." She started to close the door.

"*Momento,*" he said, putting his right hand against the door. "It is for María Maite that I am looking. Can you tell me where to find her?"

The girl's eyes were deeply socketed; they became brownly opaque under the heavy shadowing. "She is gone."

"Gone, yes, but where? When? Why?"

"Do not know. Gone." She tried to shut the door but he kept pressure on it.

"Aren't you a friend of hers?"

She hesitated. "No."

"But you must know where—"

"They moved away. In a truck. This morning. But I do not know where, and you must leave or there will be an inquietude."

He kept the door open another instant, watching the set of her face and the eyes turning even darker, dimmer; and then took his hand away. The door closed firmly and he stood looking at it. Blocked. What the *hell* had happened? He was positive Maite had intended seeing him. What could have made her go away in such a hurry? Had she been frightened; made to leave? Paid to leave? Was this part of the racket? *What* racket?

He looked up as if for inspiration, just in time to see the biddy upstairs dart away from the railing, where she had been watching.

"*Perra!*" he shouted up at her, and started down the stairs, vaguely taking in the graffiti on the walls telling everyone where to go and what to do. Let the bitch upstairs do it.

Outside, the brilliant glare of the sun dazzled him, and he moved against it as though he were encountering a giant shield of brass, burnished and reflective. . . . There would be no quick letter to the Swiatskis, he thought, as he crossed toward the shimmering red VW. And there was plenty of time now before meeting Villalta.

Getting behind the hot steering wheel, he decided to drive to the Vegas. He could get a table in the shade there, have his shoes shined, drink a long *ginebra con naranja,* maybe pick up yesterday's overseas edition of the *Times* or *Herald Trib.*

The Plaza de Toros in Zaragoza was located just off the Paseo de María Augustín in what must have been once the outskirts of the old city. Villalta directed him to park near the main railroad station and they walked the three or four blocks in between.

The streets were congested with people who spilled off the sidewalks, pouring out of cafés and cars and buses and *tranvías.* Near the big four-story-high amphitheater there was a backwash of a crowd waiting to filter into the numbered gates. Mounted police in gray-and-red uniforms sat on their horses like statues. Men sold cigars and little bottles of *manzanilla.* Women sold fans, eyeshades, and flowers.

Villalta led him to one of the gates and they went inside the prison-brick structure, under the stands of the stadium. It was dank and cool there, and long tables were covered with cheap stem glasses of cognac and wine. They rented two damp-feeling cushions and drank a quick cognac and then headed up a ramp toward their seats.

"*Aquí.*" Villalta winked at him: "The best."

They came up into the light and squeezed past three or four people getting to their seats in the first row.

"That's why the cushions," Villalta said.

They put the cushions down on the narrow concrete seats and sat. About two feet in front of them was a double railing and in front of that a narrow alleyway or outer track of the ring itself. There were policemen and a few men in blue pants with red shirts along with some photographers in the alleyway.

"That is the *callejón,*" Villalta said. "And that red fence is called the *barrera.*"

The fence was four or five inches thick and about five feet high. It was a brilliant red, as though it had been painted that morning. Spaced around it at quartering intervals were vertical lines of white, marking the baffled escape gates.

Curt had not been very responsive since meeting Villalta back at the hotel. He couldn't help but feel that the Spaniard was somehow responsible for Maite's departure. He was suspicious at how anxious Villalta had been to get him to take Lois Harte home, and how secretively and officiously he had acted after the Pardee fiasco. So when Villalta had greeted him exuberantly with a Spanish hug and kidded him about looking so tired after a night with the *rubia*, he had claimed the quieting privileges of a heavy hangover.

"You feeling better, Curtis?"

"Yeah," Curt said, with a reassuring smile. "I am." And he was. It was a fine afternoon and there was the pleasant feeling of a hot day fading slowly into massed excitement. In front of them was the perfect circle of the bull ring, repeated by two concentric lines of blue described in the sand, about twenty and thirty feet respectively away from the *barrera*. Everywhere you looked you saw color and movement, all of it seeming very close because you didn't have the wide separation or oval shape of a football field. Up above, the red and yellow Spanish flag floated from the double tier of boxes that ran completely around the amphitheater. This inner rim was pasted with signs in red and blue and white, advertising NARANJA KAS, ANÍS DEL ASTURIA, FUNDADOR, CERVEZA SAN MIGUEL.

Villalta had taken two cigars from his breast pocket. "Here," he said, " 'tis a custom. Everyone smokes a *puro por los toros*."

Curt lit the long cigar self-consciously, but as he looked around he saw that many men were already smoking their *puros*. This was something he hadn't known about bullfights. It was as though he had read about all this and yet never really understood it. Now this was real—the sun and the shadow, people in good suits and fine dresses sitting in the galleries and in the shadowy section of the stadium; coarsely clothed men and less good-looking women sitting in the sun section.

"These seats we have are called *barreras* also. Behind us are the *contrabarreras*," Villalta was saying. "And you see that man there."

"Where?"

"Across the aisle, with the black beret."

"Yes."

He was a man without a tie, but his white shirt was buttoned all the way up. He looked out of place among the more fashionable people sitting around him. There was a mourner's black band around his left sleeve.

"He has probably saved for a year to have a *barrera* for this *feria.*"

Curt looked at the man more closely. He was sitting quietly, patiently, intent on the preparations in the ring and in the alleyway. There was something devout in his attitude. He fell just within the shade, where the sun made its own line. Everything was collectively circular except for that shadowy line of distinction. The stadium and the galleries and the rows of seats, then the *callejón*, then the barrier fence, then the first blue line, then the next, and the center of the ring—all as circular as lines on a target. And across these the sun threw its conflicting arc.

"Up there sits the *presidente*. In a little while he will throw down the key to the doors to let the first bull in."

Curt looked where he was pointing, up to the top tier, where some bunting hung.

"And there you see how the fights are timed. The matador must make the kill before his time is up."

There was a huge round clock set in concrete above the tier opposite the president's box.

When the hands indicated four-thirty, a blast of trumpets came forth from the band seated in the lower tier—about six notes, drawn out long and held. Then the entire band came in, sharply rhythmed, lighter and more trilling than a marching band.

From under the stands came four horsemen in velvet costumes, their mounts arch-necked and stiff-striding in slow muscular containment. And behind them the *toreros* in three files of four each, with six picadors mounted on horses that were poor relatives of those out front. Villalta explained that the first three of the *toreros* were the matadors, the killers—Fermín Murillo in the gold-and-black brocaded suit, then Paco Camino in white in the center, and beyond him in red and gold, Diego Puerta.

They walked easily, with the naturalness of professional athletes, left arms slung, as though broken, in the folds of short capes. Behind them came their squads of three cape men and the picadors. The outfits of the *cuadrilla* members were not nearly so brilliant as those of the matadors, which scintillated like broken mirrors.

"*Trajes de luces,*" Villalta said. "The suits are called suits of light, and they cost hundreds of dollars."

The procession halted, the music stopped, the stadium hushed. Then one of the lead horsemen caught a twinkling object in his plumed hat dropped from the box above.

"The key," Villalta said.

The neat formation broke up and the crowd began shouting and clapping. The matadors exchanged their dress capes for big yellow-and-magenta jobs that they flared out in practice twirls. The other members of the *cuadrillas* got behind the escape panels. One of the red-shirted men took the key from the marshal, who then rode out, and everything hushed again. No movement at all in the stands. All eyes fixed on a door leading into the bowels of the stadium. Red shirt swung the bar up and opened the door, hiding behind it. Nothing happened. Fifteen thousand people waited, hardly breathing.

One of the *toreros* stood beside a skinny man holding swords in the *callejón*. They were just four feet away and Curt had just noticed the albino lack of coloration in the *torero's* face, when a giant voice hurled two syllables across the stadium: "*O-lé!*"

The black bull had come out at a soft trot but when the sun and the shout hit him at the same time he bolted into a massive charge that was absolutely beguiling because of the speed and grace and dexterity with which the massive body moved. It was like seeing a three-hundred-pound sprinter or ballet dancer. Only this one was closer to a thousand pounds.

One of the *toreros* stepped out, flapped a cape, and the bull pivoted and charged and split the wood of the *burladero* with the sound of a double-bladed ax—CHOCK! The sound carried to all parts of the stadium.

The bull swerved. Took a long stride toward the man, who turned, ran and vaulted the *barrera* with inspired speed.

When Curt looked again, there was Fermín Murillo, positioning himself. He stood with the long cape, his feet now set, the little balletlike slippers planted in the sandy earth. He held the cape chest high, the way a woman might hold a sheet before hanging it on a line to dry. He offered it to the bull. "Huh, *toro,* huh!"

The bull caught the chromatic flash of yellow and purple. It turned: squared, pawed, and, bringing its horns down, charged.

As it went by, Curt could see elements of diarrheal filth fouling the rump and tail. It had splattered out in one of the earlier moments of jet propulsion. Never read about that either, he thought.

Murillo made three passes. Each time he kept the bull way wide of him.

"Is that good?"

"No, he is just testing him to see how he charges."

Murillo swung behind one of the *burladeros.* The other matadors, Camino and Puerta, worked the bull a couple of passes. Meanwhile, without Curt's having noticed them, two of the picadors had stationed themselves on their crow-bait horses across the ring from each other. They looked like elderly, heavyset uncles who had come to help, sitting on their rickety nags with feet jammed hard in the enormous stirrups as though awaiting a storm.

Now the nearer picador spurred his blindfolded mount out away from the *barrera.* He held the reins in his left hand and a lance, about twelve feet long, with a pronged hilt about two inches from the point, in the other heavily gauntleted hand. The bull's head was up high. He looked around, alert, and saw the strange two-headed animal in front of him now, and charged—three, four, five galloping strides and, bang, into the padded side of the horse, the lance having skipped off target. He bulled the horse up and back, up and almost over and back against the barrier, and up again and the picador was lifted off his seat and lost his flat broad-brimmed hat, which went over the fence, and then he was following it like someone diving for a football, his lance dropping harmlessly inside the arena in the sand under the bull's grinding feet.

"Huh, huh—*toro, toro!*" One of the red shirts had come into the ring and was trying to get the bull away from the frenzied horse.

Several members of the *cuadrilla* had entered the ring and were spreading their capes and calling the bull away, and finally it gave up on the horse and moved toward them, trying to pick out one of the fleeing targets.

A few moments later a trumpet shrilled and everyone left the ring, including both of the pics, who had made their way to a gate while the bull was accepting a new cape.

One of the *cuadrilla* stepped into the ring, carrying two *banderillas*, red-and-blue decorated sticks with single-pronged barbs at the tips. He held these high above his head and yelling *"Toro"* began to run on a slant toward the middle of the ring. The bull came running out as though to oblige. At the last instant before collision the *banderillero* arched his body, swerved, and placed the barbed sticks just behind the hump of muscle. The bull swerved fast, almost falling to its knees, shaking its head to free itself of the double affliction, and then chased the *banderillero*, who squeezed behind the bulwark as though drawn there by elastic bands. From across the ring appeared another *banderillero* and he repeated the feat, and the crowd roared approval as he vaulted to safety.

The bull now stood pawing, twisting its neck, acting dumfounded at all this noise and trickery. It had not only the blue-and-white ribbon anchored in its hide (the mark of the estate that had raised this particular bull) but also the four long darts, swaying crazily, like two-foot quills. Blood streaked the bull's neck and side from the *banderillas* and where the pic had jabbed him. The horns were down almost parallel to the ground, instead of high at a forty-five degree angle, the way they had been when he first charged into the ring.

"Many people do not understand about the pic and the *banderillero*," Villalta was saying. "They think that they are supposed to tease the bull, or infuriate the bull, but what they do is make it possible for the matador to work the bull. That bull could leave here now and be perfectly all right in a few days. He is not hurt bad. But one can see how the horns are down now. And that is how it should be. If the *preparación* is not done properly, I have seen matadors *cogida*-ed in the neck and chin and face."

"I see," Curt answered, and as he did so vaguely realized that he had lost his anger and frustration. He was caught by the spectacle of sun and shadow, of man and beast, within the pale of a blind alleyway, where Murillo draped a very small red cape over a short stick and took a sword from one of the handlers.

"Now he works with the muleta."

Murillo stepped into the ring and called once, twice. The bull caught sight of the brief red flag of vanity. Hunching its neck and head, it charged. As it approached Murillo, he took two tiny shuffling steps, planted himself, offered the muleta with his left hand, the sword held in his right pointing toward the ground. He did not move his feet any more, just twisted at the waist, letting the bull whoosh past his hip and under the upward sweep of the muleta. The bull turned like a giant cat and came back, swept under the leading and evading cape again. The *banderillas* thwacked against Murillo this time, and when the bull passed him there were long smears of blood on his jacket. Shuffle, shuffle, he stood planted again, choosing his own ground. The bull came back and charged and swerved and the cape stayed in front of his dripping muzzle, and now the charge looked continuous, circular, with Murillo pivoting slowly, and again slowly, almost wrapping the bull around him as though they were partners in some unequal dance.

Finally the bull stopped, its head down. Murillo turned his back on the animal, no more than two or three yards away. He held his arms up, defenseless, and the crowd yelled approval of his mastery.

The bull stood tired, idea-less, its sides working like bellows.

"See how the front legs are even and the head down?"

"Yes."

"This is what the matador has worked for. Now comes the hard part of the job. Very hard on the *cojones.*"

Murillo placed himself about three yards in front of the stock-still animal. He stretched himself up on tiptoe, like someone trying to sight a billiard shot from up around the ear, the sword angling down. At the last instant his left hand lowered the muleta to keep the bull's head down and he stepped in over the right horn, pushing down with his right hand, the sword flashing fast—and then it was Pardee all over again!

You couldn't see and comprehend that fast. All you could do was remember that Murillo went up and over, a big rag doll thrown with an incredibly quick jerk of the bull's neck. The crowd was roaring. Murillo started to get to his feet, saw the horns coming, fell to the ground with his arms wrapped around his head. There was a long rip in the fancy pants, a slash of widening red. The bull ground at him with his horns, then tried to trample him—until finally it whipped around at the *monosabio* who was pulling its tail, and then shunted off after the flaring cape of one of the *cuadrilla.* Two of the *monosabios* took Murillo under the arms and dragged him to the *burladero.* His right leg looked useless and the foot left a line in the sand as they pulled him along. The stocking was now red as well as pink.

Soon everybody was out of the ring except the bull. It trotted around, looking for further taunters and victims.

"Do you think it's bad?" Curt asked, realizing that somehow they were standing and that his cigar had gone out.

"I don't know. Fermín was wounded last week in the chest. You could see how up straight stiff he was. But this of the leg I do not know. . . ."

"Jesus!" Curt said, and began clapping. Everybody was standing and clapping. Someone had tied something around Murillo's leg. He was shaking off handlers, getting a new sword from the *mazo de espadas*. He half walked, half shuffled out into the ring again. Quietness settled over the place like dust.

Murillo picked a spot. He wasn't going to do much moving around. The bull looked a little tired and worn itself. In a moment or two it saw the waving muleta. It trotted forward and stopped, pawed once, twice, and then made a run. Murillo kept the muleta a bit wide. The bull's right horn splintered into the barrier, riping a white scar in the red-painted wood. Murillo ran him under three or four times, keeping the angle right, never getting very far away from the barrier. Then the bull stood still again, just a few yards away from the man, saliva stringing down from its tongue. It was a black square with curved white handles that pricked the air, glinting more brightly than the eyes.

Murillo lowered the muleta again, the way he had before, went in over the same horn that had done the damage, and suddenly the sword disappeared in the bull's neck, almost up to the hilt.

The crowd had been chanting *"O-lé . . . O-lé . . . O-lé . . ."* with each of the passes. Now it murmured satisfaction with the entrance of the sword.

The bull looked much too heavy for its legs. The knees began to buckle. Blood pumped out of the mouth every second count. A hell of a lot of blood, gushing out into the sand in a widening stain of red. Who's working the handle? Curt wondered.

Then the animal fell, sledged over by some kind of internal blow. The legs moved spasmodically, climbing the air, stiffened, froze.

White handkerchiefs fluttered around the stadium. The *presidente* took them into account as a kind of vote, Villalta explained. Then came word from on high. Murillo was awarded one ear.

The other fights were good, according to Villalta, but they palled on Curt. Something about the sheer repetition of killing according to a set plan dulled his senses. It was a task and then the finish over and over again, with slightly different colored bulls, and slightly different deaths, at the hands of slightly different *trajes de luces.* Puerta and Camino were top-notch pros; they killed the remaining five bulls, Camino taking the extra one. But it was Murillo who had caught Curt's imagination and sympathy. There were two more gorings, but they were cartoon comics following near tragedy. One of the *banderilleros* got a horn right up his rear, lifting him (to a communal groan of "Oooh") about eight feet in the air, and he hopped, skipped, and vaulted to a new world's record and to safety. And one of the picadors received a horn in the side and was thrown from his mount. It took three *monosabios* to lift him over the *barrera,* where he fell with a thump into the *callejón,* a fat man in distress.

"Well," Villalta said, as they started out the gate and headed toward the car, "what is your opinion?"

"I don't know—yet. It's not like any movie or book. The bull is a tough baby." He shook his head, wonderingly. "So is somebody like Murillo. They aren't fooling out there." He remembered what Villalta had said inside: The matador must master his fear; he is afraid; he knows that his chance of dying in the ring is one in ten, his chance of dying or being crippled is one in four; and no one escapes goring.

"But you have reservations?"

"I guess I'm like the girl who's just lost her virgini~v. Not sure how I feel about it."

"You cannot tell from one *corrida*. I must teach you more about the *parar*, which is the style, and the *mandar*, which is the mastery, and the *templar*, which is the timing."

"*Gracias, maestro.*"

"*Nada, niño.*"

In the car Villalta said he would be busy that night, and Curt confessed to a date with Lois Harte at the base.

The Spaniard smiled and deliberately echoed his earlier sentence: "And what is your opinion?"

"I am still checking my sensations."

As they drove in the slow traffic toward the hotel, Curt was several times on the point of asking about María Maite. It was as though he knew his companion was expecting the question, offering opportunities of silence to allow for it.

Villalta got out at the corner near the post office. "*Adiós, guapo,*" he said, leaning down toward the window on the driver's side. "I will call tomorrow. Have a good time." He winked and started away.

"Francisco."

"*Sí.*" He turned back and leaned down once more.

"You remember Maite last night?"

"Of course."

"I was supposed to see her today. At her place."

"*Ai qué hombre con las chicas!* Lois *and* Maite."

"But she's left, left her apartment. Just like that, overnight. Can you explain it?"

Villalta's crooked smile seemed a mask. "Why me?"

"Well, I mean, you know how an *artista* like that lives. That's all."

"Of course—they work a month or two in Zaragoza, then a few in Barcelona, then Málaga, Madrid, San Sebastian. Like that."

"It is important that I see her."

"Important?"

"Yes, I—ah—wanted to talk to her about the article I'm writing. She's known a number of Americans, and I wanted her opinions especially. The woman's point of view."

"That's too bad."

"Do you think Pepe could tell me where she might have gone?" As soon as he asked the question, Curt mentally kicked himself. He should have seen Pepe first, himself.

"I'll be glad to ask, *amigo*. But I think you want something else with Maite, no?"

"What do you mean?"

"*Hombre!* Don't you think I know?"

"Know what?"

"You. You like the type. She is a beautiful woman, and not a *puta*. So 'tis normal." He winked and gave the roof of the car a smack with his hand and went into a *natural* as though he were moving a bull past him. "*Adiós.*"

"*Adiós.*" Curt let the clutch out and pulled away from the curb. He felt dimly that he did have something to learn about style, timing, and mastery. He also had plenty to learn about Francisco Villalta, who might very well hold a short sword behind the velvet cloth of proffered friendship.

10
Base Privileges

Lois came out to the main gate to escort him in. At her insistence Curt parked his VW at her place and they went on to the club in her MG. The top was down. The night was balmy, with a light breeze off the Moncayo. As they rode over the smooth asphalt streets, past neatly plotted houses with bicycles and Fords and Chevys in the drives, Curt had the impression that an American town had been plopped down here in the arid fields of Spain. He thought of the night of his farewell party at the Beaverses. It had been just three weeks ago but it seemed ages. Pennwood was far away and yet close. In his head, like Mary and Helen, and now this. . . .

Lois' voice competed with the soft rush of air and the muffled roar of the motor.

". . . twelve lectures over a period of six weeks. Your students will be officers and enlisted men, as well as some wives and nurses. The pay's not much, as I told you. A thousand dollars. But you'll be eligible for base privileges."

"Including you?"

She smiled back and shifted down for a corner. "Including the AFX, and APO postal service and gasoline coupons—"

"And you beside me—"

"And hospital facilities, and the golf club, and the class-four store—"

"Whoa, whoa. I know the AFX is the PX. But what's a class-four store?"

"Liquor, my dear. With Chivas Regal and Courvoisier at four dollars a fifth."

"*That* does it. Even without you I could manage on those."

"Also, of course, you'll have a pass to come on base when you want. And I won't have to vouch for you, like tonight."

"You're opening new worlds."

This was working out fine, he thought. The lectures would be top-of-the-head stuff. He'd be able to come out and get a bit of America any time he tired of Spain. And what Lois couldn't know was that this would give him exactly the opportunity he needed to check on Teddy.

He glanced across at her. The moon had chastened her; her blond hair glimmered like platinum. "And how do I qualify for this slice of paradise?" he said.

"You'll begin by impressing the base commander and the education officer with your professorial abilities. We're meeting both of them at the club. I've already talked things over with Major Stafford—he's the education officer. *Also*, if we see him, you'll be nice as pie to Tom Pardee, being sure *not* to mention anything about last night."

"What does *he* have to do with it?"

"Nothing much, except *he* will run the security check on you. And if you come out clean, *he* will issue your base privilege card and sticker for your car."

She cross-armed the steering wheel and they turned abruptly into a parking lot, which must have had a hundred cars in it. At the far end stood a long, low-roofed building all lit up. Lois gunned the car in that direction, and over the sound of the motor they caught swelling bursts of music from inside the building.

Near the entrance they approached a section of parking slots marked off by a sign OFFICERS ONLY. Lois angled in sharply, aiming between a Buick and a Mercedes. She jabbed at the brake, once, twice, and they stopped about six inches away from a cable bearing the sign.

Curt had braced himself against the dash. Now he looked across at her. "You've learned to drive Spanish, huh?"

"*Y por qué no?*" She leaned over and pecked at his cheek and then wiped away the mark.

As he came around to her side of the car he tried to formulate a sentence dealing with masses of lives and active desperation. This little blonde in a white dress, clutching a beaded white bag, was riding things out by the seat of her pants. In a world where there was no peace she practiced her own brand of brinkmanship.

He took her arm in a momentary impulse of protectiveness and they went up the walk to the glass door entrance.

Just inside the club, to the right as they went in, was a bar. It was jammed with forty or fifty people. Maybe one-fourth of the men were Negroes. Some of them, as well as the whites, wore uniforms. Curt was surprised to see they were enlisted men.

"How come?" he said.

"What?"

"I thought this was an officers' club."

"Was. It's all-ranks, since the phase down."

"Well, the Air Force always was the most democratic service."

"Maybe so, but we go out there." She pointed across a room filled with enough chairs and tables to accommodate several hundred persons. Beyond was a long side room separated by folding plastic doors that had been left partly open.

"Officer territory?"

"Right. Drink there, dance here." She nodded toward a dance area in the main room. A number of couples shuffled around the slippery-looking floor, following the beat of a six-man band that huffed, puffed, and thumped its way through a sluggish "Tea for Two" cha-cha, while circles of red and blue and yellow and green replaced each other on the floor as colored disks revolved beneath a spotlight attached to the ceiling. All this was somehow at odds with the large wooden plaques that dominated three walls of the room, like stations of the cross, stiffly depicting the exploits of Don Quixote and Sancho Panza.

"Come on."

As Curt followed her around the tables and down an aisle, he noticed that all the men in this room were dressed in civvies —looking stiff, high-shouldered, ill at ease in suits and sports jackets. Most of them were accompanied by their wives; and the place might easily have passed for an Elks Club in Scranton, Pa.

That wasn't true, he had to concede, as they now approached a group of young airmen occupying a section of tables off to one side of the dance floor. They had rounded up a seraglio of twenty or thirty Spanish *chicas*—some of them truly wild, if he was any judge, and way beyond the pale of amateur standing.

Lois whispered in his ear as they passed by: "The ladies in waiting."

"Whatta ya mean?" he whispered back.

"Later."

They went into the long, narrow outer room, like a glassed-in veranda. Lois waved a hand in response to greetings as they made their way toward a small table by the richly draped windows. A dark-suited waiter angled over and helped seat them.

They gave their order for double Scotch and sodas. The waiter was dutifully pleased with their Spanish. When he had gone, Curt offered Lois a cigarette, taking a look around. A thick rug cushioned the floor from wall to windows. A silky slubbed drapery screened out the night but not the moon. Everything in here seemed richer, softer, more subdued than in the other sections of the club; the music sounded less raucous; civilian suits, well cut, hung less awkwardly from officer frames; some of the women were elegant.

Curt offered a light. "Definitely *sombra*," he said.

Lois puffed, puffed. "What do you mean—*sombra*?"

"You know, like at the *toros*."

She was uncomprehending for a moment, then said, "Oh, yes, but don't forget this is all they have left of their own club."

"Are they allowed to dance with enlisted wives?"

"Certainly."

"And do they?"

"More than *that*, dear. Didn't you know a SAC base is just one big happy family? Especially overseas."

"Does it ever happen the other way round?"

"Now and then."

Curt was interested in the people sitting at a long table at the end of the room, opposite the portable bar. He pointed his cigarette in that direction, saying, "Seems to be a state occasion."

There were three American officers at the table, diplomatically splendid in their white mess jackets, butterfly collars, black ties. The Spanish officer with them wore a dull, heavy, olive-green uniform; but at his side sat a woman who reflected enough splendor for both of them. She reminded Curt of an older María Victoria. Her hair was perfectly coiffeured, towering like a bee's hive. Her head was held high, nose and chin atilt, neck arched. Among the three American women present she carried her beauty as though it were a dueling pistol.

"That's where we go later. Colonel Bolen is entertaining as part of the fiesta week. That's Colonel Ogondez from the Spanish side of the base. And his wife."

"Some wife."

"I thought you'd notice."

"Worth noticing. Definitely not one of the 'ladies in waiting.'"

"Oh, those."

"You were going to tell me about them."

"There isn't very much to tell—except that half of them are prostitutes and the other half are waiting for their papers to marry airmen, and nobody can tell which is which."

Their drinks were brought. Curt was surprised to find that together they cost only fifty cents. He gave the waiter a dollar and told him to keep the change.

"You mentioned papers," he said, taking a strong pull at his Scotch. "What kind of papers?"

"Well, to marry an American boy—in the military, I mean —a Spanish girl has to have several kinds of affidavits. I'm not sure I know them all, but there's one she must have from her parish priest, which is hard to get if the boy happens to be Protestant, and just about impossible, I guess, if he's Jewish, although really there aren't many Jews here, and I certainly don't remember one ever wanting to marry a *chica*.

"Also there's a health certificate. The Spanish health authorities have to make out an affidavit to the effect that the girl is in good physical and mental health."

Lois took a sip of her drink, as though considering her next statement. "I guess the one that causes most trouble is the one that has to do with the girl's moral character. But you've seen some of the girls, so maybe it should. The Brigada Social handles that, along with our Air Police."

Curt found himself wondering whether Teddy and María Maite had contemplated marriage, had tried for such papers: the querulous tone of her letter stuck in his mind—some complaint about the American and Spanish police.

"What you seem to be saying is that it's difficult to arrange one of these marriages."

"Well," she said, "what everybody notices is that there aren't nearly so many here in Spain as in Germany, or France, or Italy."

"Why not, do you think?"

"I don't know exactly. But you just don't find Spanish girls so hot after American husbands. I should say *good* girls. I think our poor airmen get hard up and marry the bottom of the barrel."

"Maybe you're just being catty."

"I honestly don't think so."

"Maybe part of the answer is that the country's so strictly Catholic."

"Italy and France are Catholic, too."

"Yes, but in a different way."

He took another long drink again, thinking that this subject might well develop into a point for the *Phaeton* article. You'd have to consider marriage as part of the inevitable American pursuit of happiness.

Lois said, "Why so pensive, dear?"

"Well, what you said about the ladies in waiting interests me. I have a chance to do some writing for a magazine, about the American image abroad—and I'd like to get some solid information about this business of marriages in Spain. Got any suggestions?"

"You might be able to—"

"Good evening." A short stocky man stood beside them. "I hope I'm not intruding."

The blue trousers and white mess jacket made him look like a refugee from a musical comedy, but his face belied that impression immediately. The skin was leathery, the liquory blue eyes wide-set, the nose stumpy, once broken.

"Hello, Albert."

Curt stood up.

"This is Dr. Fielding, whom I was telling you about. Major Stafford."

They shook hands. The major's grip was firm.

"Pleased to meet you, Doctor." Like most nonacademicians he used the title without the name. "But please sit down. I just came by to invite you over for a drink. Colonel Bolen would like to have you join us. So whenever you're ready, please feel free."

"That's very nice of you," Curt said, still standing.

"We'll be over in a few minutes, Albert."

"Good. We'll have some chairs set up."

He nodded and left. Curt sat down. "A royal command," he said.

"You'll wow 'em, darling. Just remember—heaps of professorial dignity. And try to pay as much attention to the American wives as to the *señora*."

"What if I don't?"

"They'll scratch your eyes out. Then the colonel will shoot you."

"Which colonel?"

"Her husband, dopey."

When they had finished their drinks, they made their way to the head table. Major Stafford handled the introductions. The base commander was a large man who talked with a Midwestern flatness. His wife was thin and angular. Colonel Ogondez was a coffee-colored *moreno*. His mustache, slow smile, and round face reminded Curt of a large cat. His wife spoke little or no English. Curt addressed her in Spanish, telling her he was enchanted. She smiled icily, without offering her hand. The other couple were Captain and Mrs. La Rosa: he was a slender man in his thirties, nice looking, almost boyish, with a pencil-line mustache; his wife, Rita, had a pretty face, turning pudgy.

La Rosa, it turned out, was an engineer. He was of Italian extraction and spoke Spanish fairly well, doing much of the translating for the party, since Colonel Ogondez had only a basic understanding of English. Curt and Lois had been seated between the La Rosas and Mrs. Stafford, a quiet woman with sagging bags under her eyes, and a puckish face. She wore thick lipstick—an outmoded fashion—and Curt suspected that she drank heavily.

Conversation was sporadic for a while, hampered by the necessity to translate. But then it settled around Curt, who explained what he was doing in Spain, where he'd come from, what his impressions were so far of the country. He was complimentary, phrasing some of what he had to say in Spanish from time to time, noticing that the Ogondezes were appreciative, though reserved.

Finally Colonel Bolen cut in bluntly. "Mrs. Harte tells us you might teach a course for us."

"He's kindly consented, Colonel," Lois put in.

"Yes," Curt added with a smile, "Mrs. Harte has explained that it is my patriotic duty to do so."

"What he means is that we don't pay his usual price, Colonel."

"Well, you know we'd allow you to have base privileges also," the colonel said. "But I'm sure a man of your background wouldn't do something like this just for the material rewards."

Like hell I wouldn't, Curt thought. He said, "If there's any hesitancy on my part, Colonel, it's because I have to get permission from the Fulbright Commission before accepting."

"Yes," Major Stafford said, "you'd have to do that."

La Rosa was busy explaining to the Spanish contingent what was being said.

By the time they had finished a round of drinks everything was going smoothly. Matters became less formal. When Colonel Bolen discovered that Curt had played football at Nittany, he gave a short history of his own career as a blocking back at Illinois under the old single-wing system. Lois winked at Curt to assure him that *this* clinched it.

When the next round of drinks came, they drank a toast to the Ogondezes. It seemed the colonel was being sent to Washington in six months as a military attaché. Curt offered his congratulations. He was sure the *señora* would like Washington: it was one of the most cosmopolitan and sophisticated cities in the *Estados Unidos*, and she would certainly feel at home there, adding her own presence to its charms. It was fulsome, but it sounded all right in Spanish, and some of the *señora's* ice cracked. She said that the Fulbright authorities seemed on this occasion to have selected a man who might bring both knowl-

edge and understanding to the university. Her husband con-
curred with a smile and a nod, saying, "I-ham agree weeth my
woif." Lois lightly kicked Curt's shin under the table.

When the colonels switched wives for a state-occasion dance,
those left at the table had another drink. Major Stafford asked
Curt to come into his office sometime early the next week.
The La Rosas said they would all have to get together at their
home soon, when things were settled. Curt felt that they were
glad to have someone from outside the military come into
their midst, as though military isolation made civilian intrusion
a sometimes necessary thing.

About twenty minutes later, when he and Lois stood up to
take their leave, Tom Pardee appeared at the sliding doors.
He came to the table in a rush and drawing Stafford and
Colonel Bolen aside, went into whispered conference with them.
In a few moments, Stafford and the commander returned to
the table. Stafford made an elaborate apology to the Ogondezes
and the others: something had come up; he had to leave, with
regrets. His wife said she would stay; the La Rosas would take
her home. When Stafford had gone, Lois and Curt smiled their
good-byes and went into the main room to dance.

"What do you think that was all about?" Curt asked, as
soon as they were out of earshot.

"I don't know," Lois said, "but I think we can find out."

The floor was crowded and the band sounded better,
smoother; the lights were softer. They moved in an alcoholic
glow, now red, now blue, green, yellow.

"Don't move away from me," he murmured in her ear, "or
I'll be disgraced."

"Don't worry, darling."

"Let's get out of here soon."

"Yes, darling."

They danced for a few more moments, then she moved
away slightly, saying, "Do you really want to know why
Stafford left in such a rush?"

"Ask me tomorrow. I'm in no mood to think."

"Seriously." She moved a little farther away.

Anything that made Pardee look disturbed was more than interesting, he thought. "Seriously, I would."

She took his hand and led him toward the main entryway. Standing against the wall was a man in a dark gray suit, watching the proceedings, a drink in one hand, a cigar in the other. Lois made straight for him.

"Hello, Ralph," she said.

He looked somewhat suspiciously at Curt before replying. "Evening, Lois."

"Ralph, this is Dr. Fielding. He may be teaching that course we were talking about."

"Oh, hello, Doctor." There seemed to be relief in discovering Curt was not an officer. "I may be one of your students."

"Good," Curt said.

"Ralph is the first soldier of this yere base. First Sergeant Sterner."

"Pleased to meet you, Sergeant."

"Listen, Ralph." Lois lowered her voice. "Can you give us a little unclassified scoop?"

Sterner looked at Curt again, then said, "Depends."

"Well, we were sitting at the colonel's table when Major Pardee came in and took Stafford away, and all we want to know is why."

"That's all, huh?" Sterner winked at Curt. "You think all you have to do is crook your little finger and I'll spill the beans."

"Oh, c'mon, Ralph, don't be sticky."

He looked from Curt to Lois, squinting his eyes as though trying to make up his mind. "Swear you won't squeal?"

"Swear," Lois said.

"Right," Curt said.

"Cross your heart and—"

"Oh, Ralph!"

"Well, this'll be all over the base in a couple of hours anyway. What happened is that three of our boys made a quick run on Andorra. Seems their car was loaded with black-market stuff. Only thing is they ran themselves off the road and down into the river—all three killed. Major Stafford, of course, has to go up there and take charge."

In the car, on the way back to her place, Lois explained that occasionally some of the airmen made black-market runs to Barcelona or to the little country between France and Spain called Andorra. Curt knew about it, knew it was a duty-free place frequented by tourists and others as a free market, a place about as large as Liechtenstein and maybe more mountainous.

Back at her place, she went into the kitchenette to make a nightcap. Then they went into the bedroom.

Lois put the drinks and cigarettes on the night table. As she began to undress, Curt asked about Stafford.

"Why would he take charge of that sort of thing? You said he was the education officer."

"He's also the mortuary officer."

Curt laughed. "The Air Force certainly has a sense of humor."

She pulled off her second stocking and began unhooking her dress. "Almost all the officers have to double up on jobs now." The dress came off like a moulted skin.

He felt himself warming to the situation, seeing her in pants, bra, and garter belt. "I'd like to talk with him about his duties sometime," he said, one part of his mind still on the Swiatski matter.

"I'm sure that could be arranged." Her breasts tumbled free of the harnessing bra, then trembled tautly as she threw it toward the chair containing his things.

He concentrated on Teddy, returning to the idea of marital papers; but his body seemed to have ideas of its own as he watched Lois step daintily out of her pants.

"Back at the club you started to tell me—"

She was not listening to him, but moved like a small dream, an image made to measure, and then was beside him, stretched pinkly out on the clean white sheets, and they touched and moved, and moved, and then for some long time there was no thinking. . . .

Afterward, Lois lit cigarettes for them, and offered him a sip from one of the glasses. Then they lay back, her head resting on his arm. They smoked without talking.

Finally, Curt said, "I'm still curious about something."

"Ummmmm?"

"At the club you started to tell me how I could find out more about those marriage papers, but then the major showed up and you never finished."

"Oh, that. Why *are* you so interested?"

"I told you—I'm doing an article."

"Then you can get the information from the horse's mouth, or mouths, I should say." There were still small beads of perspiration on her forehead.

"Which horse?"

"Your buddy."

He wiped the perspiration away with his left hand. "Not Pardee again!"

"Uh-hum. And your other buddy."

"Who, for Christ's sake?"

"Francisco."

He hiked himself up onto one elbow. "Francisco!"

"Sure, didn't he tell you? He's the liaison man between the base and the Brigada Social. I thought you knew, since—"

"I knew he was a lawyer; that's all." He reached across her for his cigarette in the tray.

Villalta had never given the slightest indication he was connected with the base. Just a civil lawyer, associated with María Victoria's father. Now that Curt thought of it, of course it made sense: a man trained in the States, capable of practicing on both sides of the legal fence. But why the hell hadn't he mentioned it? The question stung. He felt duped. Every time he looked around, there was Villalta staring him in the face. Even Lois had once been his bed partner (he could hear Villalta asking how he had enjoyed the *rubia*).

Curt sat there in bed, taking a deep drag on the cigarette.

"What's the matter, dear?"

"Nothing," he answered, rather harshly. María Victoria, her father, Pardee, María Maite, Pepe, the ladies in waiting—they all revolved around Villalta. Maybe the whole damn base, he thought.

"C'mon, Curt, lie down."

He put out the cigarette in the ashtray and then lay beside her again. She reached up and turned out the lamp. He didn't think about Villalta or anything else until four in the morning, when she said he really ought to go.

11
María Victoria's Parlor

Vía de la Cruz was in the inner city, just a block away from the Coso, in a neighborhood crowded with boutiques, jewelry shops, and fashionable clothing stores.

As he turned into the narrow entry of number 16, Curt checked his watch. It was two minutes to eleven, and María Victoria had said eleven. The idea of being on time pleased him. Back home it wouldn't have mattered much, but here in a country almost devoid of punctuality he felt a Prussian urge to be precise.

An old campaigner came out of his cubicle to assist, or challenge. The man's bulbous nose appeared to have been marinated in wine, and he peered around it parenthetically, suspicious of the *extranjero*.

Yes, he admitted reluctantly, the family Mandar did reside in this building, on the top level, *el último piso*. And yes, certainly the *ascensor* was functioning. To prove it, he pressed a large black button and the elevator cage began to vibrate with rheumatic vigor. Opening the accordion-action door, he let Curt into the walnut-and-glass cabinet, then pressed another button that made the elevator creak, groan, shudder, and finally start up at glacial speed.

Like much of Spain, the elevator was a combination of the baroque and the moderately functional. It was not so much a timesaver as a legsaver. There was a plush bench to sit on, and four narrow mirrors to aid vertical primping. Curt timed the trip—over two minutes to go four floors.

The Mandar apartment occupied the entire top floor. The entrance consisted of two dark oaken doors. He twisted the manual bell. He rang again, and in a moment one of the doors swung open. The maid who answered looked like a hefty farm girl, with dusky cheeks and mottled flesh, but she was immaculately proper in her uniform of black dress, white apron, cuffs, and cap.

"La Señorita María Victoria está en casa?"

"Sí, señor," the maid said, lowering her eyes as though it were amusing, or embarrassing, to deal with a foreigner. "If the *señor* will follow me."

They left the high-ceilinged vestibule and entered a small sitting room, one of whose walls consisted mainly of folding glass doors. The maid opened these and indicated he was to enter. "If the *señor* will accommodate himself. The *señorita* will present herself in a few minutes."

"Muchas gracias," he said in a dignified tone.

She stole a glance at him and then left with the speed of a reporter meeting a deadline. He smiled at the thought of her news bulletin in the servants' quarters.

The room he entered was a large parlor, as sumptuously appointed and richly inlaid as a coffin. He took a tentative step forward onto an ancient oriental rug: its bordering tassels were worn to the point of nonexistence; its angular pattern meandered into the dull central brownishness of a dried-out river.

There seemed to be a lack of air in the room. It smelled musty and perfumed. His nose, as much as his eyes, reminded him of other rooms he had known as a boy back in Hazleton, rooms he hadn't thought of in twenty years. "Polish parlors," his father had called them. They were usually closed off from the rest of the house except for occasions such as marriages, christenings, and funerals. Acting as home museums for whatever was considered precious, they contained all the family photo-

graphs and the few heirlooms destiny allowed steerage-class im-
migrants—perhaps a lace tablecloth, a musical instrument or
two, a small jewel casket, or simply a black shawl thrown over
the back of an overstuffed sofa, whose velure was as shiny and
fully piled as the day it was bought.

Not that María Victoria's parlor was exactly like those Hazleton rooms. It was much more luxurious. The provincial furniture was as fragile looking and voluptuously turned as a violin.
The divan, which was covered in floral satin, seemed incapable
of supporting anything other than ethereal bodies; and the three
chairs spaced around the room—feet splayed out, legs bowed—
were more to be admired than sat upon. Yet despite its being
Spanish, this room might have been an idealized Old Country
archetype of the Polish parlors. It, too, was a treasure-trove, a
repository of memorabilia. At least a hundred years of Mandars
lined the plastered walls; there were daguerreotypes and mezzo-
tints and small oils for some, oval-framed photographs (turned
brown) for others.

Curt made his way across the rug to the holy of holies. Against
one wall stood a glass-faced cabinet, whose shelves were laden
with mementos and *objets d'art*. He examined each item separately: an ivory elephant, with a splintered trunk and broken
tusk . . . a silver caster supporting two fragile bottles . . .
six miniature Toledo rapiers, their points invaginating a red
plush ball . . . a curved Moorish dagger with serpentine pattern etched into its hilt and sheath . . . a roll of parchment
tied with a faded purple ribbon. . . .

He kneeled down to see the contents of the lowest shelf. On
one side was a row of tarnished medals set against a velvet
plaque; on the other a small chalice with a platen; and in between, a bowl of dwarfed flowers embalmed in some kind of
sugary wax.

He stood up, feeling rather faint, and decided that he needed
fresh air. Two casement windows rose from floor level to a
height of about seven feet. He made his way to one of these and

drew aside the heavy silken drapery by pulling on its brass rings. Beyond, however, were wooden shutters with a tricky latch. Finally, he managed. Pulling the shutters in, he opened the casement windows and stepped out onto a tiny balcony. Immediately his ears filled with the sounds of life below. He looked down and saw pedestrians and traffic moving at varying speeds in random patterns. At the corner of Coso and Vía de la Cruz he could see a white-helmeted policeman exercising his power, like a puppet come to life. Curt drew fresh air into his lungs, felt his eyes fill with tears in the sun's glare, and sneezed heavily, so that an almost electrical shock tingled one elbow.

"Dr. Fielding."

He turned and tried to ease himself back into the room but couldn't; the shutter was caught somehow on the drape, and he was afraid to push in for fear of tearing the fabric.

"Oh, don't push," she said. "Just a minute."

He could hear small ejaculations of exertion as she stretched herself. Then the brass rings clinked on the supporting bar and the shutter opened wide enough for him to enter.

As he moved back into the gloom he bumped into the girl and felt her tense under his steadying hands.

"I'm sorry," he said.

She shrugged her shoulders gently out of his grasp. "Not at all," she said. "But won't you sit over there?" The room seemed lighter now, some of the mustiness gone. He could see she was smiling, pointing toward the divan. "It is much safer."

He made a mock bow. *"Muchas gracias, señorita.* Your beauty is exceeded only by your mercy."

Her soft laughter echoed off the walls. *"Qué caballero!"* she said, arranging the window so that an arrow of sunlight cast itself across the rug.

Curt sat on the divan, hoping it would not crack under his weight. *"No caballero,"* he said. *"Toro."*

María Victoria perched herself on a chair. She was wearing a light gray skirt and a sweater that was green up to her pert breasts and then gray to the rounded neckline. "What do you mean—*toro?*" A series of silver bracelets clinked on her right wrist as she put a loose strand of hair back in place.

"Nothing, except that we have a saying about a bull in a china shop."

"Oh, we do, too! But you are certainly not a bull—even if this place is a china shop." She waved a hand in admission, taking into account all the contents of the room, including a tray, decanter, and two liqueur glasses, which she must have brought in and placed on the leather-topped coffee table. "My sister Lola calls this room *el museo*. But it is private and will make a good place for the tutoring, no?"

"Just fine," he said. "And I hope someday you'll give me a guided tour."

"I shall."

"I'd like to know all about those Mandars on the walls."

"And shall I tell you who are the skeletons in our family?" She pretended mystery.

"Closet." He smiled. "Skeletons in the closet."

"The black sheep."

"Right. But I would like to know the living Mandars also—your family."

She hesitated a moment, then said, "You shall meet them—someday." Her tone of voice indicated there would be no hurry to introduce him; it insisted their arrangement was professional, not social. If they happened to be meeting here in this parlor, it was because his office at the university was crowded, and because his apartment, which he had suggested, was absolutely taboo.

He studied her closely for a moment. As in Madrid, when he had first seen her with Marta Torres, and during their brief conference earlier in the week at the university, he was once again impressed by the coppery quality of her beauty. It was not simply the complexion; it was as though she were warm and soft and yet cool and hard, an alloyed piece of living statuary:

the eyebrows arched, the nose arched, the lips curved into lines that seemed cast, the hair pulled up and back like a proud crest. One moment she could be relaxed and human, and the next stiffen into a mold of Spanish pride. The virgin, he thought, past twenty-five.

He offered her a cigarette. "I shall be grateful for the opportunity"—he paused as she took one, noticing how long her hand was, the tapered fingers tipped with almond-shaped nails—"whenever you feel I'm worthy of meeting your family."

Her eyes registered the ironic flick of his voice, but she said nothing. Accepting a light from him, she drew on the cigarette, and then asked how things were going at the apartment and the university.

Accepting the change of subject diplomatically, Curt told her about moving in from the hotel, getting a temporary maid to clean up the place, and needing a regular one to keep it clean.

"You will have to find an older woman. A young *criada* will not work for a bachelor."

"So I've found out."

"Do you like the apartment?"

"It's modern, convenient, plenty large. The furnishings provided by the Commission are rather cheap and ugly, but that's to be expected, I guess."

"And what about the *departamento de inglés?*"

He described the veddy jolly English department: Collins, a tall, thin Sherlock Holmes character, who was chairman; Tupper, a fat, pipe-puffing fellow from the North Country; Utley, a rotten-toothed little mouse of a man, very friendly, very difficult to understand; and Bromwich, Utley's close friend, nervous and academically incapable, with a Spanish wife and five little 'uns.

She softened as he talked and, by the way her eyes came alive and her body relaxed, he sensed that she might like him. She laughed softly at his British accent, his exaggerated up-and-down scale intonations, and his sibilant puffings as he imitated poor Utley, who spoke Spanish, French, and English as though suffering from incipient lockjaw.

Finally, she said, "What of the Vice-rector, Señor Durán?"

"He's a very exceptional man." Curt was glad he hadn't said "Spaniard." Durán was over six feet tall; he was energetic and efficient, and liked to get things done immediately. Not afraid of impairing his dignity, he had helped Curt move from the hotel into the apartment. The luncheon he had arranged for Curt to meet the department had been well planned and beautifully brought off.

"I like him very much," Curt concluded.

"He is among the most admired men in Zaragoza."

One of the things he wanted to do on this visit was unobtrusively get her talking about what might be a delicate subject, and now he thought of a way of doing it.

"Is Señor Durán a close friend of your family?" he asked.

"Not exactly. My father knows him, of course."

"But not like Francisco Villalta?" The transition was made.

"Oh, no. Our family has known Francisco since when he was a little boy. He was sent here to the Jesuit school during the war. And now, of course, he is a business associate of my father's."

"You mean they're law partners?"

"No. Just that sometimes they consult about cases."

"How long has Francisco worked for the air base, do you know?" That was a little blunt, he thought. Better take it easy.

"Well, I don't think he really works for the base."

"But for the Brigada Social?" No use easing off now.

Victoria turned her large, slightly slanting eyes on him. He could feel her tensing up again.

"Haven't you talked with him about this?"

"No, I haven't. The peculiar thing is he never mentioned it to me." He watched for a reaction. There was none. "I discovered it just by chance."

Now her left eyebrow twitched up. "Are you trying to tell me something about Francisco—that he has not been open with you?"

Curt's first impulse was to say: "You could say that!" He was thinking of María Maite, and of how Villalta reported that Pepe had no information about her at all. She had just vanished.

"No," he said, "and I'm certainly not implying any criticism of you. I'm really grateful to you for bringing us together. Francisco has been a wonderful cicerone, and in many ways has acted as a friend. But—" He let it hang there, trying to find a way out.

"But what?" she demanded.

"Well, to give you an answer I'll have to ask you a question. Do you mind?"

"I will have to hear the question first."

He offered her another cigarette. She refused. He lit one for himself.

"Something has bothered me ever since I met Francisco. It has to do with you. Is he more than a friend?"

Her smile was broad, an answer in itself. "If you mean is there romance between us, the answer is no. We are not each other's type."

"I'm glad, Victoria," he said simply, and his own sincerity surprised him. He felt that this was a good time to address her in the familiar Spanish fashion, omitting the ubiquitous María.

Again her left eyebrow twitched up, but this time she was smiling. "And now, Dr. Fielding, I have a question to ask you." She paused dramatically. "Would you like to drink some Calisay?"

They laughed together. The pressure was off. "*Me gusta mucho,*" he said, aware of the ambiguity that included both her and the drink.

She poured the liqueur like a ministrant at the altar, her movements delicate and precise. There was a lithe and lovely body under the gray skirt, the half-green, half-gray sweater, but it seemed to be more line and form than substance, like something out of El Greco.

"Here is to our agreement," she said, lifting the tiny glass. "To student and tutor."

"To Héloïse and Abélard," he said, sipping the Calisay, finding it sweet and heady.

"But they came to such a bad end!" she protested.

"Do you really think so?"

"Of course." She put her glass on the tray. "And it was because they did not attend to the lessons. So permit me."

She went out into the sitting room and in a few moments returned with two books and a sheaf of papers. Sitting beside him on the divan, she handed over one of the books.

"This we do for review, even if it is too basic."

He looked at the title: *El Español Práctico.*

"I have used it before and we can use it now to brush up."

"O.K., teacher."

"This one is more advanced. It is used in our universities. A kind of rhetoric, no?"

"Uh-huh, fine. And what is this?"

She held out the mimeographed sheaf for his inspection. "From this you can see what I must prepare for. Out of these *tópicos* I will have to pick two by chance. Two little balls we choose, with numbers that correspond with the numbers here."

He flipped through the seven sheets of topics, which began with philology and ended with twentieth-century English and American literature. It was a very thorough listing of materials, even more comprehensive than most American doctoral exams.

"Well," he said, shaking his head, "they sure expect a lot for the equivalent of a master's degree."

"I don't think it is the same. Our five years at the *universidad* is like the master. The *oposiciones* is more."

"How many persons take it at one time?"

"About four hundred each year."

"For how many positions?"

"About fifty."

"Wow."

"It is not easy."

"We will have to work hard."

She smiled, her teeth showing very white against her coppery skin. "O.K., teacher," she said.

They set a schedule for their meetings: he was to come at eleven three days a week. They would devote the first hour to his work in Spanish, the second to her *oposiciones*. He promised to bring his copy of Baugh's *Literary History of England* on Wednesday, and a double-volume anthology of American literature with head notes and special essays. Her assignments would come from these.

"Good," she smiled. "We progress."

He looked at her closely, feeling real pleasure in her presence. "I really hope so," he said.

"Then let me give you one more *copa* before lunch."

As she poured the Calisay he sat back in one corner of the divan, relaxed.

A puff of air billowed the curtain at the still open window. The arrow of sunlight had shifted and now pierced the glass of the lowest shelf in the memento case, illuminating the wax flowers.

He felt calm, content. This is not like you, he thought.

"Here you are," she said, handing him the delicate glass.

"Yes," he said, "here I am."

PART
THREE

12
Fried Monkey

The next weekend it rained throughout the province. Twice. To the outsider's eye the rain was a double miracle. Usually the countryside around Zaragoza looked as though it had never known such benefits, but now the parched wheat came alive, and some late poppies stuck up their drooping red heads. The Río Ebro rose almost a foot between its low banks, neither more nor less muddy than before, moving with the vigor of a man who has gained strength in his sick bed and is determined to go on.

On Sunday afternoon Curt wrote letters to Mary Masters and Eddy Stone, and as he did so he realized that certain things were beginning to fall into place. After a full week of teaching at the university, he felt the stabilizing pull of people and places; he was involved in a new pattern of existence, measuring time mainly by his classes at the university, his tutorials at Victoria's, and his nocturnal visits to Lois at the base.

Twice that week he had had brunch with Tupper and Collins at a café near the campus called El Mirasol, where they discussed the English program and what could be expected of the students. Only once did he meet Francisco Villalta—for coffee at the Vegas. On the surface, at least, their meeting was friendly enough; the Spaniard continued to exert that kind of charm necessary for either a good friend or a lover—the ability to make someone feel he was the only other important person in the world. He apologized for not being able to spend

147

more time with Curt, having promised to make some short excursions around the province, but at present he was up to his ears in "a certain matter."

Almost without doubt, Curt figured, it was the same matter that had Major Stafford all tied up—the three black-marketeers who were killed on their run to Andorra. That was all people were talking about at the base. The junked car had been added to an exhibit of such object lessons on a grassy plot behind the motor pool, where a small billboard warned: DRIVE CAREFULLY—OR!

The story of the accident had run as straight news in the regional *Stars and Stripes,* without mention of any black-market activity. Not a word had appeared in the Spanish press, and Curt marveled at the tight grip military liaison and civilian censorship had on each other. He tried comparing the present incident with that of Teddy Swiatski's, assuming that there was some kind of racket involved in both. But so far as publicity was concerned no real comparison could be made, since Spanish newspapers had reported on that death within twenty-four hours, even if there had been some confusion. The question was: Would they have done so if it hadn't been for the involvement of a Spanish citizen, that is, Cipriano Farlo?

He had to admit that he was making no progress in that direction at all. His latest notes in the Swiatski folder proved that things were not falling into place:

Tues. night, 13 Oct. Back to Cancela to find girl from MM's apt. She's gone too! Talked Pepe for half-hour—nothing but pederastic hints and same story as V's: Maite just disappeared. Not on usual entertainment routes. Neither is Pepe.

Wed. 14. Back to Farlo's printery. Same business—deserted. Used directory at *Heraldo de Aragón.* Found four Farlo addresses, traced three families that name. Know nothing, not related my Farlo. Checked fourth address. Widower name of Farlo *did* live there. Left two months ago, according to neighbors. Old crone says to Jaca, husband says Huesca. Everygodamnbody leaving town!

That about summed it up. Farlo was gone, María Maite was gone, her big-breasted girl friend was gone, and Farlo's relative —if relative—was gone. Villalta certainly was still around, but he seemed like the friendly bastard who might be stacking the deck.

Curt felt that somewhere along the line he had to get a break. For a while he thought of Teddy's anonymous friend, the one who had written the "something stinks in Denmark" letter, but chances of finding him looked slim. There was a much better chance of using this present accident case as a lever against the past. And to do that he had to get to Major Stafford.

He had already told Lois Harte that he was very much interested in seeing Stafford, saying that the way in which the Spanish and American authorities worked together on something like this accident would be good material for the *Phaeton* article. She agreed Stafford was the man to see. As mortuary officer, he was the only one who would, along with the base commander and Tom Pardee, have the inside stuff. The other two were out: the base commander was dense and militarily stiff about such matters; and of course Pardee didn't like civilians in general and Curt in particular. But Stafford, she thought, might very well prove co-operative: he was an off-the-cuff sort of guy, an ex-pilot who was not overawed by regulations. So she had agreed to make an appointment with him as soon as possible. Since Curt was supposed to see him about the lectureship anyway, ostensibly the appointment could be for that; she would mention the article in passing, and Curt could then take it from there.

Monday evening he drove out to see Lois, posting his Penn-wood letters on the way. It was still raining, and the Paseo de Calvo Sotelo sparkled under the early lights, with here and there puddles of water shimmering in between the streetcar tracks.

Lois was waiting. She had prepared some chicken salad sandwiches, and they ate them with some beer at the kitchen table. There was no word about Stafford yet.

Afterward they went to bed and took it nice and easy, an old married couple. After they had dozed and wakened and made love again, Lois began talking in a low voice. She wanted him to know about the boy she was seeing, she said; she thought it only fair he know. Curt said it didn't matter; he had suspected she had more than one thing going for her.

But she was in a confessional mood and just had to tell about Joe, her Joe, product of an Italian ghetto somewhere in deepest New Jersey. She wanted to educate Joe. She was helping him decorate an apartment in town, teaching him about the beautiful things in life. He was so young, she said, so capable: "Jesus, Curt, he nearly drives me out of my mind, on the hour by the hour."

"Give him my congratulations," Curt said, but she ignored him.

She wanted to be honest about it all, she said. She wanted him, Curt, also, but in a different way. He was mature and worthwhile.

It seemed that together he and Joe supplied something her husband had not. She said it was understanding and a sense of really being needed. Calvin Harte was an all-American boy, a VMI graduate who had become a hot-shot pilot, absolutely sure of himself on the ground and in the air. After a year of marriage, she had gone through a round of psychoanalysis and had come to realize she had married a younger version of her father—a by-the-numbers colonel of marines, now retired somewhere in Virginia.

Curt smoked a cigarette and let her talk. She lay on one side like an odalisque, head propped up on one hand, her right breast plumb-bobbing across her rib cage in a concave slump. She expanded on her own Sunday-supplement analysis, and as he listened he realized she was still in the same bind. She had acknowledged Joe the way a sexy little aunt would admit to a bed-partner nephew. She was using both of them to round out her desires. What she wanted was a father-son-husband-lover all rolled up in one. Like Mary Masters and other women he had known, she was a kind of female Sisyphus who kept trying to push her lust into the region of her heart, while it kept slipping down.

"So that's why Calvin and I broke up," she said. "And I hope you understand about Joe." Her innocent blue eyes searched his face for an answer.

"Well," he said, flicking her lightly, "do you think there's enough there for both of us?"

The muscles in her face twitched. He couldn't tell whether she was going to laugh or cry. Finally she smiled a tight little smile and said, "You know damn well there is. Just don't shoot your mouth off about it." Her face went serious. "He needs so much to think someone *really* cares."

What the hell, Curt thought, unless this Joe was a dummy he must have known she'd been spreading it around. Of course, the story might be she had stopped for *his* sake. Whether he believed it didn't matter. What mattered was that she at least *wanted* to care.

"Don't worry," Curt assured her, thinking that as long as she felt like that there'd be no spilled bottle of pills and the long, long sleep.

She scrunched over and pressed her pink-white warmth against him. Her face loomed large and went out of focus as she kissed him open-mouthed.

"You're quite a man," she said, as she let her blond head fall to a nesting place on his arm.

"Not right now I'm not."

She smiled faintly, letting her eyes close. The bluish lids locked her inside some kind of contentment. Her face looked unprotected, like that of a corpse. He despaired of ever knowing anyone, vulnerable or invulnerable.

Tuesday he found a message waiting for him at the university. Lois had arranged the appointment with Stafford. It was for the next day at three-thirty.

Curt reached the main gate of the base at three-fifteen. The American guard on duty recognized him and, after phoning headquarters, allowed him to drive in on his own. Progress, Curt thought, we're making progress. He drove carefully at the regulation fifteen miles an hour—past the earth-humped bomb shelters, the nine-hole oasis of a golf course, past the housing area, the club, past the gym and hospital, into the headquarters parking area. From where he parked he could see the operations tower about a half-mile away, and then beyond that the airfield, bordered on the other side by a low huddle of buildings, which belonged to the Spaniards.

Inside headquarters, impeccably uniformed men walked about with the quick steps of office efficiency, folders and papers in hand. They were as neat and crisp as female secretaries back home; and it occurred to Curt that all the headquarters personnel he'd ever known were like that: something like male nurses. The guard in the entry was representative of a different order. He broke his wooden pose long enough to direct Curt to Stafford's office, down the corridor to the right, the fifth or sixth office.

It was really two offices in one. Out front sat a crew-cut young sergeant hunched over a typewriter. There was hardly enough room in the cubicle to accommodate him and his desk, a file cabinet, and a single chair for visitors. Behind him was the closed door of an inner office, with a placard stenciled MAJ. A. L. STAFFORD.

The airman looked up from his typing. "Yes, sir?"

"I'm here to see the major. Dr. Fielding."

"Just a moment, sir."

Curt gazed around the cubicle. On opposing walls hung color photos of bombers, whose designations he didn't know. Atop the file case a potted philodendron flourished with shiny green leaves. Everything else was institutional grayness.

In a moment the airman reappeared. "You can go right in, sir."

It was much roomier and airier inside. Three windows faced away from the afternoon sun and presented a partial view of the tower and some hangars. The major was standing at one side of his large metal desk, a welcoming smile on his face. Behind him on the wall were black-framed photos of fliers and their planes: a composite of smiling faces, scarves, fur-trimmed jackets, and insignia that ran the gamut from Indian heads and giant dice to champagne glasses and Grable-like nudes.

As he and Stafford stood there shaking hands, Curt thought he could make out a younger version of Stafford in most of the photos. Nodding toward them, he said, "The good old days?"

"Hell yes," Stafford said. "And no." He indicated the chair beside his desk for Curt to sit in. "Were you in the service, Doctor?"

"Worse than that," Curt smiled. "Infantry."

"Oh!" The major had obviously expected something else. "Where?"

"Italy. The big war. Thirty-eighth Division."

"Good outfit."

"You know it?"

"Sure. I was in Italy myself, Foggia."

"I never made it to the Adriatic side."

"What I'm curious about is, did *you* think those were the good old days?"

"I see what you mean." Curt smiled like a man caught in his own trap. "But I thought the Air Force had more fun."

"Yup, they did. But when they died they stayed dead, too."

Stafford was still standing beside his desk, one hand resting on a small box, which he now picked up and handed toward Curt. "Have a Schimmelpennig," he said, "they're nice and mild."

"Thanks," Curt said. He took one of the small cigars, about as long and thick as his index finger. Stafford held a wing-encrusted lighter ablaze until he got a light, then he lit one of the Schimmelpennigs for himself and sat down in the swivel chair.

This time Curt had a better chance to look him over than he had at the club. Stafford was short, chunky. His nose had obviously been broken and some of the cartilage had probably been removed. Around his eyes were two white circles where glasses had protected him from the sun. The rest of the face was a reddish-tan, showing the effects of weathering or drinking, or both, but there was nothing swollen or mottled about it; it was not the face of a sot. The muscle tone seemed good, the eyes clear and intelligent.

"I guess I owe you an apology," Curt said. "I thought all of you old flyboys were romantics at heart."

"There was a time, Doctor, when I thought handling a P-51 and a good pair of knockers was all the happiness a man could get. But I've lived long enough to realize the error of my ways. Here I am at forty-four ready to retire from the only life I've really known, and I don't know what I'm going to do."

"How about commercial flying?"

"I've been off flying status for five years now. And for good reasons. Physical. I won't bore you with the details, but I was lucky not to have to resign my commission also. Nope, you're in a much better spot than I am. In your job you're supposed to get better as you get older."

"Only to sixty-five, then they bounce us, too."

"Well, I still think you picked a better line of work. I once considered being a teacher myself, back in college."

"Why not now?"

"The thought of going back as a forty-five-year-old sophomore doesn't exactly thrill me."

"It's done every day, believe me." Curt wanted to switch the subject and he suspected Stafford did too by now. People sometimes turned resentful after small confessions, and he didn't want that happening after what looked like a favorable start.

"Isn't that why you have these college courses on base?" Curt said. "So that people can catch up?"

"That *is* what you came to discuss, isn't it?"

For the next fifteen minutes they talked about the lectureship. Stafford outlined salary, side benefits, and hours. He explained what Lois had already gone over—the minimum security check, and academic confirmation from Heidelberg, which was the center for all such matters. Curt said he understood all this, and had already written Madrid for permission to take the lectureship.

"Now," Stafford said, snuffing the stub of his cigar out in an ashtray that sported winged holders, "Mrs. Harte mentioned something about an article you're writing for a magazine."

It was a good sign, Curt thought, that Stafford himself mentioned the article. It smacked of co-operativeness. But the "Mrs. Harte" sounded phony, and he wondered whether Stafford had ever gotten to little Lois, or whether this sudden formality indicated the major was going to be on his most official behavior.

"Yes," he said, "I've been commissioned to write a piece for *Phaeton*." The name of the magazine and the word *commissioned* seemed to have a good effect. Briefly Curt outlined the kind of article he intended to write.

"And you think that I can help?"

"On anything that's not classified. I know you have to be careful. I used to work for *Stars and Stripes* after I got out of combat; so I know something about public relations. But it's not military information *as such* that I'm after. What I'm interested in is our relationship with the Spanish, both from a military and civilian point of view. For example, Chrysler Corporation has been dickering with Franco to put in one of their assembly plants, the way Fiat and Renault have; and as soon as I can, I'm going to try to talk with someone from Chrysler. For the military, I've come to you."

"But why me? Why not the base commander—or someone like Tom Pardee?"

"Several reasons. One, I think Pardee sorta hates my guts. Two, base commanders are notoriously sticky. And quite frankly, one of your duty areas interests me."

Stafford said nothing, just raised an eyebrow.

"As I understand it, you're the officer who takes charge of the mortal remains of—"

"You mean I'm the mortuary officer."

Curt nodded.

Stafford leaned his head back and smiled toward the ceiling. "Yes, sir, that's me—Digger O'Dell, the happy undertaker." Then he came forward, no longer smiling. "And I suppose all you want out of me is the story of what's happening in our present little situation."

Curt knew that even the wrong intonation here would get him politely kicked out on his can. "No," he said, raising his right hand in a gesture of halting something. "I know better than that."

"Because it's absolutely off limits, strictly *verboten.*"

"I realize that. But what I'm interested in is the way you work with the Spanish authorities on such cases generally, not this one specifically. I'd be lying if I said it wasn't this latest case that caught my interest, but what I'm asking is if there aren't some *past* incidents that are discussable."

Like the Swiatski case, throbbed in his mind, and he was conscious of trying to hide the thought.

Stafford stared at him a long time. It was a watershed moment and Curt decided not to push any further. Stafford would either co-operate now or weasel out with some kind of official-sounding excuse.

"I can't see any harm in that kind of information," he said. "It is unclassified and you could find most of it in news reports if you wanted to. But there are some things I'd have to insist on if I'm going to talk to you."

"O.K."

"First of all, I will not name names. Secondly, I don't want to be mentioned or quoted. I'd want to see what you wrote; and if you try to nail me down in print, I'll deny everything and let you bury yourself."

"I'm in perfect agreement. But"—he paused—"that's a hell of a line coming from a mortuary officer."

Stafford laughed pleasantly, his flat nose pulling to one side. There was something perfectly American about him; he was exactly the kind of man Villalta would never understand, and Curt felt some regret in tricking him.

"By the way, how does someone get to be mortuary officer?" he asked.

"You mean, how the *hell* does someone get to be mortuary officer," Stafford said. "It's easy. Used to be a job that got shoved off onto junior officers or foul-ups, but this didn't work out too well, as you might suspect. So they made it a regulation that the matériel officer of any given command is automatically mortuary officer."

"So you're matériel, mortuary, *and* education officer?"

"Some parlay, huh? It's all because we're phased down so much. Even the old man has to wear two or three hats."

"Sounds like a book I know."

"What's that?"

"*Catch-22.* It's about the Air Force."

"I've read it. Zany but true."

Curt thought it was about time he tried to make his own story sound true. He consoled himself with the idea that lying and fiction were often means to eventual truth. "Listen," he said, "when we were talking about your present case—this was the other night, Lois and some of her friends at the club—they mentioned a case you had some months back that involved mistaken identity."

"Uh-huh."

"From the way they talked about it, it seemed to have almost fictional qualities."

"I suppose it did." Stafford was not taking the bait, and Curt decided again not to push hard.

"Well," he said, "suppose we start with jurisdiction. Who investigates what? And how do you work with the Spanish authorities?"

"Unless the accident takes place on base, we always work with them. As far as American jurisdiction's concerned, we divide the country into three tiers—northern, middle, southern. Torrejón in Madrid has the big middle section; Morón de la Frontera has the southern. In the north I cover all the way from Irún on the west to Barcelona on the east. I don't go any farther south than Calatayud and Teruel."

"Still quite a territory."

"It is, and I've got to be ready any hour of the day or night. That—as I guess you know—is what happened at the club the other night."

Curt nodded and said: "How do you work it, exactly? Do you travel with the Spanish? Is there a medical officer with you?"

"No—on both counts."

"Well, how does it go?"

"Maybe the best thing would be to pretend something happened right now—I mean the off-base death of any American military person or persons—and I hope nothing does." Stafford knocked on his desk for luck. "The Spanish authorities would call the base and be put through to Señor Alfara, our official interpreter. He's in the office next door and he lives on base. He'd notify me, and I'd hop in my car and get over to the motor pool. We have a Spanish civilian over there named Luis who's really something—hell on wheels with an ambulance and knows every road in Spain. He does all my driving and lots of my interpreting, since I know the language only *poco*. Luis and I would take off in the ambulance for wherever the place might be, but not until I put through a call to the Air Police. In theory, at least, they're supposed to do most of the investigating for our side; I'm supposed to take care of the bodily details. But I'm usually the officer in charge, so the responsibility falls on me. They have a Sergeant Alvarez, who's of Mexican parentage and speaks the language perfectly. When he and whoever's been assigned with him get on the scene we work together."

"Who do you usually find from the Spanish side?"

"Depends. If it's close to a city, all kinds of city detectives. If it's out on the *carretera* chances are it'll be the Civil Guard."

"The co-operation good?"

"Pretty good most of the time, yes. Just six months back we had an American soldier shot by a Spanish soldier. Then it was just us and the Spanish military and no trouble at all. Everything worked very smoothly. With the civilian police, sometimes it's tougher. You know how the Spanish can be. You can't tell them very much. You can talk to them, but they'll act when they're ready and the way they want to. Can't be pushed."

Curt nodded in agreement. "What about the medical situation?"

"The Spanish handle that. We don't have anything to do with it. They're pretty sticky about examinations, because by Spanish law any accidental death must be subject to an autopsy. Here in Zaragoza a member of the medical faculty acts as coroner. We can witness if we want to."

"Say an American airman dies on the highway, obvious victim of a crash. Do they forget about the autopsy in such an instance?" He wanted to be sure about this point.

"Negative." Stafford shook his head sideways to emphasize his answer. *"Neg-a-tivo.* Their attitude is that there's something suspicious about any death that doesn't take place in bed under a doctor's care. Must be something left over from the good old days of *mucho* poisonings. Anyway, we've never gotten back a body that didn't have an autopsy done to it."

"So this would be true with your 'burnt-out case'? The one with the Polish name." Curt was surprised at how calm he could make his voice sound. He kept his eyes on the major's ribbons: there were some good ones—a Silver Star and a Purple Heart. . . .

"Absolutely," Stafford said. "Especially with what was happening."

"I understand you had quite a little mystery going."

"You said it."

"Are you free to talk about it? Without names, I mean." Curt hoped his smile was reassuringly innocent.

"Sure. It was in all the papers, and it's not classified." Stafford paused, blowing a memory cloud of smoke. "There were a few things that were off the record. Nothing important, but I don't want to talk about those. They might seem a little libelous."

Uh-huh! Curt thought. "I understand," he said.

"Fact is, I'm not sure the relatives of—ah—airman X realized all the trouble that case gave us. We saw no reason to bother them."

Jesus, that's close, Curt thought, and for a moment wondered whether the man facing him was somehow playing cat and mouse with him. But how could that be? Couldn't. He was imagining things: his own duplicity made it hard for him to believe a man could be as open and obliging as Stafford was. Even so, the nagging thought remained. This was too easy. . . .

"I'd like to hear the story." *That* was the truth.

"It's a beaut," Stafford said, taking a long draw on his Schimmelpennig.

Curt said nothing. From what he had gathered about Stafford, he thought he'd be better off telling the story as he wanted. He seemed a man who liked to talk.

"Well," Stafford began, pausing, loosening the top button on his jacket, straightening his legs out full length in front of him. "It all began when this young airman we're talking about got a three-day pass to Barcelona. First thing he did was go into town and pick up a friend of his, a Spaniard about the same age. Somewhere near Lérida they stopped to have a drink and picked up a hitchhiker. Our airman had his own car, a fifty-nine Chevy convertible, plenty of room.

"Anyway, when they got to Barcelona the two friends rented two rooms in the *barrio gótico:* that's the old section of the city, and I don't know if you know about it, but it's quite a place. Just loaded with dives and babes. You name it, they've got it. You can get anything there but religion.

"From what we gathered then, X and his buddy had themselves a time. Usual fun and games, shacking up, getting loaded. Now the last time they were together, the Spaniard went out like a light—very unusual for a Spaniard. Our airman took almost all the money he had on him, plus his wallet and identity card, leaving just enough for the girl to be paid off. In other words, he didn't want him to get rolled, and I guess he was too busy with another babe to stick with the friend. Exit airman X.

"Enter the hitchhiker. All of this, by the way, we pieced together later. Seems he had brought them to the *barrio* and had been acting as a kind of guide—you know, lined them up with babes. His own expenses were paid; he got a couple of cartons of cigarettes. An exchange of goods and services. The hitchhiker turned out to be a seminary student who had given up the idea of the priesthood, although his parents and teachers didn't know about it. This is why he gave his new friends a fictional name, and why it took him some time to come forward with his information. And it's a damn good thing he did."

"Why?"

"His was the only information we could build on."

"There was the other friend."

"There was but there wasn't."

"Whatta you mean?"

"He never showed up. Skedaddled. That was one of the reasons for the mystery, the mix-up."

"You mean the airman's friend—the one from Zaragoza—has never been questioned about this matter?" Curt tried to keep his incredulity within bounds.

"That's right. And he probably had good reason for staying away, as we found out later, but that's one of the things I'm not free to go into."

"And no one knows where he is?"

"Theory is he may have slipped over the border into France."

Curt stifled several questions, forced himself to calm down, and said, "So what happened?"

"On the eighth of April this year, approximately 0300 hours, X's Chevy failed to negotiate a particularly bad turn between Lérida and here. This was the coroner's estimated time. The car wasn't discovered until about 0800 by two motorcycle Guards. They always travel in pairs, do a damn good job, too. This pair saw that a section of guard fence had been bent flat, and when they investigated they could see the burned hulk of a vehicle about a hundred yards down in a gully on the rocks below. When they climbed down they found a burnt-out mess. The body was trapped inside and burnt to a crisp. From the license plates they could tell immediately that it was a serviceman's car. You've probably noticed we get our plates issued in Madrid, and all vehicles owned by American military personnel have an M as the first letter and a zero as the third marking. So, as I said, they could spot that immediately, even though the plates were scorched.

"What bothered them was what they found in the glove compartment. That had stayed closed and the stuff in there wasn't burned. There were the usual things, plus some extras— an Esso map of Spain, a Michelin of Western Europe, a pen, a pair of glasses melted from the heat, a flashlight, *and* the wallet and papers of X's Spanish friend.

"So the question was, whose body was in the car? As I said, it was burnt to a crisp." Stafford grimaced in recollection.

"Pretty gruesome."

"You said it. Have you ever seen a burnt corpse?"

"No," Curt responded, thinking back to Stanley Swiatski in his office.

"Well, I've seen three now. One during the war, plane crash victim. And two here in Spain. The peculiar thing is how they go into a kind of boxer's crouch." Stafford pulled his hands in close to his chest, clenched, hunching his shoulders and back, with his chin tucked into the resulting hollow near his breast bone.

"It's also the womb position."

Stafford stared dumbly ahead a moment, then relaxed from the crouch, nodding his head in agreement. "Yes, by God, that, too. But no matter how you look at it, it's not very pretty. The face looks like a monkey's, crinkled all over, the mouth grinning—"

"You saw the body while it was still in the car?"

"Yes. The Guards didn't want to disturb things; they radioed in for a Zaragoza *forense*—a coroner. Each judge has one on his staff, and whatever judge is on duty, as it were, sends out his *forense*. A city detective accompanied this one. They called us and waited for us and then made a pretty good examination on the spot. The papers on the corpse, whatever they might have been—money or whatever—were completely burnt along with the wallet. Most G.I.'s carry their wallets in their hip pocket. This was the kind most Europeans carry, up in the inside pocket of the jacket. No help at all."

"And no other identification?"

"One thing."

"What was that?"

"A wristwatch. Bulova. And the damned thing was *still* running!"

"Keeping *time?*"

"Affirmative."

"How could that be?"

"Well, in the crash that wrist and arm were broken; the wrist was tucked somehow under the body and I guess the watch was protected from the flames and heat."

"Didn't you take the watch as evidence that the body was American, then?"

"Yes and no. Anybody can wear anybody else's watch. Something else was needed. The shoes were no good—too burnt. You can usually tell a lot from the shoes, although, again, there's nothing says a Spaniard can't be wearing American shoes from the base. There wasn't even a belt buckle or anything of the sort. The corpse had on the kind of slacks you don't need a belt with. So we had a real problem: was this the American who had taken his Spanish friend's money and identification papers in the wallet? Or was it X's Spanish friend?"

Stafford let his questions hang in the air for a few moments. He was enjoying his own story, setting out a course for hares and hounds. Curt waited to see where the next track was placed.

"It got even more complicated. In the wallet that had been in the glove compartment they found an address scribbled on a piece of paper, and it turned out to be the *pensión* that the two had been staying at in Barcelona. The next day we got information through the police there, who checked out the address. The *portero* remembered our two friends *and* the hitchhiker. And for a couple of days, until he came forth, we thought it might even be him in the car."

"How about bone measurement? Isn't there some way of measuring the bones and getting at least the size of a man?"

"Sure, but we knew that X and his friend were about the same size."

"How about teeth?"

"Right. Teeth are almost as good as fingerprints—especially in the service, because each serviceman has a consolidated medical record. So we got hold of X's and took it to the *forense* at the university—this was the day after the body was found. I read the stuff off the chart and the *forense* felt around inside the mouth. And things didn't tally! I couldn't understand it and I said so to Sergeant Alvarez. When he translated my doubts, the *forense* turned Spanish. He had made his examination and by God that was it! After all, he was a trained medical representative of the court and above questioning. And I think it was he who gave the story to a couple of reporters to the effect that a Spanish citizen had been killed in an accident driving a borrowed American car. It was stupid, and he's no longer doing any forensing."

"Obviously something was wrong."

"There sure as hell was. I told Alvarez that since an American citizen might be involved in all this, I was demanding that we have one of our own medical experts examine the body. The *señor* doctor nearly threw a fit, but our lawyer talked to him and, eventually, the judge, and they decided to keep the body on ice for another day. Which gave us time to fly up a man from Madrid."

Curt wondered whether "our lawyer" wasn't Villalta— probably was. But he decided against asking. Instead he said, "And this man succeeded in making a positive identification?"

"Yes, and it was just a simple-ass thing."

"What?"

"Well, we had quite an audience. Even the judge came along with his *forense*, who was all dressed up in his fullest dignity. Alvarez and our lawyer and I were there with our doctor. Before he did anything else, Foley, our man, took a wicked-looking instrument out of his bag—looked like a set of small ice tongs. It's used to rupture the jaw. I didn't exactly watch when he used it, but I could hear the bones go. Then I looked, and he just reached in and, after fingering around for a second, took out some metal with porcelain nubs. And you probably guessed it: it was a partial plate that X wore; it was marked on the records, but in a note down in one corner. On the *diagram* it showed missing teeth. I guess the Spanish doctor had been feeling the false teeth and thinking they were real. I don't know. But anyway this partial was identified as being absolutely American, because of some alloy used and the way it was made. Too technical for me. But that was that. We got the body and shipped it home. The newspapers printed retraction stories."

Stafford held out his hands to indicate the game was over. He was struck by an afterthought. "There are two things I'll never forget about that day: the sound of that jaw snapping, and the look on the *forense's* face. He just looked stupid, as though he had somehow been tricked and didn't know how."

Curt couldn't help feeling the same way. If you believed the evidence that Stafford brought forth, the body in St. Mary's cemetery belonged with the other Swiatskis. And there were so many officials involved, so many witnesses from both sides, that the evidence couldn't be questioned. On the other hand, there was "our lawyer" Villalta and his mysterious control over the situation. There was María Maite and the anonymous friend. And more than anything there was the fact that Farlo had never showed up.

Stafford awaited reaction to the story. Curt shook his head, saying, "That's more than I'd expected. It may amount to only a paragraph in my article, but it's worth something by itself."

"It's the wackiest one I've ever been on."

"I owe you a drink for letting me in on it."

"As I said, you could have got most of it from the papers."

"No, I don't think so." He *knew* that wasn't so, because he had done his homework on the papers.

Stafford shrugged as though to say "O.K., you're welcome to it."

Curt got to his feet and shoved out his right hand. "Thanks," he said. There were two more questions already nagging him. Was the accident really an accident? Where had it actually occurred?

"There's one other thing," he said.

"What's that?" Stafford said.

"Can you tell me exactly where the accident took place?"

Stafford's eyes shifted with suspicion; he tightened his tie into place once again. Curt was sure he was going to ask him why the *hell* he wanted to know. But he didn't.

"About eighty kilometers this side of Lérida," he said. And then: "That was peculiar, too."

"How so?"

"Because it happened right near a spot that they call a *punto negro*. A marker on the side of the road showing where a fatal accident has occurred. Now there are two of them."

13
Punto Negro

Thursday night he sat at the small, high desk in the study of his apartment. He had pushed to one side a half-finished plate of *tortilla*—cold but good—prepared by the old woman, Isabella, whom Victoria had helped him obtain as a maid. From time to time he picked at the potato-and-egg concoction and took a gulp of the wine which he had poured into a water tumbler. But he was hardly conscious of eating, drinking, or smoking. With a ball-point pen he scribbled agitatedly on a pad of yellow lined paper, and by the time he was finished there were ten pages of nearly illegible writing, and five cigarette butts heaped in the ashtray.

He went out to the kitchen and returned with the bottle of *tinto*, pouring himself another healthy portion. Then, settling himself in the armchair alongside the desk, kicking off his shoes and propping his feet up on a straight chair, he lit another cigarette and read what he had written:

Thurs. Oct. 22. Christ, at last a break! How can you figure? Everything's coincidence. Anything that happens to you—marvelous coincidence. Just take a look around you'll see. Birth—coincidence; death the same. Absolutely. Used to think less of Dickens and Balzac because of their coincidences. Never again. Should be a law of literary criticism: author must handle raw coincidence, blind, unmotivated happenings.

About T. S. (never noticed those initials) and the accident at *punto negro*. That phrase kept bothering me from the time Stafford

168

mentioned it. (Swiatski, Stafford—need more proof?) Kept pumping through my head: *punto negro punto negro punto negro negro punto negro punto* . . .

Had to find the spot. Reassuring to see place where he was killed. Snoop around a little. Somehow convince myself it *was* an accident.

So: this morning back to *Heraldo de Aragón.* Got issues of April 9, 10, 11. Apr. 9 account like that in the *Verdad*: short, not detailed, announced death of Cipriano Farlo. Apr. 10 nothing. Apr. 11 full story: says mistake about Farlo (he's just missing); says Airman Theodore Swiatski killed—*near Bujaraloz junction of Nacional II!*

To the road again. Again on N. II—this time in easterly direction toward Lérida and Barcelona. On map Bujaraloz shows up approx. 70 kms. away from Z. Lérida about 140.

All you got to do is hit the road, keep traveling, things'll happen to you. Boy, will they happen. Still can't get over it.

Left Z about noon in trusty VW. Picked up bottle of Careñina, loaf of bread, and hunk of Manchego. Make it a little outing. Like the idea of having provisions on road in Spain. Feel flexible. Nothing against drinking while driving in this country. No speed limit. No shopping centers. No package book clubs. Primitive.

Jesus, I'm wound up!

So what *happened?*

Crossed over Puente de Piedra. Ebro looked like lima-bean soup. Traveled first 10 kms. over stone, then brick, then stone road. VW did Teutonic cha-cha. Then N. II settled down to plain broken-up, bumpy tar road, narrowing in few outlying towns to lane and a half— and God bless car meets truck in some spots between houses on narrow streetway!

Finally, out in clear. Big reddish-gray bluffs off to the left, Ebro valley with Lombardy poplars to right. Then lost sight of river, climbing up some four-five hundred feet onto high tableland. All clear. . . .

Reached first turn to Bujaraloz in little over hour. No *punto negro.* But map shows second road angling in a couple of kms. further west.

Jack pot. *Punto negro. Punto negro.* No more than fifty feet apart. New sign fresher. Wire fence newly repaired. Red-and-white striped posts sharp in color.

Pulled VW off road onto little lane about fifty yards away. Walked back. *Punto negro* sign like target: white outline circle, big black bull's-eye. Underneath, an oblong plate with words announcing this is a "black point," where someone's been killed.

Easy to see how it could happen. Blind section of S-turn. Below— about two hundred feet sheer drop—gully. Rocks at bottom with sluggish creek, or ditch. Path going down, of sorts, leading down through chalky-looking outcroppings of rock turning to sand. Thick clumps of gorse scattered around.

Went back car, got wine and stuff. Net bag over shoulder, started down slope. Slide, stumble, slide, keep feet moving. Old culm bank training. Can't fall if you keep going.

Stopped near bottom where slope gentled. Looked back up, could see two gashes where car must have bounced and cut in. At very bottom scrub growth near creek had been scorched out. When I got there, on *the* spot, could see outlines of activity muddied over by recent rains. Off to the right was draggy trail of where tow truck must have come in and pulled out remains of the Chevy. Also some tracks of jeep or Land Rover kind—probably way they took body out.

Saw bits of brownish dirty glass scattered around. Also charred bits of what might have been seat material, innards. That's all. Not very much. Detectives always finding clues. What would Sherlock Perry Lupin do?

Upstream saw clump of small beech trees. Underarms all sweaty. Fast clouds moving aside let sun hit me. Feel tired but alive. Someone died right here. I'm alive. Air clean. Suck it in. Sit on flattish rock under saplings throwing strips of shadow.

No clues, but the Careñina tastes good, grapey. Manchego cheese sharp, cuts tongue alive. Bread softens and absorbs. Bread and wine, Jesus and Silone.

Cigarette and more wine, thinking again: is this where Teddy Swiatski became fried monkey? Hands clenched against chest. Was it really him? If so, where's Farlo? Where are snows of yesteryear? Yes, and the girls?

Swear I'm hearing a bell. Can see dilapidated town or village about three miles off to the north—stuck up on a gorse and rock bluff. But this is no town bell. Just tinkling, not donging.

Then hear the feet, and smell them. Must have been fifty of them. One black, the others white—or gray, really, dirty gray. Skinny, graceful legs—bodies wrapped in curly gray wool. Man almost black from the sun. Pants stiff and black as cast iron. Gray woolen shirt. In this heat! A blanketlike cape thrown over one shoulder. Black beret. All solid looking under the sun, against the blue scallop of sky behind him.

The sheep spread out along the ditch nuzzling into the muddy waters hardly more than a trickle.

Greeted him. Greeted me back. Offered him some wine. Displayed his own supply in *bota* underneath the cloak. Asked him join me, indicating bread and cheese on the rock.

Point, point, *point*.

Finally induced him join me in repast. Talked. Difficult. His dialect partly Catalan. First American he'd ever talked with, first *extranjero* of any kind. Didn't realize *norteamericanos* spoke Spanish. Always been shepherd. Takes his *rebaño* to territory as far as 100 kms. away, but works for *gran patrón* in Bujaraloz.

The point.

He knew this place had been "disturbed" once again by a "*coche*." There had been a death two years before, now this one.

What did he know? He knew that this time one had been killed—AND ONE HAD BEEN SAVED!

Was he sure? Oh, yes. He'd been grazing his *rebaño* only a few kms. away. Brought flock in close when he saw a vehicle coming down the gully path from the village. Military vehicle. Small. Then he saw them helping a man. He walked. WALKED. They put him in the *coche* and took him away. Later that day more men came, many more. Small *coche* returned and a giant truck. They put something into the small vehicle. Had to be the body. The giant pulled away the wreck.

Asked him please repeat everything. Told it the same. Great dignity. No reason to lie. Told him it had been one of the great privileges of my life to meet him. Asked whether he would please take the rest of the food and wine. Was indebted to him. He had given me hope.

Shook hands. Black with dirt and sun. Probably makes love with his favorite sheep. But an honest man. Trust shepherds to bring good news!

So: just a couple of small questions. One—who the hell walked away from that wreck? Two—who took him out?

Better make it three—how could anyone have come out of completely burnt-out car? Thrown free? I guess.

Four—*how* do I find *him?*

14
Old Farlo

"He could have been stringing you along," Stafford said. "They love to do that to foreigners."

"I don't believe so. Neither would you if you'd been there. This man was just telling what he saw."

"Or *thought* he saw. These shepherds get pretty lonely."

Curt laughed harshly. "The Freudian view of the Bible, sexual compensation instead of divine afflatus. But this shepherd was no prophet, just a solid citizen."

"You might have misunderstood him. You said he spoke a dialect."

"Don't worry, I understood. It's you who're refusing to understand."

Stafford turned his gaze away from Curt, looking toward the other side of the room, where weakening twilight came through the windows. There was no one else in the officers' section of the club at this hour, and in the silence Curt could hear the major sigh in small capitulation.

"All right," Stafford said, "let's assume there *was* somebody else in the car that night, and whoever it was came out of the accident alive. Then who the hell would have taken him away, and where, and why?"

"That's what we have to find out."

Stafford drank some of his bourbon as though it were an antidote for something he couldn't stomach. "Not me!" he said.

"Look, Major," Curt said. "I didn't have to come to you

with any of this. I was taking a chance. You could have been part of whatever the hell's going on. But you seemed straight to me the other day, and I thought it was about time I began trusting someone, someone who might try to do the right thing. I thought you might be able to provide information that would make this shepherd's story believable—something that caused *you* to wonder before."

While he spoke Curt could see the other man soften under the effects of his testy speech and the compliment it offered.

"That case was as much out in the open as you could expect," Stafford said.

"But there was the mix-up about who was killed. The shepherd didn't dream that up. And nobody dreamed up the fact that Farlo has not been seen since the accident."

"So what? Farlo's a Spanish citizen, completely out of our jurisdiction. So what would you expect me to do? We've already ascertained that the body—"

Curt didn't let him finish. "Are you telling me," he said, "that an American airman is killed under peculiar circumstances, that there may be someone who could say what those circumstances were, and that *you* are not interested in that information!"

Stafford's face flushed. "No, goddamn it, I am not saying that."

"Well, what are you saying?"

"For one thing, it's not my job to investigate. It's a job for the Air Police and our legal liaison."

"You mean Pardee and Villalta."

"That's right. Take your goddamn shepherd's story to them."

"I would prefer not to," Curt said in a flat tone, and drained the remainder of his Scotch.

"Why not? I know you and Pardee don't see eye to eye, but I thought you and our counselor were buddies."

"I'd rather not talk about it."

"Ooo-h?" Stafford sustained the syllable in a musical glide.

"And the fact is, I'd rather you said nothing about this to anybody else. I want it to be just between the two of us. Period."

Stafford's eyes were on him, steady and serious. After a moment he said, "I appreciate the fact that you came to me, but if you don't mind my saying so, Doctor, you sure don't behave like a man with just a passing interest in this Swiatski thing."

Curt realized that it was the first time the name had passed between them, and he took it as a good sign.

"I can't shake the feeling," Stafford continued, "that you suckered me in the other day. You're not just interested in writing some article. I have a few questions to ask you, and I sure as hell want the truth."

Curt looked at him. "All right."

"*Are* you working with some agency?"

"No, I am not," Curt said, remembering John Bowers had asked the same question. "I'm a Fulbright lecturer at a Spanish university. That's it. I have no other official ties. You'll certainly see that when you run your clearance check."

"Don't make me laugh. This wouldn't be the first time somebody like the CIA or CID used a legitimate professor."

"Not this time. Not me."

Stafford smiled. "This is stupid. What makes me think that if you were with some agency that you'd tell me?"

Curt smiled back at him. "That's right. And if you were mixed up in any of this, you wouldn't tell me, either."

"Then we're back where we started."

"Not quite. I'm willing to stick by my hunch."

Stafford looked at him squarely, rubbing his nose where it had been broken. "Tell me one thing," he said. "Are you writing an article for *Phaeton?*"

"Yes."

"And if I asked you to show me something to prove that, would you do it? I mean right now, not next week."

"We'd have to drive into town. I'll show you my contract

letter and the notes I've made." Curt understood what Stafford was doing. If the *Phaeton* article was legitimate, then he was, too, in all probability.

Stafford weighed matters for a moment. "O.K.," he said, finally, "that's good enough for now. The only thing I can think is you must have some personal interest going. I guess you wouldn't want to go into that, huh?"

"Let me put it this way, Major. I will not be lying to you if I say my only real concern is to find out the truth of this case. Nothing more, nothing less."

Curt realized his answer established limits of trust and Stafford got the message. "We'll see," Stafford said, establishing his own lines. "And what is it you expect of me?"

"For now, nothing, except maybe moral support. I have some checking of my own to do, and if it works out I'll be back to see you. If in the meantime you hear something or remember something that might help, I'd appreciate knowing about it."

They walked out to the parking lot together, Curt hoping Stafford might add something on his own initiative, but he didn't speak until they reached his Mercedes, parked near the club entrance, and then he simply said, "Keep in touch."

"Of course," Curt said, and headed toward his VW several slots farther down the lot.

There was a stiff breeze coming off the Moncayo, almost cool enough to make it topcoat weather. Back home Pennwood was probably playing Syracuse or Army, with the football season half over. . . .

He rolled the window up before putting the key in the ignition. As Stafford drove by he tooted his horn lightly and Curt threw a loose salute.

The man who answered the door was short, thin, bowed, at least sixty. Although he was almost completely bald, he had long slashing brows that jutted out over watery eyes, a gray mustache that was brown at the droopy tips, and a ragged beard that was perfectly white.

"Señor Farlo?" Curt asked.

"*Sí.*" The voice was as weak as the eyes.

"It would please me to speak with you."

The old man peered down the dingy hall as though expecting more than one person to make such an intrusion.

"*Conmigo?*" he said, unbelievingly.

"*Por favor.*"

He pushed the door open another foot and said, "*Pasa.*"

The place inside was a hovel. The old man indicated a lumpy armchair the Salvation Army would have refused. "Accommodate yourself," he said, waiting until his visitor sat down before seating himself in a chair near the table.

"I have come from Zaragoza to speak with you."

"*Conmigo?*"

"*Sí, señor,*" Curt said. "You are Manuel Farlo, who resided in Zaragoza until this year?"

"*Verdad.*"

"And you have been a resident in Huesca since September?" It sounded as official as the listing in the town hall that Curt had checked. Farlo looked apprehensive; he seemed to get smaller, like a dog before a beating.

"True."

"Why did you come to Huesca?"

"For a position."

"What kind of position?"

"In a bodega. I pour wine."

"I see," Curt said, holding to an official-sounding tone. "And you came to Huesca for such a position?"

"It was arranged for me, *señor.*"

"And do you not care to return to Zaragoza?"

"*Quién es él que pregunta?*" The question was delivered with hope and disbelief. Who is it who asks?

"A friend of the family."

"Cómo?"

"Of Cipriano Farlo, I believe."

"I do not recognize you," old Farlo said in a muffled voice.

"But you are the uncle of Cipriano, *verdad?*"

"Sí."

"Then I offer my help."

"That is what the others said. And here I am." He waved a hand to indicate the apartment. "Help is what others want to give, not what one needs."

"If you will give me some information, I will help you, truly."

"If it is about Cipriano, I do not know where he is. That is what I have told the others. That is what I tell you. I do not know."

"I am also a friend of a North American military, Theodore Swiatski. Did you know him?"

"I know nothing of the North Americans," the old man said, and then added bitterly, "or of their police."

"I am not of the police." Curt pulled out his passport folder and took out his Fulbright identification card.

The old man hesitated, then stuck out a blue-veined hand and took the card. His lips moved as he read. He handed it back, saying nothing.

"You see, I am a professor and nothing more. A man who would help the family Farlo."

"Then go away," the old man said. "Do not molest me."

"Why? What is the trouble?"

"Trouble, trouble, enough trouble. When a man lives his life in his natal city for sixty years, and when he behaves himself and works properly as a man should, and when he becomes a widower who would visit the grave of his wife and say his prayers before the Holy Mother of the Pilar—" The old man's voice broke, his eyes brimmed with tears, his tongue licked the scraggly tip of his mustache.

"Were you asked to leave Zaragoza, Señor Farlo?"

"Asked!" Anger saved him from self-pity. "The Brigada Social does not ask!"

"They forced you to leave?"

"They found me this magnificent position and told me I would be happier in this city, which may be perfectly all right for those of this province, but for a Zaragozano—"

"If you had an opportunity to return to Zaragoza, would you do that?"

Old Farlo looked at him, his eyes glowing like coals in the gloomy room, until despair dulled them once again. "A man must have something to live on. I helped my nephew, but I have only a small pension from the syndicate now that he has gone."

"Suppose I got you a position?"

"They would not permit it."

"Who?"

"They, they."

"I have friends with much *enchufe*," Curt said, thinking of Durán and perhaps Victoria's father. "It might be possible."

The old man sat up straighter. "I do not believe it possible, but if it were, why would you do this for me?"

"No one gives without taking, *verdad?*"

"Clearly."

"I told you I need some information."

The old man shrugged. What information did he have that was worth so much in return?

"Listen, *viejo*, all I want to know is who made you leave Zaragoza and what has happened to Cipriano."

Farlo sat still for some time without answering. Curt took his cigarettes out of his jacket pocket and offered one. Finally, the blue-veined hand reached out and accepted.

The same wind that had pushed the VW along like a shell on the trip to Huesca now pressed against the windshield, whistling through a partly opened air vent, and occasionally buffeting the car so that its inverted cones of light wavered against the darkness ahead. Otherwise the drive back to Zaragoza was easy. Road 123 held to the naturally flat bed of intervening mesa land. Curt drove for long stretches without having to slow for a curve or dim his lights for approaching vehicles.

At least a half-dozen times he went over in his mind what old Farlo had told him until he tied the various strands of conversation into a neat bundle of memory.

What it amounted to was this: The old man had known Theodore Swiatski, had met him on a number of occasions at the printery. The American and Cipriano were good friends and carried on some kind of business together. What kind, the old man didn't know; Cipriano was a good and loving nephew but hadn't confided in him.

The old man had learned about the accident from the police, who asked some questions, and then revealed that Cipriano had been killed. The next day he read the story in the paper. He didn't know what to think or do. His wife had died two years before, now his nephew. He had no children. What was to become of him? The family had been decimated by the war; there was really no one left.

He resigned himself to the inevitable, making plans for the funeral. His nephew deserved a proper burial. He could sell the paper stock in the shop. The two presses would go back to the factory because they hadn't been paid for yet. There were some bills due that might be collected, as well as several jobs remaining to be delivered.

Two days later, while he was waiting for the body to be delivered, a man from the Brigada Social came to see him.

And that man's name?

Señor Villalta.

Check, and double check!

According to Villalta, his nephew had not been killed, after all. It was a North American military that had died in the car. But Cipriano was mixed up in something illegal. Villalta did not think the old man was involved, was he? He was *not*. Good, Villalta said, then what he should do was leave this printery. The man who owned the property would return two months' rent. The police would take care of closing everything out. He could collect the debts and deliver the remaining jobs. That was all.

The old man had asked about his nephew: Where was he? What kind of illegality was he involved in?

According to Villalta, Cipriano had left the country. If the old man heard from him, he was duty bound to inform the authorities.

And then what happened?

Nothing. There was enough money with the pension, for a while. But by September Villalta had returned. He wanted to be helpful, he said. Had Señor Farlo heard anything from his nephew? He had not. Was he sure? Absolutely.

Villalta said that he had a position for him, and that it would be good for the old man to leave Zaragoza. The position was in Huesca. There would be transportation, Villalta would see to it. Was the old man positive that it was September that Villalta had returned? He was.

And *had* the old man heard anything at all from his nephew? Curt asked. No, he had not. Was he sure? Positive.

It was of greatest importance that he remember and speak out, Curt said. Whatever he remembered could be of great help to them all. . . .

By now Curt had reached the northern outskirts of Zaragoza. To his right ran a long stone wall behind which stood the grounds of the officers' academy, where once Francisco Franco Bahamonde had been commandant. Off to the left the streetcar line ran parallel to the road. Ahead in the glare and shadow of the street lamps, Curt thought he could make out Farlo's face, quivering as it had when the old man finally decided to speak out.

Farlo hoped to God that he was dealing with a man of honor.

He wanted no trouble with the police. Someone, a friend who knew of things at the police station, had picked up a rumor. Just a rumor, you see. He himself had wanted to check on it, but how could he?

What was the rumor?

That Cipriano had also been in the car and injured. He had been taken to a hospital somewhere!

For God's sake, where?

That was the difficulty. This friend could not say. All he knew was that it was probably in France.

Could he give the name of the friend?

It was a matter of honor; he could not.

A hospital . . .

15
Clearance

He awoke the way he had gone to sleep, seeing old Farlo's wet mustache, white beard, and beetle brows, hearing his hoarse, whispery voice. As he turned over on his back and stared up at the ceiling, he determined to fulfill his promise.

After his lecture at the university, he went to María Victoria's, where she tutored him in the uses of preterits for an hour and he worked in turnabout with her on Skeltonic verse. When the lessons were done, he asked whether she could meet him somewhere that afternoon for an *aperitivo*. Something important had come up, he said, and he needed her help. It was Farlo he was thinking about, but he knew that he wanted to see her for her own sake also. No matter how deeply he became involved in the Swiatski matter or, for that matter, the affair with Lois, it was Victoria who stayed uppermost in his mind. She resided there like something framed in silver.

"I don't know," she demurred.

"It really is important," he said, letting his right hand touch lightly against her shoulder.

Her eyes looked violet in the muted light of the parlor. "We should not go again to the Vegas."

"How about the Hotel Gran Vía? They have a nice cocktail lounge there."

Her left eyebrow shot up, forming something of a comic question mark. "Don't you know about this place?"

"It looks respectable."

183

"Very 'respectable' and very chi-chi, a rendezvous place. It is where the governor's wife sometimes meets her star *futbolista*, by accident, of course." The eyebrow wiggled.

"Well, let's us meet there at four. Accidentally."

She removed his hand from her shoulder and turned to face him, studying his face seriously for a moment. "All right," she said, smiling, "accidentally."

The sergeant on duty at the main gate did not know Curt. He called Major Stafford's office, making him wait until an enlisted man came out in a jeep to escort him in.

Stafford's reception matched the guard's formality. As they shook hands Curt sensed stiff politeness. Stafford had obviously made up his mind to play it cool. His lips were set, eyes steady and unblinking. Curt had the feeling that if he said the funniest thing in the world, the major would submit it through channels in triplicate, and only if the right answer came back, would he laugh.

They both sat down without relaxing. Curt decided to start right in.

"You said you'd like to hear if I got anything that supported the shepherd's story, and I think I have. I took a trip yesterday to a town about fifty miles from here and was able to locate a relative of Cipriano Farlo's."

"Which relative? Which town?"

"An uncle. Living in Huesca. In fact, he was transported there by the police."

"Why?"

"He doesn't know, but you can draw your own conclusions. He's a man in his sixties, born in Zaragoza, lived here all his life until now. At the time of the accident he was working for his nephew. The police got in touch with him, questioned him, and then told him Cipriano had been killed. Then they returned and questioned him some more, told him there'd been a mistake—his nephew had not been killed but had skipped out of the country. They said it was the old man's duty to inform them if he heard anything from the nephew."

"So?" Stafford showed no signs of getting down off the judge's bench.

"So, several months later the police got in touch with him again. This time they told him things would go better for him in Huesca. They had a job for him there; they'd supply transportation."

"I still don't see the connection. The police in this country are always moving people around, or not letting them move around."

"But why this old man? He's no political agitator or trade unionist."

"To get him a job."

"As wine pourer? Why not get him one here? Why bother with him at all?"

"All right," Stafford said, shrugging. "You tell me."

"I'll try. On April eighth Cipriano Farlo was supposedly killed in an automobile accident. It was so announced in the papers the next day. A day or so after that, with your help, it was ascertained that the dead man was really Theodore Swiatski. The remains were shipped back to the States, and everything's settled."

"And still is as far as I'm concerned."

"Let me finish, please. I've done some homework and I'd like you to hear me out. Some five months after the accident—the fourth of September, to be exact—the *Heraldo de Aragón* carried a good-sized story of my coming to the university as a visiting professor. A couple of columns with photo."

"That's nice."

"Yes, that is nice, especially when you consider that two days after *that* the police visited old Farlo and asked whether he wouldn't like to live in Huesca."

"Oh, brother!" Stafford's face screwed itself into distasteful incredulity. "You're not going to try to tell me—"

"Oh, yes, I am. He was moved out of town—"

"So you wouldn't get to talk to him? *That* it?"

"I know it sounds peculiar but—"

"Why the hell would anyone be worried about some visiting Fulbrighter?"

"Because *that* story gave details and one of them was the fact that I came from the same home town Theodore Swiatski did— Hazleton, Pennsylvania. And somebody who has to be careful, who notes details, decided there just wasn't any use taking chances."

Stafford squinted his eyes and scratched the tip of his nose. Curt assumed that by now he understood Curt's interest in the Swiatski case from the start. That was probably what he meant when he said, finally, "I see. . . ."

"There's more to it than that. The same man in the Brigada Social, the one responsible for getting old Farlo out of town, lost no time in getting to know me when I arrived in Zaragoza."

"You mean—?"

"I mean Villalta." Curt considered adding María Victoria's name as a possible link but decided against it. Instead, he said, "And it looks as though he was responsible for getting someone else out of town that I wanted to talk to very badly."

A slight hesitation. Stafford's official mask seemed to soften. "Who are we talking about now?"

"Swiatski's girl."

"I guess I knew he had one, but assumed she was just—"

"I think she's better than that. I met her at the Cancela one night. She was working there as a singer. I was with Villalta. Later I got her alone and made an appointment to see her. When I reached her place the next day, she had gone. Moved out without a trace."

Stafford was watching him curiously. "Isn't it possible she stood you up? Had no intention of seeing you?"

"I don't think so. I told her who I was and what I wanted to talk about, and she seemed very anxious to see me."

"So it's your idea Villalta got her to leave town? How would he do that?"

"I'm not quite sure how, but I think I know *why*. I think he decided I would be asking questions and he got rid of her."

Stafford looked off toward the wall where the photographs of his flying days hung; in a moment he returned from the wild blue yonder, saying, "There's something wrong with your reasoning."

"What?"

"Why wouldn't he get her out of town earlier, the way he did Farlo, before she had a chance to talk to you?"

"That's a good question," Curt said, as though praising a bright student. "I've thought about it myself and there are several possible answers. One, *he* didn't know whether *I'd* know about the connection between the girl and Swiatski. Two, he wanted to see whether I would really be nosing around, and he used her as bait."

"And when he saw that you nibbled, he got rid of her?"

"Right."

Stafford blinked his eyes in consideration.

"And I figure," Curt went on, "that he must have had some absolutely sure hold on her. He'd have to be able to get her out of the way exactly when he wanted to."

"O.K." Stafford nodded. "It's pretty circumstantial all the way. But possible."

"It seems more possible when you tie it to what that shepherd told me near Bujaraloz. According to old Farlo, it was an open secret among the police that Cipriano Farlo was *also* in the car when it crashed!"

Stafford looked stunned. His official attitude wilted. If what he heard was true, not only he but also the entire American investigating staff had been tricked. "How the hell would he know?" he asked resentfully.

"He wouldn't say exactly. But I think there's a friend working at some menial job at police headquarters."

"Pretty weak stuff, then, isn't it? I mean, hearsay and rumor."

"That's true. But think what a strange kind of collusion there'd have to be; you know, between old Farlo and his friend, and some shepherd a hundred miles away."

"All right. Let's say that's what happened. Farlo was in the car, and we were kept in the dark about it, for what reason we don't know. Now, the question is: What happened to him? Where is he?"

Curt's smile twisted ruefully. "I'd like to know that myself. All that the old man heard was that he was hurt, that he got out of the country, and that he was probably hospitalized." He paused and pointed at the major. "That's where you come in."

"I do?"

"I hope so. What I want is a list of private hospitals and clinics near the border on the French side of the Pyrenees. Say from Bayonne over to Andorra, including Andorra, if possible. Maybe Pau and Oloron-Sainte-Marie up to Toulouse. Could you manage that?"

Stafford thought about it for a moment, then said, nodding his head, "Yes, there's an army base at Angoulême, and I could request the information from them—make it sound like a survey for use in case of accidents."

"Wonderful. But may I make one suggestion?"

"Shoot."

"Send your request for information, as ah, unobtrusively as possible." *Unobtrusively* wasn't exactly the word he wanted, but *secretly* sounded too melodramatic.

"Not teletype?"

"Whatever you think best."

"I'll make it a letter, type it myself."

"Good."

"Which means you think somebody here is mixed up in whatever the hell's been going on."

"I haven't any idea, really—not as much as you might have."

"You're talking in riddles."

"Well, I think Farlo and Swiatski were mixed up in something, as a team. And I think you have a better idea of what it might be than I do."

"There were some rumors about black-market stuff, but I don't have any facts. Not enough for official action, anyway. Swiatski seemed to have a lot of dough to spend. That's about it. He was off base as much as possible, lived in an apartment. . . ."

"There was never an official investigation of his activities?"

"None that I know of—not by the Air Police."

This wasn't turning out to be informative or entertaining, but it somehow left Curt with the impression that Stafford was leveling with him. He believed that if the man had more to say, he'd have said it.

"O.K." Curt got to his feet. "How long do you think it'll take for that list?"

"Maybe a week. I'll get the letter out this afternoon."

"Thanks." He put his hand out, feeling some Spanish formality in the act.

Stafford rose, shook his hand. "There is one other piece of news I have for you," he said. "We got clearance on you for the teaching. Seems you're an American citizen in good standing."

"Always nice to know," Curt smiled.

"I hope you keep it that way."

The bartender returned with a snifter of brandy on a silver tray, and placed it carefully on the table. Curt smiled and said, "*Perfecto.*"

After he had taken a long sip, he leaned back on the divan, swirling brandy in the warm glass. Somewhere inside he felt a final kink loosen.

"María Victoria, María Victoria, María Victoria." The name

burbled through his mind and spilled out quietly across his tongue. A series of liquids punctuated by a consonantal hiccup: "María Vik-toria."

If things went as well with María Victoria as they had with Stafford, he'd be in business. And that was what he'd better start thinking about—business. He began arranging in his mind things he wanted to say, questions he wanted to ask.

About ten minutes later Victoria walked into the lounge, entering hesitantly, cautiously. One false move on the hunter's part and she would bound away. He raised a hand and waved it carefully. He stood up as she came toward him, tall and lithe in a grayish knit suit. She looked impossibly real, the way beautiful women do outside movies or magazines.

"Didn't I tell you?" she said in a stage whisper. "It is a place for rendezvous." Her voice was low and vibrant; she tried to make it sound comic, but he detected in it a basic seriousness, whether of anticipation or social concern he couldn't tell.

"It's a wonderful place," he assured her. He offered his hand and they sat down together. "It's a fine place for all the arts of venery."

"Venery? What is venery?"

"The gentle art of the forest—and of the boudoir."

"Aha! Already I see that it is dangerous."

"Can be, yes. Benjamin Franklin warned that it should be practiced only for health's sake or for progeny."

She smiled and said, "In the forest?"

"No, no, in the boudoir. You see, old Ben was a pretty healthy chap; he practiced venery at home and abroad. He was our ambassador to France, and he tried for a little venery with Madame Helvetius. It was a famous case."

"I think I am beginning to understand this venery!"

"Comes from Venus, you see, and the shooting of deer with bow and arrow."

"In the boudoir?"

"No, señorita, in the forest."

"And is this why all the American men come to Europe—to be like Benyamin Franklin?"

"That's an interesting question. I think I'll ask our State Department to issue a white paper on the subject."

"I am sure we would all be interested in reading it."

The bartender arrived and María Victoria turned serious immediately, speaking in a crisp, polite manner, asking for a Calisay and demitasse coffee. The man said he'd have to get the coffee from the hotel dining room. *"Por favor,"* she said insistently. Curt ordered another Carlos Primero.

When the barman left, Victoria turned playful once again. "I see that you have already discovered our best brandy."

"Oh, sure," he said. "Democracy teaches us that what's good enough for a Spanish king is good enough for an American citizen."

"Aha!" She nodded her head. Then, as though struck by a thought, she added, "Since you have been so good to tell me about Benyamin Franklin, I will tell you about one of our kings."

"You mean Carlos Primero?"

"No. Felipe Segundo."

"Don't tell me old Felipe was a great venery man also?"

"He was a spoiled man, Felipe Segundo. Always he must have what he want, in all matters, including even sport. He considered himself quite a sportsman, especially for the billiards. He loved to play billiards, and always his opponents must assure that he win. No matter how good they were they must miss on purpose and arrange for the balls to be just right for Felipe Segundo."

"Damned nice of them. And does this little account have a moral, *señorita?*"

"Yes. Because even today when somebody makes it easy for you to win, we say '*Te lo dieron como se lo dieron a Felipe Segundo.*' You understand?"

"I sure do," Curt laughed: " 'They have given it to you the way they gave it to Felipe Segundo.' "

"That's right."

"Well, I have to tell you it sounds better in Spanish."

"Why?"

"In English it sounds a little dirty."

She didn't seem to understand the connotation and Curt was saved from having to explain by the reappearance of the barman, who now arranged their drinks neatly on the table before them.

When they were alone again, Curt lifted his brandy glass toward her. *"Salud,"* he said.

"Gracias." After a sip she put the glass back down on the table and turned part way on the divan to look at him. "You told me there was something important."

"That's right."

"And that you want my help?"

"Yes. But I'm not sure I'm going to get it as easily as Felipe Segundo."

She smiled beautifully. "You are *muy listo,*" she said. "Very clever. I see that you have understood the story."

He watched her enjoying herself, perched angularly there on the divan, with her lithe legs neatly crossed.

"What I want to talk about *is* serious. And I hope that you won't in any way be offended, because I want to ask some questions. They may seem silly to you, but I assure you they have a purpose."

"All right," she said, sounding curious, but also a little perturbed.

"First of all, I'd like to know about our meeting in Madrid, with Marta."

"Yes?"

"Had you just arrived in Madrid at about that time?"

"Maybe two or three days before."

"And you knew about my coming to Zaragoza before you visited Marta?"

"Oh, yes. But I told you about that. There had been a notice in the newspapers."

"Did you read about it on your own, or did someone draw your attention to the story?"

She looked at him quizzically her left eyebrow hooking up the way it often did. "I cannot remember. I am not sure. But why is this important?"

He waved aside her question. "Just think," he said. "Did anyone talk to you about the story, about my coming?"

She thought a moment, then said, "I think we all talked about the matter at dinner."

"All?"

"Yes. My family."

"Was it then that you decided to come to Madrid and to meet me?"

"No, no." She shook her head decisively. A streak of silver hair fell across her brow in a perfect slash of disarray. "That was decided much later."

"When later?"

"I think just a few days before I went to Madrid."

"And was it your idea?"

"Well, we all talked about the possibility."

"You and your family?"

"Yes. And I think that it was my father who made the suggestion. He said that he knew I was wanting to go to Madrid for shopping, and that I could visit with Marta and maybe that way meet the visiting professor. . . . Yes, I think that was how it was."

He'd been more than half-expecting to hear Villalta had made the suggestion. If his reasoning was right, Victoria had been set up as an unsuspecting contact, someone through whom it would be easy to keep tabs on the visiting professor. But if it hadn't been Villalta who arranged matters directly, then what about Victoria's father? Had he acted on some hint or suggestion of Villalta's? That would be almost impossible to find out and it didn't seem that important now. What *was* important was that the girl seemed genuinely baffled by this line of questioning: she was either innocent of all complicity or she was a fine actress.

"Why do you ask these questions? What is it you wish to know?"

"Did you ever hear of an American airman named Theodore Swiatski?"

"No."

"How about a Cipriano Farlo?"

"No, I don't believe so."

He explained who they were and what had happened; and even before he finished talking she began nodding: she remembered the story in the newspapers; she just hadn't remembered the names.

"But," she concluded, "what do they have to do with all these questions?"

He told her that he was interested in finding out exactly what had happened to the two men. He said that the family of Theodore Swiatski had been confused about his death and mystified by the varying reports of the accident.

She herself looked mystified; she listened almost unbelievingly. Finally, she said, "And you, what exactly do you have to do with all this?"

He knew she probably wanted to ask him the same question Stafford had about whether he was working for some agency or other.

"I have promised the family that I would look into the affair. They are friends."

"Oh!" She pushed the stray slash of hair back into place. "I see."

"And the favor I want to ask you is connected with a relative of Cipriano Farlo's. For some reason or other the old man was urged to leave Zaragoza by the police, or one member of the police. He's very unhappy where he's living now, in Huesca, and he'd like to return to his native city. What he needs is some kind of job that will keep him going."

"Why would the police want this man to leave?" She wasn't getting any of this, and he could understand why.

"It's not quite clear, to tell you the truth. But I don't think they're much concerned *now* one way or the other. So what I wanted you to do was to see whether you or your father might not find a job for the old man. He's working as a wine pourer in a bodega now; he helped in the printing shop of Cipriano's, and he worked for the railroad before that."

"I do not want to seem unkind, but why do you want to help him?"

"Because he did me a favor and I made a promise, and he's a very unhappy old man."

She turned on the divan and reached for her drink. She sipped some of it deliberately, taking her time, trying to make up her mind.

He watched her as he drank some of his cognac. The pearl earring on her left ear swung gently in anticipation of her turning toward him once again.

Her eyes were on him fully. "I will do what I can," she said. "I will talk to my father, and we will see."

"*Muchas gracias, señorita.*"

"It is nothing. But I must tell you that I don't quite understand your position. It is as though you have not told me everything."

"You mean about Farlo?"

"That, yes."

"What do you want to know?"

"I suppose that you do not want to tell what favor he did for you."

"He gave me some information."

"I see," she said, understanding that was all he was going to say.

He waved to the bartender and they had another drink. She seemed to relax after more of the Calisay, and she allowed him to hold her hand.

Later she sat up a little straighter and said, "You know that I think you are very nice—"

"And I think *you're* very nice."

"Be serious, Curtis."

"I *am* serious, María Victoria."

The eyebrow shot up. "As serious as with Lois Harte?"

"Lois Harte?"

"Yes."

"She's just a friend."

"Are you sure?"

"I'm sure."

She looked at him and said nothing for a moment, then she said, "That is not what I am told."

"And what are you told?"

"Quite frankly?"

"Yes, quite frankly."

"That you practice—venery."

He put a hand on her left shoulder and gripped her. "Look, I'm a forty-year-old man, not a boy. But I am in no way in love with Lois Harte. There's only one woman in the whole world that I'd be willing to start over with—"

"Don't say anything foolish." She pulled away from his hand.

"I hope there will be a time when it does not seem foolish to you."

She sat looking straight ahead as he went on speaking in a low voice.

"I must tell you that my life already seems worthless to me. I keep going through the motions. I seem to feel—up to a point. Then I go dry. When I laugh, I laugh halfway. When I cry—

well, I don't cry. I don't seem to do anything fully. I'm halfway through my life, and I'm more than half done with it."
He reached out and took her shoulder again and she turned
toward him. "Do you understand what I'm saying?"

"Not exactly."

"I've known many women in my life. I've read many books.
I'm supposed to have educated tastes and ideas. But the ideas
have all gone flat. I don't give a damn about Spinoza or Bishop
Berkeley, Goethe or Milton. Knowing another philosopher or
poet is like knowing another woman, like eating too much—
too much meat. One way or the other it all seems to come to
so much meat."

"You *are* sick," she said, sympathetically.

"Of course I'm sick. We're all sick. I'm sick from eating too
much. You're sick from eating too little."

She looked at him as though to speak, then said nothing.

"I mean it. It's unnatural for someone like you to have
lived to your age, someone as lovely as you are, to be drying
away to spinsterhood. Your face is starting to look as waxy as a
nun's."

Her lower lip trembled. Her eyelids fluttered as she answered,
"You are assuming too much. I have many things to do in my
life."

"Yes, you've told me. You have lunch and dinner every day
with your family. You go shopping, you have the dressmaker in
for fittings. You go to the movies with your sister or María-
Pilar. You attend social functions with your father."

"I could have dates. Many of them."

"Don't I know that? I'd have to be blind not to know that.
But the point is you don't. Listen, I know something about
women, and I know when one of them is afraid of men, and the
truth is you are."

"Ho-no!" she said, with a forced smile.

"Oh, yes. And it comes from what you've told me about—
about your mother."

"Let us not discuss it."

"Why not? I would like to leave this place having some kind of understanding with you. And this is part of it—making sure you have the right man, because otherwise you will spend the rest of your life reading, reading in bed alone, like your mother, like an invalid—"

"Please, don't," she pleaded. "I have confided in you, but please don't."

"All right," he conceded. "But one of these days we've got to straighten things out. I'm not trying to play Prince Charming to a sleeping princess. I'm the one needs awakening. Being with you makes me want to grab my own shoulders and shake myself into some kind of awareness. . . . Well, it's useless maybe to try to express—"

"Not now," she said. "Not here."

"All right," he said. "But can we at least see each other once in a while, not just during the lessons. I'd like to take you out to dinner at least."

"We shall see." She put her right hand on his and smiled gently.

16
Sindicato

"Buenos días, Señor Fieldee."

"Buenos días, Jaime."

It was a ritual. Every day after class he stopped by the faculty *portero's* cubicle and asked for his mail, and almost every day the *portero,* who was fat and wore a long gray smock that made him look like a surgeon, said he was sorry but there was no mail for Señor Fieldee. In the two months Curt had been with the university no more than two or three pieces of mail had reached him there. The Commission usually forwarded everything to his apartment.

"Hoy," the *portero* said, holding the word dramatically— *"Si!"* He whipped a letter from behind his back with the gusto and flourish of a magician, smiling like those hard-bitten sergeants Curt had known who used to light up at mail call when some sad sack in the outfit finally received a letter or package.

Curt smiled back. *"Muchas gracias."*

On his way to the English department he turned the letter over examining it. It bore a Madrid cancellation of November 30. The envelope was purplish-gray, and the handwriting seemed oddly familiar.

None of the others had yet returned to the office. Curt plugged in the electric heater which they used to reduce the damp chill of the room, and sat down at his desk, looking at the letter, vaguely troubled once again by its familiar appearance. With a straightened paperclip he opened the envelope and then un-

199

folded the single sheet of paper inside. His eyes clicked down to the signature. He muttered "Maite," and began to read:

Dear Sir Professor Fielding,

I no can say much in the letter. I am have to leav Zaragoza and for that I am sorri because I wan much to see you and talk. Now I wan see you. There is much for to tell. Before I no can tell. Now I think so yes.

I no that you will come because you must be friend for me and Teddi. I work for Club Veinte-Una, Calle de San Tomaso, Madrid. Every nite but no Lunes.

Con much respecto,
María Maite Xavier-Peralta

Curt read the letter a second and third time.

Collins and Tupper walked in from their classes, plopping books on their desks and chirping English greetings.

"Morning," Curt answered.

"Care for a spot at the Mirasol?" Collins said.

"As a matter of fact, I would," Curt said. "I want to talk to you about taking a couple of days off."

He paid the cabdriver and walked across the narrow street to the Club Veinte-Una. The big *salas de fiesta* were mostly located near Avenida de José Antonio. This was several blocks away in a welter of clubs, cafés, and small restaurants. They were all just coming alive with pimps, prostitutes, entertainers, waiters, bouncers, and rake-off artists.

Inside the Veinte-Una there was only a handful of patrons. Things didn't get started for another hour. Curt felt like an anxious John until he had relaxed with his first drink.

He deserved to rest, he thought. He'd been through a hell of a rush. Everything had gone all right with Collins, who was taking his classes. But the VW had been in the garage for its two-thousand-mile checkup, and the mechanic, finding slippage in the clutch, had stripped the mechanism. So Curt had checked with the railroad, found there was a fast train leaving at four that afternoon and decided to take it. From the station he had called Victoria, telling her he'd be back in a couple of days and would explain matters then.

Now here he was, after checking into the Fénix, showering, and grabbing a bite to eat. María Maite couldn't complain about lack of interest or action: those North Americans sure could move.

The only question now was where was she? Seven or eight of the girls had already shown up and were beginning to circulate. Maybe the entertainers appeared later.

He signaled the barman for another, and just as he handed over his glass caught sight of someone entering the front door. It was Maite. She was carrying a hatbox and wore a silk scarf around her hair. He waved. She stopped short of a door that must have led into a dressing room, and then walked quickly toward him, all action. Under the belted white raincoat was a figure no cloth could muffle.

She shifted the box and put out her hand. "How prompt," she said, *"Muy pronto."*

"I've been hoping to find you for over a month."

"And now," she said, "you must wait a little longer. This is not a good place for to talk. Let me change and we will have a drink—for appearance. Then after the show we go to my place, yes?"

"Yes," he said.

By the time she did her numbers he had been rubbed and titillated by at least five or six of the club girls. He was flushed with liquor, and as he watched Maite in her tight, sequinned gown, he had trouble remembering he'd come all this way to discuss another man.

As she passed him on the way to the dressing room, she murmured swift instructions to meet her outside in fifteen minutes, with a cab.

From the Veinte-Una to her place was a warm, smothery ride

of ten minutes. The apartment was two flights up. She searched in her purse for a key, found it, and they went in—to the sharp yapping of a small terrier.

She led him in and indicated an overstuffed sofa, saying, "Wait here."

Curt looked around. The apartment was small and cramped. There was a bedroom off to the left, a kitchen, and beyond that a maid's room. It was there she went. She spoke to someone in low reassuring tones. He was confused until he remembered the old woman.

She came back through the tiny kitchen, shrugging off her light coat. "My aunt," she said. "I just tell her I am home." The terrier followed her protectively. "Let me change and put Bobo in his basket."

"O.K."

She went into the bedroom, not bothering to close the door. He could hear the sliding of hangers, the opening and closing of a drawer.

"There is some beer in the 'frigerator," Maite said, poking her head around the doorjamb.

"O.K.," he said, and tiredly got to his feet, taking off his suit jacket, hanging it over one of the two chairs at the table. Above, a canary in its cage chittered and scratched seed in a flurry of protest.

Curt took out a bottle of El Aguila. "Would you like one?" he asked, addressing the bedroom.

"Yes, please."

"Opener?"

"In the drawer of the table."

He opened the beer and slumped back onto the couch. He was tired. The long day was beginning to take its toll. As he took a swig of the beer his mind rolled as though he were aboard ship. It rolled toward Teddy Swiatski and Villalta, and then it rolled toward Maite's rounded hips beneath her sequinned gown.

She came out of the bedroom, wearing a loose tan robe that

was neither stylish nor sexy. Her hair was no longer piled up in intricate layers, but hung down naturally to her shoulders. The glamour of the stage lights was gone. But as she walked toward him, her slender legs were revealed almost to her crotch and he felt himself warm.

As she picked up the beer on the table, the canary fussed and chirped again, and she put a finger to the cage. "Don't be a bad boy, Chi-chi," she said, and then came to the sofa and sat down, covering her legs carefully.

"Now, we must talk," she said.

"All right," he said, wondering if she could see the film of desire that had made his eyes go out of focus.

"Do you have a cigarette for me?"

"Yes." He stood up rather awkwardly and fished his cigarettes out of the coat pocket.

They lit up and he found himself calming.

"You came to Madrid very quickly," she said.

"As soon as I got your letter."

"Good. I have many things for to tell you."

"Let's begin with you and Teddy."

"All right." She drank some beer and settled back against the cushions. "Teddy and I meet almost two years ago. Then I was singing at the Capri. The base was full at that time and many of the Americans try for to make me. Sometimes I let them. I have always like American men. They are not like the Espanish. They are like boys. They have a good time. When they find that a girl makes love they are still nice. Espanish men treat you like *una puta*. They think anybody that make love is very bad."

"Did you do this for money?"

"Oh, yes."

"As part of your job in the *salas*?"

"No, since I am *una artista*, it is as I wish. I do not have to drink with the men. And I do not have to go to bed."

"But there are those in the *salas* who must do these things?"

"That is the work of many. They must share the money

204 THE SPANISH SEASON

with the club. If they do not, they are fired. Or much worse."

"How worse?"

"They can be hurt. Even it has happened to be killed. We are not supposed to speak of it, but we all belong to a *sindicato*. And the *sindicato* is very powerful."

She seemed ready to add something but then didn't.

"Well, we were talking about you and Teddy," Curt said.

"*Sí*. Teddy I like most of any man. Even from the Americans he was different. Not so much like the boy. *Muy macho*."

"Did he know about you and other men?"

"Oh, yes. He know how I am and what I do. But he say, 'From now on, baby, just the two of us,' and I say yes, and that was how it was. I no let other men touch me."

"Truly?"

"As God is my witness," she said.

"Good."

"It was very good, for over a year. I don't go to Barcelona or Madrid or the other places. I get *sindicato* permission for to stay in Zaragoza. After the Capri I work in the Pigalle and then the Orchida."

"In your letter to his family, you implied that you and Teddy were going to get married."

"*Sí*, it is true. Teddy say to me, 'Baby, I have one year to go, then we get the hell out of this country.' And I say, 'How we can do that?' And he say, 'You know damn well, we gonna get marry. We live in Pennsylvania, have some kids, be good peoples together.'"

Curt glanced sharply at her. "He was serious?"

"*Sí, hombre*. I know when a man is serious. Many time guys say, 'You know, baby, you too good for this life, I take you away,' and I say, 'Sure, sure,' and we make love two, three times, and I no take it serious. Because I know. Four, five times I have men serious. I no agree. Until Teddy. Don't worry, he was serious. We already making out papers. He give me money. Some for every day, some to keep for going America."

"How was Teddy with money? Did he have quite a bit?"

"Is that important—to you?"

It was the first time she had come close to telling him to mind his own business.

"Yes," he insisted.

"I do not want to hurt the family of Teddy."

"Neither do I."

"Then you must be careful of what I say." Her large eyes studied him.

"I will do nothing to hurt his family."

She tightened the sash of her robe and began to speak in a low voice.

"About two years ago, even before he know me, Teddy is mixed up in some way to make money, and he make much money. He's never tell me everything, but he say if something happen to him, watch for Francisco Villalta and the *Mayor* Pardee."

She paused to see the effect of her words. Curt nodded his head in acknowledgment.

"He say anything happen to him, I talk with Cipriano Farlo, he tell me what is important. This Farlo—"

"I know about him."

"Oh, yes, because of the newspapers."

"Yes, and I've been in touch with his uncle, who's now in Huesca."

"It is very important to find Farlo."

"I'm trying to do that now with the help of someone at the base." He explained briefly about the hospital check he intended to carry out.

"*Bueno.* You do the right thing."

"Thanks, but let's get back to Teddy and you. You must have some idea what he was involved in."

"Some kind of black market, yes. But more. It have to do with gasoline coupons . . . and . . . also with the girls."

"Prostitution?"

"Not exactly. But with the marriages."

"Spanish girls marrying airmen?" Curt had a fleeting vision

of the ladies in waiting, as Lois Harte called them, that first
night he'd gone to the base club.

"Every one of the girls must have the certification, and to
have this, they must deal with the Brigada Social, you know,
and with the *policía* American at the base."

"Villalta and Pardee."

"*Claro*. Many of my friends that work for the clubs have
marry the American airmen."

"I was told there weren't many marriages—that Spanish
women were not eager to marry Americans."

"Maybe so, but the girls from the *salas, sí*. They do. And
they must all pay."

"For the certificates."

"*Sí*."

"How much?"

"Two, three thousand dollars."

"Why doesn't somebody complain?"

"If they complain—that's all. They do not get certificates,
they do not get married. Also, it is dangerous."

"How widespread is this racket? Just Zaragoza?"

"No. All the bases. Somebody from the Brigada and the
sindicato have this all planned."

"In your letter you said the police gave you and Teddy
trouble. Was this what it was about—the certificate?"

"No, not at first."

"What do you mean?"

"They do not ask me for money. But my sister wanted to
marry an American. She also has a young child, and Teddy
say he take care of everything, but they want money. He say
go to hell to Pardee, and he have troubles. They no want to
give my sister the *certificado*. Then some way Teddy get a
certificado. But it is no good. And my sister went away to a
pueblo with her son. Then two weeks later Teddy is dead, and
I do not think this was an accident."

Curt pieced together the fragments of what the girl was
saying. Obviously Swiatski had been involved in a ring that

handled various black-market items. Pardee acted somehow in co-operation with Villalta. They made money as marriage brokers of sorts. Swiatski had tried to intercede for María's sister, had even gone so far as to forge a certificate, which hadn't worked. Why hadn't he just paid the girl's two thousand or so dollars? And how did he fit into the whole scheme? And Farlo?

"María," he said, "what was Teddy's job at the base?"

"At first he was *mecánico*, then when the base phase down, he work for the base *policía*, in the records."

Curt nodded slowly. "I see."

He gave her a cigarette and lit one for himself. After a moment, he said, "Why are you telling me this now? And why did you leave Zaragoza so quickly?"

"A man from the Brigada come to my apartment that night. He tell me get to hell out fast and not to leave any notice."

"Was it—?"

"Villalta? No. But you can be *sure* he sent him. I think he get suspicious at the Cancela when he see us together."

"And why did you leave? Afraid of what he would do?"

"To me—" her head came up—"no. But to my sister, yes. She had return to the pueblo we come from, Taffala. And she stay in the house of my aunt. The Brigada tell me I don't go away they take her son from her; she is bad womans, they say, and they take her son."

"If that's the situation, why did you write to me? Aren't you taking a big risk in talking to me?"

She smiled bravely. "Now it is only me to worry. My sister and her child are now in Francia. Some friends helped to get her over the *frontera*. She is all right, and maybe the American is come for to take her to Switzerland and marry. I don't know yet."

"Who is this American?"

Her eyes clouded. She took a deep breath and said, "This one thing I do not wish to say."

"All right. I just thought he might be able to help me."

"No, don't bother about him." She sounded determined, almost angry.

"All right," he said again, consolingly. "What will happen to you if it is discovered you've talked to me?"

She shrugged her shoulders. "I don't know. Maybe the *sindicato* no let me sing any more."

"*Sindicato?*"

"*Sí*, the *sindicato*. Villalta is one of the heads. He can do it."

"He sure is involved in many things."

"Many."

"Have you thought of getting out of the country also? Now that your sister's gone, he'll know they have less hold on you."

"Maybe yes. I have friends on Mallorca. Perhaps I can get to Italia, you know."

"Will they have any way of knowing that we did talk?"

"I think nobody at the Veinte-Una can know who you are."

"But we'd better not be seen together."

"Do not come to the club again."

"O.K."

She had stretched back against the cushions. The robe had slipped open at the legs. She wore nothing underneath.

"But you can come to the apartment if you like." Her eyes were watching his watch her.

"I'll be here for a couple of days."

"The old lady will let you in."

She stood up slowly and began unloosening the sash of her robe. "C'mon, baby," she said. "Since Teddy, I am lonesome."

Afterward as she lay in his arms, she said, "You are much like him. I like you very much."

"I like you very much," he said, wondering whether the brothers Swiatski would approve of his consoling the widow.

17
Middle of Her Forehead

Sunday night he boarded the late train for Zaragoza. It was called the Rápido but was not very rapid. According to the schedule it took over six hours to make the same trip the Talgo did in four, but what it lacked in speed the Rápido made up for in comfort, at least in the first-class compartment which Curt had all to himself. Green carpeting, red plush seats, and glossy walnut paneling indicated the manner in which twentieth-century grandees expected to travel.

Not long after they pulled out of the station, the *revisor* stopped by and checked his ticket. He suggested the *señor* might be more comfortable if he aired the compartment. The *señor* said that would be perfect, and the man lowered the window part way.

When the *revisor* had gone Curt relaxed in his plush seat, his head against the rest, his eyes closed, turning the events of the past three days in Madrid over in his mind. He had packed as much activity into those days and nights as he might have done in three weeks. He was leaving Maite with real regret; she had been pleasant and exciting, entertaining him with her life story, with all of its various "loves" and escapades, recounting it all with some kind of inner grace, as well as a realistic sense of humor. Hers had been the education of a *pícara*; not only had she known men who were like de Sade and Montesquieu, but she had read Cela and *La Celestina*.

She had taken care of the nights, like some Spanish Scheherazade. Marta Torres had arranged his days, providing him entry into the homes of several pro-Franco writers who had written about the Civil War. He had interviewed Laura Suerte, who had been Franco's English teacher during his period of exile in the Canary Islands, and who had stayed on in Spain to become head of English-language radio broadcasting. He had also interviewed Kemp Baker, dean of foreign correspondents in Madrid, an Englishman who'd been living in Spain for some thirty years, a personal friend of Roy Campbell's and of Franco's. From these two Curt had gathered a sizable list of authors and works, which he sent along to Eddy Stone for his book. Now he sat content in the compartment, letting these events dissolve into memory.

A little later, feeling restive, he reached up to his jacket, which he'd hung on a hook across from him, and slipped a paperback book out of the pocket. It was a copy of Hemingway's *relatos:* the front cover pictured a man in turtleneck sweater, with a day's growth of spiky beard, holding a nearly burnt-out cigarette close to his forehead in a gesture of worried thought.

Curt had spotted the book in a kiosk at the station and picked it up thinking it might be interesting to try his Spanish out on well-traveled paths. He began by reading *"Un Lugar Limpio y Bien Iluminado,"* and found that after the title, it went well, maybe even better than in English. The author had pulled his clean, well-lighted story out of the murk of Spanish life, so that reading it in Spanish was a little like watching a trout thrown back into its native waters, swimming with new vigor. But *"Los Asesinos,"* which he tried next, went badly. After listening to the Chicago killers, George and Al, talk to the *"vivos"* and joke about the little pueblo where everyone ate the *"gran comilona,"* Curt dropped it. He never even got to hear how Nick Adams sounded in Spanish. The last thread of his attention was snapped by a little golden-haired girl who walked past his compartment door.

She had gone by once or twice before, and Curt had dimly wondered, even while he was reading, whether she might be English or American, because of the hair. Girls in Spain didn't become blondes until they reached their twenties, when they emulated New York and Paris and Rome, so that in resorts like Sitges or Palma de Mallorca it was hard to distinguish them from the phototropic Teutons and Scandinavians who swarmed around the sea coast.

He decided to speak to the girl if she went by again, returning from the W.C. or wherever it was she'd been going. He sat watching the passageway, and when she came whisking by his doorway he shot out a "Hello there!" Impetus carried her past the door but in a moment she returned, hesitantly peeking around the jamb. "How are you?" he said. Getting no response, he began to wonder whether after all she might be neither English nor American.

The girl stood there, her face blank. Then it broke wide open with a jack-o'-lantern smile, several of the front teeth missing. "You speak English," she said, as though she had stumbled upon a lollipop mine.

"Yes, I do."

"Are you an American?" She fidgeted back and forth from leg to leg in a natural twist movement enhanced by the swaying of the train.

She couldn't have been more than nine or ten years old, Curt thought, but, oh, dear!, she was going to be a heart-smasher in a few more years. "Yes," he said, "I'm an American. Are you?"

"Can't you *tell?*"

"I'd say yes."

"Well, I am."

"And are you traveling on this big train all by yourself?"

"What do *you* think?"

"I'd say yes."

Her giggle was wild. Finally she settled down enough to say,

"I'm with my mommy and my daddy and my baby brother."

"Oh, I see."

"Are you traveling all by *yourself*?"

"I'm afraid I am."

"That's a shame, isn't it?" She said this with a little wave of her right hand, like a hostess faced with the problem of getting someone to accompany a bachelor to dinner.

"Yes, I guess it is at that," he answered, feeling that the girl's sympathies, learned by rote to fit various social exigencies, were nevertheless natural.

She stared at him for a moment, wavering in the doorway, and then dashed off. Curt felt somewhat the fool, wondering whether something in his manner had startled her. She reminded him of deer back in the forests of Pennsylvania at night; the way they would stand, fascinated by headlights or a spotlight, and then bolt. She was back, though, almost before he could finish the thought, dragging by the hand a tall man with sandy hair.

"There he is, Daddy!"

The man reminded Curt of Ralph Beaver, the same kind of angular basketball build. He put out his hand, saying, "I'm sorry if my daughter's been bothering you. I'm Bob Markle."

"Curt Fielding. She hasn't been bothering me at all. Won't you sit down?"

The girl sat on her father's lap, beaming with the pleasure of her discovery. She was very pretty, with regular features of the kind that win children's beauty contests, but she was saved by having the glance of an imp, with lips that turned up at the corners in an indication of a budding comedienne.

"This," the tall man said, jouncing his daughter on his knee, "is our Dory."

"My right name's Doris but everybody calls me Dory."

"How are you, Dory?" She took his proffered hand, wrinkling up her nose, shaking his hand as though it was the silliest thing in the world, and yet pleased to be doing it.

At this point she hopped from her father's knee and ran to give the latest news to her mother. Markle asked Curt to come to their compartment to meet his wife, Margaret.

Margaret was a splendid-looking woman of thirty. She had a boy of about three lying half asleep on the seat beside her with his curly head propped on her lap.

As they talked for an hour or so, Curt was once more amazed, after dealing with Europeans for something like two months, at how open Americans were. Of course, they were country-men of his and that might account for their willingness to speak of personal matters, but that was only part of the answer.

Eventually he learned all about them. Margaret Markle had been an education major at the University of Illinois. Bob was a chemical engineer with a master's degree from Purdue. They had been in Spain two months. He was working for Monsanto's Barcelona plant. And this was their first trip to Madrid. They were returning from three days of the Prado, El Escorial, University City, Botin's and the Castellana Hilton. They were the kind of American family Curt had several times seen in restaurants or museums or sitting between meals in the lobbies of places like the Hilton. They were all eyes. They brought with them naïve intelligence and a way of looking at European life which was half suspicious and half delirious with the joy of finding themselves—the Joneses, the Smiths, the Markles of West Lafayette—here abroad in Spain with all those castles, in the land of Don Quixote and Washington Irving. Dory must have separated them from all the other tourists in the mind of one guide, when, as Margaret related the incident, she had peered up at him, squinting her eyes, asking why one of the male figures in the Prado hadn't put his pants on to have his statue taken.

As it turned out, Bob and Margaret knew some of the same people Curt did at Purdue. They talked of them and of the States and what they missed; of the food in Spain; of means of travel; of this slow train. Curt tried to explain some of his own experiences and how he was beginning to find something in Spain that affected him deeply, but their looks were too ingenuous for him to penetrate, their homesickness for the States too real for him to have any serious effect on them. They could no more understand what he was saying about the honesty of a gasoline attendant near Medinaceli, the way the people around Calatayud came home from the fields in the evening, or María Victoria's fragility and dignity, than his friends and family had been able to understand about combat when he had first come home from Italy and tried to explain what the places were like. So the talk once more returned to Stateside matters—football, Thanksgiving, the National Homes Construction Company in Lafayette. . . .

"It is getting late," Curt said finally, seeing eleven-thirty on his watch. "You folks probably want to have your beds made up, and I'll be getting off in an hour or so."

They exchanged cards with addresses scribbled on and Curt promised to visit them on his next trip to Barcelona.

"Do you really *promise?*" Dory said, surprisingly alert at this hour. She had sat in the corner near the window at her father's side during the long conversation; and at times Curt had the strangest feeling that she was the only one of the Markles who understood his feelings about Spain. Maybe this was because she had been induced by her mother to say a few phrases in Spanish she'd learned in school. Her pronunciation and flexibility were amazing. Her parents, by comparison, were stiff and tentative in trying out the snatches of language they'd learned.

"I promise," Curt said, reaching over and patting her golden hair, remembering suddenly how, somewhere in a French play, a count waits ten years for a child to grow up in order to marry her.

The boy was now fully asleep in his mother's lap. Madonna and Child in Train Compartment. Margaret smiled her good night.

Bob accompanied him into the passage and hand-signaled a waiting attendant to get their beds ready. Curt spoke in Spanish to the man to help matters along. Bob shook hands with Curt for the second time. "We really mean it about coming to see us in Barcelona," he said. "We have a nice little villa and I'm sure Margaret will be delighted to dish up a home-cooked meal for you. Besides, I'd like you to meet some of our people at Monsanto. They're quite a bunch. Some of them've been here for five or six years."

"I'll do it, Bob. Good night, and *buen viaje.*"

"Good journey?"

"Yes."

"Thanks, 'bye."

Back in his own compartment Curt luxuriated in the left-over aura of the family. He had been trying to tell them something about Spain but they had left a deeper impression on him simply by being what they were. They had left a haze of warmth and shared love. He felt lonelier than at any time since leaving the States. He wondered what it would have been like with Helen if they'd had a couple of kids. What would kids of theirs have been like? Maybe one of the great sins in this world was to keep life from something out there—he looked out into the darkness of the Spanish sky—waiting to be born, the way we all had waited, waiting for some combination of chance, passion, and if we were lucky, love, to pluck us off the float of nonbeing.

He opened the window a little more, surprised at how easily it came down, especially in comparison with windows he'd tussled with on American trains.

Sometime later the lights of a small town, probably Calatayud, interrupted the dark. The train stopped briefly, puffing—neither with impatience nor the desire to be off to more important places, he thought, just puffing. Then it picked up speed once again and they moved out of Calatayud, only an hour or so away from Zaragoza. He watched the lights disappear, the lights of life, he told himself. All anybody needed was a clean, well-lighted place. Maybe that's all it took— "*Un Lugar Limpio y Bien Iluminado.*"

Once again he picked up the Hemingway stories from the seat beside him and selected an old favorite, "*La Vida Feliz de Francis Macomber.*" For a while he puzzled over why the translator had left out the "Breve," or "Short" from the title: "The *Short* Happy Life of Francis Macomber." Certainly it had been an important consideration of the author's, for in another book Hemingway had said some men lead more of a life in seventy-two hours than others do in seventy-two years.

Dropping the problem of the title, he began to work through the story itself, and had finished about two-thirds when he was interrupted by Bob Markle.

He folded down one corner of the page at a line that said: "*Macomber sentía una felicidad salvaje e irrazonada, como nunca la había conocido antes. . . .*" It was the beginning and the end for Macomber; he had reached a savage and an unreasoning happiness, like nothing he had known before. . . .

At first he thought Markle had come to borrow matches or a cigarette or something, but his appearance and his manner belied that. The tail of his shirt was partially out of his trousers. His hair was rumpled and he was trying to keep his voice low.

"I'm sorry to bother you like this, Curt, but you speak the language and maybe you can help. We've been looking all over for Dory and can't find her. I know she must be on the train someplace but Margaret's beginning to get panicky."

And so are you, Curt thought, seeing the sweat standing out on Markle's forehead. "Of course, I will," he said. "Let's go together. She's probably in one of the johns. You know the way kids are about johns. In fact she came down past my compartment twice earlier—"

Bob was shaking his head: "No, I've looked in all the toilets. She's not in any of them."

"Well, have you checked with the conductor?"

"I haven't been able to find him, much less talk to him. Besides I wouldn't know what to say if I did find him."

"O.K. Let's find him. There's nothing to get excited about. She's probably gotten into someone else's compartment by mistake. We'll find her in a few minutes."

"I hope so. Margaret's beside herself."

On second thought, Curt asked Bob to go tell his wife that he was helping with the search, and then to head for the front of the train to try to locate the *jefe de tren*. "He's the trainmaster," he explained; "you'll see *jefe* printed on his cap."

He himself went to the end car to see if the trainmaster might be there. He found only two *revisores* playing cards in an isolated compartment. After he told them what the trouble was, the fat one said he thought he knew where the *jefe* was and set out to get him. The other accompanied Curt and they made a systematic search of the toilets once again. The *revisor* also checked all the exit doors to see whether they were solidly locked. Curt felt his stomach knot—but each door was locked. And all of the toilets were free except one. The *revisor* did as he did with all the others; he knocked once, then again; then turned the handle. It was locked from inside. "Who is here?" the *revisor* said, two or three times. No answer. He banged on the door. He asked Curt to help him force the door, when suddenly it opened to reveal a flushed and angry woman of perhaps fifty. She was a heavyweight and there were drops of perspiration on her forehead.

"What an idiot! What an imbecile! What an animal! Do you call yourself a gentleman? Do you call yourself a proper conductor?" Her stays had not been put back in place; the ends of her skirt were ruffled. "When the door is locked it is locked. Must one also shout the news to the world? Must a woman in distress, an ill woman, also fight off a ruffian? The trainmaster will hear of this indignity. Idiot." Then she went off in search of the *jefe*. Which makes three in all, Curt thought.

Bob appeared once more and relayed the news that the

trainmaster and the other *revisor* were looking through the cars. So far the only unusual thing they had discovered was a chicken in third class; a woman there had carried one on board inside a cardboard suitcase with holes cut in one side. They heard a suspicious, muffled sound under her seat and came up with the chicken. But that was all, and Bob was more worried than ever.

"You don't think some pervert could have—" Bob began, but looked too sick to continue.

"I really don't think so. There's very little of that here. But"—he looked at Markle to see how he would take the suggestion—"if we don't find her in any of these sleeping compartments, I think we should have the train stopped."

Bob stared at him. Then the *jefe* entered the car and for the moment prevented any questions Bob might ask that Curt couldn't or didn't want to answer. He and the other *revisor* had checked the compartments, he told them. *"Qué sobrina!"* the *revisor* said.

"What's he say?"

"He says, 'What a niece!' "

"What's he *mean?*"

"Did you find the girl?" Curt demanded in Spanish.

"No, we did not find the little *norteamericana,*" the *jefe* said, with dignity. "This imbecile should keep his mouth shut." He withered his assistant with an official glance.

"What niece is he talking of?"

The *jefe* explained that they had found a girl about eighteen in one compartment. She was traveling with her "uncle," the mayor of a city on the east coast, near Tarragona, and she had been discovered in the berth with him. But there was no sign of the little *norteamericana.*

Curt relayed the message, sparing the details, telling Markle simply that an unmarried couple had been routed from their bed. Then he turned back to the *jefe.*

"I have an official request to make of you," he began, trying to sound as important as possible.

"What kind of request, *señor?*"

In English he said quickly, "Look, before I ask him to stop the train, I should know when you last saw Dory and how she disappeared."

Bob seemed ten years older. His eyes sagged, his lips looked puffy, his chin trembled. "Well," he began, "well, Margaret and I were sleeping in one compartment and Dory and Tommy in the other."

Oh, no, Curt thought. Jesus, no.

"About a half-hour ago Dory came to our compartment. The lights of some town we were going through interested her, and she wanted to know where we were, whether we were near Barcelona. Margaret told her no, we weren't anywhere near Barcelona, and to get back to bed." He took a deep breath. "That's the last we saw of her."

The lights must have been Calatayud, Curt figured. That was about a half-hour ago. He glanced at his watch, saw it was after midnight.

"O.K.," he said. "I don't think there's anything to get upset over, but let's have them stop the train." That sounded like nonsense even to him. He turned his attention quickly to the *jefe*, outlining as much as he thought necessary, and concluding with a line meant to appeal to the man's sense of importance, saying that it was his understanding that it was within the authority of the *jefe de tren* to stop the train in such an emergency.

Yes, the conductor said, he was empowered to stop the train if there was an emergency. He could, for example, stop it at Morés, which was next on the line. But he could not do this without evidence that there was an emergency.

"What do you want, blood?" Curt asked in Spanish. "A child is missing. The evidence of emergency is that she cannot be found. If she could be found there would be no emergency. Clear?"

There was some logic to what the *señor norteamericano* said.

Clearly. But this was not evidence. A man in the trusted position of *jefe de tren* could not stop an important train at an unscheduled siding without evidence. That also was clear.

"What's the matter?" Bob asked.

"Nothing. I'll handle it." Curt took out his Fulbright identification card, which instructed all Spanish citizens to treat him as an invited guest to their country and to afford him all the privileges his position as member of a special exchange deserved. When he had first received the card from the Intercambio in Madrid, Curt assumed it had as much influence as a library card or a Little Orphan Annie button. But it had worked wonders in hotels and at banks when his American passport failed to impress. It had the desired effect on the *jefe* as he flashed it now. Spaniards were trained, like many other Europeans—only more so—to pay attention to official language and governmental stamps of approval and privilege. All Curt had to do was give another push. He said he was attached to the American Embassy; he had had the great privilege of meeting El Caudillo in person; and this man Señor Markle, was a nephew of the American ambassador. . . .

The conductor had the train pulled onto a siding at Morés. There the search began again, this time with yardmen and the *jefe de estación* checking the exteriors of the cars, looking among tie rods and axles and coupling plates. Luckily, Margaret saw none of this and Bob was saved from most of it by accompanying Curt and the *jefe de tren* to an office telephone. Spanish telephone connections being what they were, it took almost fifteen minutes for the *jefe* to get through. He spoke briefly to the stationmaster in Calatayud, listening mainly. Then he handed the phone to Curt, with a respectful *"por favor."* His mustache was stiff and hid his thin lips. The visor of his cap shadowed his eyes.

"Yes, regrettably, a child has been found," the voice at the other end was saying, "just a few hundred meters from the station. A motorist saw something fall from the train near a crossing. He thought it was a valise." There was a pause, and then: "Who is it that I speak to? The father?"

"No, a friend of the family."

"Well, it was a child, and—Mother of God!—she is dead. Her skull was broken. . . ."

The word was *rota*. Broken. Like a machine.

Curt listened to this the way a deep-sea diver gets bad news about his air pump, feeling it directly through the weight of the water pressing upon him, the weight of his shoes holding him stock-still at the end of a death line, a mist circulating around his eyes in a warm mask, and the oxygen dwindling to nothing.

Bob Markle was separated from the truth by the language, and by the *jefe* who now spoke with merciful rapidity to Curt as he hung up the phone. He sensed that Curt might want to break the news in his own time and way to the father.

Curt looked around him, hearing Bob repeating, "Well, what is it? Tell me. Did they find her? Is she all right?" The station was dark and dirty, with scraps of paper and bits of orange peel in the corners. It smelled of urine. The walls of the little *despacho* had been stained by years of human poverty and misery, but Curt wondered whether it had ever contained this much misery before, the potential misery he held in his cracking head.

He decided he couldn't tell Markle the truth here, this way. There were too many things to do: to get Margaret and the boy off the train, and hire a car to go back to Calatayud. He could pick a time, but not now.

"Have they found her?" Bob was now shouting.

"Yes."

"Is she all right?" The voice lowered a bit, in anticipation of a shock if it should come.

"Yes," Curt said. The biggest lie of all, he thought. "Yes, she'll be all right. But we have to go back to Calatayud."

Bob searched his face, wavering before the demands of his

own logic and his desire to be appeased. Finally he accepted the news that he wanted to accept, pushing horror down into a mental box not quite large enough to enclose it—or not for long.

The ride back in the car from Morés to Calatayud was an eternity of torture for Curt and an eternity of vague terror for the Markles. The car was an old SEAT, a Fiat assembled in Spain. It was driven by someone's nephew. Curt told him not to hurry, to drive safely. There was no real hurry. But the request had had a perverse effect on the nephew, who was now intent on setting a new record for imbecile drivers on the curving, treacherous road.

For some time the boy cried steadily, having been awakened from his comfortable sleep in a lower berth on the train. When Dory had taken her fatal plunge out of the treacherous, down-sliding window, the boy had probably not even been disturbed.

"I don't know what it was made me check," Bob was saying for the third or fourth time.

"Yes," Margaret answered, also for the third or fourth time. "If you hadn't checked we might have gone right on to Barcelona before finding Dory. I hope they're taking good care of her. She must be frightened to tears."

Curt had almost blurted out the truth the first time Margaret said this. But he got better at the lying as they went along and his answers were pat—cuts and bruises, no broken bones discovered, Dory was being taken care of at the station. Even though his heart seemed to burst all its attachments, flopping around like a dying rat inside his chest, he had himself set. He would tell them at Calatayud. He would *not* make them ride this hellish stretch of road, with a champion idiot at the wheel, knowing that their child lay in Calatayud with a gashed head, drained of all that had made that small body move, made the small intelligent brain function, made those comic lips talk, smile. And you'd better stop thinking about it yourself, you stupid bastard. You've heard of death before and seen it plenty.

Yes, but they were in uniforms, mostly. They were paid to die. It came with the uniform. He could never get over the idea of civilians dying, especially women. And little kids—that was somebody else's sin, by Christ, and not his. It was the sin of whoever or whatever made a world that he, Curtis Fielding, had never made.

Finally, it was over. The lights of Calatayud—the ones that had probably piqued Dory and made her pull down the window for a better view—greeted them. The nephew got the checkered flag at the station and slowed to a stop in the parking lot. Curt gave him a *mil*, a thousand pesetas, and told him to keep the change.

"Now, here," Bob started to say, belatedly. "I should pay this—"

"Never mind, Bob. It's all right." Curt waved the driver off. Then he took Margaret by the arm and headed her toward a little café in the station. "You stay here with the baby, Margaret, while Bob and I find out about things."

"No," she said, suddenly resisting his hand. "I want to see my baby, my Dory. I want to be with Dory."

Dear sweet and loving Jesus, Curt thought, that will never happen again. "Just sit in here with the boy," he said. "We'll take care of everything. Now *sit* there."

Something in the way he said it made her will collapse. She found a hint of what she had been dreading away down in some twisted curlicue of her brain, pushed into a knot of excruciating fear. She walked into the café on legs that moved like stilts.

Curt led the way, Bob behind him. As they were about to enter the glass doors to the station proper, Bob suddenly stopped, refusing to enter the door which Curt held open for him.

"Wait a minute," he said.

Curt let the door close. Bob looked at him, his eyes pinpointing with the dread of what he was about to ask. "You haven't told us the . . . the whole truth, have you?" He almost choked.

"You haven't told us the whole . . ." he said it in a lower, weaker tone, at a loss for other, less safe words, "the whole truth. . . ."

Curt had no way of knowing what his own face looked like, but he could feel the stiffening go out of the mask. He was shaking his head and watching the effect of his unspoken answer on the man in front of him.

Suddenly Curt remembered a model airplane he'd worked on as a boy; he'd put it into his mother's oven, thinking he could bake it into toughness, but the glue had just let go and the whole thing went to pieces. That was what was happening to Bob Markle. He was shrinking from six feet three and might never straighten out again. As Curt grabbed him to keep him from buckling to the concrete platform, he caught sight of Margaret. She was peering through the café door. She must have seen their little pantomime under the lights of the entry. In a moment she was out of the café, running across the platform with her boy flapping like a tail of a kite caught in a gust of wind. Then she was there grabbing her husband, looking at Curt as though he were a monster not to be believed, something from another planet, not that solid globe, where once lived the Markles, an American family. Now an American family, minus one.

"Oh, no. Oh, no, oh, no, no, no . . ."

"Margaret, don't." Markle had straightened to nearly full height, the boy in his arms. Now she threw her arms around him and the boy. They formed a kind of pyramid. Curt took five or six deliberate steps away, just to blow his nose and clear his head.

In doing so, he spied an elderly Spanish couple, sitting on one of the outside benches with their valises at their sides. They were staring, staring, and Curt felt a dull resentment rise up in him. What the *hell* were they staring at? Couldn't they respect grief? What the hell *were* they staring at? He took a step in their direction, all his anger at the universe ready to boil over into a tirade against Spanish clods and their goddamn staring ways.

But even this wasn't going to work out, because as he got closer to the door he could see tears streaming down the Spanish faces. He couldn't even be sure they knew what they were crying for. They had just seen pure grief and couldn't hold back.

Of his own grief he was not too sure. Later, when he reviewed the whole affair, he realized how objectively, in a comparative sense, he had observed much of what took place. He saw himself as someone not within the frame but outside, wielding a case-hardened camera which separated him from the actors in the tragedy. Since *she* had ceased to exist, he had automatically resorted to a trick he'd learned in combat, pushing her out of existence entirely, as though he'd never met her. Or at least he had tried to do this and partly managed it. What he had to admit was that at the station in Calatayud, where, except for a bit of nose-blowing and a desire to bawl the Spanish couple out, he had pulled himself in tight. Just because a humpty-dumpty world had cracked open a golden-haired child it was not going to crack him. . . . My God, he told himself, you've come so far in battling off sentimentality that you've also thrown away sentiment. Maybe this is why you can't love, really love. Nothing is really going to touch you, boy. You'll kill off part of yourself before the rest can get to you, and in that way you can't really be taken, can't be suckered in. You're too smart for that.

That was the way he had got through the rest of the formalities with the Markles. He never allowed himself to think how he and Bob had taken possession of the body. It was a harsh and unremitting formality, all the way to Barcelona. He went with them. All the way to the S.S. *Augustín*, a small liner, which was the first boat out for New York. Good-bye to the Markles, all three of them. And the other.

They thanked him, they told him he was a true friend. And Curt said yes, and yes. But he could see in their eyes, especially Margaret's, that he was somehow mixed up in their daughter's accident. They were hating everything about Spain, about ever having come abroad. He doubted they would ever really want to see him again. He was both a harbinger and a reminder of horror; a reminder also that Bob and Margaret had been taking their bliss in one compartment while the kids were in another. That was probably the worst of it. As though he didn't know that kids could always make any parents feel guilty inside twenty seconds.

Certainly the Spanish knew this. They said the devil must watch after kids; no one else could possibly keep up with them. Sayings, sayings, sayings. What the hell good?

He said his good-bye on the *Augustín* and went down the gangplank fast. He did not look back. Not then.

The next day he left Barcelona in a rented SEAT. He traveled on N. II again, this time heading west. Out near Montserrat a white dust, like fine snow, scintillated under the beating sun. Off in the distance the great monastery shimmered among the white molar rocks.

Some three hours later he stopped at a restaurant on the outskirts of Lérida. He ordered some paella and the regional red wine. As he ate, he remembered that it was here, near Lérida, that George Orwell had been hospitalized during the Civil War. He thought of Orwell, wounded in the throat by the Falangists, then hounded by the Communists. . . .

His thoughts slid to Zaragoza. He had phoned Durán and everything was taken care of at the university. But Victoria would probably be wondering what had happened to him. And maybe Lois Harte and Stafford. Yes, and even Villalta. . . .

During the rest of the trip he didn't think of Dory Markle more than five or six times, and only once after Bujaraloz, where he passed the two *punto negro* signs, wondering where the good shepherd might be.

PART
FOUR

18
Almost the Season

She leaned forward and put the book on the coffee table and then sat back on the divan. For some time neither of them said anything. Silence hummed in their ears, while the Mandars on the wall stared mutely from their frames, and the sunlight slanted through the partially open shutters, plunging noiselessly into the tan-colored rug.

Finally it was Victoria who spoke: "What is the matter?" she asked softly.

Curt looked at her without seeing her face—just the black skirt with a wide black patent-leather belt, and above that a silky white blouse with lace cuffs and collar.

"Nothing," he said.

"I think something," she said. "For some weeks now."

How could he tell her that he had been moving in and out of touch with reality "for some weeks now," had been swimming with heavy arms and legs through urine-warm currents of despair, when he wanted nothing more than to sink without a struggle until, refreshed by some fresh change of current, he braced himself, felt energy return, caught a glimpse of the sun, breathed freely, and moved on toward the other swimmers. How?

"I don't know why you say that," he said. "We've been moving right along." He hitched his chin in the direction of the volume she had placed on the table, a leather marker protruding

229

from the middle pages: it lay inert, next to the tray with Calisay and the two stem glasses.

She watched him intently for a moment or two, and then with a hardly audible sigh said, "Shall we have our *copa?*"

"All right," he said.

As she leaned forward to pour the liqueur, he allowed himself to look at her again. It was a profile view, and from her left ear to the frilled collar, a line in her neck stretched taut, subtly undershadowed by a blood vessel that ran close to the surface. The skin at her temple looked waxy and parchment thin.

She was fragile, he thought. She, too, would break.

She turned then and handed him a glass of the liqueur. She picked up the other and raised it, thin wristed, saying, "*Salud,*" and sipped some of the Calisay.

"*Y amor,*" he offered, weakly echoing a response that had become a ritual between them—conscious of wanting her to question him, to be concerned with him and what it was that ailed him. He drank a little of the Calisay and put his glass down on the tray.

"You have lost your taste for it?"

"Maybe I've lost my taste for taste." It sounded dramatic and self-pitying; but in this room, in this light, and with her, maybe it was all right. What the world really needed were more nurses, not doctors.

"Curtis," she said softly, "you have not been the same since Barcelona."

"How do you mean?"

"You are just not yourself."

"Is anybody?"

"That is what I mean. You did not talk like that before. Before you were *galán,* you had force and *energía.*"

"*Energía?*" he said. "I've been working like hell—my classes at the university, the new one out at the base; here, with you. I haven't said anything about it, but I've sent off two interviews to my friend Stone, the man I told you is doing the book on your Civil War. And I have completed almost all the notes I need to begin my article. . . ."

"Yes, but—"

"And, thanks to you, I even went up and brought old Farlo back."

"You know," she said, "that is not what I mean at all."

There was more he could tell her about how busy he had kept himself: he could tell her about the three trips he had taken over the border to Orloron and Pau and Lourdes, using Stafford's list of hospitals and clinics to check on admissions corresponding to the time of Cipriano Farlo's disappearance; he could also tell her that he had discovered nothing—except that Pau had plenty of hospital facilities, once having been a haven for British tuberculars; and that Lourdes had more cripples and invalids per capita than any other place on the planet, with the possible exception of a leper colony.

"You keep busy," she was saying, "but you don't seem to have your heart in things. Before you were *muy caballero,* and *divertido.* But now, I don't know what to say. I don't want to hurt your feelings, but you are some way, ah, *dividido.* You understand?"

He shook his head. According to his nurse, he was no longer diverting, he was divided. Her diagnosis wasn't much different from what Lois had said a week or so ago, complaining that he was either a split personality or going through menopause.

"Don't you want to talk about it?" Victoria asked.

"I've already told you all about it."

"And at first I thought that it was natural for you to feel that way. Now I am not so sure."

"I'm not so sure about things, either," he said, thinking of how he had simply been going through the motions, keeping busy. He had added a number of roads to his map—through Canfranc and Candanchú, into France, and back again over the high pass, where the snow had already begun to cover the craggy mountains. It was almost the skiing season, almost Christmas, too. But he wasn't sure he wanted any of it. He wasn't even sure he wanted to find out any more about the Swiatski matter. What good would it do, his going around checking hospitals that way? The main business of life was to stay away from hospitals . . . and trains.

"Curtis." She let her left hand fall onto his on the divan. He looked at her hand, brown and tapering, almost as long as his. "I must say some things to you that I did not wish to."

She wasn't making much sense, he thought, feeling vaguely that somehow he had an advantage in a situation where he wanted no advantages. "What do you mean?" he said neutrally.

"I think that you are making yourself sick with this accident of the little girl. After all, it is only a death. And God makes us all to die."

"Doesn't He ever though!"

"But you were a soldier. You saw people die."

"People, yes, but not little kids. Listen, Victoria, you realize what a rotten place this world is when you think of what happens to kids, and I personally don't find very much use in it all. No theology helps. No gathering of little lambs to God's side. No pastoral paradise. No big picture that makes everything right, if we could only see it. That's all *merde* to me—something the living use to salve their own minds. To make ourselves understand, we're supposed to say, 'It passeth all understanding.' " He took a deep breath. "Then there's Art, and Intellect. And what do they give you? Wrappings. Fancy decoration around the *merde!*"

"Oh," she said, "oh, oh, oh. And what about *love?* Don't you know that if you could hear the way you are talking you would know that you are loving that little girl?"

"Sure. Curtis Fielding, age forty, loves Dory Markle, age nine, and not getting any older." He made a noise part way between a laugh and a snarl.

"You act bitter. But you know that what I say is true. What bothers you is that you truly care."

"About what—myself or the girl?"

"You care what happened to the girl."

"I know what happens to girls—they die young or they pile into a bed."

"Oh, *don't* talk like that. You just say these things to seem an *hombre duro,* and we both know that you are not. Also not all girls grow up to be the way you say."

"No. Some become nuns and old maids."

"Yes."

"They're dead, too."

"Or they need to be awakened."

He looked up at her. "Anybody we know?" he said.

She lowered her gaze. "Yes," she said.

Well, he thought, isn't it crazy how things work? You put out a sign saying *Closed for the duration,* and people come rapping at your door.

"You should have come around before I declared bankruptcy."

"I don't understand." She looked confused.

"Are you trying to tell me something about us, *señorita?*"

"Must you ask?" she said, her voice softly resentful.

Therapy, he thought. Was the nurse offering herself as therapy? Too fragile: she'd break.

"You're a lovely nurse," he said, "but I don't want to burden you with my problems."

"I don't know what you are talking about. But I am trying to tell you something very important in my life." She placed a hand on his sleeve, clutching it lightly. "This has not happened with me before. I mean you . . . you are the first man I am not afraid of. . . ."

She let go of the sleeve and turned away, almost as though contradicting her own statement. He watched her for some time. She looked two-dimensional, as though something were missing, some breadth of intention or motive as well as something physical. Or was it some lack of his own that refused to accept her as a whole woman? Had he in his own mind placed her inside a glass cabinet, like the wax flowers? He should be touched, moved. She was trying to come alive.

"You know," he said, wondering what his voice would say, "you know, I have been half in love with you for months."

"You don't show it."

"I have a hard time showing things." That was the truth, he thought, and so was the half-loving. It was like trying to talk to Mary from Kennedy Airport. The same thing that had drawn him into a shell when Dory died.

"I do not want to force you to say anything."

"You're not forcing, Victoria. Christ, if it hadn't been for you the last few weeks, I'd have jumped out of my skin."

"I think now that I need you, too."

He looked at her sharply, trying to see into the person that lay behind the beauty. "You mean you would consider—*everything?*"

She turned to face him, looking flustered. "I don't know what you mean."

"I mean marriage." It was as though he were trying out the word to see how it sounded.

"It is possible. It remains to be seen."

He watched her closely, trying to imagine what she'd be like back in Pennwood, say at the Beaverses'. He found it impossible to picture her in that setting.

"But I'm divorced," he said. "You've reminded me of that at least twenty times."

Her eyes were serious and patient. "I have discussed this with my mother and we do not think that it is important. After all, the church does not care because your wife was not Catholic, you were not married in the church, and there were no children."

He began to laugh softly. She looked bewildered. "What is the matter?"

"Nothing," he said, suddenly aware that the room and all its objects and the girl beside him had become tangible, fully focused, cleanly distinct, and somehow interconnected with whatever it was he could call reality.

"Why did you laugh so?"

"Nothing, only it sounded funny that you would have figured things out so thoroughly before you talked with me. Now, don't get sore, please." He reached out and grabbed her wrists. She struggled to get up but he held on. Her face was drawn close to his and her eyes looked a little wild and trapped, and then she stopped pulling away and somehow he had an arm around her and she leaned toward him and gave a small gasp and he was kissing her, not hard, and he felt there was a possibility that it would all work out. . . .

Moments later he became aware of her hands pushing against his chest and a shuffling noise coming from near the folding doors.

"*Perdóneme, señorita.*" It was one of the maids, and she looked as though someone had shoved her out to the end of a high diving board.

Victoria was on her feet, unconsciously brushing a wrinkle out of her skirt and hitching her belt around so that the buckle was centered. "*Qué quieres?*" The familiar form subjugated the maid to the level of a child or chattel. What she said was "What do you want?" but what it meant was "How dare you enter like that?"

"*Perdóneme, pero su padre acaba de llegar y desea hablarle a usted.*"

God, that was quick, Curt thought.

"*Bueno,*" Victoria said, dismissing the maid, who vanished around the corner, and could be heard in a moment or so talking in the anteroom.

"My father has come home early for lunch. Would you care to meet him?"

"Certainly. But I hope he's not carrying a shotgun."

She handed him his blue portfolio from a side table. "I don't know what you mean."

"It's an American joke."

"Oh," she said, intimating this was no time for American jokes. "Come."

They went out to the anteroom together.

Judge Mandar stood before a small oval mirror set in a high cabinet; he was smoothing his gray hair at the temples. His coat and hat hung from wooden pegs set in one side of the cabinet.

María Victoria went to him and kissed him on the cheek and said, "*Muy buenas, papá.*"

The judge was no taller than his daughter, though almost twice as broad. He was dressed in a dark gray suit, which gave boxy form to a body that looked soft and sedentary. His face was a shade darker than Victoria's; his eyes were almost black, agate hard and opaque.

As she began the introductions, Judge Mandar advanced toward Curt, offering a well-manicured hand. "*Mucho gusto, Señor Fielding.*"

"*Es un placer conocerle, Señor Mandar.*" They shook hands, and Curt added: "*Siento no saber la forma adecuada de saludar a un juez.*"

Victoria had come to her father's side and, taking his arm, said in English, "The judge is just Papá in this house. We do not let him wear his robes in judgment on us."

"That is right," the judge said, spacing the words out slowly. "At home I am Papá or Mister."

"Ah, you speak English well, Señor Mandar."

"Thank you very much. Victoria say it is barbarous."

"Oh, no, Papá. I say it is original."

They all laughed.

It was going smoothly, pleasantly. The girl obviously loved her father, and as a favorite was allowed to twist the lion's tail. Curt had expected something different, with ambassadorial stiffness, a series of movements and countermovements, like the openings in chess. The judge, however, had let him know he was certainly welcome; using a slow, painstaking English of that sort was a true gesture, offsetting the dictates of pride.

Judge Mandar switched now to Spanish for a statement that was formal. He told Curt that he was very much pleased to welcome a *catedrático* who had been of such great aid to his daughter; he and his wife were aware of the favor and honor that had been bestowed on a member of their family; they wanted it to be known now that Señor Fielding should enter their house as a friend; the *señor* should understand their natural reluctance to intrude on what had originally been a professional arrangement; but now that they understood from the lips of their daughter what a gentleman and a scholar he was, and what a student of Spanish life, they could do no less than open their doors in friendship. It was a tie, he concluded, not only between them but between their two countries.

Curt thanked him, saying that he was also aware of the honor done him. The judge offered his hand again. The black eyes met Curt's squarely. *"Bueno,"* the judge said, smiling, giving a little bow as they shook hands. *"Hasta pronto."*

"Yes," Curt said. "See you soon."

Judge Mandar patted his daughter's arm and went down the hall that led into an inner suite of rooms, the domicile proper, which Curt had never seen. It contained a mother and two sisters and a brother whom he had never seen, either.

"He liked you."

"He seems like a very capable man," Curt answered, feeling that he himself had passed some kind of an examination, with a partial verdict in. "Did you discuss all of what we were talking about with him, too?"

"Oh, no. Not entirely."

"Not *entirely?*"

"We cannot talk about it now."

"No, of course."

She offered her hand. "You will not be so unhappy now?"

"No," he said, watching her brown eyes. Somehow she had touched him, with the combination of her timidity and practicality. And now he wanted to be tender.

He reached forward quickly, took hold of her shoulder, and kissed her lightly on the coppery cheek.

"*Adiós, Señorita Mandar.*"

"*Adiós, Señor Fielding.*"

Curt walked slowly down the stairs to the ground level. The elevator in this building, as the *portero* had informed him, was safe to use only on the way up.

On the first floor, in his cubicle, the old grenadier sat hunched over sausage and a tumbler of red wine. The way he went at them showed his interest in living.

That was what was needed, Curt thought, an appetite for life. Even the carnival could be raised to a level of communion.

He threw the *portero* a half-salute as he walked by. The old man nodded, wiped his mustache with the back of his hand, and said, "*Buenos días, señor.*"

19
The Season to Be

It was Merry Christmas out at the base, *Feliz Navidad* in town. The way things had been progressing with Victoria, Curt had expected some of the *Navidad*, thinking the Mandars would at least invite him in for a drink. But they hadn't, even though he had sent them, as was the custom, a family basket packed with bottles of champagne and cognac, interspersed with fruit and sweets, and covered by transparent amber paper.

Instead, he was celebrating Christmas at the base. It started with late brunch at Lois Harte's. Afterward they drove over to the club, which was festooned with red and green decorations looped from the walls and ceilings. In the main room stood a twenty-foot Spanish pine, branches drooping under the burden of shiny ornaments, strings of lights, and candy canes. Heaped beneath the tree were a hundred small boxes colorfully wrapped and ribboned—presents to be handed out to the children of the base later that afternoon.

Santa Claus was warming up for his task by serving free drinks at the bar, collaborating with Uncle Sam in the task of transplanting good cheer and peace on earth militarily.

When the kids began to arrive, Lois and Curt went on to the Staffords', where they were expected for cocktails. Albert Stafford met them at the door, sporting a necktie whose colors would have impressed even a man with cataracts. He kissed Lois and took Curt's hand in an exchange of Merry Christmases.

As he ushered them into the living room, he asked Curt, "How're things going? Anything new?"

He was referring to the list of hospitals and Curt's search. "Not a thing," Curt answered.

Lois gave them a crinkled-brow look, as if to say, What are you two talking about?

"Well, something may be happening here. Tom Pardee was called into town a couple hours ago."

"Oh?"

All the senior officers and their wives were present. Curt and Lois mingled and merged, and the afternoon wore its way into a mixed memory of small talk, new ties and dresses, some selective kissing under the mistletoe. In the background Bing Crosby gave way to Johnny Mathis, who in turn gave way to an English quartet that sounded beautifully castrated, as the hi-fi musicale moved in three-minute shifts the entire distance between "White Christmas" and "Good King Wenceslas."

At about four-thirty Colonel Ogondez arrived in full uniform with his beautiful *señora*. No one dared to kiss her under the mistletoe, although she stood under it several times, unaware of the custom and the lack of military courage surrounding her. After one drink, they left and, in the subsequent lull, Colonel Bolen and Captain La Rosa felt it necessary to show their stuff out on the driveway with the La Rosa boy's new bike. La Rosa had just managed a one-handed, figure-eight turn, which drew mock applause from the spectators, when Tom Pardee pulled up in his officially stenciled jeep.

They all came into the house. Pardee's face looked even more puffy and red than usual. With a drink pressed into his hand, he began to explain where he'd been and why he was late: four of their men had been "shacked up" with two professional *chicas* for a couple of days and nights, and when the girls insisted on going home for the *Navidad* all hell broke loose. Pardee had to get the airmen out of the local hoosegow and deposit them in the stockade.

"Is Villalta taking care of it?" the colonel asked.

"Yes, he got the charge changed from kidnaping."

Someone said, "To what? Disturbing the piece?" They all laughed.

Not long afterward the party at the Staffords' began to break up. Colonel Bolen and his wife left first, releasing the rest of them. Curt drove Lois to her place, where she got her MG, and then they drove separately the five or six blocks to Sergeant Sterner's house in the enlisted men's area.

It had all been arranged.

First Sergeant Sterner was now one of Curt's star pupils in Overseas Instruction 105: Introduction to Literature. For a twenty-year man, Sterner had displayed a surprising streak of romantic appreciation for the poetry of Keats and Shelley, as well as a more predictable admiration for the fiction of Kipling, whose "The Man Who Would Be King" became his favorite story. His wife, Ruth, had written to Lois and Curt asking them to "come spend an old-fashioned Christmas dinner with us and our son, Ogden." Lois had accepted, but only after making a separate arrangement with Curt: At about ten she would beg off and say she had to return to the Staffords' to help out there because of Polly. It was a plausible excuse, since Polly Stafford hardly ever felt well; she almost always drank too much and became ill. But Lois would not be headed on any mission of mercy. She had a date with her Joe in the apartment they had so tastefully decorated together in town. "Joe's become more important to me than ever," she told Curt, "especially since you've retired from the field."

Dinner over, Lois helped Ruth Sterner clear away. It had been a good enough meal. Air Force Exchange food had a peculiar taste, as though someone had managed to preserve it in sawdust. Ruth had served the AFX special—turkey stuffed with chestnuts. It came close to what you remembered. The canned cranberry sauce was better, and the Spanish champagne helped.

Almost on schedule, Lois made her escape. With knowing looks about Polly's condition, Ruth and Ralph said they certainly understood. Under the mistletoe at the front door, Lois took a kiss from each of the men. She threw one to young Ogden, who was too busy with an Erector set near the tree to notice, and had to be coaxed by his mother to say good night to "Aunt" Lois.

Lois' hand now fluttered like a released dove. "Good night," she said, "and Merry Christmas."

"Merry Christmas."

And give my respects to St. Joseph, Curt thought.

"Do come and see us more often," Ruth said at the open door. She stood there for a moment watching. Then she closed the door reluctantly. Turning toward the men, she said, "Well," and clapped her hands lightly together, as though to signify that one thing was over and another about to begin. "Can I get you two gentlemen some more coffee to go with your cognac?"

Curt watched her move toward the kitchen, a figure of forced merriment. Her left hand reached out automatically to pat a decorative doily on the alcove table into place. From outside came the metallic harrumph of Lois' MG. He wondered whether Ruth would like to change places with her, heading for a rendezvous of sensual thrills and mind-easing entanglement. Not much chance, he thought, not with that dried-apricot face. If he was any judge, little Ogden was Ruth's only love. What was wrong with people who could love only children? Curtis Fielding loves Dory Markle . . . loves María Victoria?

Ralph had busied himself at the hi-fi, an intricate and expensive outfit, and now waved his guest to a comfortable armchair in the living area. "Bach and Courvoisier," he said.

"Good," Curt said, rather absently, and sat down. Sterner gave him his snifter and sat on the sofa.

There was no need to talk. The music had started. Curt

thought of earlier Christmases back in Hazleton. The distance between the sad-faced Ruth and her husband reminded him of his own parents, when he was Ogden's age and perhaps as spoiled. Children and parents. Dory Markle. Golden hair, turned-up nose—starting to rot by now. . . . He felt chill perspiration seep into his shirt and trousers, which turned sticky against the flesh. How were the Markles celebrating their Christmas? *Celebrating?* He drank deep of the cognac and felt it warm someone or something inside. He shoved his legs out as he slumped down in the chair and let the music fill the crevices in his brain with nonmessages. . . .

When Ruth returned with the coffee and placed it on the table before them, and then turned her attention to shuffling little Ogden off to his room with a promise to read him asleep with the rest of their Christmas story, it was as though her actions and the boy's wheedling complaints took place on a side stage, in another dimension of time and space, away from him and Landowska, who never wavered in the process of pouring Bach through her finger tips.

Later, some time later, when the last of the Bach seesawed to a tremolo conclusion, Ralph Sterner rose to his feet, put the machine to rest, and turned triumphantly: "Can you tell me, Doctor, what the hell is better than that!"

Curt roused himself, sitting up. "Nope, I can't."

"I used to think women," Sterner said. His pencil-line mustache seemed out of place on his square face; it made him look like a detective-turned-floorwalker.

"Well, old Landowska was a woman. Wanda."

Sterner smiled. "I *know,* but you know what I mean."

"I do indeed."

"Then I thought cars for a while."

"Cars?"

"Uh-huh. They're still a kind of hobby, but I don't race them any more."

"You're a bundle of hidden interests," Curt said, thinking

there'd been no first sergeants like this in any of his outfits.

"Well, it wasn't big time. I did some of the minor circuits in France and Italy."

"What was it like?"

"Hell of a fine feeling. Over a hundred miles an hour driving's an entirely different thing."

"Why'd you stop?"

"Don't know." Sterner shook his head. "I saw some people killed, some crippled. But you expected that, like the fear. I don't know—suddenly it just seemed silly, useless. In fact, I began to lose interest in a lot of things about the same time."

"It happens to everybody."

"Maybe so. And maybe that's why I'm giving this literature stuff a chance. Lately I been thinking what to do when I get out of this man's army, and I've come up with the idea maybe I could get a job, maybe in a military depot or something, near a college, and I could get an education. Pretty stupid, huh? I mean for someone over forty."

"Of couse not," Curt said, and delivered a short, encouraging speech about how old many graduate students were, as well as all those ex-G.I.'s after World War II.

Sterner listened with the attentiveness of a freshman. When Curt finished, he nodded his head. "I know you're right," he said. "Let me get us some more of this." He poured the shallow remains of the decanter into Curt's snifter and then went off to the kitchen.

Curt could hear a short, muffled conversation in the other room. His mind went back to Sterner and his interest in cars. The nub of a question formed itself into a line of inquiry.

Sterner returned with a full bottle of Courvoisier, holding it up like a trophy.

"Just this last drink," Curt said, letting his host add to his glass, "and then I think I should be going." He looked at his wristwatch. Twelve-thirty and no longer Christmas. How was Joe liking *it* by now . . . ?

"Hell, no, Doctor, you don't have to go so early," Sterner was saying. "You're part of the family tonight. Isn't he, Ruth?"

Ruth had entered the room. "That's right," she said, sitting in the other overstuffed chair, legs folding under her like retractable gear. "We're really proud to have your company, Dr. Fielding."

The way she said it embarrassed him: What she meant was that socially you'd expect a professor to buddy with the officers, not enlisted men and their wives.

"Where else could I have gotten such a splendid meal?" he said. "And a touch of home-style Christmas?"

"Oh, I'm so glad you feel that way," she said. The erosive lines of her face parenthesized her smile like a series of infinite ripples.

Jesus, she was sad, Curt thought. Obviously Ralph's fading interest in life included her. What she had left was little Ogden; for him she fought the daily battle of maintaining a gay spirit and the house beautiful.

"Ralph," he said, "I wanted to ask you something about cars, since they're your hobby."

"Oh, that *is* Ralph's fort-ay. He'll soon be too technical for either of us."

They all smiled.

"I'm curious about what happens to the cars of base personnel when they're wrecked—you know, like this one up in Andorra a couple of months ago."

"Depends," Sterner said. "Some are just scrapped. You've probably seen some of the hulks up by the motor pool."

"Drive carefully—or."

"Right. Some go there. Some are bought by Spanish garages."

"No one on base ever buy them?"

"Yeah, now and then. And we have the facilities for them. You know the old man had a double garage built for guys to tinker with their cars. Fact, I'm in charge of it, and we've got as good tools as any hot-rod shop. Even a crane for lifting motors."

"Sounds great."

"Ralph spends hours there in the evening, but Ogden doesn't seem to take any interest. I guess he's not going to be a grease monkey."

"It's a fine setup," Sterner said, ignoring his wife. "We have to schedule it just right to keep people happy."

"It is mostly maintenance and repair work?"

"Yes, but some of the wrecks you're talking about we strip, use the parts, do complete overhauls. I took a Chevy-8 motor out of one myself and put it in my little Pontiac Tempest. I can get that baby up from stop to one hundred and ten miles per in twenty seconds."

"When you can get it to go."

He gave her a quick, hard look. "Well, I had to machine some of the parts with a Spanish joker in town. The motor's too big, and the torque is tremendous for that setup. So there are still some bugs in it. It stalls now and then. But when I get it right, there won't be anyone around with as much car for under six thousand."

"Where'd you get the Chevy motor?" Curt was again trying to keep his question casual.

"Two of our guys missed a turn up near Morato. They spun, came out of it, and smacked into a big tree—backward!"

"Backward?"

"Yup. Only thing saved them. And the motor. Car was a total. Except for the motor. I dickered with Crosby for it before they shipped him down to Torrejón. Got it for seventy-five. Crosby didn't much care. He was pretty bad off—"

"Was it a convertible? Or would the motor have been more powerful from a convertible?"

"Depends. In 1963 Chevy began putting a 327 into some of its convertibles and other models. Deke Smith latched onto one of those about a year ago—from a wreck that killed one of our boys."

Curt felt his own motor miss slightly. "Who was that?" he said, trying to keep the excitement out of his voice.

"A kid by the name of Swiatski. One of the best in the outfit until—"

"I remember him, Ralph. The one who was so brusque and polite at the same time, and real nice looking."

"How did the wreck come in?"

"Bad. Burnt out. I helped Deke try to get the carbon out of the hardware, but it never did work right after . . ." He stopped for a moment, rubbing his chin. "Funny thing about that car."

"What's that?"

"Well, it looked like a brake-failure job, but you couldn't tell anything about the lining or fluid—you know, a mess. But the emergency linkage had been disconnected."

"You mean broken."

"I don't think so. I remember Deke and me looked that over for a long time. We figured some Spanish mechanic didn't know his elbow from a grease pan got monkeying around, screwed up the works, and then just left it that way."

"Did you ever say anything about this? I mean officially?"

"Oh, no. What was the use? You couldn't show anything more than that."

Curt didn't agree, but he wasn't going to say so. Instead he tried to cover his tracks. "And so the motor never worked out for this other fellow?"

"No. We must've put in a couple hundred hours apiece on that baby and it never did anything but cough and sputter. Deke finally bought a VW Microbus from a guy shipping home."

"That's what we should do, too. Ogden would like one of those, Ralph."

"Maybe, dear."

"Well, listen, you folks," Curt said, getting to his feet. "I want to thank you for a wonderful meal and the Christmas cheer. It was like being home for a while." He felt the shaft of unintentional irony.

At the door, making his farewell, he brushed Ruth's eroded cheek with a kiss. *"Feliz Navidad,"* he said. "And many thanks, Ruth."

He thought she was going to cry. "You're always welcome, Dr. Fielding."

Sterner walked out to the car with him. They shook hands in the snowless Spanish night. There was a skyful of moonlit clouds, streaked gray and black and purple.

"Funny kind of Christmas," Sterner said.

"You said it. But I want to thank you for taking care of me."

"Nada, hombre," Sterner said.

As Curt slid into the VW and was about to close the door, he felt the opposing pressure of Sterner's hand holding the door open.

"Something just crossed my mind," he said. "About that Chevy convertible."

"Swiatski's?"

"Yeah. He had a real good buddy on base. Still here, as a matter of fact. Deke and I were having a drink at the club one night and we told him about this emergency brake stuff, and he took it real hard. Couldn't figure him out. He swore it wasn't an accident. So I told him to see the provost marshal if he felt that way."

"Pardee?"

"Yeah."

"And did he?"

"I dunno. As I remember, all he said was 'What the hell good will it do?' "

"What's this friend's name?"

"Mike Dalton."

Curt could sense the other man's wanting to ask why he wanted to know. "He's not a tall blond-haired kid, is he?"

"Yeah. You know him?"

"I think I saw him in the Cancela once. He got into some trouble with Pardee. That's why I asked."

"Oh." Sterner didn't believe him, but wasn't going to push. "Well, good night, Ralph."

"Night, Doctor, and Merry Christmas."

Back in town Curt found a place to park about a block up the Gran Vía from his apartment. The streets were quiet, except for a late *tranvía*, rattling loosely along with only a few passengers aboard. Everybody was home with their everyones, he thought. E. E. Cummings.

He walked past the travel agency and the SEAT salesroom and the place that sold the books and cards, and then past the Italian *gelatería* and the *bombonería*. Standing in the doorway of the *bombonería*, like a gray ghost, was a *sereno*. For a moment Curt thought he was asleep standing up, leaning there in the corner; but out of the gray muffler came a greeting, low and reassuring: *"Buenas noches, señor, y Feliz Navidad."*

Curt wished him a Happy Christmas and a New Year of fortune. The *sereno* rustled himself out of his nook and fell into step with Curt, his huge ring of keys jingling every other step they took.

"Do you find it cold tonight?" Curt asked.

"Cold enough," the man said. "Colder than some Christmases, but not so cold as others."

"In my country there is almost always the snow. Much snow."

"To the north there is much snow in the Pyrenees, and to the west on the Moncayo, and to the south in the Guadarramas."

"But here along the Ebro, no."

"No. Here in Zaragoza it is more like the real Christmas."

"True," Curt said.

They had reached his apartment. The *sereno* jangled his ring and found the right key. He drew the door open and stood aside. Curt gave him a hundred-peseta bill.

"No, *señor*," the man protested. "It is too much."

"For the many times, and for the New Year."

The man shifted his wooden truncheon to his left hand with the ring of keys and, touching the brim of his gray cap, said, "Good. I am at your service."

Curt walked into the lobby and up the half-flight of marble stairs that led to the elevators and the *portero's* glassed-in cubicle. Out of habit he went into the cubicle to check for mail, and just as he reminded himself there had been no deliveries today, he caught sight of a white envelope in his box. He unlocked the box and took the envelope out. It bore no stamps, just his name scrawled in black ink.

Amigo, the note inside said: *I came to see you on this Nativity, but you were not home. I hope you are having a Merry Christmas. Can you meet with me tomorrow? The Vegas at eleven in the morning. It is important, but not to worry about. We must talk.* It was signed Francisco.

20
To Candanchú

The next morning Curt found the Vegas packed with day-after-Christmas patrons. Some twenty of them stood at the pastry counter waiting for take-outs. Others gathered around the serving counter in a welter of hands, arms, and coffee cups. By pressing through to the back section of the restaurant he managed to get a small table just as a couple were leaving. It was underneath the spiral stairs that led to an upstairs dining room, but by craning his neck he could keep watch on the bustling entryway.

Some five minutes later he spotted Villalta, easing himself through the crowd, shucking off his trench coat. In his dark blue suit he looked very sharp and very Spanish, like something left over from the Armada and the conquistadors. He stood looking around with that captured hawk's glance of his.

Curt stood up and waved. Villalta saw him and started toward the table. As he got near, his voice cut through the intervening noises.

"*Hola, hombre, que tal?*"

Curt endured the Spanish embrace, wondering what María Maite would say if she saw him now.

"*Bien, bien,*" he said, in an effort to sound cheerful.

They sat down, Villalta flopping his trench coat over a nearby chair.

"You are looking good, Curtis." He gave Curt's face a

mock physician's examination. "Only a little bit tired. You been traveling too much?"

Curt looked at him sharply. Villalta's expression was ambiguous; his smile could have meant anything.

He tried to smooth ruffled feathers as he went on. "I mean, Victoria has told me about the little *americana. Muy triste,* Curtis."

"It wasn't very nice."

"You should have called me to help."

"There wasn't anything to do."

The waiter brought their *completos.* Curt put sugar and cream in his coffee, broke a croissant, and began buttering it. Talking about Dory Markle depressed him. He wished Villalta would get the hell to the point. Hadn't his note said important!

But Villalta seemed to be in no hurry. With a piece of croissant in his hand, he said, "I understand how busy you must be. I know you are teaching out at the base, too. Lois has kept me informed."

Curt felt his patience dissolve into resentment. "Seems you're always well informed."

"Well." Villalta smiled. "I just hear things from friends."

"Me too. And what I hear is that my friend Francisco Villalta is a man of many parts. He is not just a lawyer; he works for the base *and* for the Brigada Social, and God knows what all."

The smile on Villalta's face broadened. "Now," he said, "you have discovered how it is with us poor Spanish. We cannot do with just one job. It is the *economía.*"

"It must be tough on you. I hear it's hard to serve two masters."

"Ah, yes. 'For you will learn to love the one and hate the other,' no?"

"That's right."

"But doesn't the Bible also tell us we must render unto Caesar what is Caesar's?" Villalta spread his hands wide. "And here we live in the old city of Caesar Augusta—Zaragoza."

"Caesar is the state. I think it's possible to render too much to the state."

"*Claro, hombre,*" Villalta said, wiping some butter from his upper lip. "But we must have a strong state to hold the passions of the poor Spanish people in control."

"I know all of that argument. I've heard it before. The Spanish aren't ready for democratic freedom. They are too passionate, too ignorant. What they need is a strong paternal regime. Big Papa. Even the people themselves admit it. The Pope in Rome, the Caudillo in Madrid, and Papa in the home."

"What would happen if the anarchists were in power here, Curtis? Maybe you would not be here. Maybe in Greece or Italy."

"Is that what you meant in your note?" Curt said, impatiently. "You wanted to discuss Mediterranean politics!"

Villalta laughed good-naturedly, wiping his hands on his napkin. "No, I do not want to discuss politics. I wish to talk about us. I must confess it, *amigo,* that I have missed your company. And the other day when I was talking with María Victoria, I got wonderful idea."

"Namely."

"Well, she happened to mention that you have an *afición* for to ski."

"Yes," Curt said, somewhat taken aback. "I mentioned I was thinking about some skiing over the holiday." He had asked her what she knew about La Molina, Andorra, and Candanchú.

"Well, that is my idea. That we all go to ski together."

"All?"

"*Sí.* You and me, Victoria and Lois Harte. With the four it is correct. Lois is the *compañera.*"

In spite of himself Curt had to smile. The system of companions had replaced that of the *dueña* in preserving a girl's reputation. "Some *compañera,*" he said.

Villalta smiled back in collusion. "It will be all right."

"I knew Lois skied, but not Victoria."

"She wants to learn."

"And how about you?"

Villalta twisted his right hand—like this, like that. "I ski a little."

"Which must mean you're *un campeón de las pistas.*"

"Oh, no. But I took my military training with the mountain troops, in Jaca."

Curt felt some of his resentment against Villalta dissolve. He was unwillingly attracted to the idea of a ski party, especially since it meant having Victoria with him. Just one thought bothered him at the moment, and he voiced it.

"Why didn't either of the girls mention this fiesta in the snow to me?"

Villalta winked, held an index finger up in the air, and said, "It is a surprise party. María Victoria told me that you very much need a holiday. I make the plan. Everything is all arranged."

"For where?"

"Candanchú. Do you know it?"

"Yes. But I was thinking of Andorra. All I had sent over were my ski boots, and I understand Andorra's the place to buy equipment cheap."

"Listen, don't worry about equipment. I have a friend who owns a shop in Jaca. There you can get all kinds of equipment, very good and very cheap. Also, I have arranged for reservations. The first night in the Gran at Jaca, then four nights at the Hotel Somport up in the pass."

Suspicion nagged at Curt again. He had become accustomed to seeing shadows wherever Villalta moved, and he couldn't help wondering why he had gone to all the trouble of arranging everything.

Villalta had taken something from his inside pocket and now placed it in front of Curt. It was a tourist folder with CANFRANC-CANDANCHÚ printed on the outer fold, along with a picture of the Somport Tunnel, which led into France. The inner folds contained more photographs and a map. There was a picture of the huge combination railroad station and hotel at Canfranc, and another of the major ski mountain, El Tobazo. Candanchú, which made Curt think of something Chinese, was a spot on the highway just a few hundred yards from the frontier; it was also the name of a deep valley that fell some six thousand feet from the pass to the foothills below. Spanish prose advertised the *pistas*, or trails, as excellent for the "practice of skiing by *aficionados* of the sport." These *pistas* were "extensive and various, proper for national and international competition."

"Looks good," Curt said, looking up from the folder. He said nothing about having been through the pass at Candanchú less than two weeks ago, and seeing the early snows piling up on Tobazo. If Villalta knew about the trips into France, then he knew; if he wanted to mention them, let him. Now.

"Good," Villalta said. "I have arranged for us to leave Wednesday if possible. Is that all right for you?"

"Fine."

"*Bueno.* I will call and confirm the reservations. How about tonight we have a drink here with the girls, and we can complete the plans?"

"All right," Curt said, with only the smallest of nagging doubts.

According to plan, Lois arrived at Curt's apartment building at ten-thirty Wednesday morning. He was downstairs waiting, and helped bring her stuff into the foyer from Rita La Rosa's car. Then they went out to say good-bye to Rita, who wished them a perfectly wonderful time and said she wished she were coming along. When Rita finally pulled away, with Lois at the curb waving, Curt saw that they had attracted quite a little attention.

"We'd better get inside," he said, "before there's a slaughter on Calvo Sotelo."

Lois giggled appreciatively. She wore a tight blue sweater and a pair of cerise *après-ski* pants. Several men stopped to stare, and an old lady looked as though she might attack her. Girls did not wear slacks of any kind in Zaragoza, and these pants were threatening the lives of pedestrians and motorists.

"You're getting to be quite the Puritan," Lois said, as they entered the foyer.

"Just trying to prevent an international incident," he said. "Besides, you told me there's a military directive against women from the base wearing slacks in town."

"These aren't *slacks*," she said, running a hand down one leg.

The *portero* had stationed himself on the first landing near the elevator. He bowed toward them now, his eyes popping like grapes.

"Our friend thinks you're good enough to eat," Curt said.

"I wish you still did." Her eyes slitted almost shut. "We could run upstairs right now."

"Cut it out."

"I'd like you right now, Curt." Her lips rounded and kissed the air. "One way or the other."

"Forget it." He busied himself by lashing her ski poles to her Head "Standards" so that they could be transported together. As he did so, a sudden thought struck him. Was *that* the way Villalta figured this trip? He'd get all hot and bothered by Lois somewhere along the line and ruin himself with Victoria. Was that it?

"Listen," he said. "All that's finished. We talked it all over."

"I know, dear. I just want you to know you can have it whenever you want."

"Thanks," he said flatly.

"You really are sweet on her, aren't you?"

"Who?"

"Oh, come on, darling. Victoria."

He straightened up from the skis. "Yes. I am 'sweet' on her."

"I guess I knew all along it would happen. The other night I was sure. I just hope you know what you're getting into."

"I'm not getting *into* anything."

"Poor boy."

A few minutes later Villalta and Victoria pulled up in front of the building in his four-door SEAT, one pair of skis and poles in the rack mounted on the roof. They both got out of the car. Victoria, Curt noticed, was wearing a gray skirt and navy blazer. She looked lithely severe, her hair piled into a tight coil, making her appear taller than usual.

"Hola, esquiadores," Villalta greeted them in his grand manner. *"Vámonos a las montañas."*

The two men packed the trunk and latched Lois' skis and poles into the rack, while the girls admired each other's outfit and told each other how badly they would perform on the ski slopes.

Villalta's Rossignol metal skis and long-thong bindings convinced Curt he was no novice. "Very nice," he said.

"Not bad," Villalta admitted. He walked around the car checking the ski rack. Then he slapped the roof and said, "O.K. We are ready for the mountains. Come on, little *rubia,* you sit up front where you can see.

"Oh, *gracias señor,"* Lois said. "You are so considerate of little old me."

That seemed to settle something, Curt thought, getting into the back seat with Victoria. His eyes sought hers and she smiled contentedly. Before they had crossed the Puente del Pilar, they were holding hands, listening to the two up front chatting about what the snow would be like at Candanchú.

They went out past the Estación del Norte and the Academia Militar. Just outside town they stopped at a gas station, with the usual bar-restaurant attached. Villalta went into the bar while the attendant was filling the tank, and came back out with a bottle of red wine and another of Quarenta-y-tres, a tawny-colored liqueur. He handed these in to Lois and from his pocket took a map, which he unfolded to a certain section and passed through the open window to Curt.

"This is the route we take," he said. "National twenty-three. We go through Huesca, then to Ayerbe, then straight north, you see, to Jaca. Then we are only thirty kilometers from Candanchú."

"Uh-huh, I see," Curt said, feigning interest in a route he knew almost by heart, trying to decide whether there was any irony in Villalta's voice.

They reached Huesca by noon and opened the Quarenta-y-tres to celebrate. Lois got two small metal cups out of the glove compartment, filling one for Victoria and the other for herself. The men drank from the bottle. Villalta offered a toast to them, their holiday, and the ancient city of Huesca, which he informed them had a venerable history that went back some four hundred years before Christ.

As they drove through town, Curt caught sight of a certain street off to the right, where old Farlo had lived. . . .

Beyond Huesca the landscape quickly changed. Suddenly they were out of the lunar hills and dusty mesas of the lower Aragón. They passed by large sections of evergreens that rose tall and full-limbed. After Ayerbe the piedmont gave way to abrupt, twisting descents and tortuous rises. Deep down in a river gorge they saw the remains of a bombed-out bridge, a crumbled reminder of the Civil War.

Soon the temperature in the car began to fall and Villalta turned the heater on full force. They were not far from Jaca now. After cutting through a range of mountains, they drove for some ten or fifteen kilometers along a stretch of road that paralleled the low banks of a river. White boulders shone through the slate-blue water. Thin shelves of ice edged the shores. Here and there in the shade of pine trees lay patches of crumpled snow.

"Now I'm beginning to think it's really Christmastime," Lois said.

"And for the first time I truly believe we are going to practice the ski," Victoria said.

As they came within sight of Jaca they saw much of the wall that surrounded the city, as well as a series of high-roofed buildings off to the right.

"My old home," Villalta said. "Those are the barracks of the mountain troops."

They entered the town, and it was as though they had passed into another country. Here the streets and buildings were moistly dark, not powdery gray like those of Huesca and Zaragoza. The roofs here were steeply pitched. Pedestrians wore heavy, informal clothing. As they drove toward the main plaza they passed several cars with racked skis. This was the New England of Spain, or perhaps the Nevada, where the mountains to the north loomed as high as the clouds and squeezed the horizon shut.

At the plaza Villalta turned left and drove down an avenue lined with snow-tipped poplars. Then he turned left once again and they entered a graveled courtyard, where the snow had been shoved into angled banks against the walls.

"This *is* lovely," Lois said.

"*Muy moderno, no?*" Villalta said.

The hotel was a white, two-storied building with red-tiled roof. Out front was a porte-cochere, and behind that a wide expanse of glass window walls. Double glass doors led into a brightly lit lobby. The place couldn't have been more than two or three years old, and it struck Curt as the most clinically clean and functional building he had seen in Spain. Two uniformed porters came out under the porte-cochere to handle the baggage and skis.

Villalta led the party to the desk inside. A heavy-set man in dark coat and striped trousers came out of his office to greet

Villalta, who introduced him to the others as his good friend, Señor García-Echague.

García-Echague shook hands all around. He assured them that their rooms were ready, and that he would have some *tapas* and sandwiches prepared for them at the bar, if they wished. He had called the sports shop to tell them of their coming, as Señor Villalta had instructed. Also he had phoned Candanchú that morning and inquired about snow conditions. *"Estupendo,"* he summed matters up, drawing out the third syllable.

As they followed the porters down the hall to their rooms, Lois said, "Our Frankie really takes care of everything."

And will probably take care of you, Curt thought.

"It is my job," Villalta said, "as the *administrador* of the expedition."

After washing up, Curt went out to the bar. It was a pine-paneled room, light and airy. None of the others were there. He ordered a Martini, and a few minutes later was joined by Lois, who asked for the same. Here in this setting her *après-ski* outfit seemed more appropriate.

"Lovely," she said, twitching her blond pony-tail as she looked around the room. "I'm really glad we didn't go to Andorra now."

Curt felt something go click inside his head. There had been nothing said about Andorra the night they had made their plans at the Vegas. The talk had all been Candanchú.

"Had you thought of going to Andorra?" he said carefully.

"Well, I suggested it to Francisco. I heard it was a wonderful ski area where you can pick up darling outfits practically at cost. But he thought we'd be better off coming to Candanchú."

As he took a sip of his Martini, Curt made a mental note to ask Victoria sometime whether she had wanted to go to Andorra also. That, he thought, would have made it three to one. . . .

21
Somport

The cable rattled through the pulley wheels overhead and the chair swung up level with the landing platform. Curt kept the heads of his skis tipped up and in a moment felt the tails scratch on the icy snow. He stood, pushing against the seat, getting free of it and then, with his skis spread slightly, schussed the steep ramp to the bottom—there making an abrupt stop-turn, so that he was facing down the mountain. At one side of the path stood a wooden post with a blue-circle placard that warned skiers this was a most difficult trail. He slipped his gloved hands into the straps of his poles, yanked on the grips, and pushed off, skiing down a short dip, and making another stop-turn.

From here, using his poles like short crutches as he leaned forward, he could look out over the rim of the mountain. The wind hummed in his ears and the sun beat warmly against his back.

This was one of the moments in skiing he liked most of all, and he often forgot to enjoy it, because when he skied with friends, they usually just got set, picked a line of descent, and pushed off. Now, alone, he had a chance to gaze out over the three-thousand-foot drop of El Tobazo. It was like standing on the ledge of a building, getting ready to leap, feeling that through some miracle of free fall you could still make it to the bottom unharmed.

Before him Tobazo sloped down some two miles to where a

creek wound its way alternately black and white through the narrow valley. Beyond the creek the Somport rose to form the last, sharp ridge between Spain and France. He let his eyes follow the twisting climb of the highway, up from the bridge that crossed the creek, past the cluster of three hotels, up to the Spanish customs shed, and then up beyond that to the very top of the pass and the French *douane*.

He scanned down the highway to the loading area of the big *telesquí* just below the hotels. There miniature dolls attached themselves to invisible seats and came swinging gently out across the creek. At the halfway station they were believable midgets; up beyond that they achieved a stature and a completeness that included ears and noses, as well as voices that could be heard like the occasional cries of birds.

Again his gaze shifted across the valley to the left of the highway, where their hotel stood in its own small clearing—a squat box of dark wood whose tiny glass slits glared red in the falling sun. Up beyond that were four larger boxes, the barracks of the mountain troops—some of whom now formed a brown thread of a line, where tow ropes operated on a gentle slope for beginners. He squinted hard, searching the civilian area, trying to make out which of the colored ants might be Victoria. Just a half-hour ago he had been there teaching her snowplow turns; but now, even knowing she must be there, he couldn't rid himself of the feeling that life below was impossibly silly and futile. Nothing that small could matter to the gods. It was the view from Olympus that distinguished gods from men; and later, when he made his descent, he too would become one of the ants; his titanship was temporary.

He picked out a line of descent: the snowy slopes fell away in fields of varying shades—white, gray, bluish-gray, purplish-gray, and in places, where boulders and hillocks threw shadows, black. El Tobazo gave no sign of tree or bush; whatever small vegetation it supported was blanketed for the winter. Even the huge humps of rock and corniced outcroppings, which he had

seen on his early trips to France, were now giant fists and knotty
spines gauzed and furred over with snow. For a moment, poised
there, he felt caught in the grip of a glacial world—like that
small puff of a cloud a thousand feet below, and the dark V
of a hawk just there to the north. . . .

Behind him the pulley wheels of the chair lift squeaked and
someone said in Spanish, "*Jesús,* is it heaven?" and another voice,
feminine, exclaimed, "Ayiie, how high!"

Curt turned to watch the man and woman schuss the ramp,
pause, and then ski down the path to where he stood.

"*Hola,*" the man said. "How is the slope?"

"*Enorme,*" Curt said.

"*Es difícil?*" The girl was small and neatly made; she wore
a tan one-piece ski suit and a conical fur hat almost half as tall
as she was.

"Not very difficult," Curt said. "Only here in the first section. The . . . chimney." That wasn't the right word for it,
but he couldn't think of the Spanish for chute.

"It appears very perilous," the girl said, sucking her lower lip,
"and we are not skiers of the first category."

The man looked unhappy with her confession.

Curt said, "I watched you come off the ski lift and you do
the parallel turns very well. If you go softly down the chimney,
the rest of the trail should not be too difficult. You will see
where the others have traversed."

"Do you descend now?" the man said.

"No, I wait for a friend."

"Well," the man said. "Many thanks for the information. We
will go softly." He turned to the girl, saying, "*Vamos a ver,
chica.*"

The Spaniard slipped over the ledge and schussed the narrow
path down to where the chute began, making a quick check
turn there. Then he was in the chute, flicking his poles fast,
doing very well for the first fifty yards until, seeming to lose
his nerve, he tried to stop, and his feet went out from under

him and he began sliding and then twisting and finally rolling, all for some thirty yards, until finally, his hands clawing like brakes, he got some purchase in the side bank of loose snow and came to a dragging stop.

"Ayiie . . . ayiie . . . ayiie," the girl kept saying. "Poor Felipe!"

"I believe he is well," Curt said. "See."

The man was already waving, signaling he was all right.

"Thank God!" the girl said. "But I will descend on foot."

"Better to go back and ride the ski lift," Curt said.

"*Sí,*" she said reluctantly.

"However, you could try it this way." Curt did a side-slip and a stop. "*Comprende?*"

She looked doubtful. Then she executed the same maneuver.

"Good, perfect," Curt said.

She gave him a comic grin, tugging her hat down firmly. "We are going to see. *Gracias, señor.*"

After some five minutes of careful side-slipping she had almost reached her companion, who was bending over, adjusting his bindings, when she fell and took him with her, so that they slid the remaining twenty yards of the chute in a revolving clutter of skis, poles, and limbs, until they were deposited in some deep snow in an open section of the slope. A few moments later they were floundering around, then standing, seemingly unhurt, two whitened creatures fallen from Olympus.

A group of four skiers had gathered above Curt without his having noticed them. They were speaking French.

"That is definitely a novel method to descend a trail," one of them said, and they all laughed.

"And here is another!"

The man who said this shoved off fast, skating down the path, and the others followed his lead. They cut down the chute in formation, no more than ten yards apart, in a tight snaky line that looked almost vertical. The last of them stopped momentarily near the Spanish couple—then with a push of his poles set off after the others.

Curt hiked his black metal skis back and forth in practice edge-sets. The new Sohlers had a tight camber and beautifully sharp edges, so sharp that he had spent most of the previous day falling, trying to get used to them and the Look bindings with the Gran-Prix heel, which was a spring-and-roller device with a silvery piston that ran up the back of the boot and kept you tighter to the ski than any other binding he'd ever used.

"*Hola, Curto!*" Villalta waved from an approaching chair.

"*Hola, esquiador.*" Curt lifted a pole in salute.

In a few moments the Spaniard came off the lift and down the path, shoving his heels out into a quick stop a few feet above Curt. "I left Lois at the bar. She told me you would be waiting. How was Victoria doing?"

"Fine. She's got natural balance and grace."

"And you, how are you doing with the new skis?"

"They're still a bit sharp and stiff, but I'm getting used to them."

"*Bueno.* Shall we go, then?"

"*Pase, hombre, pase.*"

"O.K."

Villalta took two skating steps, pushing with his poles, out over the lip of the path and then down the chute, with a disjointed hippy movement of the body, angled in alternating comma positions, the poles acting as turning points, his skis cutting a series of tight herringbone turns.

Curt planted both poles, jumped so that he was facing down the mountain, and pushed off. He hit the chute with his ankles jammed tight against each other, knees locked for mutual support, and began the rhythmic experiment in motor control and body physics that produces parallel turns, reversing the shoulders, torquing the hips, setting the edge of the downhill ski, really the outside ski, on each sharp turn. There was no thinking, hardly any breathing, as his poles flicked and came away. His body rose and fell, leaning out and forward, as his rear moved like that of a disjointed rabbit—hump, and hump, and hump. The edges of his skis cut precisely into the packed snow. He kept his heels together, edging tight every time he came up the side of the chute, getting the tails of his skis up so that they did not snag on the concave turn of the path. It was like roller skating down a sharply inclined barrel with the top half removed. One final check, hump, past the struggling couple, and then out over a ledge, where he planted his poles and jumped clear through them up into the air for ten or fifteen feet and smacked down with his skis flat. He started a long S-turn on the grainy field of snow that was icy underneath but covered with two inches of tiny pellets that resembled rice and made for perfect skiing. He remembered now to breathe, and saw Villalta a hundred yards ahead pull to a stop with a flurry of snow pushed up in front of him like a lace curtain. Curt turned . . . turned . . . turned, and humped, edges set hard, and came to a stop at his side.

"Isn't this something!" Villalta said. His black hair was blown straight back, his nose cut out from under his goggles in a proud curve.

"Marvelous. The way skiing should be."

"*Claro,*" Villalta said. "And now that you are used to the skis, we gonna do some real skiing tomorrow. Tomorrow we do the Calle del Diablo." He lifted one pole like a sword and pointed off to the right where snow-covered rocks rose and fell like huge teeth.

"Why not today?"

Villalta pushed his sweater sleeve up and looked at his watch. "It is quarter after four. By the time we get down the Diablo the *poma* is closed, then we have a long walk up the highway."

"O.K., tomorrow."

"If you want some excitement, why don't we do the straight fall?" He pointed to an area just this side of the Devil's Path.

There the slope dropped in a series of gray and purplish hillocks that resembled multiple breasts. The snow was wind-swept and crusted, with no ski tracks showing. Villalta described a way they could go down to near the bottom of the valley and then still be able to cut back over the bridge and get to the inter-mediary lift.

"*Vamos a ver,*" Curt said.

"Let's go."

They traversed across the slope to the steep fall line. Curt followed the path Villalta was cutting. In places their skis rattled loosely on gray icy surfaces; in others pulled tight in six inches of wind-blown powder. Sometimes their poles hardly made a dent in the surface, sometimes they threatened to sink beyond the baskets. Pretty soon Villalta cut straight down the fall line, picking up speed. Curt followed, and at the first of the hillocks tried to turn and, catching an edge, cartwheeled two or three times until he came to a stop, his goggles frosted over, one wrist smarting from a pole strap, his left ear pounded full of snow.

He got to his feet and found that his right ski had come loose. As he started cleaning his goggles, he saw that Villalta had pulled up about thirty yards ahead.

"You all right?" he yelled back.

"Yes!"

He brushed his blue jacket clean, wiped a smear of snow from his right hip, then worked on the ski, getting it back on, feeling the heel of his boot snap into place.

They started down the incline again. Curt fell in some thick crud about halfway down, this time consoled by Villalta's falling right in front of him.

"It's tough going," he said.

"Very uneven," Villalta admitted.

"Is the Diablo like this?"

"Much steeper, but much better, because it is skied."

By the time they got back to the Somport bar, the place was mobbed. The pine-paneled walls reverberated with voices calling in several languages for more drinks and lost friends. Beer bottles and wine pitchers clinked. Everywhere there was excited laughter, and everywhere bodies exuded a warmth that made the place mildly steamy.

It was less crowded out in the sunroom, where a piano, sax, and guitar were working their way through a rhumba. There was a second bar out there, just off the main dining room. That was where they spotted Lois, sitting with legs crossed on a high stool at the bar, hemmed in by several admirers. She had a cigarette in one hand and a drink in the other, her elbows propped back on the bar, her breasts jutting out in two firm cones. Her blond hair, tanned skin, pink lips, blue eyes, white-sweatered breasts, and cerise-covered legs vibrated with an energy that lit the swarthy faces of her admirers.

"Some *compañera*," Curt said.

"She never looked better," Villalta said.

They waved to her. She saw them and threw a kiss. The faces of the men around her darkened. As she started to get off the stool, several hands reached out, touching her shoulders and elbows to detain her, but she shook her head and a warning finger and disentangled herself with a smile. Then she started across the room toward them with a hippy stride that picked up the rhumba beat. They found space at the end of a long table near the windows and sat down, Lois waving a final ta-ta to the men at the bar.

"Quite a rooting section," Curt said.

"They're nice boys," Lois said.

"Have you seen Victoria?" Villalta asked.

"No, she hasn't come in yet."

"She must be working hard at her lessons."

"*I* got absolutely bushed about an hour ago," Lois said.

"You didn't look bushed at the bar."

"Oh, a couple of Martinis do wonders."

"Which makes me think we're not going to get served. So what you want from the bar?"

"I'll do it, Francisco."

"No, tell me what you want."

"I'll take another Martini, dear."

"*Whisky-sifón.*"

"*Bueno.* Be right back." Villalta slid off the bench and headed for the larger bar in the dining room.

"Have a good day, dear?"

"Fine. But not as good as yours."

"And what does that mean?"

Curt nodded toward the men at the bar.

She laughed. "I could stay in bed for the next seventy-two hours and come out of it with a Porsche, a Citroën, an Alfa-Romeo, and my pick of husbands."

"You're all heart."

"Don't turn nasty, dear. Besides, you have your own true love to concentrate on."

"Just hate to see a countrywoman go wrong, or be used."

"You should know I do my own share of using."

"Yeah, I guess I should."

"Don't look like that. I didn't mean you."

"How about Francisco?"

"How *about* Francisco?"

"I mean last night. I heard you when you went into your room."

"Well, for Christ's sake, if it isn't the house detective! We *are* grown-ups, you know."

"And old friends."

"Of course, you knew that."

"Just tell me one thing. Who's using whom there?"

"Even Steven, chum. But what *is* eating you? Having troubles with your girl?"

"No, it's just that in a crazy way I guess I care about you and I hate to see you going to hell with yourself."

"Oh, that *is* rich, Curtis. You want to save *me* from myself?" She stopped smiling by stages until her lips pressed into a straight line. "Forget it. Can't be done. I just like one thing and we both know what that is. It's what keeps me going."

Villalta came back out to the sunroom and Victoria was with him, helping to carry the drinks. People turned to stare. She was wearing a powder-blue outfit she had bought in Jaca, filling it with a lithe vibrancy. As she moved across the room you had the impression that she might be someone famous, someone you must have seen before: black hair severely pulled back, chin and nose and wide brows perfectly molded. . . .

"You're glowing, dear."

"She's not bad, is she?"

"She's beautiful, you dog, and you know it."

Curt stood up and Victoria handed him his drink. "They have lovely waitresses here," he said. "Could you sit down with us a while, *señorita?*"

"Oh, *gracias, señor.* Do you think it proper?"

They all sat down, Villalta handing a Martini to Lois. "Let us drink to the *ambiente* of the Somport and Candanchú," he said, raising his glass.

"And to the *duende* of our foursome," Curt added.

"Oh, if you say that, we don't have *duende*," Victoria chided.

"It's Spanish lesson time," Lois said, and sipped at her Martini.

"*Ambiente* is proper atmosphere," Victoria said, and *duende* is what you call—ah, class, no?"

"Well, I agree with Curt, I think we've got class."

"But *duende* is like luck," said Villalta. "You must not say you have it, or it will vanish."

"This schoolwork is tiresome," Lois said. "Let's you and me dance, Frankie."

Villalta led her to where several other couples were dancing in the corner near the combo. Lois' rooting section at the bar watched the liquefaction of her cerise rump as it began rolling and swaying, just below Villalta's guiding hand.

"She dances very well," Victoria said.

"I'm assuming you'd rather sit and rest."

"For the present, yes. I have not exercised so much in my whole life. Now I have a pain here and here, and my feet feel like someone squeezed them in a—"

"I think you're doing very well, though. Tomorrow I could take you up the chair lift to the trail."

"Oh, I would be afraid, Curtis."

"No. I'll take care of you."

She looked at him seriously, her brown, wide-set eyes on his. "All right."

He smiled. "You know, this is the first time we've really been alone on this trip."

"We've been together on the *pista*."

"I know, but I mean together, in a tête-à-tête. Do you think we could break loose from the others"—he nodded toward the dance area—"and be by ourselves for a while tonight?"

She took a long sip of her Calisay. Her lips came away from the glass liquidly warm and shiny. She put the glass down next to his so that her hand brushed against his. "All right," she said, in a low voice. "If we find the proper opportunity."

"You're lovely," he said, and then began to tell her about the Olympian feeling he'd had up on the top of El Tobazo.

"And now, do you mind being down in the valley?"

"No," he said, "I want to live in the valley."

She looked at him under her shading lashes, saying nothing, taking another sip of her liqueur.

"Let's dance," he said.

They joined the others in the corner, and she was lithe and warm against him, letting her body touch his lightly, not pulling back.

"Let the gods have the mountains," he said in her ear.

22
Valle de la Luna

Across the way El Tobazo loomed, obliterating the world to the south. Behind them the Somport barricaded the north. Moonlight flooded the narrow valley. Alongside the road the snow was banked high in gleaming walls of silver and slate.

Neither of them had spoken since leaving the Hotel Candanchú. Their boots squeaked on the tightly packed snow. Their breath left thin vapor trails in the night air. Occasional bursts of party noises from the Candanchú echoed across the valley. A hundred yards down the slanting highway stood their own hotel, quiet and subdued, everyone having gone either to the party or to bed.

Victoria held onto his arm with both hands, clutching tight whenever she started to slip. A few paces farther on she stopped and made him turn to face her.

"I am so sorry that it had to happen, Curtis." Her words came out in gray puffs, as though drawn forth by some cartoonist.

"So am I," he said flatly.

" 'Twas so silly, no?"

"It was silly."

"Why didn't you just walk away from him?"

"Because I was stupid, and because he was an insulting bastard."

He started walking down the road again. Victoria caught up with him, grabbing his arm.

272

Things certainly had gone fast, he thought, and began to re-cast events from the time, some two hours ago, when he had encountered Pedro and Marguerita Henares, the couple he had tried to direct down the chute of El Tobazo. They had thanked him, assured him that their run down the rest of the slope had not been bad, and then invited him and his friends to join them and their group. There were seven of them, all from Pamplona, all members of landed families, including the Conde del Man-char y Cortes.

"Those people must know what he is like," Victoria said consolingly.

"Just because he's some kind of third-rate nobility doesn't give him the right to talk like that."

"Like what? That is what I want to know."

"I'll tell you sometime."

All of his crowd called Cortes Juanito. He had the smooth good looks and movements of a cat. From what Curt could gather, he had been everywhere, done everything. He spoke three or four languages, had a string of horses, a bevy of mis-tresses, and a garage full of racing cars. The others obviously looked up to him, and even Villalta seemed to acknowledge his ascendancy, smiling at Juanito's witticisms, agreeing with his observations.

It wasn't until after a round or two of drinking, more danc-ing and conversation—when Cortes discerned Curt was really with Victoria—that Curt sensed there might be trouble. The first inkling of it came in a discussion over whether, in un-weighting skis to turn, you raised your body up or let it drop suddenly. Curt was an "up" advocate, Cortes a "down." It was a classical skiing argument, one on which the experts disagreed, and Curt knew there was no logical way of settling the question, but Cortes' assured, offhanded superiority trapped him into a childish " 'Tis-'Tisn't" kind of wrangle.

"You didn't like him from the beginning, did you?" Victoria asked.

"That's right. Too goddamned superior. But I notice you liked his style all right."

"Well, he was very nice and polite. He is from a fine family and seemed to be a gentleman."

"Yeah—a real gentleman!" He quickened his pace and she almost fell, having to clutch tight to his arm.

When they reached the steps leading up to the hotel entrance, he stopped and faced her. The air had cut away some of the effects of alcohol and anger, but he still felt nerved up, agitated. Suddenly he wanted to break the chaste silvery film the moon threw around her. He grabbed her by the shoulders, feeling the bone underneath the jacket and flesh.

"I want you to come to my room," he said bluntly, making it an issue rather than an invitation. He had wanted to feel her loyalty, or love, back at the Candanchú and found it lacking, or at least unexpressed. Villalta had been even worse, he thought, a referee rather than a friend. Poor Lois had remained gaily unaware.

"I cannot. I would be afraid." He let her go and started up the wooden steps.

"Curtis!"

He stopped part way up.

"Please don't do this."

"I'm not doing anything." He started up again.

"Curtis!"

He stopped again; she came up almost to where he stood. "What will they say?"

"Who's they?"

"Inside. The clerk."

"My door is unlocked. I left it that way. *You* said this afternoon we'd be together if there was an opportunity. This is it."

"You are being cruel."

"And you're being frigid." He swung his right arm in an arc. "This is your kind of territory. The frigid moon girl."

Her eyes glinted in the light from the doorway. "This is not the way it should be."

"You mean if I were a Spanish gentleman, like Cortes."

"You are both very proud men, I think, and perhaps cruel."

"You come to my room and I'll tell you what kind of gentleman your Juanito is."

"You know that is not why I would come to your room."

"Why would you come to my room, Victoria?"

"Because I think that maybe I love you, and that maybe you care for me—or at least I did think so."

Her statement sobered him, and he stepped down, leaned forward, and kissed her lightly on the forehead.

"I really do care for you," he said, "and I know you're right about this. Let's forget it."

"No, I don't want to forget it," she said softly.

"You mean you're angry?"

"No." She took a deep breath. "I want to come with you."

Her voice was as simple and resigned as that of a child. Her face looked as innocent as—as Dory Markle's when she had sat beside her father listening to them talk.

"Look, you don't have to do this."

"I want to. Just to be with you—but nothing more. All right?"

"All right," he said.

They walked in past the sleepy night clerk, went down the hall to where their rooms were, said good night in loud voices, and then turned in at his door.

The room was small. The moon shone through the tiny window; a ray of light passed over the rug and up the bed to the wall. He could hear her quick, nervous breathing. He reached for her, and kissed her gently, letting his right hand fall to her hip and pull her close.

Her lips broke away from his and she said, "No, Curtis, don't."

He let her go and whispered, "Take your jacket off." He fumbled with the zipper of his own jacket, finally managed it, and threw it over a chair.

"You sure you won't do anything?" she whispered, as she removed her jacket.

"I promise, let's just lie down together." He sat on the edge of the high, narrow bed and slipped off his boots. She sat in the chair and took hers off. Then she stood up and walked through the path of the moon and stood at the edge of the bed. When he reached for her, he found she was trembling. He pulled her down beside him and kissed her awkwardly, turning her slowly, until they were lying beside each other.

"Let's get this off," he whispered huskily, pulling her turtle-neck sweater up to her bra.

"Oh, no! Curtis, you promised!" She tried to pull it down again, but his hand caught hers.

"Just this," he said.

Her hands let go, and he pushed the sweater up, but it got stuck until she sat up, and slid it past her head and off, her perfect coiffure becoming a shambles. She sat there with the sweater in one hand, seeming dejected, defeated, her white-cupped breasts silver in the moonlight. He reached up and fumblingly, while she sat absolutely still, managed to unhook the bra, and it fell slack, sliding down to her elbows. She slipped it off and with a sob threw herself beside him, and began sobbing steadily, tears coursing down his shoulder, her two pear-shaped breasts crushed into his woollen sweater.

"Don't cry," he whispered, "don't cry, baby," while he tried to undo his belt.

"Oh, no!" she whispered hoarsely, trying to sit up, as he pulled her back down. "No, no, no, no. . . ."

"All right," he said, "you're right."

She began to sob even harder than before, completely limp, and he knew that she had made all the efforts necessary for a definite refusal and now was resigned. It would go whichever way he chose. There was only one temporary defense left, and she used it.

Her lips buzzing close to his chest, she said, "If you really love me, Curtis, don't."

"O.K.," he said, thinking—the lover's dilemma: if you love her you don't make love to her, and if you make love to her you don't love her, and if you make love to her and don't love her you may learn to love her, and . . .

He held her tight and stroked her hair and said nothing and did nothing else, and they lay that way for quite some time. Just the pale moonlight and their breathing.

"What did Cortes do that made you so mad?" she whispered, now looking up at him, adjusting her head against him and the pillow.

He laughed. "You're a true woman," he said.

"You don't have to tell me if you don't want to."

"If you really love me . . . you won't make me tell."

He could see her lips part in a smile. "All right," she said.

"Then I'll tell you. But you may not like it. *Es una cosa muy sucia.*"

"Must you tell it as—as a dirty thing?"

"If you want the full effect; if you want to know what kind of Spanish gentleman Cortes is."

"Tell me, then."

Pandora's box, he thought, feeling her tight against his leg.

"Well, it began when you were dancing with one of their crowd, and that little fat guy with the mole—"

"Ramón."

"Yes—was dancing with Lois. Cortes was watching her and he began expounding on the difference between Spanish morality and other kinds. He wasn't talking to me. I was busy with Pedro and his wife. But I knew he was talking for my benefit. Well, one of them asked what he meant, and he said he would give them a demonstration."

"A demonstration?"

"Yeah. He got up from the table and cut in on Ramón, and began to dance with Lois. He did everything but make love to her right on the floor."

"Oh! I didn't see that."

"Well, Lois certainly didn't object, but I thought it was a pretty scurvy trick. I still wasn't going to say anything, until someone else asked her to dance and Cortes came back to the table with a grin on his face. He said in a voice I could hardly hear—'You see, all of these *Suecas* are the same, whether they come from Sweden or Norway or Germany or anywhere.' "

"Oh!"

"You haven't heard the best of it. He said all these foreign types were no better than *putas—coños*—for the easy use of Spanish gentlemen."

"Ahh! How horrible!" She shook her head as though getting rid of something.

"That was when I asked him if he considered himself a gentleman, even a Spanish one. He smiled and said he expected that since I was an educated *norteamericano* I probably had some vague idea of what a gentleman was, but that América del Norte was not a nation of gentlemanly qualities. And I said—'Like Spain, the hero nation of Latin America, of the Spanish-American War, and of World War Two.' "

"That was when Francisco and I came back to the table. I heard you say that."

"Then you heard me tell Cortes that I would demonstrate certain gentlemanly qualities of América del Norte if he would step outside."

"Yes, and *now* I know why."

"That was all of it."

"And are you going through with the other?"

"Of course."

"Oh, I think it is silly, and dangerous."

"We'll see."

"I think Francisco was wrong to suggest it."

"Maybe he was just trying to ease the situation."

"I hope you don't get hurt."

She moved her head toward him and kissed him, and he knew it would be all right if he wanted to try. But he did nothing more, just held her, warming her. Later he covered her and himself with a blanket from the foot of the bed. And they lay for almost an hour together, saying little, content simply to be sharing the same room, breathing the same chill air, and watching the moonlight pour through the window.

Still later, when she had scurried quietly back to her room, Curt lay in bed with his clothes on and smoked a final cigarette. It was silly, he told himself, to think of morality as a matter of puncturing or not puncturing someone's mortal flesh. And yet, it was vital to see that other flesh as human. Women and children also died. Somehow little Dory Markle and Victoria were tied to him by bonds that transcended the attainable.

23
Calle del Diablo

Curt checked his watch again. "It's after one-thirty. You think he's going to show?"

"You kidding? The Conde de Manchar y Cortes?"

"He might think it's silly, too."

"Thank you very much."

"I didn't mean it that way. I know you saved the situation last night, but—"

"It is a sensible solution, Curtis, believe me. When it is over everybody is going to feel better." Villalta's face turned dumb-innocent as he added, "Unless, of course, *you* want to call it off."

"Go to hell."

"That's where you are going, down the Calle del Diablo."

"Very funny," Curt said, searching the chair lift again for any sign of Cortes.

"You just remember what I told you this morning, and follow the plan we discussed."

They had made three runs down the Calle that morning. From the eastern summit of Tobazo it dropped a mile and a half down to the *poma* lift shed near the creek. It was the steepest, shortest, fastest, and most dangerous *pista* on the mountain. The first half-mile was a sharply stepped corridor running between rows of snow-covered boulders that rose thirty and forty feet in the air. The initial face was about as steep as it could be and still be skied. There was only one strategy for taking it—double-pole turns, checking, turning, checking, making sure you didn't let your edges slide out from under you.

At the bottom of the face there was a natural shelf. Beyond that the corridor widened somewhat and the fall line was not so precipitous, but you had to watch for boulders that resembled moguls. Here the job was like that of a canoeist taking white-water rapids, having to stay away from rocks that were hardly distinguishable from waves. Also, as you picked up speed in this section you had to prejump a series of spaced steps, or get thrown way the hell up in the air.

The second half of the Calle del Diablo gave you a choice of about five trails that cut through parallel sections of boulders. He and Villalta had tried two different trails. And on the last run, when they had stopped to talk over this area, Villalta suggested that if Curt fell or lost much time anywhere above, he could still perhaps win by taking the path farthest to the left. But only as a last desperate choice, he said, because although it would save time, it was dangerously steep and narrow, and required a long jump across a brook.

About a quarter of a mile above the creek the Calle opened out wide into a regular slope that could be taken almost straight in a schuss, with just enough shallow turns to keep under control. On the last practice run Curt had done it in a tuck position, and flashed by the *poma* lift shed in fine form. Villalta had smiled and said if he did even a little better he had a real chance.

"*Mira*," Villalta said.

Curt looked down the lift and saw Cortes coming up with Pedro Henares. Henares waved, Villalta waved back.

While they waited for the others to get off the lift, Curt felt his mouth go dry. Perspiration collected in the armpits of his ski jacket, and his stomach behaved the way it used to before football games, quivering as though he were going to retch.

"How you feeling?"

"Fine."

"Don't forget, don't push too hard. And if you fall, remember the short trail, but be careful."

"Right." Curt grinned to show he was all right and wouldn't forget.

The others came skiing across toward them. Cortes moved gracefully, easily. He was wearing black ski pants and a black sweater ringed around arms and chest with gold stripes. He was about five nine, solidly made. With his long black hair parted to one side, thin black brows above dark glasses, a rather long and twisty nose, flashing white teeth, and jutting jaw, he made Curt think of Mack the Knife.

Everybody said, *"Buenos días."* Cortes nodded coolly and Curt nodded back, noticing that his opponent's equipment was all first-rate and looked damn well used.

"Do the principals understand the terms of the competition?" Pedro Henares delivered his question slowly, enunciating precisely, his tone somehow implying he was sorry to have involved Curt in all this, even indirectly.

"Señor Fielding comprehends perfectly," Villalta said. "Does our distinguished rival have any question?"

Cortes allowed himself a superior smile and shook his head.

"Bueno," Henares said. "Then the Conde de Manchar y Cortes will start first, true?"

"Sí, exactly one minute before Señor Fielding."

"And they are to continue on the course until they have passed the *cabaña* of the *poma* lift."

Cortes nodded, so did Curt.

"That is where the judges will be waiting with their watches."

Cortes nodded again. Curt looked ahead stonily. All the details had been worked out at breakfast with Pedro Henares, including the size of the wager: the loser would make out a check for five thousand pesetas to the Candanchú hospital. It was an honorable way to work off a grievance, Villalta had assured Curt, better to put money into the hospital than to pay doctors' bills. Besides, he had added, after Henares left them, if Curt fought with Cortes, there was a chance he might be kicked out of the country, since the family had very powerful connections.

"Let us proceed," Villalta now said.

They pushed off across the summit of the mountain to the eastern rim, first Cortes, who skated his skis easily; then Henares, pushing hard with his poles; then Curt and Villalta.

At the lip of the descent, Cortes relatched the top buckles of his Trappeur boots and slipped his hands into the straps of his poles. After a few edge-setting hops from side to side, he said, "*Bueno, estoy listo.*"

"*Yo también,*" Curt said.

Villalta and Henares huddled over their watches, trying to synchronize them to the second.

"*Bueno,*" Villalta said to Cortes. "I will proceed by counting five, four, three, two, one—then you go."

"*De acuerdo.*" Cortes slipped his skis on the rim, getting rid of any snow that might have adhered to the bottoms. Then he set himself, with the tips of his skis out over the rim. Villalta pointed a finger at Henares and began counting.

"Halt!" Henares said. "Stop."

Cortes had been crouched, ready to take off. Now as he stood up Curt could see that he quivered from tension, and it made him feel better to know he was nervous, too.

"I am sorry." Henares' forehead wrinkled with concern. "But my watch seems to be some seconds different."

Again they huddled. Curt avoided looking at Cortes. Instead, he gazed out over the Calle, picking the line he wanted to try for, thinking over the steps he had to jump, the paths he had to select. Already he could imagine bursting out onto the final open slope, tucked hard, schussing—and then past the shed. There'd probably be quite an audience gathered there, not just Victoria and Lois and the Pamplona crowd. The news of the grudge race, involving a *norteamericano*, had spread throughout the hotel. . . .

They were ready again. "This time for a certainty," Villalta said.

"*Sí*," Henares said.

Cortes grimaced, and once again got himself set. After pointing a finger at Henares, Villalta began to count. "*Cinco, cuatro, tres, dos, uno. . . .*"

Hump—and Cortes was out on the face. After the first four or five turns, which he handled cleanly, Curt could see that he was a damn good skier. He attacked the slope with both poles, the tails of his skis coming up a few inches above the surface of the snow and then down, edging, and hump, hump, hump, all the way down to the initial shelf, which he jumped, and then he was out of sight down in the second section amid the rocks.

"*Pronto*," Pedro Henares was saying.

Curt stationed himself at the lip, shuffled his skis, got his sweaty hands clutched tight around the poles. Henares now did the honors in counting, and when he reached "*uno*," Curt pushed off. He took the first three or four turns well, but as he lost his initial rhythm the face seemed to threaten him. With his turns unconnected, his descent became a series of erratic jumps, and two-thirds of the way down the face he almost pitched over sideways. As it was, he had to stop to avert a fall, and when he pushed off again he felt as though he had lost entire minutes.

By the time he hit the first shelf he was back under control, feeling a rhythm in his turns, in the up-and-down unweighting. He prejumped three of the steps and could hear the wind whistling past his ears. Things were a blur off to the sides, where the huge boulders lined the way. The whole world was concentrated in the next thirty or forty yards. He felt his skis slap on the well-packed snow, felt the edges hold as he shuffled his feet and tilted his knees left and then right and then left as loose snow fluffed up from his pricking poles and his shoulders swung in counterrotation and his knees rose and fell in the process of weighting and unweighting. Rhythm, rhythm, rhythm, he told himself in a subliminal hum: you're going good, going good. . . .

He came down one side of the Calle where the snow was banked high against the boulders. Ahead was the last of the steps. He crouched to jump just before he reached it so that he'd come down quickly, and everything went perfectly—until he landed and one ski hit some loose snow and he tried to pull out of it and was almost under control when he rolled over and came up on one knee. His skis had not come off in the sprawl. He lumbered to his feet, got his poles gripped right, and pushed off again, saying, "Goddamn it, goddamn it."

One part of him continued skiing while another tried to think: he had lost time up on the face and then more in the fall—at least twenty seconds. The only way to make it up was to try the short cut that Villalta had mentioned. He'd have to make his choice very quickly now, because he was rapidly approaching the section of multiple corridors. He felt good on his skis again, everything was working; his breathing and his turns were timed together, the huff of intake and the up-unweighting. *Which way, which way?* Any of five or six corridors. *Tell me!* His skis edged hard, his left pole flicked, and without having made up his mind he was headed there—to where the short cut dropped off. He could hardly see it, narrow and darkly shadowed under a ledge of rock.

Swoop—and he was down in it. And, Jesus, what a mistake! He braced to avoid sideswiping the narrow walls of rock along the way, keeping to an almost perfectly straight line down, picking up one hell of a lot of speed! And then—Christ!—he could see how the path simply broke off—six or seven feet higher than the slope below. He'd have to clear what looked like some large lumps of foam, which he half-realized must be the brook that . . . He crouched low, got set, pushed up and out with his legs and poles and was air-borne and cleared the brook, only to come down heavily off balance, so that his left arm shot out automatically for protection. He went down, crumpled and dazed for a moment, and felt something torn and limp in his wrist. Somehow he shuffled to his feet. His skis were still on, the bindings having been tightened beyond the safe point for the race. That could have been dangerous, he caught himself thinking. *Could* have been!

He was moving again, but when he touched down with the left pole he yelped involuntarily. The hand was worth nothing; the pole trailed listlessly from it, like the broken antenna of an insect. As he came out into the clear he finally managed to slip the pole off and let it fall behind. You've really done it, he told himself, crouching down into a tuck position, feeling lopsided with just one pole. You have really done it, not only lost the race and the bet, but you've probably busted your goddamn arm. . . .

Down by the *poma* shed he saw a cluster of reds, pinks, blues, and whites. Soon he caught sight of two men who were studying their watches. *That* was the finish line. He made one final angled turn, took the last hump, and then lined down in a straight schuss, crouched, feet slightly spread to maintain balance. As he neared the shed, the run flattened out; he stood up and took a few last skating steps, past the two men with the watches, and almost fell when he poked his right pole down, making a heavy turn, coming to a ragged stop, leaning in against centrifugal force.

Poor race, poor finish, poor form. Most ignoble. Down with América del Norte!

Lois and Victoria came clumping over the snow to him, their faces bearing dutiful smiles.

"Nice try, Curt," Lois said.

"Are you all right?" Victoria asked.

He merely nodded, trying to keep self-disgust from showing. Cortes had five or six people standing with him, and Curt tried to figure out from his bearing whether he was sure of having won. Of course he must have, but he couldn't tell from Cortes' attitude.

"What happened to your other pole?" Lois asked. "We *thought* you were skiing with just one."

"I lost it after a jump."

Just then the two timers broke their consultation. The Frenchman from their hotel, who had agreed to help judge, came toward Curt. He smiled. "Monsieur must 'ave 'ad some difficulty. His time was thirty second less good than that of M. Cortes. I'm sorry."

"That's nothing. Thanks for helping."

"*C'est rien.*"

By now Villalta had skied down to them and caught the last of the conversation. "You lose?"

"Yup, I lose."

"He even lost a pole," Lois said.

Curt told Villalta what he had tried to do, how he had fallen.

"Let me see this." Villalta slid down beside him and took hold of the wrist. Curt winced and closed his eyes against the pain. "Boy, I think you have done it."

That night as he struggled into a sports jacket there was a knock on his door. He threw the sling around his neck and placed the fractured wrist into it. Opening the door, he saw Pedro Henares.

"I am sorry to hear of your unfortunateness."

"Thanks. It's not bad."

"Juanito Cortes is down at the bar and ask if you will join him for a drink."

The Christian knight, Curt thought. After some hesitation, he said, "All right."

Cortes stood up from the stool when Curt approached with

Henares. He offered his hand and Curt took it. "I would like to buy a drink for *un caballero norteamericano*," Cortes said, quite formally.

"I'd be honored."

They both ordered a cognac. Henares excused himself, saying he had to find his wife.

"I think we are both sorry about last night," Cortes said.

"Yes," Curt said.

"And when I discover about the hand, I admire your attempt to continue in the competition. It *was* the act of a gentleman."

"Nice of you to say so."

"I do not consider that I have won the competition; so I have also sent my contribution to the hospital."

"You didn't have to do that. You won fair and square, as they say in my country. But I appreciate the gesture."

"*Bueno, y salud.*"

They drank off their cognacs. Curt wondered whether he was supposed to smash his glass in the fireplace. It was something out of *El Cid*, or the Flying Circus.

PART
FIVE

24
To Another Country

The trip back to Zaragoza was subdued. Nobody did much talking. Curt sat in the back seat with Victoria, and she held his hand for long intervals. If he seemed quieter than usual, she and the others probably attributed it to his defeat and his wrist. What really bothered him was Villalta. After dinner the night before, he had discovered from Victoria that she, too, had wanted to go to Andorra instead of Candanchú—which made three of them who had gone where Villalta dictated. Once again it was Villalta pulling the strings. Of course, it would be paranoid to think he had also set him up by advising that short cut out of the Calle del Diablo. But why did he want him to stay away from Andorra?

They crossed the muddy Ebro around four-thirty and dropped Victoria off at her place. Curt said he would see her the next morning as usual.

At Curt's apartment Villalta helped the *portero* handle his stuff. Lois leaned out the window of the car and said, "Take care of that wrist, dear."

"I will," Curt said.

Villalta came back out of the building. Shaking Curt's hand, he said, "*Adiós, amigo.*"

"*Adiós,*" Curt said. "It was a fine trip. Thanks for arranging everything."

291

"It was nothing, *hombre*. Why don't we have dinner to-morrow night? I meet you at the Gran at nine, eh?"

"All right. See you then. 'Bye, Lois."

He did not have dinner with Villalta the next night. When he awoke that morning he decided to go through with the plan he had worked out before falling asleep. He shaved, showered, and dressed in his dark blue suit. Then he made two phone calls; the first to the base, the second to Victoria.

He told her his wrist was bothering him and he had an appointment at the base hospital, so he wouldn't be able to see her that morning. Also, he said, there was a chance he might have to run into Madrid, where he could receive expert treatment at the Torrejón hospital if necessary.

"But can't you be treated here at the municipal hospital?" She made it sound as though he were rejecting both her and the Spanish medical profession.

"Sure, I could," he said, "but this way everything is taken care of free; and more importantly, if anything goes wrong with the wrist later, my government will assume full responsibility. Also, it would be a good time for me to see a friend in Madrid, about some additional material for my article."

She tried to sound lighthearted. "I am beginning to think you have a 'friend' in every city."

Curt laughed and said, "For that note of jealousy I promise a present. You're my only 'friend,' and you know it. I will see you Wednesday morning at eleven, unless something goes wrong."

"What can go wrong?"

"I just mean I might be delayed somehow."

"Oh."

"Listen, *querida*."

"Yes?"

"We will have much to discuss when I get back, *porque te amo mucho*."

"I love you too, Curtis."

"Truly?"

"Truly."

"Then my trip will seem both long and short."

"*Adiós*, Curtis. I hope they don't find anything bad with the wrist."

"*Adiós*, Victoria." He started to place the phone back on its cradle but heard her voice still buzzing.

"Curtis, Curtis—"

"Yes?"

"You are not going to try to drive to Madrid with your wrist that way, are you?"

"No, dear. I'll either get a ride from someone at the base or take the afternoon train."

"Oh, good. All right, then."

While he packed, he continued to think of the concern in her voice, and it increased his feeling of guilt at having to lie to her. When he was finished with his bag, he put some papers, a guidebook, and a road map into his blue portfolio.

Then he made another call to the base. It lasted about five minutes and he took notes on a slip of paper, which he then folded carefully and put into the portfolio.

Downstairs he told the *portero* he would be in Madrid for the next two or three days, if anyone should ask. Then he walked around the block to where he had the VW parked.

Driving through traffic with one hand proved tricky, but he improvised a method of steadying the wheel with his left elbow while shifting with his right hand. In a few minutes he pulled up in front of the Gran Hotel. He left the motor running and gave the doorman twenty pesetas, promising he'd be right out. Inside, he wrote a note at the desk for Villalta, telling him he was sorry about dinner but he had to run into Madrid to have his wrist looked at and to attend to some business. He would get in touch as soon as he returned.

From the Gran he drove down a side street to the Paseo de

Marina Morena, which he followed around the city to the
north until he came to the Puente del Pilar. As he crossed the
Ebro he smiled at the thought of what any Spaniard would say
about his going to Madrid by this route: another of those
crazy *norteamericanos*. Well, even the *norteamericanos* eventually learned that the shortest distance between two points is
not necessarily a straight line.

On the other side of the river he was delayed by heavy
industrial traffic on the Avenida Cataluña, but soon traffic
thinned and he was out in the open. Within an hour he had
reached the *punto negro* sign near Bujaraloz, where Teddy
Swiatski's car had plunged down into the arroyo. He pulled
the VW onto the berm and got out. He stood looking down
over the drop, noting where the grass was still scorched, seeing
the stone near the trees where he had sat and talked with the
shepherd, hearing his words again: "One was saved. He walked,
and they put him into the car."

Somewhere Cipriano was alive. Find him and you'd get all the
answers. It was as simple as that. And now he felt that he
might finally be on the right track, ironically enough because
of Villalta and his reluctance to go to Andorra.

National II ran a fairly even course to Fraga; then, as it
approached Lérida, it dipped down. Curt crossed the bridge over
the Río Ségre and stopped on the eastern outskirts of Lérida
at a fashionable motel, the Hostal Condes de Urgel, where he
had eaten on the way back from Barcelona.

He left the VW in the care of an attendant at the gas station,
telling him to fill it with gas and check the oil, and asking
how long a drive it was to Andorra.

About two or three hours, depending, the man said, eying
his sling; and the best way to go was to continue on National II
until Tárrega, where you turned north to Artesa and Pons.

Inside the *hostal* Curt ordered the smallest lunch he could
without insulting both the waiter and Spanish cooking: chicken

soup, mixed beans and vegetables, paella, flan, and a half-bottle of the regional red wine.

While he waited for the food to come he took the road map out of his portfolio and opened it to the northeastern sector of Spain. He found Tárrega on N. II, and then traced a yellow vein of road that swung north to Artesa and there joined C. 1313, which wrinkled alongside a blue line marked as the Río Ségre. The road ran almost directly north to Pons, Basella, Seo de Urgel, and just above that into a triangle of black dots that resembled a droopy eye—the principality of Andorra. A spot of red near the center of the eye stood out as the city of Andorra la Vella.

Curt estimated the entire distance at about a hundred kilometers' drive, about seventy miles. It was now only two-fifteen, so he had plenty of daylight left. But if what he'd heard about the route into Andorra was true, he did not want to drive it in the dark. It had as many cars to its credit as Gravesend had ships.

When he finished his meal, Curt poured a final glass of wine and lit a cigarette. Putting his map away, he took the guidebook out of the portfolio, opened it to the marker he had put in the night before, and began rereading the stiff, informative prose that mixed history, geography, politics, hotel information, and shopping tips:

Andorra is an almost independent territory, measuring some seventeen by twenty miles, roughly. It was given in feudal fief in 1278 to the French Count of Foix and the Spanish Bishop of Seo de Urgel. The Bishop still theoretically holds domain, as does the co-controller, the President of France, who superseded the Count; but in actuality the Andorrans, an old and tough line of smugglers and sheep-raisers, have achieved virtual autonomy, capitalizing on the no-tariff sales of articles from all over the world—everything from pearls and gold coins to ski equipment and automobiles. You can buy a Cadillac for less in Andorra than you can in Detroit. The main trouble might be in driving it out: The only road you can rely on in the winter is that through Seo de Urgel; the others leading into France are often closed by snow at the passes some ten thousand feet up in the Pyrenees.

For the tourist, the two principal points of interest in the tiny country are Andorra la Vella (sometimes spelled Vieja, or Viella) and the neighboring spa of Las Escaldas (Les Escaldes). The international sightseer and shopper will find many hotels and hostelries to suit his pocketbook; ditto restaurants, which tend to be more French than Spanish in cuisine, though producing in some instances rare and delicious concoctions bespeaking a double heritage. Francs and pesetas are both official currency, with Swiss francs and American dollars in great demand. The traveler is urged to visit Andorra even if just to mail cards or letters with the much sought stamps and cancellations, or simply to say he has been in one of the smallest and least visited countries in Europe.

When the waiter returned with the check, Curt asked if he knew for certain whether the road to Andorra was open. The waiter said he himself was not the possessor of such information, but he would find the manager, who would certainly know. A few minutes later he returned, his round brown face creased by a moony smile. According to the manager, some skiers had stopped off a few hours earlier, returning from Andorra. The road was clear.

"*Gracias,*" Curt said, tipping him.

"*Nada, señor. Buen viaje.*"

Curt put the guidebook away and took out a folded sheet of paper. The book mentioned nothing about hospitals, but Stafford had come through with the necessary information. When he had compiled the list for southern France, there'd been nothing on Andorra. But after Curt's first telephone call that morning, Stafford had really gone into action, working through the American Embassy in Madrid, and ascertained that Andorra contained not one but two hospitals.

Curt opened the sheet of paper, and studied the names once again:

Clínica de Santa María de los Remedios (Las Escaldas)
Hospital de San Juan de Dios (Andorra la Vella).

"*Vamos a ver,*" he muttered to himself, slipping the paper back into the portfolio. "We are going to see what there is in another country."

25
Andorra

He left N. II at Tárrega, swung north onto C. 240, and followed it for twenty miles through low rolling farm country. For long stretches there were no other cars—just barns and farmhouses and hay carts and men working off in the grain. The fields went up the hillsides. The pueblos he passed through all looked the same, with circular plaza, communal water fountain, and staring women and children.

The sun stayed behind him, and the VW kept running its snubbed hood into its own shadow. For a while he thought of Dory Markle and how he had driven back from Barcelona. He imagined her golden hair, impish smile, intelligent eyes, and he wished hard that she were with him now, seeing this country-side, breathing this clear blue air, flecked with pollen from the cut wheat. Perspiration broke out on his forehead, and he let Dory dissolve into Victoria, with thin brown wrists and slender neck and dark, wide-set eyes, and he thought of how it would be with him and Victoria, how he would perform the rite, baptizing her and confirming her, and perhaps himself. . . .

At Artesa he followed the sign on a stone column, turning right onto C. 1313; a quarter of an hour later he passed through Pons. Outside Pons the country changed considerably. The road climbed up into foothills and left the grain fields below. Now there were cattle and sheep grazing on sparser vegetation. When the road made a broad swing he could see things spread out behind him. The fields were squares of brown and tan.

When the road finally came over the crest it entered a forest of oak and pine, and the sun came through the trees in patches. The VW ran over a series of saddles and humps like a toy, and Curt was reminded of a stretch of road in the Pocono Mountains that ran from Hazleton to Stroudsburg. Often he had driven that route with Helen, on their way to New York. How long ago? And how had that road led to this? He wondered about Teddy Swiatski. *He* would have known that stretch through the Poconos, but had he ever taken C. 1313 and noticed the similarity here? Forget him, he's dead. How about Cipriano Farlo? *That* was the big question: had *he* taken this road nine months ago—or been taken over it, burned, battered, and probably unseeing? *Vamos a ver.* . . .

The VW came out of the woodland suddenly and swung wide around a curve. Up ahead was the first high ridge of the Pyrenees, almost touching a bank of gray clouds. For a mile or so the road dipped down before beginning its climb. He passed through a village where the terraced grapevines came right to the houses. Then the road started up, following a water course. The mountain loomed blue-green in the slanting sun, with here and there gray slashes of outcropping rock. The VW whined and groaned in second gear, then in third. The horizon was nothing but the tops of trees, some ragged peaks, and the low-hanging clouds. It grew cold in the car and he turned the heater knob to high. He began to think of John Bowers and their flight over. John Bowers. Why the hell couldn't he write to him and see if there were any leads on Villalta? Why hadn't he thought of that possibility before? If Villalta were involved in anything, wouldn't someone like Bowers . . . ? Good idea, he'd write him tonight, greet him from Andorra and then get down to business.

At about six or seven thousand feet C. 1313 went through a pass cut into stratified stone, and he could see then how the road twisted in a series of S-turns down to a narrow gorge below. A silvery-gray river—that would be the Ségre—glinted in the gorge, running like a deep ditch through tented-up mountains. The VW cruised down through the turns with little acceleration and much braking, until finally the road leveled off and began its parallel course along the river.

Like no other river he had seen in Spain, the Ségre ran swift, deep, and blue, with plenty of white-water passages where it shoaled or narrowed. The gorge was almost perpendicular on both sides. The highway ran along a narrow ledge that canti-levered out over the boiling water a hundred feet below. For mile after mile it ran like this, on the western verge of the river, and Curt thought of nothing but driving. There were no guardrails; in places recent erosion had scalloped the outer edge of the road so that even parts of the macadam surface had crumbled away. He straddled the middle line and hoped there'd be no cars from the opposite direction as he rounded blind turns. Sometimes he had to swerve suddenly to avoid chunks of rock and mud that had fallen from the dripping wall of stone to his left. At other times it was like driving through a partial tunnel—with a beetling ledge above, then the rock wall to the left, and finally the base ledge of the road itself. Without thinking, he had begun to use his left elbow to help steady the wheel. His wrist was now throbbing with pain, his right hand jerked spasmodically. Luckily, he met only three or four cars coming from the north. Each time he was forced out to the right edge of the road and felt a strong spurt of adrenalin. As he slewed around one corner that was particularly scary, he wondered whether this was the way the black-marketeers from the base had made their final exit— off into the rushing water below.

An hour later, after passing through the gloomy town of Seo de Urgel, he crossed the border into Andorra. Customs inspection on the Spanish side was perfunctory. On the Andor-ran side it was nonexistent. Curt searched the shed but found no guards on duty. Andorra was obviously committed to the ideal of free trade. It was also, he thought, the perfect place into which to smuggle a man and to keep him secreted, way the hell up in these mountains.

He drove through two villages that were little more than double rows of shops, with large placards in the windows advertising the low prices of their goods.

Finally, he found himself entering the low open end of a triangular valley. Lights from the town down in the cupped bottom of the valley glowed pale orange in the twilight. On three sides jagged mountain peaks rose, snow brimming gray against the darkening sky. Andorra la Vella. And about time.

Soon C. 1313 became the main street of the town, which seemed to be not so much a national capital as some county seat in Idaho or Montana. There was no evidence of Spanish plazas or arcaded quadrangles. Andorra la Vella appeared to be no wider than a couple of city blocks, with everything concentrated on the main thoroughfare. For almost a mile he drove past scores of shops and cafés, all modern and brilliantly lit. Everything looked prosperous, thriving. Pedestrians were dressed mainly in ski and *après-ski* outfits. Traffic was thick and slow; buses threatened to block the narrow street.

As the street dipped and then began to rise, he discovered he had left Andorra la Vella and had, according to a sign, entered Las Escaldas. It was just as well. According to the guidebook, Las Escaldas was "an adjacent spa in which the modern-day traveler will probably find accommodations more to his liking than in the capital." He watched for signs of the two hotels most highly recommended. Another block and he caught sight of them both: the Endor Roc and the Catalunya. They were off to the left in a U-shaped court, of which they formed the base and one wing.

The Endor Roc was full but the Catalunya had a vacancy. Up in his room, he tipped the man for his baggage and, taking a look around, credited the guidebook with being right: modern, efficient staff and service, well-appointed rooms. He hung his topcoat and suit jacket in the closet but didn't unpack his bag;

instead, he slipped off his shoes, loosened his tie, and lay back on the double pillows of the bed, his sore wrist throbbing at his side. Closing his eyes, he told himself the hotel heating system was also efficient. Warm. Maybe he should turn the thermostat down. Too much trouble. All he needed was five minutes rest, just five . . .

Memory rolled inside his eyelids like an erratic film: road, rocks, river, and VW flashed across the inner screen, imposing themselves in a montage of red, black, and gray. And then suddenly the VW was plunging off into space and he was in it, letting go of the steering wheel and holding onto Dory, who materialized in the grasp of his sore left hand, and then Victoria in his right, and they all fell together, their hair streaming up and back, as he heard his own long-drawn-out wail—"IT WOOON'T HUUURRRT . . . !"

When he awoke, Curt thought he was back in his own apartment until he saw the patterned drapes on the windows and the light-grained wooden bureau against the wall. His mouth tasted rotten and his teeth felt too big. He checked the wrong wrist to see what time it was, winced with pain, and he looked at the other: six forty-three. Christ, he'd been asleep more than an hour. He sat up slowly, his stomach grumbling with hunger. The first thing to do was get out of these sweaty clothes.

By seven he had brushed his teeth, showered, and changed into a fresh outfit of navy blazer and gray slacks. He slung his arm in the blue-and-red silk scarf Lois had given him for Christmas. As he stepped out of the elevator and into the lobby he felt like the nattiest and most refreshed cripple in Andorra. The young clerk at the desk eyed him with approval.

"*Bon soir, monsieur,*" he said with Catalan intonation. "Do we have here an accident of the ski?"

"That is it," Curt said in Spanish. "And perhaps you could be of assistance."

"Anything, *señor*."

Curt opened his portfolio and took out the slip of paper on which he had copied the names of the two hospitals. What he wanted, he explained to the clerk, turning the paper so that he could see the names, was directions for getting to both places, and if possible the names of the medical directors in charge.

"The directions are simple," the clerk said. He bent down and pulled out a small tourist map of the environs. "Here we are here," he said circling with his pen a building marked X. "All that is necessary to go to the Clínica de Santa María de los Remedios is to continue here on the highway for three kilometers. You will see a sign and you will then turn to the right on a private road which goes on for two or three more kilometers." He made another circle with his pen. "Here."

"And for the Hospital de San Juan de Dios, you return into Andorra la Vella, and you go to here." Another mark with the pen. "This is the Callejón de Foix. And then you turn again here, and within a few hundred meters you will see the hospital."

"Very good," Curt said. "May I have this map?"

"Certainly, *señor*. As for the names of the medical directors, please allow me a few moments."

He went into the manager's office and a little later emerged smiling, a piece of paper in his right hand.

"Here we have the information." He handed the paper over to Curt, who examined it.

"If we can be of any help in the *señor's* obtaining medical aid," the clerk went on, "we will be pleased."

"That won't be necessary," Curt said. He fished a hundred-peseta note from his jacket pocket and laid it on the desk. "But let me contribute to the medical fund of the hotel."

"*Gracias, señor*. And may I say that although the hospitals are open at this hour, it would be difficult to see the directors until morning."

"Clearly. A thousand thanks."

He decided to hell with dinner, had one Scotch and soda in the small cocktail lounge off the lobby, and went out to where he had parked the VW.

He would go to the San Juan de Dios and do what he had done in all those hospitals in Pau and Tarbes and Lourdes: say that he was a friend of the family of Cipriano Farlo, sent to find him and bring him some money the family thought he would need—had anyone by that name been admitted on or about April eighth or ninth?

The Hospital de San Juan de Dios was not hard to locate. The clerk's diagram and the smallness of Andorra la Vella made it easy. He entered the three-storied stone building, and found himself in a cavernous hallway, with a main desk in an alcove off to one side. There were several uniformed nurses near the desk. He approached and asked who was in charge. The oldest one, who had a whiskered mole on one cheek and looked like an overgrown dwarf, admitted with pride that she was the head nurse.

"May I speak to you in private?" Curt said, as charmingly as he could.

She looked at his arm, inquiringly; then she motioned to the others and they left on duties suddenly remembered.

"Is it about your arm?" she said, indicating a chair beside the desk.

As they both sat down, Curt said, "No, the wrist was hurt in a skiing accident, but it has been properly attended to, and is doing very well, or I would not have been able to drive to Andorra on this mission of trust. You see, *señora,* I have for a long time been the family friend of a man from Zaragoza. This man once did me a great service, and now I am trying to help him and his family. It is a matter of money to be delivered. The only trouble is that the man is very proud, and the family has not been able to find him. Now we have received word that he is here, has been here, in your hospital. I have come to visit him, bring greetings and love from his family, and deliver this money which he must need."

The head nurse's face looked unimpressed. She was an ugly woman, used to the facts of life and its physical debilities. She spoke curtly: "What is this man's name?"

Curt's heart throbbed. It could be the end of the line. One honest answer. "Farlo," he said, "Cipriano Farlo."

The nurse's smile was final, self-satisfied. "We have no Farlo. We have no one here from Zaragoza."

"That's just the trouble, *señora*."

"Not *señora*, *señorita*."

He forced a smile. "You see, *señorita*, the man is very proud. We have reason to believe he does not want to trouble his family with his misfortune. It is almost a mental illness with him. Also he believes he is in trouble in Zaragoza. The fact is he is not, and his family is full of grief at not knowing whether he is alive or dead. They have searched in many hospitals, and now they think there is some hope here."

"We simply have no patient here by that name."

Goddamn, Curt thought, she just liked saying it. "I know, *señorita*, that your mission is one of mercy and help to the unfortunates of this world. I know that if you could help this man and his family you would do it. May I ask if you would check your entries for the eighth or ninth of April to see if a man, age thirty-two, was admitted as an accident case. Perhaps this would be of some help."

He took his passport case out of his inside jacket pocket and fished out the photograph of Cipriano that old Farlo had provided him with.

The nurse looked at the photograph. She pursed her lips.

"No," she said, "we have no one who looks like that."

"Could you check your records for that date?"

"It is not within my power to give out such information."

The mole, black and hairy, stood out in taut relief as her jaws
set.

"Look, *señorita,* I have traveled this long distance. It is not an
easy trip into your country. I can naturally talk to your director
tomorrow." He unfolded the paper with the name on: "Señor
Antonio Pasquarro."

"Naturally. That is what I suggest you do, *señor,* since you
do not appear to be satisfied with my answers."

"All I ask is that you check your records. And for this I am
prepared to make a donation to the hospital."

Her eyebrows came up.

He took three thousand-peseta bills out of the passport folder.
The nurse's mouth turned up into a smile, the mole pulled into
a curl of wrinkles. She pushed one of the buzzers on the desk,
and in a moment one of the others came hurrying around the
corner of the hall.

"Señorita Barrata," the head nurse said. "This estimable
gentleman wishes to contribute to our hospital fund. Will you
please witness the receipt of three thousand pesetas."

Taking a pen from a stand she wrote out a receipt on the
note pad in front of her, and handed it to Curt in exchange
for the money, which she put inside a desk drawer.

"*Gracias,*" she said to Curt. "You may return to your duties,"
she said to the other nurse, who nodded and left.

From a file case, the head nurse now took a folder and placed
it on the desk. She turned to the pages she wanted and asked
Curt to come look at them. They were marked April eighth,
ninth, and tenth. He checked through to the eleventh, hoping
to find something of help, but there was nothing that looked
like an automobile accident case. No name, no indication,
nothing that looked as though Cipriano Farlo had been a patient
in San Juan de Dios.

"You might try at the Clínica de Santa María de los Remedios," the head nurse said.

He nodded. *"Buenas noches,"* he said, *"y gracias."*

"Nada, señor."

You said it, he thought—nothing, and more nothing. Contributing to hospital funds was getting to be a habit.

He decided to have something to eat, and to drink. The Clínica de Santa María de los Remedios could wait until morning.

26
Los Remedios

After the desk rang him at nine, Curt lay in bed watching the sun filter through the patterned drapes for a few moments. He began to review the plan he had concocted at dinner the night before. After canvassing all those hospitals in France with negative results, and after paying the dwarfish head nurse of San Juan de Dios more than fifty dollars for equally negative information, he was now left with the Clínica de Santa María de los Remedios. It all amounted to a loose process of elimination, and if he found no trace of Farlo at the Clínica he probably would not find him at all. So, assuming *this was it,* the plan could very well work. And if it didn't, what the hell was there to lose?

A half-hour later, having dressed, breakfasted, and made a phone call, he walked across the parking court to his VW. The air was clean and bracing. An inch or two of snow had fallen overnight, but under a brilliant sun it was already turning to slush. As he pulled out onto the highway, he found that it had been scraped clean, the macadam surface shining like washed coal.

The road climbed quickly out of Las Escaldas in a series of steep escalations and soon he could see how snugly the two towns lay in the base of their valley with snow-crested mountain peaks rising all around to form a jagged crown. Alongside the highway the snow embankments were now ten to fifteen feet high, and every so often a tall pole rose up, painted in red and white spiral lines, showing motorists and snow-removal crews the safe edge of the road.

About a mile out of Escaldas, at the third leveling-off place, he saw a side road branching off to the right. It ran through an iron gateway that had an arching sign above: *Clínica de Santa María de los Remedios.* He turned off the highway and went through the open gates, his heart thumping for a moment at the thought that this could be it, the end of a very long road indeed. . . .

The clinic road was hardly more than a shelf on the mountainside. It ran for about a quarter of a mile through snow-covered pines. One final bend and it suddenly opened up into a circular parking area, which contained some twenty or thirty cars. The clinic was at the far end of the lot and, surprisingly enough, the two-story building was built in Swiss chalet style, with steep eaves hanging down over ornately scrolled and brilliantly painted wooden balconies. It looked more like a ski lodge than a clinic, and Curt had the feeling that if a clock were to chime, dozens of giant cuckoos might pop out onto the balconies to deliver their message. And, he thought, maybe that was what his efforts deserved. . . .

He parked the car, walked across the snow-impacted lot, and mounted the banistered steps to the main entry of the clinic. Just inside the door he was met by a uniformed attendant, who seemed as much guard as *portero.*

"May I be of service, *señor?*" The man's Catalan accent edged over almost into French.

"*Por favor.* I have come to see Dr. Cerdat. I am Dr. Fielding and called earlier this morning."

"*Bueno.* Will you come with me, Doktor? Herr Dr. Cerdat anticipates your arrival."

Curt followed the man down a corridor to their left, thinking how much of a linguistic effort the "Herr Doktor" had been, as though the *portero* had had to be trained to say it precisely that way. Which meant Cerdat was either a Mittel-European type, or, with that name, maybe a Catalan full of Teutonic credentials and aspirations.

The *portero* ushered him into a reception office, saying that if the Herr Doktor would accommodate himself Herr Dr. Cerdat would present himself directly.

The office was monastically severe. There were no decorations on the walls. A bank of fluorescent lights hung in a white grill frame from the ceiling. The floor tiles were white with faint swirls of black-and-gray marbling. The furniture was all metallic—desk, revolving chair behind it, tubular chair beside it, and two straight-backed chairs set against one wall. Atop the desk were a blotter with black leather corners, a tear-away appointment calendar, a silver-edged traveling clock, a white block of writing paper, and a pencil next to it, sharpened to perfection.

Although Cerdat was probably responsible for the office decor, Curt thought, he could hardly be responsible for the architecture of the building. Old Sherlock Freud analyzed this man as a precise, anal-compulsive, someone who was not going to take kindly to having been duped by a telephone conversation that included phrases like "a professional matter of great importance."

Just then a thin, angular man wearing a white laboratory coat bustled through the doorway. "Dr. Fielding?" he said, sticking his right hand out stiffly as he advanced.

"Sí," Curt said. *"Mucho gusto, Dr. Cerdat."* Cerdat looked like a cross between Groucho Marx and Leon Trotsky, with horn-rimmed glasses, mustache, and neatly cut Vandyke. As they shook hands, he looked at the arm in its sling quizzically.

"You are English or American?" he asked.

"Norteamericano."

"Very well, then, we can speak English if you would prefer. Won't you be seated?" There was no warmth in the invitation, just ingrained politeness.

Curt sat in the tubular steel chair and, pulling out his

cigarettes, offered one to Cerdat, who refused with a grimace of a smile. Curt lit one for himself, sensing the other man's disapproval and impatience.

"You are a doctor of medicine?" Cerdat said, as he took a small metallic ashtray from a drawer and placed it at the edge of the desk, where Curt could reach it.

Curt blew smoke and said, "Actually, no. I'm a professor of American literature, among other things."

"Oh!" Cerdat's eyebrows rose above his horn-rimmed glasses and relegated Curt to a lower order of beings. "Then it must be your arm you wish to see me about. What is the trouble?"

"I hurt my wrist skiing," Curt said, taking a leisurely drag on his cigarette. "But it has been taken care of, and to tell you the truth I've come to see you about another matter entirely."

Cerdat had switched their relationship from learned colleagues to doctor-patient quite easily, but now he squirmed with displeasure as once again he said, "Oh?" This time it was an impatient question rather than a judgment. "Won't you please to tell me exactly what matter?"

Obviously the man did not like surprises, especially when they occurred within his own clinic, where no doubt everything ran according to his strict schedule and dictates. Physicians were like that, and this was the worst of the lot, Curt thought, as he slowly withdrew his passport folder, slipped out two cards, put the folder back into his jacket, and very deliberately slid the cards forward on the desk for the Herr Doktor's inspection.

Cerdat did the little bifocal stunt of lifting his head slightly to read. Curt watched him closely, trying to see if there was even the slightest flicker of recognition, but could detect nothing in the man's examination or in his response: "And what am I to make of this? Who is this Señor—ah—Villalta?"

"A very good friend of mine," Curt said evenly. "We have certain business dealings in common—and he has assured me that he is a friend of yours as well."

The grimace-smile twisted Cerdat's face again, his lips show-

ing pink out of the black beard and mustache, like some under-
part of an animal. "How very interesting, since I have absolutely
no acquaintance with any Villalta."

Weird, Curt thought: the conversation was going as planned,
and he had a *déjà vu* sense of mouthing words that he had
already spoken.

"Señor Villalta assured me that you are a careful man, Dr.
Cerdat. But he also assured me that you can be a direct and
decisive man, and advised me to approach you directly, like this."
He took another puff at his cigarette, paused, and then said: "It
has become imperative, because of certain things that have occurred among the American military, that I speak to you of·—
Cipriano Farlo."

Having saved the name, he uttered it finally with a Castilian
smoothness, letting the six syllables roll out of his mouth like
polished marbles.

Nothing. Cerdat simply sat in his revolving chair staring
back. Damned cool, Curt thought, or he thinks I'm out of my
mind. The pool of silence widened. The desk clock ticked on.
Cuckoo. Cuckoo . . .

"Dr. Fielding," Cerdat finally said, his voice consolingly meas-
ured, "there has been here some enormous mistake. I assure you
that I know nothing of what you speak. There is nothing for me
to say, except that I am sorry. And now, if you don't mind, I am
a very busy man." He rose to his feet.

Curt stared at him, refusing to stand. Then, deliberately, he
dropped his cigarette to the tile floor and ground it underfoot.
So much for anal-compulsives, he thought, watching the look
of small outrage that stiffened Cerdat's face so that his beard
quivered.

"Cerdat," he said, dropping the title, letting his own face
harden with anger that was partly feigned. "I did not make this
fuckin' trip all the way up from Zaragoza just to play games.
Francisco Villalta told me to come directly to you. He said he
would have sent a note along but that it would be too risky if

anything happened. He said that his card and my possession of the facts would be enough. He also said that if you had any doubts at all, you could call him by phone and check."

Now he stood up, feeling some satisfaction in towering over Cerdat. If the feeling was irrational, the telephone remark was not. That was one of the snares he had worked on quite carefully. It was set with the knowledge that any phone call into Spain would take at least an hour, the national telephone system being a jumble of inefficiency, so that even a call between Madrid and Zaragoza took over an hour.

And besides. All he had to know was that Cerdat wanted to call. That would be enough.

Cerdat stood there observing him, arms folded across his chest, goggled eyes never wavering. Finally he said, "Dr. Fielding, I do not wish to be impolite, as you have been. Please to notice I do not approve of your behavior. Also, I know nothing of these people you speak of. You are under some delusion. Now, I do not want to hear any more about your—your problem." With a sweep of his hand he retrieved the ashtray and put it back in the desk drawer.

He *was* good, Curt thought: either awfully good or completely in the clear.

"O.K.," he said, "we'll see." He made his voice raspy hard. "Everything Villalta and I have planned depends on your cooperation. If I have to drive out of here without the information I've come for, all of us are going to suffer."

He picked up his topcoat from the adjacent chair and started toward the door. There he turned, thinking, I'm not so bad myself, and said, "One last thing. I do not find you impolite, Doctor, just stupidly bureaucratic. Now, I am staying at the Hotel Catalunya. I will wait there until two this afternoon. If I have not heard from you by then—I'm leaving."

Not waiting to see the effect of his last words, he walked swiftly out into the corridor and toward the entry. It was possible Cerdat might try to stop him before he left, like some shopkeeper in the climactic moment of bluff and bargain. But there was no call, no rush of feet behind him. So he walked past the *portero,* nodding, and out the main door. As he climbed into the VW he did not look back toward the clinic, to see if the cuckoos were out in force. . . .

On the drive back to Las Escaldas he reviewed the entire visit, trying to discover any error in the way he had handled things, and concluded it had all gone according to plan. Of course, it would have been nice if Cerdat had simply admitted knowing Villalta and Farlo on the spot. But that was hardly to be expected, certainly not with anyone like the Herr Doktor.

What was left now was Snare Number Two.

Back at the hotel he found that he had time to kill. He went up to his room and wrote a letter to John Bowers, asking if in all his experience in Spain he had come to know anything about Francisco Villalta, or whether he could dig up any information about him, quietly, because it was a really confidential matter. If he needed a lead, there was Villalta's connection with the air base and the Brigada Social. That was about it, except that Villalta had spent a number of years in the States, getting a law degree, supposedly, from the University of Texas.

After the letter he packed. It was only a quarter to twelve when he went down to check out. He chatted with the clerk at the desk until finally the manager came out of his office with a copy of the bill stamped paid. The manager said he hoped they would have Señor Fielding with them again, perhaps for the skiing when his arm was better. Curt said he would like that; the Catalunya was a most agreeable hotel. The manager smiled, directing one of the *botones* to carry Señor Fielding's bag out to his car.

It had been a successful exit, Curt assured himself, tipping the bellboy. Now he had to find something to do for the next two hours.

Traffic was fairly heavy in Andorra la Vella. There were no

places to park on the main street, which was just as well. He
turned off at the top of a rise, found an alleyway and left the
VW there. Taking his portfolio with him, he walked until he
found a neat little restaurant, the Casa de Vals. Up front there
was a section given over to cigarettes, tobacco, stamps, and
picture postcards. He bought a batch of cards and enough
stamps for them, as well as the letter for Bowers.

During a lunch of bean soup, mountain ham, fried trout,
and cream pastry, he wrote cards to Mary Masters, Helen, the
Beaverses, and Eddy Stone. The effort of writing the cards and
thinking of the people involved in each instance was tiring
and confusing, as though he were taking short, swift flights
back into a world where he no longer had a real place.

He posted the cards and the letter in a mailbox to which the
proprietress directed him. It was still only one-fifteen; he had
about another hour to go. Remembering his promise to Victoria,
he decided to do what the tourist is supposed to do in Andorra.
There were jewelry stores and gift shops everywhere he looked.
In one he bought a bracelet consisting of a golden chain, with
a large gold coin dangling from it, stamped with Caesar
Augustus on one side and a Roman eagle on the other. In
another he picked up a pure angora sweater, pink and fluffy,
in what he hoped was the right size for Lois. He made one last
stop in a grocery store that seemed to specialize in wines and
liquors, where the clerk assured him he was allowed to enter
Spain with a gallon of spirits without paying any duty. Curt
asked him to put four crockery flasks of Armagnac in a box
and he'd take them.

As he paid for the brandy, he looked again at his watch and
felt an uncontrollable tremor of anxiety. It was five after two.
Now, damn it, he would find out once and for all.

Back at the VW, he opened his suitcase and put the sweater
and bracelet in. Then he wedged the cardboard box of Armagnac
into the trunk with the suitcase—taking one of the flasks out,

on second thought, and placing it under his portfolio on the front seat. He just might need a drink in a little while. He needed one now, for that matter.

When he walked into the lobby of the Catalunya, the same clerk was on duty. The man looked dumfounded to see him. A good sign.

"You did not expect to see me again so soon," Curt said, smiling.

"No, *señor*. Is there something wrong?"

"Nothing important. I just discovered that I have lost my gloves, or perhaps left them in my room."

"Oh, yes. This we can find out immediately." The clerk, as immaculately attired as an undertaker, beckoned one of the *botones* and sent him up to the room to search for a pair of gloves that the *señor* might have left behind.

The bellboy headed for the elevator, and the desk clerk said, "He will be back in a moment," paused, and then added: "By the way, it is peculiar that you should have returned, because approximately an hour after your departure, there was a telephone call for you."

Curt's heart flopped with excitement. *Jesus—how simply and beautifully it had worked!*

"A call for me," he said. "Who?"

No need to ask, really. Not another soul in Andorra knew him. *That* was what was so perfect about it. Had to be dear old Cerdat. . . .

"I don't know, *señor*. It was a lady."

Lady? His mind fluttered momentarily. All right, Cerdat had simply had a secretary or nurse call.

"What did she say?"

"Nothing, except to ask if you are registered at the hotel. And of course I told her that you had been, but that you had checked out earlier."

Perfect. Per*fect*!

"It must have been the girl from the shop I went to this

morning. She was looking into a special bracelet for me. Not important."

The clerk looked relieved and turned his attention to some guests who wanted information about the ski lifts at Solineau. In a moment the *botones* returned and told the *señor* there were no gloves in room 206. Curt thanked him, caught the clerk's eye, shrugged, and waved good-bye.

Out in the VW he sat perfectly still, turning matters over in his mind. The first part of his plan had worked with reassuring perfection. The clinic and Cerdat held the answer to Cipriano Farlo. Had to. There was otherwise no reason to call the hotel, or have it called. Either Cerdat had been able to reach˙Villalta, and Villalta had told him how to handle the *norteamericano,* or he had not been able to reach him and Cerdat had decided to talk with him after all. Or had just decided to keep tabs on him. It didn't matter; the reason wasn't important. The only important thing was that Cerdat *had* checked the Hotel Catalunya. That was enough.

He took a combination bottle opener and corkscrew from the niche under the dash and opened the Armagnac. He took a good pull at the flask. It was a strong brandy and he felt an immediate glow signaling his senses to relax. A second pull reinforced the signal. He corked the flask. Gods have their ichor, temporary titans Armagnac. He started the motor, put the VW into gear, and pulled out of the parking court.

Driving slowly back toward Andorra la Vella, he went over what he had raised to capitals in his mind—Part Two of The Plan. What he needed was someplace to kill three or four hours. Perhaps make a phone call or two . . . ? There was some indecision.

27
A Man in White

Although he knew it was too early, by five o'clock Curt was parked in the lot of the Clínica de Santa María at the far end from the clinic. With the seat pushed back as far as it would go, he sat slumped down low, so that someone even ten feet away would have a hard time seeing there was anyone in the car. Pretty soon the lights inside the clinic went on, then two spots set high up on poles at either side of the parking lot, but little illumination reached back to where he was.

By six Cerdat had still not come out of the building, and Curt began having doubts about the way he'd planned things. When he had left the hotel that afternoon, his first impulse had been to call Cerdat's residence and ask what time the doctor was expected home, but he realized that wouldn't do because whoever answered the phone, maid or wife, would certainly inform Cerdat that a man with a foreign accent had inquired after him, and Cerdat would probably alert them at the clinic or come out himself. Then he had thought of going into a shop and, on the pretext of speaking neither Spanish nor French, asking some clerk to call Cerdat's place and check for him; but that wouldn't do either, because anyone as prominent as Cerdat would probably be well known to whomever he might ask, and the risk of arousing a third party's suspicion was unwise.

So here he sat. Waiting for Cerdat. Willing him to come out

318

of the clinic, get into one of the cars near the entry—probably the black Mercedes in the first stall—and drive away. . . .

At about six-twenty a uniformed man stepped out onto the landing. It was the same *portero* who had let him in that morning. The metal buttons on his jacket glinted in an angle of light. He stood sniffing the air like a dog; then he ran one sleeve under his nose, wiping it the way a school child might, looking around him guiltily, and then stepped back into the building.

This *portero* might be a problem, Curt thought, wondering when he went off duty, and whether it would be better dealing with him or a new man. That would depend on what Cerdat might have said to him this morning.

A little later three nurses wearing white caps and gray cloaks left the clinic in the company of a heavy-set man who looked somewhat Russian because of his black overcoat and Persian lamb hat. Curt could hear their excited chatter as they followed him to a Citroën station wagon. The man held open a front door, then a back. The nurses hopped in, the last getting a bit of assistance from the doctor, if he was one, that would have qualified him as a proctologist.

Not long after the Citroën disappeared around the bend, Curt heard the approaching whine of a heavy motor, and in a few moments a bus followed its own splayed beams of light into the parking area. The driver angled in close to the entry and parked there, letting the motor run. Some twenty people got out and went into the clinic: nurses, some older women, and five or six men wearing zippered jackets and caps.

Within ten minutes another group of people, the doubles of those who had just entered, came out of the building and clambered aboard the bus. The day shift was going home except for the *portero*, who stood on the landing waving good-bye to someone. The bus doors closed, headlights came back on, and the driver started the vehicle around in a swinging turn.

Curt ducked down as the lights swept past. The bus went by

with a wavering whine and groan, and faded from sight and sound around the bend in the road.

The *portero* had re-entered the building, which was lit up like a Christmas tree. The lot was again a place of semidarkness. All Curt could hear now was the sough of wind in the pines nearby.

Where *was* Cerdat? What the hell was he, Curtis Fielding, doing up here on a goddamned mountainside in Andorra? Back in Zaragoza he could be sitting in a café having his evening *tapas*, maybe getting ready for dinner with Victoria, or going out to the base. Back in Pennwood he could be stretched out in Mary Masters' apartment, watching her clear the table, listening to records, getting ready for a long winter's night. . . .

Jesus, it *was* cold. He considered turning the motor on for some heat, but decided against it. Instead he took a full swallow of the Armagnac, patting the flask, thinking of old Mr. Flood —"Have another drink. Don't mind if I do. . . ."

Once again he held up his watch so that it caught a glare of light and he saw that it was six-forty. A moment later, two men came out onto the landing, one pulling on gloves. They stood chatting a while, then started down the steps. They got into separate cars, but not the Mercedes, and so far as Curt could judge, neither of them was Cerdat. The sporty red Volvo pulled out first, the Renault followed closely after.

Again silence. Still no Cerdat. Doubt flashed through his mind like the first signals of a toothache: What if Cerdat made it a habit to sleep over at the clinic, this being one of the occasions? Or what if there was a rear exit from the building, perhaps a little private parking area for the Herr Doktor? Or what if he had already left sometime this afternoon?

If Cerdat was staying over, that meant delay. *He* would have to find a hotel room and try again tomorrow night. If there were a rear exit—but there wasn't: he'd have spotted it, would have been able to see the lights of the car as it came out to the road. . . .

All day long he had been patient, proceeding according to plan, but now his nerve ends were twingeing. Since the telephone call to the Catalunya he had been suffering an anxiety that came from knowing that the clinic held The Answer. Now if he could just get in there and work things right! But if he went in and Cerdat was still there, that would be the end of that. And he doubted he'd get another chance.

What about waiting until seven-thirty? If Cerdat didn't make his exit by then, he could drive back to Las Escaldas, telephone the clinic, and . . .

He sat up suddenly and then slid back down. The door had opened, spilling light onto the landing. The *portero* came out, holding the door open wide. He was followed by a man in a dark overcoat and black Homburg hat. Curt felt his pulses jump. He couldn't be sure, but it had to be Cerdat. The man came down the steps, got into the Mercedes, started it on the second try; and as he pulled out of the parking slot, the *portero* made a two-fingered salute that couldn't have been meant for anyone but the commander in chief.

When the Mercedes had gone and the *portero* stepped back into the clinic, Curt sat up straight, getting the stiffness out of his joints, remembering how he used to feel at tennis tournaments when it came his turn to play. He took his left wrist out of the sling and rubbed his forearm, then fitted the wrist back into the sling. He combed his hair and tightened his tie. Turning on the ignition, he started the VW, put it in gear, and drove slowly around the lot, pulling into one of the vacated slots near the clinic. Damn clever, he told himself, as he got out of the car. Anyone near the entry would hear the car pull in.

As he started up the steps, his feet and legs felt numb from the long wait. He hesitated at the top of the landing. Inside, across the corridor, he could see a nurse sitting at the main desk. She seemed to be writing. Unless the *portero* got into the act, she would probably be the one he'd have to deal with.

He opened the door and strode in, trying to look confident and cheerful, holding his blue portfolio so that it acted as a sign of professionalism. The *portero* was nowhere to be seen. The nurse looked at him and got up out of her chair as he approached. She was rather pretty in a round-faced, round-eyed way, no more than twenty-five, he judged. Better than some old battle-ax, he thought.

"*Buenas noches,*" he said.

"*Muy buenas, señor.*"

"Doctor," he said, smiling his best. "Dr. Fielding."

"*Perdóneme, Doktor,*" she said, her round eyes examining his slung arm. She was caught in the same small dilemma that had bothered Cerdat earlier in the day. "How can I be of service to you?"

"I hope that I am not too late to see Dr. Cerdat. Has he departed as yet?"

"Oh," she said, "I am sorry. He has just now departed."

"*Qué lastima,*" he said. "But it is no matter. He told me earlier today that if he was not here, I should simply proceed."

He put the portfolio on the desk and, withdrawing his passport folder, took from it his Fulbright card with its official stamp of identification. Handing it to the nurse, he said, "My business will not take long. Dr. Cerdat said that whoever was on duty could let me see your files for the information necessary."

The Fulbright card impressed the nurse, but as she handed it back her eyes showed some doubt.

"I do not know," she said, looking at him as if to decide. "The files are of course private, as is this clinic, and I do not want to exceed my authority. If only you had come a few minutes earlier, the Herr Doktor was still here. . . ."

"All I need to see are your entries for three dates in April," Curt said. "Dr. Cerdat assured me that as a professional courtesy there would be no difficulty."

She stood there, biting her full lower lip. It occurred to Curt that she might want to call on whichever doctor was in charge, and that would complicate hell out of matters.

Just then someone walked past and said, *"Buenas noches, Doktor."* Curt turned and nodded, dumfounded, for an instant not recognizing the man as the *portero* in street dress.

"Muy buenas," he said, heartily, seeing how the recognition had affected the nurse. "It was this good man who took me to the director's office this morning," he explained. "Only he looks less military this evening."

The nurse smiled at their private joke. "Well," she said, "I believe that we can accommodate you and give you the information you wish, Doktor. Will you come with me?"

She waved to another nurse who was passing down the corridor and asked her to take her place at the desk for a moment. Then she led the way into a side office. Inside were files and glass cabinets containing drugs. The keys hung from a hook on the doorjamb. The nurse took these down and, sorting the keys attached to a large ring, found the one she wanted. It opened one of the greenish metal file cabinets, marked with a white card on which something was typed.

"What dates of entry did you want?" she asked.

"April eighth, ninth, and tenth," he said, holding his breath, hoping nothing would foul things up now.

"Bueno, aquí." She kept one hand in the file and then removed a folder, placing it on top of the cabinet.

He opened his portfolio and took out a writing pad; then, searching his pockets, he asked if she could get him a pen or pencil to make notes. She appeared reluctant to leave him alone with the files, but then said, *"Sí, momento, Doktor."*

He opened the folder and quickly found the entries for April eighth. His heart thumped, perspiration formed on his forehead. But nothing. No Farlo.

He turned the page over to April ninth, using a finger to run down a short list of names.

Jesus! The bank robber had finally opened the vault. There it was:

Entered: Sr. Cipriano Farlo Trigo.

And, unlike all the other entries for that date, there was nothing in the column reserved for release!

The nurse had returned with a pen. She looked at him as though he were ill. "Is there something wrong, Doktor?"

"Ah, no," he said. "Everything is perfectly all right." *Perfectly,* a voice inside was shouting. *Don't you know that Farlo is in this hospital right now!* His eyes skipped across the entry sheet and caught the room number: 204.

"I just had to have this exact entry date," he said to the nurse, hoping his breathing, his voice, were not dead give-aways. He wrote on his pad, playing for time, trying to think clearly.

He returned the pen to her. She put everything back into the file case.

When she faced him again he said, "Now, if you please, I would like to visit Señor Farlo."

Something in her changed, he could see it. She had somehow sensed that things were not exactly right. Her face colored with embarrassment or suspicion, or both.

Avoiding his eyes, she said, "No. That is not possible without the presence of Dr. Cerdat. No one is to see the occupant of 204 without the specific approval of the director."

Of course. That was it. Farlo would be a very special case. And this little baby-faced nurse was getting ready to push the panic-alarm button.

"Ah," he said, "I am being unfair, *señorita*. I have put you in a very difficult position. Do not preoccupy yourself with this matter. I will call Dr. Cerdat tonight and return when he is here tomorrow."

In his mind he had already decided he'd have to get into the building some other way than through this main entrance. He knew the room: that was enough. He ought to be able to get to it somehow. He had eliminated the idea of forcing his way up. That left sneaking in or trying to get official help. And chances of getting help on Cerdat's home grounds would be mighty slim.

"*Bueno,*" the girl was saying, "*eso es mejor.*" Her eyes registered relief as she regained her composure and smiled.

Outside he got into the VW, started it, and drove away. He went out to the main gate, turned around on the highway, and headed back. As he approached the lot again he cut the headlights and drove slowly in the dark, as he remembered doing in Italy near the front lines. It was really remarkable how well you could see after the first few moments, especially on a night like this, clear, with a rising moon. He pulled into the lot quietly, parking just off the road.

He slipped his wrist out of the sling and took off his white trench coat, folding it on the floor behind the driver's seat. He was about to remove the sling, too, but on second thought decided it might be of use if he had to fake something inside the clinic. Closing the door of the VW softly behind him, he walked quickly across the road toward the bordering growth of pines.

In places the snow was two or three feet deep, but under the trees he found it easier going. About ten minutes later, huffing and perspiring, he finally made it to the rear of the clinic. His shoes, socks, and trouser legs were clogged with snow. He found a path that had been cleared out to a trash heap and followed it, hurrying across a snow-free area, and dashing under a balcony that doubled as a roof. Beneath it, stacked against the wall, were large waste containers, and a snow-blowing machine. At one side of that he found what he was looking for. A basement door. He tried it. Locked.

He took the sling off his neck and quickly wrapped it around his right hand. There were four square panes of glass in the top section of the door. He jabbed the right bottom pane sharply. Glass tinkled on the floor inside. He waited, listening, like an animal, his ears alert. He heard the wind in the trees, heard snow from a branch plop like soft dough. Nothing else.

He pulled out a few jagged sections of the window, placing each one carefully to one side of his feet. Reaching in to turn the doorknob proved awkward with his right hand. It was all backward. But finally he heard a click; the door opened. He pushed in carefully and stepped into the basement, realizing it was warm inside and that, without his having been aware of it, he was cold as hell. He closed the door and stood there trying to get accustomed to the darkness. In a few moments he could make things out and discovered that he was in a combined furnace and storage room. There were crates and sections of beds and some piled-up mattresses. He sat on the edge of a crate and took his right shoe off and emptied it of snow, brushing his sock and pants; then repeated the operation with the other foot.

Now he was ready. He picked his way across the concrete floor slowly, making sure he didn't trip or knock anything over. In the far corner of the room was a wide wooden staircase. He started up, treading lightly, letting each creak die before the next. At the top he put an ear to the door. He could hear rapid steps on the other side, and a feminine voice calling out something he couldn't understand. Then for several minutes there was nothing. He felt himself starting to grow dizzy, like a statue in an unnatural stance. He'd have to take his chances; that's all there was to it.

The knob turned under his hand with a *clack* that he was sure could be heard throughout the building. The door was ajar now. Light angled through. He was able to see out into what was obviously a corridor. But which corridor? If he stepped out, did he walk right into view of the head nurse. . . ? He remembered sneaking into movies when he was a kid; the trick was to open an exit door with a wire coat hanger. Once you heard that click, you waited a moment, and then stepped in, hoping no usher was standing there waiting to kick you right back out.

He opened the door quickly. The hall was clear. He closed the door behind him as softly as he could.

This was obviously the first floor. The numbers on the rooms opposite were 106 and 108. He looked right and left along the hall, realizing that at any moment someone could turn a corner and see him.

Just a few feet away was a double swinging door. He made for it and burst through, finding himself in a stair well. He went up one flight, turned, and almost fell over himself, slipping, catching his balance.

There near the top of the stairs, with her posterior pointing toward him, was a woman on her knees scrubbing the landing. It was too late to turn around, he thought, just keep going. How else get to 204.

"*Buenas noches, señora,*" he said.

"*Muy buenas, señor.*" She turned to look at him, pushing her hair up with her wrist.

He squeezed past her, and said, "*Perdóneme,*" as he stepped across the landing she had just washed. He was through the swinging doors and out in the corridor before she had much chance to examine his face.

And there across the hall on a slant was room 204.

He made for it. The door was closed. He turned the knob, opened the door, stepped in.

The figure in the bed didn't move. There was nothing in the room except the bed, a chair, and in the far corner near the window a floor lamp, which gave off a small tent of light.

Curt stood with his back against the door. "Farlo," he said, in a husky voice. "Cipriano Farlo."

The figure in the bed turned slowly, awkwardly, painfully, it seemed. White bandages swathed one side of the face, cutting the face on a diagonal, with the right eye showing. It blinked at Curt, seeking to identify.

There was something incomplete about the man he was look-ing at, Curt thought. Something broken, out of kilter.

"Farlo," he said, walking slowly toward the bed. "Listen. I am a friend. I have been searching for you for months. I have come to see you for your uncle, and because I am a friend of the family of Theodore Swiatski."

The single eye twitched and the body of the man under the white sheet jerked spasmodically, as though some invisible hand had stuck him with a needle. A portion of the mouth just clear of the bandages moved, but no words came out.

Curt leaned over, his face close to the other. "Listen, please. This is important. I am here to ask you about what happened to you and Theodore Swiatski. I represent his family. I am a friend of his brothers. You must tell me everything that happened."

The lips moved. They formed one Spanish word: *"Vaya."* The man turned his face away.

"I cannot *go*," Curt said disbelievingly. "You do not com-prehend what difficulties I have overcome to be here. I want to help. Don't you understand?"

Maybe the man was drugged. *"No comprendes, hombre?"*

The face turned toward him, the eye blinking. The mouth twisted into a horrible half-grin. In a hoarse voice, the man said, "You're too goddamn late, buddy. The ball game's over."

28
A Wake in 204

Curt's face went numb. He felt powerless to move. The tent of light thrown by the floor lamp seemed to dip and sway, the room echoed with words that amplified in his ears: "The ball game's over . . . *The ball game's over* . . . THE BALL GAME'S OVER. . . ." He put his good hand to his head, staring at the man, whose body formed an irregular ridge under the white sheet. A mocking half-grin protruded from the bandages around the face.

He could hear his own words, coming of their own will, sounding silly, fatuous, inevitable: "You . . . you're Teddy Swiatski."

"Right," the lips said, rasping. "And who the hell are you?"

Curt didn't answer. He stood there feeling detached, as though going back into a dream from which he was trying to escape.

Then he heard himself speaking again: "Excuse me. I have to get used to this. . . . I, ah, I've been searching for Cipriano Farlo for about three months now. My name is Curtis Fielding. I'm from Hazleton. I know your brothers, Joe and Stanley. . . ."

The eye blinked; the lips twitched, then said, "How are they?"

"They're fine."

"They are, huh? And how'n hell I know you're who you say you are?"

329

Curt moved the chair from near the wall quietly over to the bed and sat down.

In a low voice he began to tell Swiatski about his brother's coming to Pennwood and asking him to see what he could find out in Spain. He mentioned the undertaker Brutkevich and the letter from María Maite. For good measure, he told him about Joe Swiatski's daughter and about his sister, the nun, who had intended to visit them in Shaker Heights. Then he quickly narrated what had happened since he'd come to Spain, mentioning Villalta, Stafford, Pardee, Ralph Sterner. He explained about the shepherd near Bujaraloz and about checking the hospitals in France and then finally arriving in Andorra.

Swiatski watched him intently during the entire account, his eye registering acknowledgment occasionally with a blink. When Curt finished, he said, "Yeah, you've really done a job. But if you don't mind me sayin' so, you could still be a real slick operator from the CID."

"Would you like to see my passport and papers?"

"They could be fake," the man on the bed said. Then, as though struck by a thought, he added, "Tell me something about Hazleton, you're supposed to be from there an' all."

Curt thought for a moment, then said, "All right. You're from Hazle Township. So you know where North Mountain Street comes down and meets Lehigh. Well, the streetcar tracks are still there, even though the cars don't run any more. And just where North Mountain curves you can still see where cars used to jump the tracks and run down Lehigh."

Swiatski made that half-smile. "O.K.," he said, "you know the place."

"Good," Curt said. "I'm glad you believe me. Now how do we get you out of here?"

"We don't."

"What the hell do you mean?" Curt sounded incredulous even to himself.

"I got my reasons. And what I want you to do is to forget you even saw me."

"You're kidding."

"I am, huh? Let me show you somethin'. Gimme your hand."

Swiatski guided his hand over the sheets, here, then there, and what Curt felt were two stumps where the legs should have been. He pulled his hand out of Swiatski's grip, as though he had done something furtive. He remembered saying "Christ," and again, "Christ." Now he added, "I'm sorry, sorry as hell, but—"

Swiatski drew his left arm from beneath the sheet; the hand had been amputated at the wrist.

It was somehow ludicrous. All of it, like some stage joke. Curt wanted to laugh, to say, Yeah, you are pretty bad off, aren't you? Oh, *off*, yes indeed, the exact word!

"Jesus," he said, "what happened? I remember that shepherd said the other man walked away."

"Yeah, I walked away, but that's the last walkin' I did."

"What happened?"

"Burns, blood poison. They shoulda let me die. Half my goddamn face is chewed away."

"But they should be able to do something. Plastic surgery."

"That's right. That's what they did. I'm wearin' part of my ass up here." His right hand motioned toward his face.

"Well, but back in the States you could get—"

"I ain't goin' nowhere. There's only one thing I want this fuckin' Cerdat to do." His eye stared at Curt defiantly. "And there's only one thing I want you to do."

"You're crazy."

"Not *that*. Just forget that you ever saw me."

"*Why?* We can—"

"Listen, I appreciate what you done. Far's that goes, you been a real friend to my brothers. But don't foul it all up now. I am not goin' back to no States. I've had it. All I want is out —O-U-T. Understan'?"

Curt nodded slowly: "I guess I do."

"Good. You must be a pretty smart guy, bein' a professor an' all. You know I still got some rights. Sure, I screwed things up pretty good. No one's gotta tell me that. Even if I was to go back to the States like you're suggestin', you know what'd happen? I'd end up in a prison hospital five or ten years. They got that over me."

"They. Who's they?"

"No dice. Let's drop it."

"Listen, Teddy, we may not have much time. Will anybody be coming in here?"

"No. The supper's over. They don't bother me. They stay the hell away."

"All right. Now let's get this straight. I'll do anything you want me to do, if you want to get out of here and back to the States. If you don't want that, I will consider not telling your brothers or anybody else that I found you. But I *have* to get some answers. I've got to."

The eye studied him; then Swiatski turned from his side onto his back, so that he was looking up at the ceiling. His voice was conspiratorially low as he said, "You get me enough pills, or some kinda shot to do the job, I'll give you all the answers you want."

Curt thought of lines he hadn't remembered in years—something about "I knew the wreck as I knew the man . . . I stood there with a slight kind of engine in my hand . . . You wouldn't blame me, would you? I thought not . . ."

And now there was this slab of burnt meat, with nothing but pain between it and the end. No, that wasn't true. Not with what they could do these days with artificial limbs and plastic surgery. . . .

"Teddy," he said, "I can't do that."

"Then we got nothin' to talk about."

"Yes, we do, because you know that I can have your brothers and the U.S. government piling in here in a couple of days."

The man on the bed said nothing. His breathing was like that of someone with a bad cold. Curt listened to the wheezing, watched the unmoving trunk beneath the sheet. He hadn't yet sorted out his emotions, but he knew now that the man he was dealing with was somehow worthwhile. Not once had he sought pity, not once cracked open. There he lay, maybe twenty-three years old, half-dead, yet somehow a man. Jesus, but wasn't it just lovely to be bullying someone like that!

Teddy Swiatski rolled back over on his left side. All that could be seen of the face was the blunt nose, part of the mouth, a high cheekbone, and the eye. Trying to picture the whole face, Curt thought of Stanley Swiatski.

The lips moved. "What kinda answers you want? And what're you thinkin' of doin'?"

"I know that you and Farlo were mixed up in something with Villalta, and I think Pardee. María Maite says you were, but doesn't know what it was all about. Your friend Mike Dalton thinks somebody may have tampered with your car, to get rid of you and maybe Farlo as well. I think whatever's going on ought to be stopped. Somebody ought to put the skids to Villalta and Pardee."

"What would happen to María?"

"So far as I can tell she's out of it. She's in Madrid, and I don't think Villalta has a hold on her. Her sister's baby has been taken over into France. I'd keep María out of it."

"And you'd keep your mouth shut about me, here?"

"Is that what you really want?"

"You know it."

Curt looked at Teddy Swiatski steadily, still confused by the rapidity with which things had happened, and by a basic contradiction in the whole situation. If it was true that the accident had been arranged so that Swiatski would be killed, why did Villalta now keep him from killing himself? Cerdat could easily manage things—an overdose of sleeping tablets, something of the sort. *Why* was Swiatski being kept alive under the name of Cipriano Farlo . . . ?

He took a deep breath and releasing it, said, "All right. I agree. But I think you're wrong."

"Forget about *wrong*. All's I want's your word."

"You've got that."

"Which means not a hint to nobody—not my brothers, not María. Nobody, right?"

"Right."

The lips smiled tautly. "There's one other thing. You got a cigarette on you? They don't let me smoke 'ceptin' when a nurse or someone's here. 'Fraid I'll burn myself up. Stupid bastards; 'at's the *one* thing I couldn't do. They also nailed a screen over the window."

Curt took a cigarette out of his pocket and lit it. He handed it carefully to Teddy, who took a heavy drag, and began to talk in a low, steady voice:

"It all started about a month after I come to the base at Zaragoza. I had my trainin' as a mechanic but the place was phased down and they had no real assignment for me, so they stuck me in the Air Police. They put me in with a guy that was shippin' out, to learn how to take care of the files. About a week before he leaves, this guy and me went to town on a toot; and when we're about half-loaded, he says to me how'd I like to make myself a nice little bundle, and I says, sure, sure, who wouldn't? and he says he'll talk to me about in a day or two if I'm serious.

"I di'n't think much about it, but a day or so later we're in the office there, alone, and he asks me again: serious, you know? He says him and someone else's gone over my record and've seen that I been AWOL and was in a couple of scraps and that I don' look like no saint. And I says all right, cut the crap, and what's this all about. And he says just to take it easy. All's he wants to know is can I keep my mout' shut and do I wanna make some real dough. And I tell him he's already got my answer to that—yeah." As Swiatski went on, his voice flat and noncommittal, Curt felt like a priest, the way he did when undergraduate students unburdened themselves with accounts of pregnancies, abortions, cheating practices, and family splits. He wondered whether there was any therapy in the words coming out of that broken face.

Captain Pardee *was* the other man, Teddy said, and he became Pardee's trusted assistant in the file room, getting the necessary information, keeping materials in a special file in his own room under lock and key.

Pardee, in turn, worked under Villalta. They had a whole batch of rackets that paid off beautifully. They sold American military gas coupons that discounted forty per cent on all gasoline bought in Spain, and were thus as good as gold certificates. They trafficked in special AFX cards that allowed selected shoppers to buy American goods, including food, liquor, and clothes—later sold on the black market for double the price. They trucked out furniture and refrigerators and stoves from surplus housing at the base and got rid of them in Barcelona. They had a physician on the take at the base hospital who supplied them with drugs periodically. "And," Swiatski said, "old Cerdat's usin' almost nothin' but American stuff here in his clinic."

One of Teddy's special tasks had been to line up prospective car sellers, men who were shipping out and wanted to get rid of their cars. Every car bought by an American serviceman, or brought over by him, had to be accounted for when he left the country. They could not be sold in Spain unless the Spanish government collected its hundred per cent import, which was standard on all foreign vehicles; but Villalta had a system whereby the cars could be driven to Andorra, sold to a dummy buyer, provided with Andorran plates, and then brought back into Spain and sold illegally to Spanish citizens on a fifty per cent mark-up.

All of this, Swiatski said, was beautifully organized; but none of it was slicker than the operation they had going with the girls. Villalta had that all worked out. Spanish girls paid anywhere from several hundred dollars to several thousand to get properly certified as fit wives for American airmen. Since almost all of them were prostitutes, they had no real trouble raising the cash. There was a sliding scale, the more beautiful and more prosperous the girl, the more money she paid.

Swiatski stopped talking, as though he had suddenly grown very tired, and Curt wondered whether he was thinking about María Maite.

"Sounds like a well-oiled operation," he commented.

"You said it."

"Well, what happened? How did you get into this—this mess? Do you think they tried to get rid of you? Ralph Sterner said that it looked as though someone might have tampered with the brakes of your Chevy, but he couldn't tell for sure."

The eye stared at him from the bed. "I don't know myself. Cippi was drivin' when it happened. I sorta dozed off. Next thing I knew . . ." His voice trailed off.

"But why? Why would they try anything like that?"

"Because I was wise to the bastards, and because I got pissed-off."

He began to talk about María Maite how he had met her, how much he thought of her and cared for her, as "a really honest Jane, the best broad I ever met in my life." She had given up other men; they had been living together and planned to be married.

"I know," Curt said. "She told me about it. She's a fine woman." In lots of ways, he thought guiltily, remembering.

He was sorry he had interrupted. Teddy Swiatski lay still under the sheet and didn't say anything for a while. Then the scratchy voice started again.

He had told Pardee about María Maite, and about her sister, who also wanted to marry an airman, someone who knew about the half-Negro child but didn't care. There had been a terrific argument later when Pardee said that he could swing a double deal on the sisters for two thousand dollars. The sister's case, with the child involved, would take very special handling. And María Maite was a top-notch "entertainer," who couldn't be let off the hook without ruining the whole system.

Through Cipriano Farlo, who was a contact for legal forms and certain forged documents, Swiatski had gotten a true picture of how large an operation they were involved in.

"Cippi was a real good guy, and me and him became buddies," Swiatski said. "He took me to a lot of places around town and sometimes we made runs into Barcelona, and like that. He knew that I cheated a little on María now and then but that I, you know, really cared for her, and that we was serious. It was him that got us a nice apartment for her to live in, I mean nicer than the dump she was in, because it was hard for someone doin' her line of work to get a good place."

It was also Cipriano who told him how they could make some extra money of their own. He had the right kind of paper and the right printing setup to make gasoline coupons that were dead ringers for the real thing. They hadn't been greedy, printed only small batches, and let them filter out through some trusted friends Farlo had in the Tubos.

It was also Cipriano who opened his eyes to the nature of the organization they were involved with.

"You ever heard of somethin' called La Legión Azoo?" Swiatski asked.

"No."

"Means the Blue Legion in English."

"Oh, *azul*. Yes, I have. Franco lent them to Hitler in the war; they fought with the Germans on the Russian front."

"That's it. Well, they now have a kinda civilian branch, you know. The top men, most of them, were connected with the army, but they got others, too. Some very respectable people and high up in the government."

According to Swiatski's account, the Blue Legion was a secret organization: nobody knew how many members they really had, or exactly what they did. But they had their fingers in a lot of pies; they were connected with the building of the American air bases and the construction of off-base housing. They had made millions of dollars off Rota, Morón de la Frontera,

Torrejón, and the Zaragoza base. They worked with the Brigada Social in controlling night clubs and prostitution.

"Like a kinda Mafia," Swiatski said. "Only Cippi told me they're a real patriotic bunch, workin' for a strong government in Spain, and gettin' rid of the Americans and everybody else soon's they get their dough. They want all things to stay Spanish, pure and simple, none of this foreign influence."

"And where does Villalta fit into all this?"

"He's right up there—number two man in and around Zaragoza."

"Who's number one?"

"I don't know. Cippi didn't know. But he's gotta be one of the big cheeses because, Cippi said, Zaragoza's the real center for this outfit."

"Do you think Pardee knows about this organization?"

Swiatski considered the question, then said, "Tell the troot, I don't know. One thing I do know's that bastard's gonna take around a cool fifty grand home with him."

Curt tried to digest all Swiatski had said. He lit another cigarette and handed it over to him. Outside in the corridor he could hear the quick rubbery slip of feet on the tile floor. He waited until they were gone, then he said, "You must know that everyone thinks you're dead."

"So I figured."

"Stafford had an American expert come in to identify the body. He made a positive identification on the basis of some bridgework and your dental chart. Do you think they got to him?"

The lips parted in a narrow smile. "That's pretty cute."

"What is?"

"The night we crashed I remember them gettin' me into an ambulance. They put me in a Spanish hospital somewheres that night. Next day they put me in a back of a car and drove me over the border to here. Either a day or two after that, this Cerdat comes into the room, and I'm doped up to my ears, and di'n't know what's goin' on, but he took my partial out, you know, a bridge." Swiatski laughed. "How d'you like that. So that's what they were up to. . . ."

"They planted your bridgework on Farlo." Curt got a momentary picture of someone prying open the corpse's mouth—that must have been one pretty job.

"Listen, Teddy," he went on, "there's something else that's really bothering me. Do you have any idea why they've been keeping you like this? First it seems they want you and Farlo dead. Then they go to all the trouble of keeping you alive in this clinic."

Swiatski took a long pull on the cigarette and handed it to Curt, blowing a stream of smoke out between his thin lips.

"It is screwy, ain't it? If you had any idea how many times I ask myself this question. Why'n hell don't they gimme something? I asked that friggin' Cerdat a hundred times. At first, after this"—he waved his good hand weakly in a gesture that took in his leg stumps—"I thought maybe he was gonna do it. Then a week went by, a month. They put that screen in. . . . I swear to Christ, I been goin' crazy. You got any idea what it's like to be in one room? Like this! I think you ought to do something for me. I mean it. Don't be like these other bastards. You say—"

"Listen. I can't do it. I told you before that—"

"Yeah, yeah." The voice trailed off, and for the first time Curt realized how tired the man on the bed was.

Once again, carefully, he argued that the best thing would be for him to be removed to the United States; he'd get to see his family, it wouldn't be so bad even if he did have to spend some time in a prison hospital, and in his condition he might even be spared that, might be sent home.

Swiatski didn't even bother to answer, and finally Curt said, "Teddy," as though to awaken him.

"Forget it," the lips said. "Just get outta here, will you? And remember, you give me your word."

"But *why?* You're young; you could pull out of this."

"You kiddin'? You must be real stuck on life, buddy. You never had nothin' just make you sick of the whole business? If you ain't you must be one of the lucky ones. Me, I'm *not* stuck on life. You thought I was dead, they all think I'm dead. Great, 'cause I *am* dead. You just happena come to the wake a little early, that's all."

Swiatski lay limp under the white coverlet, the energy drained out of him. He had turned his face so that all Curt could see of it was the nose protruding above the swathed bandages. The figure looked shrouded, almost mummified. Maybe Swiatski was right: more than half of death had been thrust on him through those revolving doors of chance that open and close around us without our even being aware of them, until it's too late, and our own existence is called into question. So why not let him have whatever choice there was in the rest of the matter? Let the *flesh* become *will* and the carnival is over. I *will*, therefore I am, and am *not!* Little Dory hadn't reached either flesh or will. . . .

"All right," Curt said, his voice soft. "You may not know it, but the full name of this place is the Clinic of St. Mary of the Remedies. Maybe in your case, for you, there is no remedy—or you don't want it, which is the same thing. I respect your decision."

He stood up, his legs feeling numb. "If you're absolutely sure there's nothing else you want me to do, I'm going to leave."

He thought of shaking hands or gripping Teddy Swiatski's shoulder. Something. But it was useless, he felt; it would just embarrass them both.

"I'm sorry I can't do any more, but if it's any consolation, I'm going to try to nail Villalta and Pardee."

There was still no answer. Curt started to walk toward the door. The man on the bed shifted so that his good eye was on him. Curt stood with his hand on the door knob. Teddy Swiatski said, "You do what you gotta do." His lips curved into a tight smile, and he added, "I'm glad that you know my brothers, Doc."

"I'm glad I know all the Swiatski brothers."

"Good. Then just keep your yap shut about this one." The lips made that tough cocky smile again.

Curt opened the door quickly and stepped out into the hall. He made for the doors across the way, then went down the staircase to the first floor. Through the circular peephole window he saw two nurses talking in the hall. He waited behind the swinging doors. When they finally split up he went out fast, across the corridor, through the door leading into the basement, feeling like the rabbit hiding from the wolves in one of those movie cartoons.

As he left the basement, he locked the door, hoping that the broken glass might look like some kind of accident when they found it.

Outside he could barely see the moon. A light snow had started falling. He paused under the balcony, thinking of the man in white that he had left behind; it would have been possible to carry him out. . . .

He crossed the open space and went into the pines.

29
Hand to Hand

By five o'clock he had finished typing his notes, an original and two carbons, listing point by point what Teddy Swiatski had told him, and what he had gotten from Major Stafford's account of the accident, as well as the supporting statements of María Maite and Ralph Sterner. He read it over, thinking of it as "my brief." It was satisfactory. He put one of the carbons into his portfolio, another into the top drawer of the desk. The original he folded and placed into a heavily stamped envelope, addressed to himself care of the English department at Pennwood.

As he washed and changed into a fresh shirt he once more went over the procedure he had decided to follow. He had thought about it all the way back from Andorra and finally decided to see Villalta before going to Stafford. There would be plenty of time to talk to Stafford after he got some things cleared up.

From his apartment he walked toward the Gran, past the Air Ministry building, the medical college, across the Plaza del Paraíso. It was fairly cold but not windy. The Moncayo for once seemed to be taking a rest. Late shoppers hustled along through the arcades of the Independencia, lottery men stood at their posts offering winning tickets, and near every other large column a woman sat on a folding stool tending a chestnut brazier.

When he reached the corner of Independencia and Costa, he

stopped at the post office, took the envelope addressed to himself out of his jacket, and slipped it into the lion's mouth beneath the bronze sign that said *Cartas Extranjeras.*

The Gran Hotel was just two minutes away. He entered the lobby, took an elevator up to the third floor, and walked down the hall to suite 308. In all the time he had known him, this was the first time he'd been to Villalta's quarters; even when he himself had been staying at the hotel they'd always met downstairs, at the bar or in the huge, glass-domed sitting room off the lobby.

The door to 308 had been left slightly ajar. He used the little brass knocker, rapping sharply. From inside Villalta's voice boomed, *"Venga, hombre, venga."*

Curt went in. Villalta stood just inside the bathroom with a towel dangling from his hands. He wore a clean shirt but no tie. His face was red and his hair disheveled, as though he had just finished washing and drying himself. "Make yourself comfortable, Curtis," he said. "I will be with you in a minute."

"O.K." Curt took off his trench coat and dropped it over an armchair.

The room was arranged as a kind of parlor. A maroon rug covered most of the tile floor. There was a divan and a straightbacked chair, both of some period design. On opposing walls hung large reproductions of the masters—Goya's clothed Maja and Velasquez' little Bourbon princeling on a fat-bellied pony.

What made the room different from hundreds of others in deluxe hotels across Spain was a section near the windows that gave out onto Calle de Isaac Peral. Curt walked toward it. In this section were a desk, a file cabinet, and an office chair. On the desk was a sleek new Olivetti portable and behind that an imposing leather folding frame with two good-sized photos in it.

He put his portfolio on the divan, picked up the leather holder, and began studying the photographs. One showed a man of about fifty in an officer's uniform: bulky chest crossed by a satin sash; square epauletted shoulders; sharp face dominated by a curved blade of a nose; a head of black hair combed back tight and straight. From a ribbon around the man's neck dangled a military cross; and from a suspension ribbon above his left breast another medal, this one circular with rayed edges.

The second photo showed the same man, standing in profile, shaking hands with a medal-heavy officer in a white tunic, made splendid by wide gold-braided cuffs and lapels and black shoulder boards that matched his black shirt and tie. This obviously superior officer was completely bald, and he had the puffy round face of some enormous baby except for heavy black arching brows, which looked as though they had been painted on as part of a mask.

There was an inscription written diagonally across the bottom of this photograph. Curt turned the frame and was attempting to decipher it when Villalta came out of the bathroom, straightening his tie.

"Can you read it?" he said.

"Not quite." Curt replaced the frame on the desk.

"To one of Spain's illustrious Christian knights," Villalta recited from memory.

"Which one's the Christian knight?"

Villalta laughed good-naturedly as he came across the room, hand extended. Curt accepted the hand and the token *abrazo*.

"Sit here. It is more comfortable." Villalta indicated the divan, as he himself sat in the swivel chair at the desk. Picking the folder up from the desk, he said, pointing to the bald man, "This is José Solis Ruiz. Have you heard of him?"

"Sorry."

"It is nothing. We have such an insular history."

"Who is he?"

"A commander of the Falange and a trusted member of the cabinet."

"And who's the other man, your father?"

"His younger brother, Colonel Augustín Villalta y Muñoz. It is he who is the Christian—"

Someone knocked at the door. It was a waiter, carrying a tray with glasses, a bottle, and some *tapas*, which he set down on the desk. After Villalta had signed the chit, the waiter nodded to both of them, saying, *"Muchas gracias, Señor Villalta,"* and left.

"All the comforts of home," Villalta said. "I remember that you like Carlos Primero, no?" He poured the two snifters half full and then offered the tray to his guest.

"Just the cognac for now," Curt said.

"Bueno." Villalta put the tray back on the desk, and lifting his snifter said, *"Salud*—to true friendship!"

"Why not the truth?"

"The same."

"You sure about that?" Curt sipped the brandy.

Villalta's eyes watched him over the rim of his glass. "Aren't you?" he said, and then drank.

"That's one reason I wanted to see you."

"You did sound very serious on the phone." Villalta turned and placed his glass on the tray. When he looked back at Curt, his eyes were steady, his hawkish face set, as though he were willing to hunt the truth with anyone who had the nerve.

Curt took his time, getting himself set. During that long drive back from Andorra, he had thought of two things over and over again—Teddy Swiatski in the clinic, and Villalta and how he wanted to hit him with the full story. Now he thought he had a way to make his attack.

"This uncle of yours. He wouldn't be connected with La Legión Azul, would he?"

Villalta's eyebrows shot up. "Ah," he said, "I see that you *do* know something of our insular history."

"I know your Christian knights joined with the equally Christian knights of Germany to slay the Red Dragon of godless Russia."

"The same dragon which is giving you so much trouble these days."

"We won't worry about that. The question is about your uncle and the Blue Legion."

"I see no reason to deny it. He was a commander in La División Azul. A very distinguished soldier."

"And what about his nephew? Is he a member of the Division?"

"What are you talking about? You must know it was disbanded after the war."

"Militarily, yes. But I'm talking about the new Legion—the one that fights to preserve the Spanish way of life, runs most of the rackets in Spain, and uses its money and underground power to maintain the regime."

"*Ay, hombre,* you return from Madrid full of information!"

"Enough. And I'm getting more. But, in this friendly pursuit of the truth, are you denying there is such an organization?"

Villalta smiled. "Of course not, Curtis. Your information is quite correct."

"And about you, too?"

"I don't know. Maybe you know more than me."

"All I know is that in the province of Zaragoza you are the number two man in the Blue Legion."

Villalta made a clucking sound. "It seems a shame to be just number two, doesn't it? Do you also know who is *número uno?*"

"I was hoping you'd tell me."

"Who knows? Maybe I will."

"And maybe you'd also like to tell me why you did what you did to Theodore Swiatski." Curt realized his voice had gotten hard. "You've been screwing around with the lives of people, Francisco. You've played me for a jerk, laughing behind my back. But as you must know, *true* friend, I finally made it to Andorra—"

"Please, don't get excited, Curtis," Villalta said. "I know about your trip to Andorra."

He turned and picked up his brandy and, while Curt watched

him, he took a calm, slow pull at the snifter. Was the son of a bitch bluffing?

When Villalta spoke again his voice was gentle, pacifying. "You must have known, Curtis, that Cerdat would call me. After all, you told him to. And the fact is that he called me twice. The second time to tell me they discovered someone had come into the hospital through the cellar. The nurse told him how you came back that night. So it was easy to assume that it was you, no?"

Villalta did not sound like a man who was losing any points. Somehow he had succeeded in taking all the sting out of the attack. Curt wanted to knock him over at least once, upset him, ruin his confidence.

"We know the worst about me," he said. "I broke into a hospital. But let's talk about you. You're the one makes toasts to true friendship. Yet you're the one's been lying to me since I got to this city. You're the one who got rid of Maite and old man Farlo—"

Villalta raised a hand in protest, but Curt went on.

"You're one of the chief whoremongers in the country, a racketeer posing as a superpatriot. You're one of those who tried to kill two men, and when that failed, stuck one of them away as a basket case in the mountains of Andorra. Hell, you're the one probably arranged things so that I'd break my goddamn neck in a ski race."

"Please, Curtis," Villalta burst in. "I can understand you getting excited, but—"

"That is putting it mildly, friend."

"You say you want to find out the truth. Good, let us do it. But first of all, you are not being fair when you say I try to get you hurt at Candanchú. That is very stupid."

Curt knew it was, but just glared. Of all the accusations he had made, that was the one, peculiarly enough, that seemed to bother Villalta most.

"Listen, *hombre*, if I wanted for you to be hurt, I could have arranged it most easily."

"I'll bet you could. As part of our friendship."

Villalta looked exasperated. "All right," he said. "When I first met you, I just wanted to find out if you are looking for information. That is true. But then I begin to like you. No, I am not lying. If we had met under other conditions, I would still want you as a friend. And I tell you why. You think you are a pretty tough guy, an intellectual with a knowledge of the hard life. You think that you don't give a damn about things. But I know how you feel about María Victoria—and how she feels about you. And believe me, that is no small thing. She has told me that you are a good man, and I believe her. Also I know that you have some feeling for this country and for the people and the way we feel. Even your maid, old Isabella, has told me, and of course I know about the *viejo* Farlo."

Villalta stopped abruptly, then said: "But I must tell you something, Curtis. There are some things in life that are more important than friendship."

"So I'm learning."

"I think you know them—family, country, honor."

"You mean the honor of managing whores into marriage, and fixing a car so that two men can be killed. You have a hell of a sense of honor, *amigo*."

"Just a moment. It is not I that marry the whores, but your countrymen. And if you don't remove your bases, there will soon be no whores left in Spain."

"You know what I mean—selling them marriage certificates."

"*Hombre!* Don't be sentimental. They can afford it, and the money goes to good use."

"I'll bet it does."

"For this, you must take my word. And you must take my word that the decision to get rid of Farlo and your Swiatski was not mine. If it had not been for me, Swiatski would have been allowed to die."

"Do you think you did him a favor?"

"No. I am not sentimental about him. I don't know what he has told you, but he made a lot of trouble, and there could have been more. He also made a lot of money for what he was doing. Did he tell you that he got two thousand dollars a month? Not bad, eh? And all the girls he wanted. Oh, yes, he and Farlo had lots of the girls. Often it was they who drove them from one city to another."

"You're just saying that," Curt said, not at all convinced at the sound of his own words. "Teddy Swiatski was in love with Maite; they were going to get married, go to the States, along with her sister, and you put the blocks to that."

"You are more *romántico* than Quixote. This sister of Maite was a special whore of the Negroes in the *barrio corea* in Madrid —no, let me finish. She was mixed up with many men, and always to get to the States. It was impossible, especially after the baby she had. Your American military made it impossible; she was on a special list of undesirables. So when your friend Swiatski wants for her to gain permission, nothing I could do would help. As for Maite herself, I don't know, I think she is pretty good woman and maybe, as you say, truly in love— *quién sabe?*"

"Even if I believed you about all this, there's no good reason why you should have tried to kill Swiatski and Farlo. That's murder, goddamn it! And I'm going to see that you're nailed for it, one way or the other."

He reached into his portfolio, took out the copy of the chronicle he had set down that afternoon, and shoved it at Villalta.

"This is going into the proper hands for action," he concluded, "and you might as well know what's in it."

Villalta read the notes. Curt could see that in another three or four years a small bald spot in the middle of his head would probably spread into quite a tonsure. He felt regret as well as triumph in watching the Spaniard read.

When Villalta peered up from the notes, he did not look as worried as Curt imagined he would. "Have you presented this document to anyone yet?"

"I have it on deposit where it is sure to come to the proper attention."

"Good. That is good. Now listen to me, Curtis. You do not think I am your friend but I am. And this is a time when we must act properly. You have shown me something; now let me show you."

He got up and went to the file cabinet. It took him only a moment to withdraw a Manila folder from one of the drawers. He shoved the drawer closed and, turning to Curt, gave him the folder.

"Go ahead," he said. "You might find it very interesting."

Curt noticed the tab typed on the edge of the folder: FIELDING, CURTIS.

Inside he found clippings of stories he had seen in the Zaragoza newspaper morgues, announcing his own arrival at the university as Fulbright professor. Attached with a paper clip was a small note in Spanish. Curt had some difficulty with it, but finally made out the gist.

This was what we thought might happen. You were right. Now we must watch this man and what he does. Take all the precautions necessary. I think I can be of help.

Then there was a phrase that had something to do with *in the commanded adoration of our country,* or something of the sort. The note was signed, in bright blue ink, with the initial M.

Curt looked up at Villalta inquiringly, as though he were going to question him, but Villalta said, "Please, read on to the conclusion."

The next item in the folder was a list of dates; they showed his arrival time in Madrid, the day of his meeting with Marta

Torres and María Victoria at Oskar's. These were followed by dates of his talk with Major Stafford and all the trips he had taken into France to visit various hospitals, as well as his trips to see old Farlo in Huesca. There was a note of the time he had first gone to the Cancela, and in parentheses a directive to get María Maite out of town immediately. Next to this was the date on which he had gone back to the Cancela to question Pepe about her whereabouts. The last entries on the page read:

Dec. 30–Jan. 2—Candanchú. F still wanting to go to Andorra
Jan. 3—F leaves for Andorra
Jan. 4—F approaches Cerdat. *F has seen S.*
Jan. 5—F returns to Zar. Under close observation
Jan. 6—F has asked for meeting

Curt shot a quick look at Villalta, who sat watching him. "Very good," he said grudgingly. "I suppose you had reports from border guards every time I left the country."

"Of course." Villalta lifted his brandy deliberately and took a sip.

It was all here, Curt thought, except for his meeting with the shepherd and with María Maite in Madrid. It was not a perfect tally, but almost, and that "under close observation" probably meant they knew he'd not yet gone to anyone at the base.

"Who"—Curt returned to a question that was bothering him—"who is this M?"

"Perhaps later," Villalta said. "First, there is something I must know. What do you want done with Swiatski?"

"That's a hell of a question!"

"We must be truthful with each other. You see we have, in a sense, kept him alive because of you."

"Because of me!"

"Yes, read the next page in your dossier."

Curt looked at it. It was a letter on bonded paper with an

embossed insigne consisting of an eagle inside a circle. He began
to read:

After the most exhaustive investigation, everything we have discovered
indicates that the person known as Curtis T. Fielding is what he pur-
ports to be. Using our most trusted and highest-placed informants, our
office has been able to discover nothing that would connect him, even
on a temporary basis, with any of the North American intelligence
services.

> In the honor of our country,
> José Arturo Barragán

He looked at the date of the letter: December 19. That meant
Villalta had known before they went to Candanchú that his
connection with the Swiatski case was not official.

He looked at Villalta sharply. "You mean you were keeping
Teddy Swiatski alive until you found out if I was with some
intelligence service?"

"It has been an awkward situation, very difficult and painful
for us."

"For *you?* Jesus Christ, how about for him? Why didn't you
just put the poor bastard out of his misery?"

"At first there were the Civil Guards. It was they who found
him and took him to the hospital in Lérida. They had to be
managed. From them we discovered that there was probably at
least one witness, a shepherd. Then the newspapers complicated
matters with the story that it was Farlo who was killed. We
were afraid the Americans would start a full investigation, even
perhaps after the medical identification. So we took Swiatski to
our friend Cerdat in Andorra."

"Where you butchered him."

"Believe me, Curtis, everything that could be done for him
was done."

"I still don't see why you didn't just let him die."

"In Andorra we had him under our control. No matter what

your government did, we were not guilty of murdering a
norteamericano military. Cerdat has an affidavit that says it is
Swiatski's request that he be sheltered from a harsh life as a
terrible cripple. The only way the Spanish government can be
embarrassed is that a poor deserter has been smuggled past our
frontier."

"And if there were no investigation, you could just quietly
put him out of his misery!"

"Wouldn't that be better for him? That is what I am asking
you now."

"You son of a bitch." Curt stood up, his fists clenched. "You
want *me* to be partner to your crime!"

Villalta looked up at him as though he were suddenly bored.
"Curtis," he said, in an elaborately patient tone, "don't let us
play games with each other. You say you want to find the
truth. Isn't it true that he would be better off dead? Isn't that
what *he* wants?"

Curt sat down, avoiding Villalta's gaze. He lit a cigarette,
thinking, taking a swallow of the Carlos Primero. They had
known for nearly two weeks that the investigation on his part
was unofficial. But all they had done was to go on keeping
tabs on him. Villalta had figured that even if he found something, he'd be reluctant to act.

Obviously Villalta was right. He was voicing a dilemma that
Curt had not solved since leaving Andorra. To expose Villalta
and the others meant exposing Teddy. Not to do so meant
giving mute assent to killing Teddy or allowing him to commit
suicide.

"Suppose," he found himself saying, "suppose I decide to
chance it, and tell what I know to the authorities?"

"*Bueno*, then we could still get rid of Theodore Swiatski.
There would be no record of him. He disappears. In fact, you
see, he is dead, except for your word."

"What's wrong with my word?"

"You haven't finished reading your file."

It was true. There was a sheaf of six or seven carbon copies. Curt read through them quickly. They were depositions: five from students in his class, the other from Chester Bromwich. All of them said much the same thing—that Professor Curtis Fielding had expressed detrimental and dangerous opinions against the present regime of Spain, and that his influence was responsible for much of the student unrest that had resulted in demonstrations and near-riots, specifically on the dates of November fifth and twenty-fifth.

Curt thought of the times students had approached him, asking for his opinion about their cause and their need to reject state control over their organization. He had followed the line laid down by the Fulbright Commission, saying that they should do what they thought best; he would hold his classes as usual.

It had probably been easy for Villalta to get to the five students in his class, through their families, in all likelihood. And poor, nervous little Bromwich, with his Spanish wife, five children, and no possibilities back in England. . . .

"Nice work," he said, looking at Villalta. "You must have especially enjoyed twisting Bromwich's skinny arm. Make him give back Gibraltar while you're at it."

"*Hombre!* One does as one must."

"And what if I do what I must?"

"You must not make a fool of yourself. If you make any trouble, you will be revealed as an *agent provocateur*, an undesirable, a liar."

"There would still be people who'd believe me."

"You would be deported within a week."

"So what? I would have had my season in Spain. I'd make thousands of dollars writing articles for magazines begging for stuff." As Curt spoke, he had one of those clear peephole memories of himself and John Bowers, with Bowers telling the Spanish censor the same thing. "Why, I ought to be willing to pay you a percentage of the take."

"So you would be willing to sacrifice Theodore Swiatski, and relations between the two countries, *and* your own reputation?"

"I told you, maybe Swiatski's better off dead; and I don't think I'd be ruining relations, I'd be improving them. As for my reputation, you know damned well it would be improved."

"And what about María Victoria?"

Curt blinked; he snuffed his cigarette out. "María Victoria?" he said blankly.

"Yes. Also, you must know you are going to be responsible for what happens to María Maite."

"You bastard!" he said. "What do you mean about María Victoria? I know you could probably manage anything you wanted with Maite, but you wouldn't dare do anything to Victoria, not with her position and family. You're just running a bluff there."

Villalta began laughing in a remarkably good-natured way. Finally, he said, "Ah, Curtis. I was not wrong about you. You are one of the good *norteamericanos*. But you still have much to learn about this country." He studied Curt seriously, sympathetically. Don't you know who is *número uno* in this section of La División Azul? Can't you guess?"

Curt stared at him for silent moments. Then he put his left hand above his eyes, to rub away the tautness in his brows, and said, "Oh, no!"

"Of course, *hombre, el juez*. Judge Mandar. He is one of the top men in the country."

Curt saw himself in the foyer of Victoria's apartment, meeting her father, that squarely built little man, neatly attired, shorter than his daughter, smiling, pleasant . . . the Spanish chamber of commerce type.

"This is another bluff," Curt said. "I don't believe it."

"Ask *him*. He said that if there are any difficulties in our talk, he would discuss them with you."

Jesus, wasn't that just neat! Villalta wasn't bluffing. Victoria's father was in up to his ears.

Something nasty stirred his mind.

"Do you mean, then, that Victoria has been—"

"No," Villalta cut in. "She knows nothing at all of this. The *juez* and I thought that it would be natural for her to take advantage of the fact that you were a professor in her field. And since Marta Torres is a good friend of the family . . ." He held his hands out in a gesture showing how easy and natural it had been.

Curt thought of himself and Victoria in his room at the Hotel Somport, when they had almost gone all the way. No, he thought, she had not been faking anywhere along the line. She was in the clear. It was just the old man. *Just?* How could you tell her her father was a murderer, a top-level racketeer?

"What's to prevent me from going to her, explaining my position and why it's necessary to put matters into the hands of the authorities?"

"I thought that you really cared for her."

"I do, goddamn it. I've been considering marrying her, as you well know."

Villalta smiled wryly. "You mean you think there are things more important than friendship or love?"

Curt recognized the irony. "Yes, I do. And maybe she would understand."

"*Hombre!* María Victoria has been brought up to recognize the supremacy of two things—the church and the family. Do you think that if she must choose between you and her father —her family—she will choose you!"

Curt thought over his chances and, even admitting that Victoria was truly in love with him, realized that she would have no real choice.

"No," he said, "I don't think she would choose me. But I didn't start any of this. You and Mandar did. She would have to recognize that and pay the price. We both would." Curt paused, then added, "And so will you."

"I don't think so," Villalta said, his jaw line tightening as though he had clamped down on a hard nut.

"Why not? You going to arrange an 'accident' for me too, *amigo?*"

"That I do not want and that is not necessary, Curtis. And I hope that this is not, either." With evident reluctance he reached into his breast pocket and pulled out a folded document. "This can be added to your folder also," he said, handing over a sheaf of lined, legalistic-looking papers.

Curt began to read, having some trouble with Spanish legal terms for a while, but then, feeling his face getting hotter and hotter, managed to make his way through most of the document, including a deposition by Villalta and another by Juan Cortes. He turned to the last page, which was empty, except for María Victoria's full name typed at the top.

"Do you care if I keep this as a memento of Spain?"

"*Qué quieres tú, amigo,*" Villalta said. "We have plenty of copies."

"I'll bet you do," Curt said, getting to his feet, putting the folded sheets into his blue portfolio. "And now if you don't mind—"

"Curtis. *Por favor.* Please sit down. I know how you feel. I know that you may never speak to me again in your life. Let me explain something to you."

"I'd just as soon take it standing, *amigo.*"

"No, no. Please sit down."

Curt stared at him. "You mean you want to prolong your relationship with a—a *rapist?*" He shook the portfolio. "Isn't that what I am, a *norteamericano* who practices *violación?* Do you really think *she* would go through with it?"

"Believe me, I sincerely hope that we shall not have to find out." Vallalta looked as though he had just swallowed a bitter pill.

Curt sat down, watching him.

"You tell me that you want to discover the truth. Now we have come very close to it. You see that we have an impasse. You have your side of the truth and I have mine. I am working

for what I think is best for my country. I don't take any
money out of this. All of it goes into La División. And if you
think that is bad, then think of your own secret police and
organization, your CIA and others. Do you think that their
methods are so beautifully clean in Guatemala or Vietnam?"

"The CIA is an official part of the government. You're not;
you're an organized gang."

"Are you sure that is a legitimate difference? Don't be a
fool. We have as much official acceptance under the surface as
the CIA or your FBI or the CID. Don't forget it."

"So you're just a peacetime soldier in the service of your
country, is that it?"

"You do not seem to believe it, but that is the truth. I do
not want my country to become a Coca-Cola colony, with
beatniks and rock 'n roll and *béisbol* and mortorcycle rapists and
democratic criminals with the highest crime rate in the world.
So we are poor. We live as you did during the Depression. But
our streets are safe. We have a strong sense of family. Our
women remain women; our men, mostly men. Our girls do not
fall over with their legs spread every time someone touches them.
You have been here long enough to know some of these things.
You must see some of the changes; you must know that if
we are going to change, it is necessary to change for the best,
not the worst. We admire you *norteamericanos* for many
things; you are friendly, you are generous; you make a miracle
in one century of production. But you *cannot* control your
wives and daughters. You cannot control your criminals, or
treat Negroes like human beings. You do not know how to use
your great power in international affairs. We admire you and
despise you, as most of the world does. I do not want for
Spain to become a little United States. I want it to find what
is good in itself."

Curt had been trying to think of counterarguments as
Villalta went on with his little speech, but he realized that

there was no real argument against the idea of a people's self-determination. Whether Villalta represented the will of most of the Spanish people or simply of the hard-headed governing class was a moot question, or at least one he was sure he could never convince him about.

He said: "Reactionary Spain. That's what you still speak for—reaction. You never had a Reformation. You never gave democracy a fair chance. You want to linger on somewhere between the expulsion of the Moors and the seventeenth century. You're not giving people a chance to remain Spanish, just drudges. You rose to power and decayed faster than any other European nation and you want to stay in your own state of decay."

"Decay? Don't you see it in the United States? The breakdown of the family, the university, the state, all authority. The only thing that keeps you going is money, atomic power—"

"And the ability to replace what we rip down with something better."

"We shall see. When your country fails, it is going to take half of the world with it. You are already headed in the direction of France and Italy—too much food, too much drink, hedonism, plenty of everything but respect and dignity and a concept of form. You are going to break in pieces, *hombre*."

"You'll never see the day. You don't understand the process."

"*Vamos a ver*."

There seemed nothing more to say. Curt got to his feet again, picked up the portfolio.

Villalta stood up also. "I think," he said, "that you owe me one thing before you leave."

"Namely?"

"That you tell me what you intend to do about all of this."

Curt stared hard at him. His eyes blinked once, twice. He realized that Villalta had to make some kind of report on what had happened between them. He also realized that Villalta had probably argued for this way of taking care of things, rather than something more drastic, like having him run over by a car.

"I'll let you know in a couple of days."

Villalta nodded his head slowly. "All right. I hope that you will do the wise thing."

Curt turned his back and went to the armchair for his trench coat. He threw it over his slung left arm and started for the door.

"Curtis."

He paused with his hand on the doorknob and turned to look at Villalta. He was standing in front of the desk, smiling. "Don't forget what I said—there are some things stronger than friendship. But I *am* your friend."

"I'll think about it," Curt said, ambiguously, and turning the knob, opened the door and walked out into the hall.

PART SIX

30
Homeward Bound

He sat looking out at the airfield through a wall of windows that ran the length of the main dining room at Barajas terminal. A huge aluminum bird wheeled slowly out to a holding position. Free of hoses, electric trucks, and loading ramps, it was ready to do what others of its species, marked BOAC and PAN AM and Iberia, had done previously in powering their way up from the grasp of concrete into directed flight.

He watched as the TWA 707 trundled farther out onto the runway and made a circling turn. For a few moments it quivered there, motors whining to a shrill crescendo. Then the wheels began to move, faster and faster, until finally, with sudden thrust, the plane was off the ground. It climbed to a shuddering point where all was held in balance: it either flew or fell.

Minutes later there was nothing left except a jet trail, something of a visual mnemonic device, a fading remembrance of things past here, present there.

For him the past in Spain had begun here at Barajas. And although it seemed more like nine years ago than nine months, he clearly remembered Milly Bowers standing out there in the huge reception room. When she had spotted her husband coming up the ramp, she ran toward him as though he had just escaped the tiger's clutch. It had taken her some time to recover a civilized attitude and become fully cognizant of the introduction. Curt had materialized for her only after her husband's well-being was established fact. She had shaken his hand just as their stewardess, Miss Nancy Jean Jameson, clacked by with a friend, waving a little ta-ta, and smiling her eternal smile.

Good old Nancy Jean, he thought. Good old Mary Masters. Good old Lois Harte. Yes, and good old Helen Wright Fielding. Women like that do as much as Milton or good brown ale can to justify the ways of god to man. If that's true, what of the Milly Bowerses and the María Victoria Mandars? You seem out of luck there, don't you? Dead end. Little Dory Markle. Whatever *they* justify, you haven't been able to comprehend, as yet. . . .

He looked down at his wristwatch: four-eleven. If Bowers was coming he'd better hurry. The loud-speaker system had just confirmed ramp time as four-thirty, departure five-fifteen.

Actually, he thought, he had departed from Spain when he had called Villalta two days after their meeting in his suite. Things had stopped happening after that. He had not seen Villalta again, except once across the Independencia: Villalta had been sitting with a group of acquaintances, and had not seen him go by. Even at that distance he had recognized the proud set of the Spaniard's head, the carefree and yet controlled manner of the man. There had been one gesture, a simple movement of the hand in making a conversational point, which made it seem as though Villalta were pronouncing a humorous benediction. That moment on the Independencia had been, in retrospect, his true departure from Spain. Everything else had been a trailing off, like the almost dissolved jet stream in the sky above Barajas.

When he had gone to María Victoria's apartment that one last time, it was apparent something inside each of them had been broken. He suspected that her father had laid down the law about any liaison with a *norteamericano*. The honeymoon was over before it began. Her voice had been tight, her manner carefully aloof and proud, as though they had done something foolishly personal, and now she had to rectify matters under proper orders from above. As he responded in kind, making no demands, asking for no further consideration, he saw her lips and eyelids tremble momentarily. Finally, as he had taken her hand at the door, thanking her for all she had done, he paused, looking deeply into those elaborate brown eyes, and then added in a low voice: "You know, of course, that we are both fools, Victoria, because neither one of us knows what to do with love, or we don't know how to love enough. Either way, it's a shame."

If she had said or done anything to encourage him then, he might have tried to convince her, and himself. But she did not. The only satisfaction he had was that her voice cracked as she said, "*Adiós,* Curtis, I cannot thank you enough."

After that he had spent most of his free time out at the base. He saw quite a bit of the Sterners and the Staffords. One night at the club with Lois Harte, now fully resigned to the good-friend role, he had seen Pardee and was tempted to punch him in the mouth. But he hadn't, realizing that it would be a hollow and stupid compensation. Instead, he had contented himself with walking up to Pardee and telling him in a normal, steady voice, so that others around could hear, that he knew him to be one of the truly outstanding all-American bastards of all time. Pardee had turned turkey-red but, probably coached by Villalta on how to act in such a situation, had swallowed his gorge and walked out of the bar. . . .

He looked at his watch again: four-fifteen. There was a snifter of cognac on the table before him. He picked it up and drank almost to the bottom. The table he sat at was large enough for eight or ten, and it made him feel very much alone, the *extranjero.* He was headed back to Pennwood for his summer classes, but he knew he would feel just as much an outsider there as he did now. After all, he had developed something of a Spanish ear for nuance, something of a Spanish eye for arroyos and dusty mesas and high rocky mountains. The lush greenery of Pennwood would now seem strange.

Just then John Bowers, tall, angular, concerned, hustled into the dining room. He paused, spotted Curt, waved and, taking long strides, came quickly to the table.

"I'm sorry, Curt," he said, rushing his words together, "but I got held up in traffic on the *avenida*, and then I had trouble getting out past customs because some jerk had to call a superior to check my credentials."

"It's all right. Just as long as you made it." Curt caught the waiter's eye and beckoned him over.

Bowers ordered a *whisky-sifón*. Curt said he'd have the same. The waiter raised his eyebrows and shook his head, as if this were crazy, since he had just been drinking cognac.

Curt said to Bowers, "I've got to get prepared for my native land. That'll be the end of Carlos Primero for a long time." He sipped the last of the brandy.

"I hope not for too long," Bowers said. "Milly says that we're expecting you back within a year, at least on a flying visit."

"That's nice of her, but I thought you'd be leaving pretty soon yourselves. Wasn't she anxious to get back to the States for the girls' sakes?"

Bowers looked somewhat embarrassed. "Well, she was," he admitted, "but you might as well know our Peggy's engagement to Juan Espero is about to be announced. You'll have to make it back for the wedding."

"So. The Pact of Madrid is going to be tied in marital bonds."

"Well, I don't see why not. He's a very fine boy, with a good future as a lawyer. His family's one of the most enlightened in Spain—solid, liberal. We couldn't ask for more anywhere, and Peggy, God bless her, is simply in love."

"And love conquers all!"

Bowers looked at him inquiringly, slightly offended by what he took as a jibe.

"I didn't mean it that way," Curt added quickly. "Actually I was thinking of someone else."

"Oh," Bowers said, "oh, I guess I know what you mean. It just didn't work, did it?"

"No, it didn't. I don't think we ever had a chance."

The waiter returned and Bowers insisted on paying for the drinks as a going-away present.

"*Salud*," he said.

Curt smiled. "*Dinero y amor.*"

They both drank. Then Bowers said, "You never did tell me what broke it up, Curt."

"A very long story. Maybe I'll tell you someday."

"Well, when you do, maybe you'll tell me whether Villalta had anything to do with it. After I sent you that stuff on him, I decided he'd be a tough bird to fly with."

"Tough, yes. But I have known worse."

"Are you using any of that Blue Legion stuff in your *Phaeton* piece?"

"Yes, I've got about three paragraphs on it. No names, because I don't have any documentation, but a list of their activities, and a general outline of the way they're organized." Rather mild satisfaction, he thought.

Bowers drank some more of his Scotch, then said, "And you finally finished off that business about the airman—what was his name?"

"Swiatski. Theodore Swiatski. Yes, I checked that all out to the end. It's finished business."

"And did you ever find the Spaniard that was involved? I forget his name."

"Cipriano Farlo," Curt said. "I never found him."

But I know where you can find him, he thought, if you're ever in the Hazleton area.

The public address system clicked on and made its announcement, first in Spanish, then English, and finally French.

"That's it," Curt said.

Bowers said, "I'll say my good-bye here, if you don't mind. I hate those last minute jobs."

"*Adiós, amigo,*" Curt said, smiling, shaking the big Midwesterner's hand.

"*Hasta pronto,*" Bowers said. His gray eyes were steady on Curt. "Someday, if you can ever manage it, I'd like to hear the whole story."

His voice was insistent, and what it plainly indicated was that Bowers was not satisfied with the answers he'd been given.

Curt smiled ruefully, shook his head. "You do have a nose for news, John. Keep it away from the Spanish grindstone."

Aboard the plane a stewardess spoke to Curt in the dulcet tones of recorded pleasantness. "Let me take that for you, sir."

She could have been Nancy Jean's cousin: vital but not sufficient.

Curt said, "Thank you," and handed her the matador's sword that he had been allowed to bring aboard as part of his hand luggage. Two weeks ago it had been delivered to his apartment with a note from Villalta saying that this sword had been used by Paco Camino in the slaying of a brave bull. It was offered as "*un recuerdo de España y amistad,*" a memento of Spain and friendship.

The stewardess gazed at the weapon curiously. It was wrapped in brown paper, but the bandaged knob, crossbar, and guard protruded, along with an attached tag from customs. "I've never seen one of these close-up before," she said.

"Nothing to it." Curt pulled the brown paper off, revealing the sword in its red leather sheath.

The girl ran a hand down the length of the blade. "Oh," she said, "it's been used and bent."

Curt smiled. "You might say that."

"I'll take care of it for you. Put it in a little closet we have for loose articles."

"Thank you very much," he said, deciding it wasn't necessary to tell her the sword was made that way, bent so that it could enter and kill more easily.

He sat back in the plush seat, wondering how easy a kill it had been for poor Teddy. Had Cerdat slipped a hypodermic needle into him easily and neatly?

His mind returned to the same problem he had gone over a hundred times, like a tongue dragging itself over a broken tooth. *What should he have done?*

He had become involved in something that demanded a moral decision and found that there were scores of answers. If he testified against Villalta, Pardee, and Judge Mandar, he was doing the right thing. But what did he really have to go on? There was no real proof. The Swiatski car was long gone. Who could prove there had been any tampering with the brakes? If he said that Teddy Swiatski had been kept prisoner in a hospital in Andorra and Cerdat's clinic was investigated, he knew what they'd find—nothing. And what about the Swiatskis back in the States? And María Maite. *And* María Victoria? What good would an investigation do them? You couldn't even say that justice would be served. It would simply be an example of ineffectual personal honesty. And even that would be turned into a mockery, if Villalta went through with his discrediting plan. Who believes a nonrapist accused of rape?

So he had called Villalta, and had written the letter to Stanley Swiatski. A white lie out of the heart of darkness. . . .

And now here he was, flying home. Home? All flights are in-between states. All answers are anticlimactic. It had been intriguing and dangerous to search for Farlo-Swiatski, but it was harder to search for oneself. Maybe in the process of looking for others he had discovered something about himself. Through Villalta, through María Victoria. What he needed was a clean start. He would act for the best, hope for the best, and take what came. . . .

No one occupied the aisle seat beside him. On impulse he reached under his own seat, pulled out his TWA flight bag, and from it removed a package wrapped in shiny white paper. It was loosely tied with ribbon. He looked at it curiously, remembering what had happened at customs.

The inspector had opened the box and pulled the glass decanter out of its nest of excelsior. As he did so, María Victoria's card had fallen to the floor.

"*Lo siento,*" the inspector said.

"Nothing," Curt said, stooping and picking it up, reading its short message once again: *For what might have been.* V. He stuck the card into his breast pocket behind his handkerchief.

"How should this be valued?" the inspector said.

Curt smiled. "I do not know."

The man pointed to the metallic lip and ring around the neck. "*Plata,*" he said, "silver."

"Clearly."

The inspector held the decanter up to the light, examining it minutely. The faceted edges scintillated in the afternoon light.

"It is a beautiful cut glass, as good as I have ever seen. But do you know there is a fault in the neck, *señor?*"

Curt looked where he pointed, saw the fine split, running from the silver collar down into the cut-glass design.

"I see," he admitted.

"How long have you been in Spain, *señor?*"

"Nine months."

"And have you ever used this decanter?"

"I am afraid not."

The inspector considered. "Let us set the value at . . . two thousand pesetas, approximately thirty-five dollars."

"*De acuerdo,*" Curt said.

"I realize this does not measure the sentimental value."

"Clearly."

Curt decided not to open the box. He tied the ribbon more securely, placed the decanter back in the flight bag, and zipped it closed. Quietly he repeated the customs inspector's question to himself: "How should it be valued?"